# Baker and Thief

Evan Kvalvik

# Baker and Thief

The Crownsmith Chronicles
Volume 1

# By Evan Kvalvik

Evan Kvalvik

First published in the United states of America by
DimeSquare Publishing, 2024.
ISBN: 979-8-9913976-2-9
First edition.

**DimeSquare Publishing**

This fiction is dedicated to the USS Alabama (SSBN-731). You can piss the entire crew off by saying "731 Roll Tide shipmates!" Somewhere in the world, this book is being burned, ripped apart, or thrown across the room by a submariner... or a college football fan.

Evan Kvalvik

# Table of Contents

# Chapter 1

## The Spice Merchant's Daughter

I t was a long-standing tradition to send the boys of the village, on their sixteenth birthday, on a coming-of-age trek up the mountain of Asven. The mountain was close enough that the whole journey, on foot, rarely took longer than a week but usually six days. It was not common among the returned to brag about beating another's record because part of the tradition was to not talk about it.

"It only took me four days, sunrise to sunrise," Brahm bragged to the group of children. The fact of the matter was, four days ago, they weren't just children; they were his peer group.

Benj grew up with Brahm, but they were not friends as much as, perhaps, the closest in age in the nearest proximity. At fifteen years and eleven months old, Benj would be the next to travel to Mt. Asven.

"How was it?" He asked, expecting more than the "Oh fine," Brahm said in return.

"You know what I mean," Benj pressed. "Were there any wild animals? Did you pack enough food? Was the mountain... steep? You know, anything that will help me out when it's my turn?" He asked in seemingly one breath.

"I would love to help you out, kid. I really do. But you know the rule," Brahm said with a measured level of condescension. "We don't talk about it."

It was true; no one spoke about the trek. It was a tradition. You were chastised if you broke the unwritten rule that went back as far as Mt. Asven itself. Still, there were no repercussions as far as Benj knew about breaking the rule, at least a little bit to help someone you've known your whole life.

"Let's say that you didn't tell me anything but made small recommendations like 'Bring an extra blanket' or 'Don't eat the yellow berries' or anything," Benj said, trying to get any information he could.

"No, thanks." Brahm said, smiling with an amused look, "That would go against the spirit and intent of not talking about it. Besides, why would I try to help you beat the new village record?"

"No one cares about your self-proclaimed record," Benj said, exasperated. "There isn't even a record to keep. For all you know, someone beat your record fifty years ago, and no one ever bothered writing it down because it was irrelevant. Did someone write down your record?"

Brahm thought for a moment, or at least he appeared to be thinking. "If anyone had broken my record, someone would have told us about it."

Benj considered how to reframe his question.

"I have adult things to do," Brahm turned his back and walked away.

Benj was frustrated at the quality of his friends at times. He wished he had someone to share secrets, have deep discussions, or make up insults about Brahm with. He would even settle for shallow discussions. The village he lived in was feeling smaller and smaller every day.

Benj's full name was Benjos, with the adopted surname Baker. His mother was a barmaid who died giving birth to him. His father was said to be a red-haired musician who had played at the tavern passing through. His dark brown curls portrayed the fact that he favored his mother.

He was raised by the tavern owners. Not inside but outside the tavern his mom worked at before she died. Hungry and homeless, he found more food and warmth in places near the tavern than he did elsewhere. He was never permitted inside but found meals with full mugs of ale waiting for him on the back step every so often.

A baker in search of medicine for his wife noticed the young Benj. His wife told him to take the boy. The baker protested, but his wife was too weak to argue, and he relented. The baker's wife made him promise to take care of the boy. He promised, and she died.

Nine years later, Benjos Baker had learned to bake breads of every color, cakes, rolls, and tarts of every size and shape, with glazes, icings, creams, and honey. He had learned recipes he could throw together without measuring cups and make rolls so soft that they would fall to the countertop without making a sound. He could do all of this, but he would remain an apprentice to the old man Sephus until he was a "man." That is until he made the trek to the summit of Mt. Asven and returned alive.

Benj, considering his mortality as he walked back to the bakery, was greeted by a "Ho, Benjo, get your skinny behind back here and have a look!" Sephus yelled from the back.

"Sephus," he greeted.

"Master Sephus to you," he said, "You still have four months to address me properly."

"Less than one month," Benj corrected. "You're the one who decided my birthday was on the first of the year."

"Ahem," Sephus cleared his throat and raised an eyebrow expectantly.

He added, "You're the one who decided my birthday was on the first of the year, Master Sephus, you old coot."

"Now that's pretty good. Do you see how much better my name sounds when you pronounce it correctly?" Sephus said, tossing Benj a smooth black roll, "Take a look at that!"

Benj acted quickly, pulling a cloth off the counter to catch the flying roll. He learned at a young age that just because Sephus tosses something to you, it doesn't mean it won't scald your hands if you caught it.

"Oh, come now, it's been cool for a while," Sephus said behind laughing eyes. He was a head taller than Benj and had neatly cut hair around his tanned, bald head. He kept a long, unkempt beard that he would tuck into his shirt when eating or baking, however rare the latter occurred. His eyes were a cold blue that always seemed to say, "I might be an old man, but I'll outlive your children if you could find a woman dumb enough to make them with you."

Benj inspected the roll. It was smooth as glass and cool to the touch. "Dragon's bread?" He asked, not because he wasn't sure, but because he wasn't sure why. Dragon's bread was only really eaten during the new fall festival.

"I think we should sell them at the festival of challenges," Sephus said, filling his tankard to the brim with a dark amber ale.

The festival of challenges was really called the "winter festival." Mixed with food and music, the event had many nicknames centered on the fact that it was entirely overshadowed by competition. People competed over baking, racing, farming, husbandry, or famously, among other things, "feats of strength," which is why it was also referred to as the Winter Feats.

Feats of strength were ways a man or woman could gain or lose seemingly worthless but cherished titles. Some titles included the village's strongest, fastest, most agile, or best ax thrower. Every year, a claim to some obscure title from the previous year would spark a new competition. Random titles such as 'farthest to walk on hands,' 'farthest to throw a wheel,' or 'highest to jump' were won and lost. It was not uncommon to see a group of people hanging from tree branches or balancing broomsticks on their foreheads to win any title whatsoever. Possibly not as crucial as a title was the money won and lost in bets over various competitions.

"What do you think?" Sephus asked. He was either asking about selling them at the Winter Festival, the quality of his work, or both.

"In truth, I hate the idea," Benj said, tossing the smooth black roll into the air. "They're complicated-" The black roll hit the floor with a thwack! "They cost a lot to make, and there's no guarantee that people will want to buy them outside of the First Harvest."

He picked up the cracked roll off the ground, ripped it apart, and pulled a piece of dark bread from the middle. "I think we should stick to ginger sticks or cinnamon apples or something," he said and put the morsel into his mouth.

"Well?" The eager Sephus asked.

"It's good, but…"

"But what?"

"It's missing something," he said, taking the ale out of Sephus' hands and taking a deep drink. "There we go, not bad. Not as good as mine, but not bad."

"Good," Sephus said and pointed around. "Clean this up; I'm going out. I left the recipe out for you if you can't think of a better idea".

"If we need extra spices for the dragon's bread, the spice merchant is coming tomorrow," Benj recalled.

"Good thinking Benjo, take this," he handed him a silver talent "take inventory tonight and get what you think we'll need. I want the change."

"There won't be any," Benj said, knowing any change left over, no matter how much, would be just enough for a well-earned pint afterward. He would need to barter the price of the spices down first, but he was confident it would go well, like so many times before.

Bakeries made good customers for spice merchants. If more than one spice merchant made rounds through the same village, they would tend to offer better deals. Unfortunately, only one made rounds in his village, and Benj knew that it didn't hurt to show up with hot cinnamon rolls. Sephus had always said it's bad for businesses to give products away; he had no idea how wrong he was.

The next morning, Benj woke up before sunrise and started his morning routine. He got out of bed, put his trousers and boots on, and created a fire in the hearth. He placed the kettle containing a mixture of water and char leaves that had been soaking all night over the fire. It was the simple pleasures in life that made the unceasing work of a baker more bearable. He gathered some food scraps and then went outside to chop wood, placing the food he found in a small brass dish outside the door.

A moment later, a fat, homeless dog rounded the corner to find his daily breakfast exactly where it should be.

"Good morning, Chubbs," Benj greeted the dog who was already eating as loud as ever. "Sorry, there isn't a lot today; I'll see what I can do later."

The dog didn't seem to care but wagged his tail once in acknowledgment.

Benj walked towards the wood shack where his ax was hanging. The ax was worn, but he kept it well by sharpening it once a week. He swung the heavy ax with ease from years of experience. Sephus was too old to chop wood, but it seemed he had always been too old to do anything.

By the time the sun peeked over Mt. Asven, Benj was covered with beads of sweat and ready to bathe in the cool river when he heard a familiar sound. It was the low rumble of a single-horse-drawn carriage. Benj moved to get a better view of the road. The sunlight peeked onto the westward road, highlighting kicked-up dust and something that he hadn't expected for several hours — the spice merchant.

His ax dropped several feet from its proper place, and he ran inside. His cinnamon rolls were figuratively and literally his bread and butter, but he hadn't started them, and the spice merchant was already pulling up. He had gotten nearly double the number of supplies for the same price in the past for the small bribe that took the form of hot, fluffy round rolls covered in cinnamon and a honey-cream glaze. There was no time to lose.

In the kitchen, a fire grew. It needed to be hot enough to warm the oven but then die down to coals for a slower cooking and more even temperature. Too hot, and you'll have burnt dough. He spread out four of his smallest pieces of wood. The fire grew. Next, he splashed his hands in water and washed them with a dark green block of sulfur soap up to his forearms. When his hands were clean, he dried them with a white cloth. Sweat was still forming on his body, making his skin slick. He took his damp cloth and wiped his face; there wouldn't be time to bathe until after he made his purchase.

Two bowls landed on the countertop. A moment later, two wooden lids covering the flower and sugar flew up with a streaking plume of powder. An egg cracked and emptied simultaneously. The two large bowls filled and mixed with a flourish. With no time to measure, his hands became scales, scoops, and measuring cups. He needed warm water. It was common knowledge that water heats slower if you're in a hurry. He would have to cut the process short, "Char leaf tea!" he said out loud. It was hot by now. All he had to do was cool it down a little bit. He poured a measure into the bowl and stirred. He then took a jar of wild yeast that had been nurtured since he was alive and scooped a portion inside.

There wouldn't be enough time for the dough to rise fully. Panic prickled at the back of his neck. No, he would have to do something else. Scones. The batter needed adjustment. A cloud formed around him like sawdust in a carpentry shop as he worked.

Char leaf had a bold flavor; it also made you more alert. Drink too much, and your heart would pound in your chest just sitting down. It could have been a dumb idea to add it, but it was too late now. The only way out was forward. To see how the flavors would pair, he poured a cup of the tea and added cinnamon and honey. He took a sip; it was different. This all happened in a matter of heartbeats. He formed scones in triangular shapes and put them on a metal baking sheet.

The fire was burning higher than optimum despite the few logs he used. He spread out the fire, so only the coals were heating the bottom of the oven. That would have to do. The scones went in. He needed time; he wasn't sure how much he had. Hopefully, everyone in town needed spices too, or at the very least salt and dried peppers.

Outside, he saw the town gather around the wagon to make their purchases. He still had time. Then he noticed the village wives walking away, almost pulling their husbands behind them. That was odd. Usually, the town stayed and gathered news, stories, and gossip from neighboring towns. The traveling merchants doubled as a news source that didn't seem to be of importance at the moment. Fortunately, Brahm and a few others were still there, inadvertently buying him more time. A half-hour went by, and the others had left. The merchant was waiting for the obligatory ten minutes after the last customer moved on before moving forward, making his way beyond the trees surrounding the bakery. Time was money for them. The less time a merchant stays in one place, the more places they can sell their goods.

*I only need three more minutes*, Benj thought. He grabbed two tankards and filled them with the piping hot tea. The merchant would undoubtedly appreciate it for the journey ahead. He opened the oven and used the long wooden spatula to pull out the scones. With no time to taste them, he wrapped them in the bakery brown paper and placed them in a basket. He took the tankards, set everything down, put on a shirt, regained his valuable bribes, and was out the door in time to hear "Hyah!" and see a single brown horse pull the spice cart sluggishly towards the long journey ahead.

"Ho, there! Merchant!" He called out. No response. He could have run if he wasn't holding two tankards filled to the brim with scalding tea. "Stop, I have a lot of money!" He called louder. Something about the word 'money' carries farther than other words like, perhaps, 'help' or 'my house is on fire.'

The cart came to a stop right outside the town's perimeter, and a young woman peered out from the front of the carriage at him.

"Hello there. Sorry, I'm late!" Benj apologized as he ambled over to her.

"Hello, you almost missed me there." Her voice carried to Benj as he made his fast and level walk towards the cart. He arrived to see a girlish young woman with a long travel coat draping over a tight leather vest showing more skin than he usually got from the women in town.

She had messy black hair, almond brown eyes and a single dark spot above lightly colored lips. There was something about her poorly cut hair that intrigued him. She had an unrefined quality that was somehow alluring. The closer Benj got, the more fascinated he became with her.

"Here," he said, handing her the scones and tankard of tea, "I brought you breakfast for your time."

She reached out and took the basket. She investigated the contents with the gentle sound of brown paper crinkling. He handed her the tea.

"Thank you," she said, slightly taken aback. "What an unexpected surprise."

"I thought you were John," Benj replied, "Usually, he's our spice merchant. He would eyeball me sideways if I came to him without my famous baked goods."

They both took a sip of the tea. She would have politely declined back home, but these parts were safe, and — "Char leaf," she said with a smile — she needed it.

"I soaked the leaves all night," Benj said, feeling giddy and self-aware. "I feel like I should try one of these before you do," he said reaching into the basket and removing one of the scones. "It was a new idea, not sure if it was a good one."

He took a bite.

She also took a scone, blew gently, and took a small bite. Her almond eyes got big with surprise. "You put it in the roll?"

"It's a scone, and yes, I've had worse ideas," he said, taking another bite and visibly relaxed at the realization that it wasn't terrible.

"It's delicious," she said, "It's like cinnamon tea with honey. Anyway, what can I get for you?"

"I've made a list." He handed it to her. She reached out and took his hand, tilting the list towards her.

Her touch was warm, and it sent tingles through his arm. *Stay focused*, he told himself; it was the only way he would get a good deal. The second this salesperson realized she had any power over him, she would bleed him dry. He desperately resisted blushing, but she was looking at the list — close call.

"You can have it," he said, placing the list in her hand. "I don't really need it anymore."

She got to work opening drawers and cabinets and taking out sacks of spices. She bent down to pick up the scale, which revealed a strange necklace. It was a cord of rope holding a square metal plate with runes etched into it. It was not an elegant piece like women would typically wear, but bulky and crude.

Noticing the direction he was staring, he immediately looked away, facing up, left, and finally down at his shoes. "So, are you officially taking over for John?"

"My father is feeling ill, so I came in his place." she said, not looking up at him.

"John's your father?" He asked.

"Last time I checked," she replied.

"I hope he gets better," he said.

"Thanks, I'll let him know you asked about him," she said. "This is quite a tall order for such a young guy," She spoke, still measuring small piles of spices. "What do you do with all of it?"

"I own the bakery just over there," he lied. "There's a big festival coming up."

She stopped what she was doing, looked into his eyes, and then ambled towards him. "You," she placed her finger on his chest, "own a bakery?"

"Yes," he said, wondering what emotion would be more prevalent on his face, guilt for lying to her or something else? "I inherited it; it's a small-" he made inarticulate hand gestures.

"You're like fifteen, right?" She asked innocently.

"Seventeen," he lied again. The truth was he didn't know exactly how old he was, but he knew he wasn't seventeen. He also didn't know why he was lying so much and trying to impress her; there was already a girl that he liked. "How old are you?" He asked.

"Old enough," she said, turning and starting to open drawers in the cart until she found what she was looking for. She pulled out a small wooden box and removed the lid, revealing two separate compartments, each with a small, round stone inside.

"These are touchstones," She explained, bringing the box closer. There are different kinds, but these heat up when they touch." she moved closer and put one rock in each of his hands.

"Relics?" It was half question; the other half was painfully aware of her touch and how close she was standing.

"That's right," she said, taking each of his hands in hers and moving them slowly together.

"What is your name?" He asked, absorbed in the fact that her hands were holding his.

"Lucia," she said with the hint of a smile.

"Lucia," he said with a warmth in his hands, "That's a very pretty naaaaaaaahhh!!" His hands were hot. They felt like the first time he caught a roll from Sephus. Benj let the touchstones fall to the ground to blow on his hands.

"I told you," Lucia laughed at him, "They get hot!" She tested the coolness of the stones on the ground before picking them up. "I found out how hot they get the hard way, too."

"Wow," he said, trying to recover from the embarrassment, "they heat up really fast. Where did you get them?"

"I found them," she replied, touching her necklace, "I'll sell them to you for two gold royals."

*Did the rune on her necklace just glow?* He felt the urge

to impress her by saying yes, but he simply did not have the money. "I'm afraid I'm going to have to decline. How much for the order?"

"A talent and three marks, or fifty-three marks." she said, taking a sip of the tea. His heart sank. Lucia must have used the scales to an exact measure. Her father would have given him extra and still charged him less.

She must have seen the look on his face. She walked up to him, holding out the sack of spices, and said, "But because you brought me breakfast, I'll only charge you fifty." Her eyes glittered at this, and he felt his emotions pull in different directions. He was upset because he would have otherwise gotten his entire order for less than the talent she was charging, but he didn't want to seem poor or miserly. He reached for the coin bag and handed her the coins.

He watched as Lucia made a quick entry into her ledgers and pocketed the money. "I would love to stay and chat, but I have to be going," she said. "It was my pleasure doing business with you." She held out the empty basket.

"And I, you," he replied, taking the basket. The merchant retracted her hand, finished a ledger entry, and climbed up to her seat.

Benj stood dumbfounded as he heard her feminine voice, "Hyah!" and slowly moved the carriage forward. That was the most he had ever spent on spices, and it felt odd not signing for the purchase. Every time he did business with John, he had always signed the ledger. A thought occurred to him. He sprinted toward the carriage.

"Lucia!" He called, and the carriage stopped.

"Oh, yes, I almost forgot," she handed him back a

half-empty tankard.

He dumped the contents and placed the tankard in his basket, "I should probably sign for the purchase."

"It's okay, really," she insisted. "My father is just old-fashioned. They don't really need double verification for taxes anymore."

"I better anyway," he said. "Just in case."

"Oh, it's fine, I'm sure," she said.

Did she look worried?

"No, I insist," he said, holding up his hand. From a very young age, Benj was taught various ways a swindler could swindle. Sephus had inadvertently taught him how to be a criminal if he wanted. But he hated the idea of stealing and loathed anyone who took part in such criminal acts.

"Here," she said, reluctantly handing the ledgers over.

Benj opened the last page and saw his entire order was correct, except for the bottom price, which showed 'twenty-five marks' for the purchase, which was only half a talent. Next to the order, her signature swooped with two initials next to some illegible scribbles, presumably his own. Before he had a chance to speak, she cut in.

"I'm sorry," she said, close to tears, "Just listen. My dad owes some very bad people a large sum of money. They hurt him and took me as payment. The only reason why I'm out here and not in a whorehouse is because they don't know anything about spices and need me to sell them. I'm only trying to repay my father's debt and buy him medicine."

"By overcharging, skimming, and effectively stealing from people like me?" He asked, raising his voice and not waiting for a response. "I'm sure the village constable won't mind hearing how you're using that relic of yours to get people to go along with your little deceit."

She looked shocked and instinctively touched her necklace. "How did you know?"

"How did I know?" He repeated indignantly. "It takes longer than five minutes for me to fall in love with someone."

"You love me?" She asked, wiping away a tear that threatened to remove a streak of dirt from her face.

"No, it was the relic," he gestured toward her necklace, "Like how it's making me feel now even though the thought of liking a thief repels me."

"It's not doing anything right now," she said, "I'm not even touching it. Also, it doesn't make people fall in love with you; it just allows people to be persuaded."

Benj looked confused.

She hopped down from the carriage, placed half a talent coin into his hand, and kissed him on the cheek.

"Here," she said, sliding the box of touchstones under his arm, "They're mine to give, just like my heart." Then she got up on her carriage and rode off without another word.

Benj stood there dumbfounded as he watched her ride away. Should he try to stop her? He watched her go.

On the way home, Benj had no idea what happened. He had a half talent, all the spices he would need for the Winter Festival, and a rather interesting relic, or rather two. He had also gotten a kiss from the spice merchant's daughter. Thief or not, it was probably good luck.

# Chapter 2

## Sausage Bread

The morning before the Winter Festival, the village prepared to celebrate their strengths, resourcefulness, and skill. It was not uncommon in the years before to see families already taunting each other or arguing about the previous year's tied matches over the log toss, ale-drinking relay, or even the pie bake championship. Embarrassing enough, Sephus had entered Benj into the pie bake competition the prior year without him knowing. He had won. The pie bake was one of the more serious competitions, with a grand prize of a gold-plated cooking spoon. The contestants were also predominantly women. He was so embarrassed he left before the rest of the festivities had ended.

The next festival was a day away, and Benj spent his time trying to decide what to make for it. He would have to start working on a massive order of dragon's bread if he couldn't think of anything better to sell. It also seemed that everyone, especially their grandmothers, wanted one small order or another from the famous pie bake champion. Fortunately for Benj, they were mostly the same thing: the previous year's award-winning pie. This made it a little easier for him. He could keep the ingredients out and even make extra if he needed to.

The kitchen was hot, and the front bell rang again. "Hello, Ms. Gale!" Sephus' voice carried with the same pitch as the bell.

"Hello Sep! Are all the festivities tomorrow keeping you busy?" Benj heard Gale say through the door. She was a kindly older woman who had inherited a large sum of money following her husband's death. She was portly, wealthy, and easily flattered, basically Sephus' type of woman.

"Oh, yes. This time of year, oh, you know, keeps us on our toes," Sephus said, "And might I say," he continued, tracing his eyes down to her feet "Speaking of toes, you look like you've been keeping light on yours."

There was a slight pause to consider the implication. Benj had written the comment off as nonsense when Ms. Gale seemed to get it, or at least she feigned comprehension.

"Oh, you flatter me so, Seph. Do stop!" She giggled. "Don't stop?"

*Twice drowned, that man would flirt with anyone*, Benj swore, rolling his eyes and walking back to the solace of his kitchen. He could practically hear her blushing through the walls as Sephus shot compliments at her with the accuracy of a forest fire. He stopped listening.

He wasn't upset that Sephus was out there flirting away with old women while he was in the back, in the heat, and working nonstop to fill the countless orders. In fact, he preferred it this way, though he did need help getting firewood, washing bowls and pans, and kneading large batches of dough. Making a pie crust was easy enough, but after six hours of it, his arms were starting to feel like dough themselves.

The pies in the oven needed more heat and more time. He went to get more logs for the fire and found his pile depleted.

"Sephus!" He called out, "We need more firewood!"

In the middle of holding Ms. Gales' hand and talking about the healing properties of nutmeg, Sephus called out, "I'm in the middle of something!"

*Incredible,* Benj thought as he stormed outside. He's taking a break on the *busiest day of the year at the busiest time of day. He* grabbed two armloads of wood and walked them back to the kitchen by maneuvering the door with his foot.

He placed the wood by the stove as loudly as he could and looked up to where his water cup was. As he reached for it, he noticed the box on the mantle. A hot kiss burned on his cheek as he took the box down and carefully removed two small stones so as not to let them touch.

He slid open the furnace door under the oven and cleared the ash and coals from the middle. He placed the two rocks in, used the fire poker to position each in the middle, and nudged them together. A moment later, after nothing happened, he walked out to get another armload of firewood and returned, shocked by the heat on his face. The two round stones were glowing red with intensity.

"Ok, let's give this a try," he said, setting the logs on top of the others. After a quick round of cleaning, he opened the oven to find four golden pies. He set the pies out to cool and looked around. He didn't have any leftover pie crust but had enough dough for another loaf of beer bread. Instead, he separated the mixture into four small loaves and slid them into the oven.

Keeping the oven hot with such little room in the furnace below had been an art he had learned at an early age. Now, if the rocks worked as well as he hoped, none of that was necessary anymore—no more chopping wood, and no more, well, wood.

"I'll help you carry them to your house," Sephus said in the other room before stepping through the door. He looked at Benj and asked, "The pie?"

Benj gestured towards the pies, cooling off on the mantle with his golden mixing spoon. Sephus took one of the three pies in mitted hands.

"I'll help you clean up when I get back." He then added with a wink, "Don't wait for me."

Benj knew he had no intention of helping with anything; it was a mutual understanding. Less than an hour later, he came to a stopping point with the last orders plus two extras in the oven and had the whole kitchen area cleaned and wiped down. He was hungry. It amazed him how much food he could be surrounded by and not have time to eat. The four small loaves of beer bread looked like they turned out well.

He took out two of the sausages he had gotten from the butcher earlier in the morning, opened the furnace, and set them on the ledge to cook. The stones were still glowing red, but the temperature had seemed to wane. That wasn't a good sign, but it wasn't necessarily bad. From his limited knowledge of relics, he knew they were powered by physical touch. So, once they cooled, he would try holding them and see if he couldn't return them to their former glory.

Ever parched from the ever-present heat, he reached

up to grab his cup and drank the remaining water. He then refilled it from Sephus' barrel of ale. The beer was strong and warm. He felt it would go well with the sausages, which gave him an idea.

He removed one of the small loaves of beer bread, cut a hole in one side, and hollowed out the center. The aroma of the sausages brought back memories of his childhood, which gave him another idea. He took a jar of spiced mustard and layered it inside the hollowed-out loaf. When the sausages were done, he pulled one out and placed it inside the hollow.

He could easily make large orders of this for the winter festival. If it was good, he wouldn't have to make the dragon's bread after all. He immediately made another one, making a mental note of how to prepare it efficiently. He stared down at his creation. It was beautiful.

The front door opened with a ring. He wondered why it had taken Sephus so long, but then he banished the thought.

"Hey!" He called, "Come back here and check this out!"

The door to the kitchen opened, and a girl poked her head in. "Check out what?" A girl's voice asked.

"Oh, sorry," he said, looking embarrassed, "I thought you were Sephus."

The girl's name was Melisandra, but she went by Mel. A year older than Benj, she was arguably the most beautiful girl in the village and an argument Benj had made before, often enough. She had thick blonde hair that fell gracefully around her thin neck down to her lower back. She wore a wool sweater and a long skirt that left everything to the imagination. Whenever he worked up the nerve to talk to her, their conversations came easier than he expected.

"Nope, it's me," she said with a playful voice. What were you going to show me?"

"Oh, it's nothing," he said. It's just something I was going to show Sephus."

"You're not getting out of this so easily," she said, making her way through the door and walking towards him, "I'm curious now."

Benj was glad he had cleaned up the place a little before Mel came in. He would have been thoroughly embarrassed if she had seen it in its chaotic state earlier.

"Alright," he said, relenting, "Come over here."

She moved closer to him, looking around the kitchen for the first time.

"Behold," he said, making a royal gesture with a knife in hand, "Sausage Bread!" He cut one of his creations in half, revealing the loaf with a sausage in the middle.

"Is that what you're calling it?" she asked with a quizzical smile. Sausage bread?" She paused, absorbing the expression on his face, and then added, "It's so... original."

"Thanks!" He beamed while rummaging through a drawer. "Here," He handed her a fork. "You can have half," he said, pointing towards the smaller half.

"Why do I get the smaller half?" She asked, putting on a fake pouty face.

"Uh, I mean, you could, but uh…" Benj stammered.

"Relax, I'm just kidding," she said, setting her fork down and picking her piece up with her fingers. "Even offering me this much is very sweet of you."

"You're assuming it's any good," he said, stabbing his piece, "I've never made this before. I should thank you for

30

putting yourself in harm's way."

She gently blew on hers and took as big a bite as she could without burning her mouth. Benj followed suit.

"This is really good, and there's mustard?" She asked, disregarding all tact and talking with food in her mouth.

"I thought I could go through the trouble of dipping it in mustard, but decided just to put it in," he said and then finally added, "It is good!"

After a moment of silence, the two finished eating. Mel said, "What about calling it something like, I don't know, a butcher's roll?"

He remembered the pies he had in the oven and excused himself. Instead of squeezing past her, he walked the long way around the counter to get past her. He opened the oven, and soft steam billowed out. His pies were perfect.

He hurried to grab the wooden paddle to remove the two pies and set them next to the others. "I don't know," he said, shutting the oven door. "I came up with 'Sausage Bread,' and I kind of liked it.

Just then, the door opened with a ring.

"Benjos, my sweet, sweaty kitchen boy, I did it!" Sephus's voice came from the front room. "Let's just say she got some pie, and I got s—" he stopped mid-sentence after pushing through the kitchen door and noticing he and Benj weren't alone.

"Hi," Mel said quickly.

"Why hello, uh," Sephus said, "don't tell me, Margo, May, uh… Melisandra! What a pleasant surprise!"

"Thank you, Master Sephus," She stepped down from the stool she was on. "Benj was just helping me with the two pies I ordered."

Benj immediately took two pies off the shelf, checked

to see how cool they were, and handed them to her.

"Yes," he said, "That will be ten marks."

Mel set the pies down, reached into her coin purse, and produced the coins. "Here," she said, offering them to Benj.

"I can take that," Sephus said with a smile, holding out his hand.

"Yes, of course," she said before giving Sephus the money.

"Would you be needing help carrying those pies home?" Sephus asked in the most grandfatherly way he knew how.

Benj shook his head.

"No, thank you," she said, picking up the pies again. "I'm a short walk away."

Both men scrambled to open the door for her as she left.

"Oh," Mel said as she walked outside, "Thanks again for the... Sausage bread."

Benj watched her walk away. After a moment, when she was far enough away, Sephus slapped him on the back. "That's a right fine woman you got there," he said, "Gave her the ol' bread sausage and everything!"

"It's 'sausage bread,' and it's not what you think," he said, visibly flustered.

"My boy, when I was your age, we called it something different," Sephus said, "but you make me very proud you do!" He had a toothy grin.

"No, it's something I made," Benj deadpanned, "-with sausage."

Sephus' smile dropped into a somber line. "Well, I'm not surprised but I am disappointed," he said dismissively. "Show me this sausage bread."

Several moments later, Sephus had a piping hot sausage bread in one hand, a tankard of ale in the other, and a big smile in the middle. "This, my boy Benjo, is excellent!" He exclaimed, "She helped you come up with this? We need to put beautiful women back there with you more often!"

"No, I came up with it..." Benj began before Sephus cut him off.

"We'll sell this at the Winter Festival!" He said, sloshing his beer as he yelped with excitement.

"I could teach you how to do it," Benj offered, "They're really fast to make, maybe I'll have time to attend more events this year."

"Nonsense, my boy," Sephus said. "I'm not sure if you've noticed, but I haven't done anything useful in four years!"

"Oh, I've noticed."

"I'll order forty sausages, no, sixty, and you can make them all and sell them!" Sephus was drunk on excitement and ale. There would be no talking him out of this one, so he wrote the orders down.

Evan Kvalvik

# Chapter 3

## The Winter Festival

T he morning of the Winter Festival, Benj woke up to find Sephus awake and running around. There were already sausages, and a barrel of ale staged in the kitchen. The night before, Benj had barely slept. He woke up and was too excited to go to sleep, planning his great escape to explore the festivities.

"Benjo!" came the only voice that said his name that way. "Come in here and put this stuff away!"

"I can do that, or I can chop wood," Benj replied through the door. "We really should have stocked up yesterday. One of us needs to start that now."

"Never mind! You go right on ahead!"

"Are you sure? It's never too late to try something new," Benj said half to himself as he made his way outside. Chopping wood was his ritual and one he secretly enjoyed. He still wasn't sure how reliable the touchstones were, and he didn't want to explain them to Sephus, who wouldn't use them anyway. The work helped wake him up and help clear his head. After chopping the wood, he put the ax where it belonged and the wood outside the back door. It was time to get cleaned up and somehow distract Sephus. He had a plan.

Several hours later, Benj had made a small batch of Sausage bread, cut them in bite sized pieces, and set them on a tray. "Sephus!" He called, "I have the samples!"

"What samples?" Sephus asked. He was counting money in the front room.

"I'm assuming you'll want to hand out samples," Benj said, working out his plan of escape. "You know, spread the word, let everyone know what we're selling today."

"I don't like the idea of handing out free food," Sephus said, mulling it over in his head, "But I suppose it couldn't hurt for people to at least see what we're offering."

"Ok, here they are," Benj said. "One of us needs to walk around and hand them out. It could be exhausting, so it's probably better if you do it. You wouldn't want to wear out your number one workhorse before the big race."

"I'm a little busy right now." Sephus gestured towards the sales ledger. "Besides, workhorses don't race. You'll be fine."

Benj began protesting, but the old man was firm in his decision. "Go make me proud, Benjo, and stop bothering me."

Benj hunched his shoulders, took the platter of sausage bread, and lazily walked to the door. As soon as it shut behind him, he straightened his posture, smiled, and made his way to the festivities.

It was still early, but more than half the town was out in the streets, either helping set up or watching. Benj spotted Mel walking with her father past where the hammer throw would be held. He approached them with his tray of goods.

"Good morning," Benj said with a smile. "I'm handing out samples if you would like to try one?"

"Oh, Daddy," Mel said, "This is what I was talking about."

"Is it now?" Her father looked at the samples with a sincere interest. "Benj, this girl has been talking about your sausage bread non-stop."

"Well, if you would like to try one," Benj held up the tray. "I made some samples. It would help if you ate it obnoxiously around as many people as you can and then told them how good it is and where they can buy their own."

"I don't know how well I'll do," He said, taking one, "but I'll try my best."

"Benj," Mel said, "Do you need help passing these out?"

"Sure," he replied, "if it's ok with your father, that is."

"Go on, have fun," her dad said before walking off, "I'll be around."

The two talked and laughed while they passed out free samples. Brahm came over, and Mel offered him one.

"Mel!" Brahm said with a smile, "I thought I saw you over here. I almost didn't think it was you at first because you were walking with… uh," He snapped his fingers. "Baker boy... Uh, Benj, is it?"

Benj didn't understand what Brahm was up to. He clearly knew his name.

"You silly man," She smiled and slapped his arm, playfully, "why wouldn't I be walking with Benj?"

"No reason," Brahm smiled. "I just thought you would end up courting someone… Better off."

"We're handing out samples," Benj finally spoke up.

"Samples?" Brahm said, "I thought you two were planning your wedding over here."

"No!" Mel blushed. "We're just friends. Here, try one."

Brahm took one of the slices between two fingers. "Is it safe?"

"Benj made them," Mel said, "of course it's safe."

"I know Benj made them; that's why I asked," Brahm scoffed, taking a bite. With his mouth full, he added, "Just playing with you. This is almost as good as the award-winning pie you made last year!"

He was really starting to get on Benj's nerves. "Thanks," he said, not able to think of a better reply.

"Are you entering again this year?" Brahm asked with an innocent smile. He might as well have asked if Benj planned on wearing a dress to the mother-daughter dance.

"Are you?" Mel asked, facing Benj sincerely.

"No, I didn't even enter myself last year," he said, starting to feel frustrated with the shift in conversation. "Sephus tricked me by ordering a pie and then entering it into the competition. The pie bake is for women; why would I enter myself?"

"Isn't baking in general for women?" Brahm asked, leaning slightly forward, daring him to take a swing.

"Baking is for anyone who enjoys eating well," Benj pointed at Brahm's belly, "I know you've been eating well; does that make you a woman?"

"Now, now, boys," Mel cut Benj off. "Play nice."

"Of course! I'm just having a laugh with my old pal anyway." Brahm said, "I think it's cool that he won the golden spoon last year. If my mom had won, she probably would have broken it over my cheeks by now." Brahm

38

said, holding his last bite of sausage low to the ground as a fat dog approached."

"Hey, Chubbs!" Benj said, noticing the dog approaching.

"Is this your dog?" Mel asked as Brahm lured him closer.

"I think he's homeless. I try to feed him every morning." Benj said.

"That's probably why he's so fat," Brahm said, "Here, doggy, doggy." When the dog came up to eat the sausage held out, Brahm kept moving it out of reach and then finally plopped it into his own mouth.

Benj was frowning. He had to loosen his hands up before he bent his tray. Brahm was bigger than him, but he wouldn't hesitate to put the big oaf on the ground if he kept it up.

"I'll walk with you guys," Brahm said, explicitly talking to Mel. "Later, you can watch me win the ax-throwing competition again."

"I have to go," Benj said, thinking of any excuse to leave. He would probably lose his temper if he had to spend another moment with Brahm.

"But you still have two more samples left. Don't you want to hand them out?" Mel asked, concerned.

"If you're not using those, I'll take them," Brahm said, taking the last two samples and tossing them into his mouth. With his mouth full, he smiled.

Benj glared at him.

"Don't be mean!" Mel said, slapping Brahm's arm.

"I have a lot of work to do before everything starts," Benj said. "Anyway, I would love to stay, but you know...."

"You sure you don't want to walk around some

more?" Mel implored.

"I really have a lot of work to do," Benj said, "but I would like to talk to you later if that's fine?"

"I'll walk around with you, Mel," Brahm said, mouth still half full. "Let's check out the races."

"Sure," Mel said, looking at Benj. "I would like that. It was nice seeing you!"

Benj said his farewells and walked back, not fully understanding what else he could've done. He liked Mel and wanted to spend more time with her, just not while Brahm was around. Besides, he really did have to get back before Sephus came looking for him.

# Chapter 4

## Harmless Prank

E ulourus Key, or "Just Key" as he would prefer, stood in the morning assembly, completely bewildered. His armor was polished beautifully, reflecting the dim, overcast light around Grayson Hall. His plate wasn't just shiny; it was the glistening standard of perfection, and nothing could have been worse for him at that moment. The gleam on his armor was a creative and intelligently calculated attack.

*I have to hand it to the guy. I wish I had thought of it first*, Key thought miserably as he awaited his doom when it came time for his uniform inspection.

This wasn't the first attack and wouldn't be the last, but Key was far from being a guiltless martyr. He and Ansel Jory had been at war with each other since Royal Guard training camp over two years ago. How the fight happened was undeniable. It started simply and elegantly with a flower in a vase sitting on Key's foot chest. This broke the berthing standards for the Royal Guard Training Camp, or "camp" as it was called, and

Key had been punished liberally for it. After some investigative work, he found out who the culprit was.

Ansel Jory, a plump boy with dark curly hair and an appetite for cruel humor, had planted the vased flower to "see what would happen." Key did not turn him in, and they both knew he couldn't. Ratting on a fellow brother at arms or betraying 'the brotherhood of the guard' was like signing your own death warrant. No one would trust you after that, and you would find yourself in a position where you couldn't piss around the corner without someone telling on you for leaving your post. Instead, Key got even.

Two days later, love letters from Jory to his squad leader just happen to emerge, transforming their lives into an endless bout of retaliation. Attacks between the two became more random and imaginative. These attacks included anything from various animals in various places, moonlight haircuts, peppers, itching powder, sharp plants, and now, among many other things, the shiniest armor ever to plague the morning assembly.

Grayson Hall was named after General Grayson, a once remarkable member of the king's service in Royal City, reduced to nothing more than a name for one of many locations that mustered the Royal guard for the morning assembly. The hall was an auditorium that held up the sky with two stone pillars jutting out from either side of a central stage. A semi-circle of stone stairs surrounded the stage, climbing upwards, row after row, until meeting the surrounding walls and three exits. Perhaps General Grayson meant to put a roof on his hall before he died. With a ceiling open to the world, he left a legacy poorly suited for bad weather. If there were any blue skies to be seen, they were outside the preview of the walls. The overcast ceiling darkened the halls, threatening to spill rain on three hundred mustering guards.

"Are you trying to stand watch in the king's private chambers?" Alrick asked quietly as he stood at attention next to Key.

"No, but with this plate, I wouldn't be surprised if they put me there," Key replied to his friend standing next to him.

"They'll probably put you at one of the castle's entrances," Alrick said. "I'm guessing the North door. I'll make sure the boys drink to your health today."

"Thanks," Key said despondently.

There were many places a guard could stand watch in Royal City, but some places had more benefits than others. Some watch stations were so bad that they were reserved for people who got in trouble that week or, consequently, if someone else didn't get in trouble.

Bridge duty was one of the worst places to be. You had to control access to the city, taking dirty coins from even dirtier travelers coming into the city. Sick people would cough on you, poor people would cry and beg to be let in. If anybody ever wanted to force their way in, you would be the first person to die or wish you had died before wrestling down the unbathed assailant.

The only place debatably worse than bridge duty was standing guard anywhere regarding the castle. No one congratulated you for standing at attention, staring directly in front of you for hours on end, and being unable to move. Conversely, suppose someone important did notice you slouching, sleeping, drinking, laughing, or scratching your ear. In that case, you would get in a lot of trouble, and there were many important people at the castle to notice. To make matters worse, even the chamber maids acted as if they outranked you, passing you with their noses in the air and treating you with general disdain.

It was important that you didn't have the best or the worst-looking plate of armor. Either way, you would be standing watch at the castle. But the former bypassed the part where you were yelled at while you made yourself presentable first.

"You got a date tonight?" A voice came from over his shoulder.

Key turned and smiled to see Gustave winking at him from behind Alrick.

"He was hoping the queen uses the North entrance," Alrick quipped. "That way, she'll have something to fix her hair in as she passes by."

"Guards," Sergeant Dilly called to the assembly. "fall in!"

Dilly walked around the hall, taking muster reports and conducting uniform inspections. When he stopped in front of the row Key was standing in, he whistled.

"That is the best-looking plate I've seen in a long time. Why don't you switch places with someone in the front so people have a better view of what the standard should be?" It wasn't phrased as a direct order, but it was one.

"Yes, sergeant," he said and then made his way down the stairs to the front row, humiliated.

After all the muster reports were in and the inspection was over, the sergeant went to the front and called the room to attention. The sound of hundreds of heels coming together unanimously hushed the room. Solitary footsteps marched down the ranks to the focal point of the assembly. Captain Watford walked past the ranks of guardsmen crisply, eyes forward, unwavering.

When he reached the front, Sergeant Dilly gave a crisp salute, bringing his fist to his chest with an audible thump. The captain, in lieu of saluting back, dismissed him with the roll of papers in his hand.

"Good morning, sir; these are the reports from yesterday; not a lot of-"

Captain Watford quieted the sergeant with a gesture as another sergeant entered the assembly carrying a staff with a metallic eagle. "Call the men to attention," he spoke quietly to his sergeant.

"They're already at attention, sir," Sergeant Dilly replied.

"Just do it, Dilly!" the captain rasped. "You will not try my patience this morning."

"Assembly!" Dilly called out, "Attention!"

The room stayed unchanged while the unanimous sound of heels striking together echoed through the walls of Grayson Hall.

The sergeant carrying the emblem stave waited a moment after the command to attention before announcing, "Captain Castor, Entering the hall!"

"What an unfortunate surprise," Captain Watford said to himself. "I wonder what he wants this time?"

Captain Castor passed around the stave carrier towards the front. He was a tall man in his late thirties with his face fixed in a look of pure confidence.

The two captains faced each other, neither saluting.

"Good morning, Charles," Watford said.

"Fredrick," Castor returned.

"What do you want?"

"I need someone to run messages for the day, possibly longer," Castor said cheerlessly. "I am conducting an audition for a new assistant."

"I heard about the," Watford said making a stabbing motion with his hands. "I might have someone to *spear*, so to speak."

"My assistant was murdered in cold blood, serving loyally in the line of duty. It would be bad form if you were, just now, making quips at his expense." Castor said between clenched teeth. "Bad form indeed."

"Yes, quite right," Watford agreed, feeling chastised. "Bad form."

"So, do you have anyone available?" Castor asked.

"I have just the man," Watford said. "Sergeant Dilly, send that gentleman we have assigned for bridge duty and replace him with someone else."

"Gentleman, sir? You mean the red-haired tree pisser?" Dilly asked before Castor interjected.

"I'm afraid that I do not have a need for any red-haired tree pissers today," Castor spoke as if his voice, his words were the epitome of finality. "At the very least, I need someone to represent me. Someone like...." His eyes scanned the room.

"I'll send someone else then," Watford offered.

"I'll take shiny armor over there," Castor pointed at Key in the first row. "Sound good?"

"Yes, I'm sure that will be fine," Watford said, making sure the sergeant was listening. "Send him."

After the assembly, Key was sent to the captain's office - The Office of Investigations - and knocked on the door.

"Enter," the captain permitted.

Key turned the knob on the sturdy oak door and slowly opened it revealing a small room with regal decorations and weapons hanging from the wall. The captain sat behind a desk, fingers steepled. Blue smoke drifted up from a short-stemmed pipe clenched in his teeth.

"Come in, close the door." The captain managed without dislodging the pipe.

Key closed the door behind him and stood at attention. "Corporal Key, reporting as instructed, sir." He announced himself formally.

"Do you know why I called you here today?" The captain asked, taking his pipe in hand and pointing to Key with the end of it.

"To run errands for you," Key paused momentarily, "sir."

"Yes and no, corporal." The captain puffed at his pipe, "The reason why you are standing in front of me right now is because I believe you understand something that most people do not, at least not at your age and not so early in their career. You understand the simple but powerful axiom: appearances create credibility."

Key stood at attention, trying to look like he understood the word axiom.

"It should go without saying, corporal," the captain continued, enunciating as if each word was commissioned by the king himself. "whatever happens in my company, you shall ensure that you are irrevocably circumspect about it. Whatever you see, whatever I tell you, or conversations you overhear are strictly confidential. Do we have an agreement?"

"Yes, sir." Key said and then dumbly added, "Of course."

"Good," the captain said, "Do you know what happened to my last assistant?"

"Yes, sir," Key answered. "He was killed."

"He made a mistake and let out certain information. That information inevitably put him in harm's way." The captain corrected. "He was top of the line, and his death weighs heavily on my heart. I will not make the same mistake and send you out as ill-prepared as he was." He paused, collecting his thoughts. "When you are working for me, you directly represent me. It is imperative you speak, act, and look up to my standard at all times."

"Yes, sir," Key answered.

"Excellent," The captain spoke, lifting a leather satchel and setting it on the desk in front of him. "These are private correspondence that need to be delivered," he pulled out a folded and wax-sealed parchment from the satchel and pointed at the script on the front, "to these people. These letters will not be delivered to the addressee's housekeepers, wives, children, mothers, or the like. It will pass from your hands into the individual's hands that it is addressed to."

"Yes, sir," Key said, still standing.

"Go on then." The captain said with a shooing motion. "Report back when you're done."

Key picked up the bag with one hand saluted with the other and left the office.

The sun had just begun melting away the remnants of the previous night's fog, and Eulerous Key was overjoyed. It was still midmorning, and he was off the hook for the rest of the day. Sure, he had some letters to deliver, but who's to say how long that would take? If he delivered everything fast enough, he could take a midday nap, play a few games of dice, and then make the report that everything has been delivered. He would even have time to plan how he was going to get back at Jory for polishing his armor, even if his attempt fell flat.

He climbed hand-chiseled stairs to a rather large estate overlooking the borders of Royal City. Two stone statues made of wood and cast iron stood on either side of the door. An iron loop with silver and leather pierced the door like a nose ring on a pig. Key raised the metal knocker and made three simple taps on the door.

After a moment of silence, the door made a series of clicks and taps that indicated an unlocking and unlatching of the door. Another moment of silence and similar noises indicated a different lock was being pried away, then silence. Muffled curse words came through the door from a feminine voice and frustrated muffles from a younger one. Two women were arguing about how to open the door and who got the privilege of opening the door. A rattle sounding like spoons in a drawer leads to a decisive turn and click.

The door swung inward on a young woman wearing a simple black dress with white lacing. She was forcing a smile. Behind her was an old woman wearing a matching dress and a frown presumably formed from years of practice.

"Yes?" The young lady asked. The older woman cleared her throat pointedly. "I mean," she revised. "How may I help you, sir?"

"Good afternoon," Key reached into his bag and produced the wax-sealed parchment; it was the last of his deliveries. "I have a letter for a Mister Templeton."

"Thank you. I'll make sure he gets it," the young woman said, holding out her hand.

"I am on direct orders to hand deliver this to Mister Templeton himself." Key explained, withdrawing the letter from her reach. "Is he here?"

"He's down at the-" The young woman started but

was moved aside.

"He is on an errand presently," the older woman amended. "He should be back this evening, but I can set it on his desk."

"I'll come back," Key said, putting the letter back into his empty satchel. He bid the housekeepers farewell before making his descent down the stairs. There was nothing left to do but wait, so he decided to do so over a pint.

The market moved with activity. The sound of coins on countertops and mixed voices bartering over various merchandise mixed in the air with the smell of bread, wool, and sea creatures. Key stopped at a fish merchant with an idea to get back at Jory.

"Good day, sir," The fish merchant greeted with a big oily smile. "You've come to the right place for the freshest fish in all of Royal. Caught these this morning."

"Actually, I'm looking for something…" Key started slowly. "Perhaps, not so fresh. I will take anything that is at least three days old if you have it."

"I run an honest business, sir," the merchant said. "I haven't been selling bad products, and I'm not looking for trouble with the law."

"No, no, no," Key said, holding his hands out in a disarming way. "I need something extra fishy for a joke. I'm not here to arrest anyone."

"Why didn't you say so? If you're trying to have a laugh, you've come to the right place." The merchant produced a fish and held it up. "This was caught a while ago. Legally, I can't say exactly how long but look at the fog in his eyes. This be what you're looking for and for only four coppers."

"Four?!" Key asked incredulously. "You would sell an

old fish for full price? I'll give you one, and I won't tell everyone you're keeping nasty fish with the fresh ones."

"I'll sell it for three and throw it in a sack with citron leaves so you can carry it around without offending anyone." The merchant bartered.

"I will give you two and no more," Key countered back. "You're not getting a better price for that dross from anyone else."

"You drive a hard bargain," The merchant said. "You've got yourself a deal."

"I'll still take the citron leaves," Key set two coins down. "I have a reputation to keep."

Key walked cheerfully through the market, toting an old fish in a bag. He thought about all the best places to put it for optimum impact. He decided it should go under Jory's bed. That would show him. His thought was cut off by a shrill scream.

People were gathering around something in the street. Key walked over to find a dead body.

"Oh great," he muttered. His perfect day off had turned into a day of more work. Of course, he knew what to do, they drilled it into him since camp. If anything happens, blow the whistle, clear the area and if anyone arrives send for back-up. Not forgetting, of course, the most important rule: Ask questions until someone incriminates themselves.

"Everyone, stand clear!" Key said digging into his pockets to find his whistle had also been shined too. After marveling at the whistle, he blew several loud, long pulses. He then set the fish down next to the corpse and began gesturing for everyone to move back.

"Who saw what happened here?" He asked, wanting to wrap things up as fast as possible so he could drink a pint and plant the fish.

"I saw," an older woman said from just behind him. "There was shouting from the roof; this man was stabbed and then fell down."

"This roof?" Key said, pointing to the nearby building.

"Yes," The old woman said.

"Can you tell me what the killer looked like?" he asked, hoping someone would come and take over. "What was he wearing? What direction did he go? What else can you tell me?"

"I didn't catch any details," She said. "My eyes aren't as good as they used to be. Can I go now?"

"Yes, thank you," Key waved her away.

It seemed like an eternity later when, none other than Captain Castor rode up on a giant war horse with two guards on smaller mounts trailing behind. Key recognized the two as Jerome and Remero.

"Corporal Key, what a pleasant surprise," The captain spoke. "Report."

Key considered a moment, eager to deliver more than what was readily apparent, and described the circumstances that had befouled his afternoon plans. "I was searching for the last letter recipient when I heard some screams and shouts. There was this gentleman lying here dead and gathering a crowd of people around him. I acted as trained, blew my whistle, cleared the area, and questioned people. There was an old lady who saw this man fighting with another unrecognizable man on the roof just there," he pointed up towards the roof near the dead body. "The lady described a brawl; this man was stabbed, and here he landed. She was unable to recall anything else, so I let her go. Sir."

"It looks like my intuition about you was right," the captain said. "Even running errands, it appears you rise above and beyond the call of duty. You said you had one message left?"

"Yes, sir."

Captain Castor held out his hand and Key pressed the wax sealed message into it. "Consider this message delivered."

"Yes, sir. But –" Key started to ask.

"You see," The captain said, cutting off any questions. "The dead man is none other than Mister Templeton, who, as it happens, is the very man you were looking for. Now, I'm afraid I will have to draft another, more solemn, letter to his household, and I can't think of a better person to deliver it for me. However, we will let tomorrow's problems wait for tomorrow. You said this man was stabbed and fell here?"

Key replied in the affirmative as the captain circled the dead body and picked up the bag holding the fish. He put his nose directly on the fish and inhaled deeply. His face repelled. He set the fish back down and lifted the man's left arm to tilt him sideways. After observing his torso, the captain disappeared inside the building and moments later appeared at the spot on the roof where the murder had occurred. His head moved back and forth as if reading a book that was too large and too close. He disappeared over the ledge of the roof and shortly after stormed out of the building's front door, moving towards the body once more.

"This man has been dead for some time," the captain said at last. "There's no blood on the roof, there's no blood on the ground under him, and his skin is already cold. Furthermore, his fish is starting to putrefy. Whoever gave you this misinformation about a fight was probably paid to do so or a culprit. Either way, she is more than likely long gone, as is the killer."

Key's heart sunk into the pit of his stomach. He should have kept the old lady around for more questioning. He at least tried to do the right thing.

"Don't lose heart," the captain said as if reading Key's mind. "I've fallen for bad information before. Some lessons only come from time and experience. If you are fooled, always try to never be fooled in the same way again. I'm sure you will smell the fish next time before ever letting a false witness go, won't you corporal?"

"Yes, sir." Key said at attention. "I am sorry."

"Don't be sorry," the captain said. "Just smell the fish."

"I will, sir," Key replied.

"Now," the captain said after relieving the dead man of one of his rings and a coin purse. He gestured to Key and the two other guards before ordering, "Help clear the road and take the rest of the evening off. One of you get in contact with the death wagoner to have this man hauled off for burial. Pay him with these." He gave one of the guardsman two silver coins proffered from the purse.

"Corporal," he looked at Key, "tell your sergeant I will require your services first thing in the morning. See to it that he removes you from the watch bill."

"Yes, sir!" Key acknowledged. He was echoed by the two other guards in unison.

The captain turned on his heel, mounted his horse, and rode off.

Key helped move the body to the side of the road. "I have to get back to the barracks," he said, wiping his hands on his pants. "If you want, I can get rid of this fish for you on my way there?"

Jerome, the Guardsman, looked around conspiratorially. "Don't worry about it," he said, picking up the fish and throwing it on the roof of the building the captain had just been considering. "What fish?" he asked.

Key frowned. He went through a lot of work for that fish, but it was probably for the best. He didn't want a dead fish somehow linking him to a murder, or rather, a murder linking him to a dead fish. He thanked Jerome and carried on walking through the market. Even in uniform, the merchants still called out their wares to him. After a while, one of the voices stood out from the rest and perked his interests.

"Sweet-smelling perfume," the merchant called. "Perfume is the perfect gift for that special someone! Do you have a special someone in your life?" He asked.

In fact, there was a special someone in Key's life. He was surprised he hadn't gotten this special someone perfume before. Already, he was feeling better about his lost fish after all.

Back at the barracks, Key uncorked his rather expensive prank and smelled it. The scents of flowers and spices filled him with a wicked excitement. He placed the bottle in Jory's footlocker, strategically positioned in a tunic with the cork gently placed on top of the bottle. When retrieved, the tunic would spill the potion, cursing his clothes with the aura of flowers. He hoped that it would be spilled before it was smelled. He then left the barracks and walked across the courtyard to the sergeant's offices.

Standing outside Sergeant Dilly's office, he took a deep breath and then knocked three times. When beckoned inside, he stood at attention and made his report. "Good afternoon, sergeant. Captain Castor has ordered me to request you take me off the watch bill for tomorrow."

The sergeant, looking through stacks of parchments, stopped what he was doing and looked up. Dilly could not have been younger than fifty years old. His skin was the dark leather that only came from standing, unmoving under the sky and little else, in every weather condition. This man had earned his station, not from exchanging pleasantries or rubbing elbows with politics, but from allowing his hard work and determination to outshine his lack of charm. Lack of charm being the sole reason it took him so long to get to where he was. "I take it you're done with whatever the captain needed you for today?"

"Yes, sergeant," Key said, standing at attention.

"Good, I need you to eat and relieve Corporal Thomas at the castle's North entrance," the sergeant said with a sparkle in his eye. I wouldn't want to waste that shiny armor."

"The captain told me to take the rest of the day off," Key explained, hoping the sergeant would be reasonable and retract his orders.

"Oh, did he now?" the sergeant asked, making another entry on the parchment. "Well, next time the captain writes the watch bill, I'll make sure to remind him that you prefer earning your pay while asleep. The schedule I have prepared, however, looks like you will be pulling a double to make up for the time you won't be on watch tomorrow. You can prance around with the captain tomorrow after morning assembly."

"Why would I need to attend the morning assembly if I'm not standing watch?" Key asked, realizing he was treading a fine line between the logical and the petulant.

"Because," the sergeant said, suppressing his anger.

"If I don't see your smiling face in the morning, I'll have you flogged for disobeying a direct order from your superior. Does that answer your question?" The sergeant replied in a clipped tone.

Key's hopes of getting some rest were replaced with a terrible feeling in the pit of his stomach. There was no use arguing with him.

This wasn't the first time Key had fallen prey to the whims of his seniority, and it wouldn't be the last. "Yes, sergeant." He said as calmly as possible and was dismissed.

Evan Kvalvik

# Chapter 5

## Twice in Two Days

Key had enough time to scarf down cold ham and a quarter loaf of bread before making his way to the castle doors. His fingertips smelled faintly of perfume, but there was no time to wash off the incriminating evidence; the city bell had already begun ringing. If it struck a fourteenth time and he hadn't arrived at his watch station, he could make enemies with the person he was about to relieve.

The bell struck four times as Key arrived at the castle's North entrance. There were two guards, one on either side of the massive, decorative doors. He nodded at the guard on the right, whom he recognized as John Sutton, before standing in front of Thomas with a fist on his chest. "I stand ready to relieve you." He recited the formal turn-over verbiage. If he were anywhere other than the castle's front steps, he would have said something like, "Kick rocks naive" or "I got this, go drink a pint for me."

"I thought you had the day off," Thomas whispered,

returning the salute. "What are you doing here."

"Sarge had a stick up his ass," Key whispered back, not betraying the look of professionalism they portrayed. "He's got me doing a double tonight."

A grunt came from the guard on his right. It was all he could do to express empathy for his fellow man.

"Ah, blackened shields, mate. I'm sorry about that." Thomas whispered and then said in a full baritone voice, "The watch station is secure."

"It's no problem, and thanks," Key whispered and then, in a theatrical voice, said, "I relieve you of your post."

The two dropped their salute, switched places, and saluted again. Without another word, Thomas turned and left.

Unable to speak to anyone, Key stared stoically off into the horizon. As minutes turned to hours, the sun dipped below the west mountains. The sky became dark and dotted with stars. John Sutton's relief came. The proper words were spoken, but instead of leaving, John Sutton stood in front of Key.

"Do you want a piss break before I leave?" He said softly.

"That would be great," Key replied.

"I stand ready to relieve you," John said.

After they had switched places, Key used the latrine and stood to trade back.

"I stand ready to relieve you." Key saluted.

"If you want to grab something to eat, stretch your legs, or whatever. I can handle this for a while longer." John said quietly.

"Thanks, John, but I'll be fine," Key replied, risking a smile. "If you fall asleep where you stand, you'll still get less than six hours of sleep before assembly. Besides, I'm not even on the watch bill tomorrow."

John nodded resolutely and spoke. "The watch station is secure."

"I relieve you of your post."

The sixth bell rang, and the morning assembly was called to attention. The room grew quiet as Captain Watford entered the room. Sounds of shuffling feet on the floor and clinking armor squelched the sounds of foot falls as the captain took center stage next to the platoon leaders. The sergeant indicated that the roll call was complete.

"Good Morning Men!" The captain called out.

"Good morning, sir!" the men replied, followed by a pause and from a lone feminine voice, "Good morning, sir!".

He took a mental note to address them all as guards from now on because Trudie wanted to make it a point to remind him, they weren't all men. He shook off the interruption. "I'm glad to hear yesterday went without major incident," he continued speaking to the crowd, "Aside from of course, certain repeat offenders."

A few glanced at Keebler, whose blush nearly matched his red hair. Everyone knew he would inevitably be assigned bridge duty for the seventh consecutive week in a row.

"Remember these words well," The captain began pacing along the ranks. "If you have to use the latrine, send for someone to relieve you of your watch station. If you cannot wait for a relief, maybe you should lighten up on the ale. I will not stand for anything less than official turn overs." The captain trailed off. He smelled the air. "What is that smell?"

The room was silent. Having stayed up all night, Key had forgotten about the perfume bottle he had planted the night before, but he remembered now. The room did smell uncharacteristically nice.

The captain walked around smelling. He seemed to pick up on the trail as he followed his nose through rank and file, carelessly shouldering past people, including Key, as he searched for the source of the smell.

He stopped in front of a plump-looking guard with long, curly hair and an embarrassed expression.

"Oh my! That is quite pungent," The captain said, waving the air, spreading the smell further. "Sound off, dandy!"

"Ansel Jory, 4th battalion, sir," Jory announced with a military professionalism that betrayed his scent.

"Will you explain to me and the people standing within a thousand feet of you why you smell like the highest quality brothel I have ever had the privilege of walking past?" The captain asked with a stern voice, sounding somewhere between humorous and belligerently angry.

In spite of having stayed up all night miserably on his feet, this moment had made it all worthwhile. Key knew Jory wasn't going to turn him in. If he did, he would have betrayed the brotherhood of the guard. No one would trust him after that, and he would find himself in a position similar to Keebler, who couldn't relieve himself around the corner without someone telling on him for leaving his post.

"Well?" The captain asked, hovering over Jory. "Speak up so they can hear you in the back."

"I bought the fragrance for a girl," Jory said, coming up with the lie in real-time. "But the glass broke on my way here. So now I smell like this."

"Likely story, however, I will give you the benefit of the doubt on this. Just get yourself cleaned up and report to your duty station." The captain shifted his attention to the sergeant. "Where is his duty station?"

"Patrolling the west courtyard, relieving..." Dilly flipped through the papers in his hands.

"I'm sure you can all work that out later. Make sure this incident is documented," the captain moved back toward the center of the assembly. "Until then, I don't want any more perfume bottle accidents. Am I clear?"

"Yes, sir!" The Assembly joined in unison.

After they were dismissed, Key received secret smiles, winks, and pats on the back from his brothers at arms. For them, the quarrel between him and Jory was more than a routine spectacle; it was something to look forward to. It was a moment of good cheer in an otherwise monotonous environment.

Exhausted from his double watch duty, Key made his way to the office of investigations. After he knocked and was let in, he stood at attention in front of the dark, wood-stained desk as the captain made scratching noises on a piece of parchment with a long, goose-feather quill.

"You can be seated," the captain said, pausing momentarily to chew on a thought, pressing the feather to his chin. "What was the first thing I told you yesterday in my office?"

"About an axiom, sir?" Key asked uncertainly.

"Yes, I suppose I did mention something like that first," the captain mumbled to himself. "The second thing I told you then, about everything that happens in here when you are in my service."

"Oh, yes, sir," Key said, understanding what he was

getting at. "You said that whatever happens, I should keep my lips sealed about it."

"Precisely corporal," the captain said, smiling. "The instructions I give you are part of that. When I say "at ease," I don't mean stand at parade rest; I want you to forget all, and I do mean all, military courtesy. When you and I are the only ones in the room, you will make yourself at home in the most respectful definition of the idea. If someone knocks, you will pop to attention over here," he motioned towards the right side of his desk, "and you will remain there until that person leaves. I don't care if that person is the Chambermaid or General Calcutta himself."

"Yes, sir," Key replied.

"Corporal," the captain said.

"Yes, sir?" Key replied.

"At ease."

"Yes, sir," Key replied and then looked around and found a chair to sit in.

He sat as the captain continued scribbling words on a sheet of paper. Key's chair was upholstered with animal skin. Brown and white fur brushed the back of his plate armor. The comfort of sitting, mixed with the scratching sounds of the captain's penmanship, relaxed Key into a sitting sleep.

Key could have slept standing up. Anybody with military experience had developed this tactic out of sheer necessity to maintain his or her vigor. Straight-backed and high-headed, key allowed himself to slip, ever so slightly, into a peaceful rest. He was so blissful, in fact, that he failed to notice the ceasing of the pen scratches. The captain cleared his throat, and Key's eyes popped open, stature unmoving.

"I thought you had gone to sleep on me for a minute." The captain said.

"I was just resting my eyes, sir." Key admitted. "It was a long night."

"Took the night out on the town?" the captain asked, seemingly neutral.

"Sergeant made me pull a double when I got back," Key said matter-of-factly. "He said that since you were taking me off the watch bill today, I should make up for it."

"Did you not understand my direct order to take the rest of the day off?" the captain said, slow boiling anger punctuating his words. "Or did you assume that working for me was a thankless, perkless job reserved solely for the lowest of dimwits that they should think getting stabbed was the best way to avoid all of the extra responsibility?"

"Neither sir." Key stood to attention. It was an unconscious reflex drilled into him from the very beginning of his career. "I told the sergeant that you had given me the rest of the day off, but he said…" he paused, thinking better of breaking the brotherhood of the guard. If he incriminated his sergeant, his life could very well become a living nightmare. "He told me that he was short on men yesterday."

"At ease, man," the captain waved him down, anger cooling behind his eyes.

Key sat down.

"So, they had you up all night standing watch before turning you over to me?" It wasn't a question. He seemed to ponder the idea out loud before coming to a personal resolve. "We should do something about that, shouldn't we?"

Key, not knowing how to respond to the question, nodded awkwardly once.

"Take this letter to late Mister Stapleton's estate. It doesn't matter whose hands it goes to, just as long as it gets there. It's a letter explaining their unfortunate loss in hopes of clearing up some confusion. Deliver it solemnly."

Key took the letter and, after some more brief instructions, left. The sun had gotten brighter since he entered the office earlier, but the air was crisp. The breeze simultaneously gave Key a burst of energy and reminded him how tired he was. He smiled at his exhaustion the way one might smile at a child threatening them with a stick; it was no match for his ability to press forward.

It was a quiet walk through the city. A handful of birds that had not yet migrated for the winter sang to the rhythm of the clip-clap of his footsteps. The song brought him to the now familiar cobblestone stairs he had climbed the day before. It felt like an eternity ago. At the top, he grasped the door knocker and made three loud taps.

He stood there, his imagination unfurling as he thought of Jory's clever response to the perfume spilled on his tunic. He had to hand it to the man; he was a formidable opponent. If things had been different, Jory might have made a good friend. Their feud had made Key who he was today, even if he distrusted drinking anything he didn't personally pour.

His thoughts brought him back to the present. He was still standing in front of the giant hardwood doors. How long had he been waiting there? He knocked again and waited. There was no response. He had a moment of panic that he wouldn't get any sleep until his message had been delivered. He knocked furiously at the door, ten knocks in a row. He grew anxious and paced.

Determining that if no one was inside the house, it must mean they were in the back. Not wanting to waste any more time, he rounded the house. On the side, he found a path of bricks set into the ground leading into a garden. He made his way through bushes that were brown from the winter's cycle. He tried to imagine the garden looking more welcoming in the spring as opposed to the empty, haunted thing he was trespassing through. No one was around; even the birds had left this place alone.

Straining his neck, he saw that the back door was ajar. Relief washed over him. He called out, "Hello!" No one replied, so he approached the back door.

Dirt and leaves had blown into the doorway. Peering into the house, he saw there was no light, no noise, and none of the normal bustling about that took place inside estates such as this.

"Hello?" he asked the empty air, pushing the door open. "Royal Guard, your door is wide open. I'm here on official business. Is anyone home?"

There was nothing, and then a bang.

"I can hear someone inside," he said, annoyed. "I have a message to deliver, and then I will be on my way." *On my way to bed,* he thought.

Bang, bang, bang.

"Hello?" he asked the open air and then noticed for the first time the disarray of the place. Cabinets were open, plates and cutlery were scattered around, and paintings lay broken on the ground.

Bang, bang, bang.

He drew his sword and entered. Seeing nobody on the first floor, he climbed the steps, finally realizing how crazy all of it was. The banging was getting louder, so he followed the noise closer to the source, sword at the ready.

He turned the knob and pushed the door open a small amount. He then backed up, holding his sword to point toward the crack of light, and charged. His heart hammered in his chest, sweat already pooling under his clothes. He shoved the door open with his foot. Light from the window washed over him.

In the center of the room sat the two women he had spoken to the day before. Still wearing matching uniforms, old and young, the two sat back-to-back with their hands tied to a massive bedpost. He almost forgot to inspect the rest of the room as he ran to free them. Untying their gags, he pulled the saliva-soaked strips of cloth away from their faces.

"Oh, thank the creator!" the older one exclaimed, working her jaw. The younger one gave similar exclamations as Key began working on the knots that tied their arms.

"Is there anyone else in the house?" He asked.

"I don't think so," The older one said. "The bandits left while it was still dark. We haven't heard from anyone for hours. They tied us up, gagged us, and then robbed the house. How did you know to come save us? Who are you?"

"I'm Corporal Key," he said, finishing the first knot and beginning working on the other. "I have a letter to deliver. What are your names?"

"My name is Eloise," The older one said. "And this is Elisabeth."

"I am in your debt," Elisabeth said, rubbing her wrists. Color began returning to her cheeks.

"It's nothing," Key said, feeling color creep into his cheeks as well. "I was doing my job. Now, I have some rather unfortunate correspondence to deliver, and then I have a report to make."

Key handed Eloise the wax-sealed letter and investigated the rest of the house. Sword in hand, he searched room after disheveled room. Desks and bookshelves lay toppled over, and their contents were dumped in piles on the floor. Parchments mingled among cracked or chipped dishes. Only the chamber pots sat undisturbed. He unlocked the front door and swung it inward.

Stepping out into the sunlight, Key brought out and marveled at his whistle. It was still shiny. For the second time in his whole career, he brought the whistle to his lips and blew. He blew continuously in short bursts until two guards ran up the steps, one after the other. He explained the situation and sent one of them to get help. Before he knew it, the house and property were swarming with guards. He stood around uselessly, still tired from standing watch the day before.

Sergeant Allister listened to the reports Key made and then took over as the primary overseer for the crime. Captain Castor appeared, and the sergeant passed the responsibility of overseer to him and explained the series of events that had transpired. Key stood close by, making sure he got the story right.

"Corporal Key," the captain said. "It seems you have a gift."

"Just doing my job, sir." Key said wanting the conversation to get to the part where he gets sent away to sleep it off.

"But twice in two days?" the captain asked. "I'm

beginning to think you might be very good at doing your job."

"Perhaps, sir," Key said. "It's possible the two crimes were related. You know, word got out about the dead man, and thieves realized that no one would be around to protect the place, so they robbed it. I just happened to be the one who showed up because I had a letter explaining the man's death in the first place."

The captain looked surprised at this insight and instinctively reached for his pipe. "That doesn't sound like a bad theory. Thieves catch wind of the late Mister Templeton's death, so they rob his house. Allister, what do you think?"

"It sounds, sound enough for me, sir." The sergeant agreed.

Key decided to try his luck with a more direct route. "Is there anything else I can do for you today, or may I take my leave?" he asked.

"There are several things I can think of," the captain said. "But that can wait for tomorrow if you want to get some rest?"

"Yes, sir," Key said gratefully. "I would like that very much."

"Go get some rest, then," the captain said and then moved close so only Key could hear. "Don't bother checking in with your sergeant. I will inform him that you will not be attending the morning assembly. Instead, report to my office at the sixth bell. I have a very time-sensitive mission, and it would help if you left your current chain of command out of it. Do I make myself clear?"

"Yes, sir," Key acknowledged. He kept his face passive, saluted, and then made his way to the barracks.

After some cold meat and warm beer, he told the barracks watch to wake him well before the sixth bell. He then climbed the stairs to his room and collapsed on his pillow.

Evan Kvalvik

# Chapter 6

## The Journey Up

T he sun was setting, and the air was cold and dry, but luckily for Benj, it wasn't blowing yet. It was the day after his birthday when he had set out on his trek to the peak of Asven. He was just now nearing the mountain's base and would need to set up camp soon. If he didn't, he would be setting up camp in the dark.

*At this rate, it looks like I'm not beating anyone's records, he thought*, drifting forward like the river he was following. The wind shot a gust through his brown leather jacket as if to inform him that winter was upon him. When Brahm made the journey, it hadn't been this cold yet.

His pack was heavy, but Benj tried to stay optimistic; he had been waiting to take this journey for a very long time. He jumped over a small river and found a clearing of trees at the base of the mountain. Drawing closer, he saw a fire pit and a good place to pitch a tent for the night. Two hours later, the fire was roaring, and Benj was fast asleep.

In the morning, Benj woke, sat on a log, and looked around his campsite. To his right, large rocks that had toppled from the cliffs lay in a massive pile. On top of the pile sat the largest rock, which, upon further investigation, had names etched into it. Tys, Frejar, Jarlstone, "and look what we have here," Benj said out loud, eyes stopping on a familiar name written with a sloppy hand. It was Brahm's. A few scrapes with his knife later, the rock now read, "Brahm kisses sheep." He admired his artwork and was satisfied.

Without wasting more time, he packed his bags and stood looking between where he had come from and up at the new day's challenge. He really wanted to be done already, but if he never finished, he would never know if he was man enough to.

Benj turned up towards the mountain and started his slow ascent into Asven. It was surprising how often he had to decide whether to climb a rock wall straight up or take the easy option. More often than not, the slow, steady path would lead to a drop-off, causing him to backtrack.

Nearing the late afternoon, he found that there hadn't been any decent areas to set up camp. He needed to hurry before he ran out of strength to go further, or it got too dark to see. Again, he was faced with the choice to take a long narrow passage with a gentle slope or a direct climb. He tested a few handholds and decided to go up.

The chill wind tore at his face and handholds. It wasn't looking good. His pack seemed to get heavier and heavier as he climbed. He reached out with his left hand and found a hold above him. He took his left foot off, putting more weight on his hands when his left hand sprang loose, tossing rocks and dirt down the mountain's face. He held on with his right hand and foot, swinging out over the vast drop. He steadied himself and stole a glance downward. He could see down the cliff where there were no gentle landing places. He couldn't feel his hand gripping the cold stone, but the only way out was up.

His pack kept trying to pull him down as he took hold after hold trying to focus on his hand, foot, hand, foot until he reached the top. He swung a leg over the cliff's edge and gradually slid and rolled until he was lying down, facing the edge and breathing heavily. He was done for the day.

The clearing was wide enough for his bedroll with some room to spare. There seemed to be a clear enough path sloping upward to one side and a steep downward slope to the other. He set up camp and checked his supplies. He had enough flatbread and dried meat to last another twelve days without rationing.

"Why did I pack so much?" He questioned outwardly, loud enough for the mountain cliffs to repeat his question, returning his echoing voice. He ate as much as he could and threw as much down the mountain. He set up camp, but it would be a cold, restless night with no firewood nearby.

The following day, he awoke before the sun peeked over the mountain's crest and decided to get an early start. He got up and worked the aches out of his body with visible breath. He packed his bedroll and heard a snapping noise. He reached to his belt where his knife was and held it out. A moment later, a low growl came from his right, where he saw a thin mountain wolf making its way through the clearing of rocks and bushes.

Its thick grey mane had streaks of red and yellow, probably from sleeping on top of his hoarded food in a cave. Foaming saliva dripped off his bared, snarling mouth as it saw Benj and slowly stalked toward him.

"If you're ever face to face with a wild animal, make yourself as big as loud as you can," came Sephus' voice in a flash of memory.

Benj raised his bedroll in one hand and his knife in the other and yelled, "I WILL KILL YOU AND YOUR WHOLE VILE SMELLING FAMILY IF YOU TAKE ONE STEP CLOSER!!"

The beast took another calculated step closer.

"AAAAAHHHH!!!" he yelled, waving his bedroll in the air. It wasn't working, and the creature was still moving towards him. Twenty feet, fifteen feet, ten feet.

Benj tried yelling some more, but it hadn't worked. The wolf crouched, and he knew what for.

"Lord of light, don't let me die," he whispered; the prayer rose out of his mouth as frozen vapor. The wolf's eyes flickered. There was no time to think before it sprang forward, its teeth widening in a nefarious grin.

*Mountain wolves are more scared of you than you are of them,* a flagrantly false memory burned itself into his thoughts. Benj held his bedroll in front of himself as a shield and gripped it from both sides. The bite landed on the roll inches from his left hand and knocked the knife out of his hands. Benj smelled urine, blood, and hot putrid breath. He fell backward, the beast on top of him. The grip of the mountain wolf's jaws flattened the roll near his hand and threatened to rip it from his grasp.

Inches from the cliff's edge, he turned and tried throwing the wolf and bedroll down the mountain. The wolf released the bedroll, causing it to fly over the edge, but it staggered as it caught its footing. Benj turned on his back and kicked repeatedly at the animal, which toppled it over near the edge. It caught its grip and sprang forward. Reacting from instinct, Benj caught its front legs in his hands. He squirmed right, avoiding a bite to his neck. He kicked with his legs as hard as he could, pulled, and thrust the animal over the edge. The mountain wolf let out a pitiful cascading cry for several heartbeats as it tumbled through empty air and plummeted down the mountain. It landed somewhere with a loud crack that echoed from the cliff's depths.

Benj realized he was holding his breath and let out a sigh. Relief washed over him like a wave of comfort. He gathered all his belongings with shaky hands and set up towards the continuous incline. Moments later, an old song came to him. It was one he had heard Sephus sing after an exceptionally good night at the tavern. His voice rang out a smooth tenner, and with glory in his chest, he sang out:

"No, brandish swords nor clashing steal shall error to pierce my heart. Not shadows yelling: MOUNTAIN WOLVES!" He changed the lyrics. "Shall rob victory from my soul. Come away, my lads, and soldier up! Tomorrow, we will see. No bows nor bolts nor melee hands will take our victory!"

The mountain ridge pierced the sky like an ax through a log. At the pinnacle, Benj could see the tops of the clouds wisp past the mountain peaks. It was a sight to behold, but most importantly, it was finally time to turn around and start back home. The air was thin, and it was difficult to breathe properly.

After soaking in the view of all the surrounding areas, he realized something. He was on the top but not at the highest point he could go. The highest point was a good twenty-minute hike along the ridge and about a twelve-foot climb straight up a rock wall.

"I made it this far," He said to himself, "And it's not like I'll be beating anyone's record if I start down now." So, he made his way to the highest peak of Asven. It was more for himself than anything else. To become a man, you only have to reach the top; by every definition, he was there already.

The climb was a little more challenging than he'd expected. The holds were smaller and fewer between, but having left his pack at the base, he had more area of movement and an easier time navigating around to the top.

When he got to the top, he found something quite unusual. In the middle of the peak, hidden by ridges from every direction, was a circular table carved out of the mountain's stone. It was almost perfectly round and big enough that if he lay on it with his hands and legs spread out, he might barely touch the ledges, if at all. Even more interesting were the names carved into it.

Unlike the boulder at the base of the mountain, the characters here were carved into the table as if drawn with great reverence. The names seemed to spiral from the center. The most recent one was Mayor Grensald Frojor Hagen. Next was William Stoeger, the shoemaker, and other names he did not recognize, Ava Grey, Seles Laymont, and Mustava Truestorm, all forming a circular list around a central focal point.

He followed the circle with his eyes, reading each name aloud until he reached the one in the center of the table. It was the first name to be inscribed, and it read, "Zilez Kalizar," and it was written in a small waving script. He felt a shiver. Maybe it was the cold or the altitude, but even though he was reading it for the first time, he felt reverence for the name. To be the first to climb Asven and to become the forefather of a tradition he was now a part of was no small feat.

He went to the outside of the list, just after Mayor Hagen and, with the knife from his belt, inscribed 'Benjos Baker.' He wasn't born with a surname but had adopted 'Baker' soon after he was. After the final stroke of his knife, he felt something odd, like he was being watched from behind. He looked and saw nothing but vast space and distance. Still, the tingling on his back lingered for a span of a few breaths, and then it was gone.

"Hmm," he grunted and then walked toward the ledge to figure out how to get down. It was time to go. The drop wasn't more than twelve feet down. It would be no different than jumping off the roof of the bakery. Still, he didn't want to land wrong, so he hung from the ledge, kicked off, turned, and let go.

The cold mountain air rushed past his ears as he fell, except he wasn't falling, at least not normally. He was falling forward and down as if he was carried by a giant bird. He glided six feet past his intended target and was still four feet in the air. The unexpected flight took Benj off guard and off-balance, sending his body backward as if slipping on ice. His descent angle decreased as he flew almost horizontal to the ground. He touched down, slid, and fell straight onto his back, fortunately missing the jagged rocks in front of him.

"What just happened?" Benj asked himself out loud, checking his head and ribs. It didn't feel like he broke anything. After dusting himself off and going over the events in his mind, he stood up and looked back up the peek. He had to try that again.

He climbed back up the ridge, hung, and kicked off

again. This time, ready for anything, he stayed balanced as he moved through the air, coasting forward and down. He leaned back, slowing his descent, and slid to a stop. He was still standing this time, which made him smile.

For the next hour, his experiments got increasingly more reckless. There were times that, if the spell or whatever caused him to glide downward had decided to wear off, he would have fallen to his death or broken his legs and then died. He found that he could roughly steer his movement by leaning in either direction or he could fall faster by leaning forward.

He picked up the biggest boulder he dared to carry, moved to the edge of a six-foot drop along the mountain's crest, and jumped. The boulder pulled him at a steeper angle towards the ground, but he was still making a slower descent.

"Doesn't go as far with a lot of weight, got it," Benj noted to himself while he made his way down the mountain's shallowest slopes. He ate dried meat as he hiked, taking the long way down - the way he hadn't seen on the way up.

The air had only started feeling more breathable when the sky began getting dark. He found a flat piece of ground and made camp. Without a bedroll, he found a place to lay down with no sharp rocks jutting up. He made himself as comfortable as he could and went to sleep.

# Chapter 7

## Tradition

It was completely light outside when Benj woke. He was still tired, and the air was still hard to get enough of. A number of places on his body hurt from sleeping without a bed mat, so he stood up and started working the stiffness out of his joints. He decided that the faster he got off the mountain, the better. A thought struck him. Why should he bother climbing down when he could probably just jump.

He found a straight path and tested to see if he still had his new abilities or if it was some weird hallucination. He still had them. With a foggy mind, he became resolute with his plan. He opened his pack, took out his cooking pan, threw it into the mist below, and then discarded anything else heavy in the bag. He took a deep breath and soaked in his surroundings one last time. He ran towards the edge and then stopped at the last moment.

"This is a bad idea," he said to himself, turning to find a clear path. Except, there wasn't a clear path down. The shallow path he had been taking dropped off in every direction. He turned and looked up where he came from. It would be a long hike back up to find another path down. Exasperated, he took off his pack and looked inside. The only thing heavy he had left was his water, so he dumped the rest of it. Finally satisfied that his pack was light enough, he took in his surroundings one last time, took a deep breath, and jumped.

The ground fell away as he rushed over it. The pressure change made his ears pop, and the wind threatened to freeze him mid-air. Benj was afraid to shift position in case it caused him to fall. He had experimented with it on the mountain, but nothing to this degree. He didn't want to learn anything the hard way.

The ground was the farthest it had ever been from him. He had never been afraid of heights, but probably because he had never seen them with this magnitude. The view was breathtaking and terrifying as he flew through the juxtaposition of earth and air.

The ground started closing in, and Benj wasn't expecting to have been going so fast. Rivers and trees passed him underfoot. He leaned left to avoid a tall tree and maneuvered around it. He was close to the ground now. He leaned back so his flight path nearly paralleled the ground. A bush swiped at his shoes before he contacted soil and gravel. His feet slid violently on the ground for a long stretch before he hit a mud hole, causing him to roll forward on a patch of grass.

Benj lay there, sprawled out in grass and sunlight. "That wasn't so bad," he told himself. The sound of birds singing and a throbbing pain in his whole body reminded him that he was still alive. He slowly sat up and checked for damage. Despite having more than a couple of sore areas on his body and some pretty impressive thrashings on his arms and legs, he made it out completely unscathed, considering he had just jumped off the side of a mountain.

He gauged how far he had come. It looked like he was less than a half-day walk from home. He stood up, adjusted the broken shoulder strap on his travel pack, and set out at an excruciatingly slow pace.

Benj limped through the gates of his village, sore and hurting. All he wanted to do was take a hot bath, eat a hot meal, and lie down. But he couldn't yet. The bell in the middle of town had two purposes: To alert the town in the case of an emergency and, in Benj's case, to alert the town at the end of the traditional Asven Trek. The ringing of the bell was a symbol that he was old enough to be a valuable member of the village, fend off attackers, and help during the event of a casualty.

He put his hand on the thick, woven rope and rang it two good times, nothing extravagant. Other boys had wildly rung the bell for half a minute in the past, alerting a crossed-armed and, quite frankly, cross village. He would not be one of those.

The bell rang out loud and true, and within moments, the whole village was starting to come out and gather around the bell. Finally, Mayor Hagan walked out with a considerably large ale horn. Benj had almost forgotten about this part. He was to make a toast and drink until it was gone. The horn was as long as his arm and filled to the brim.

"Attention, ladies and gentlemen," Mayor Hagen said, calming the sea of mumbles. "A few days ago, we said goodbye to one of our boys, and today, a man returned. He has finished the Asven Trek and the hike to the top. But, as tradition states, there's one last thing that he must do... he has to say his piece and then empty the horn!" The mayor handed the horn to Benj.

"Go on then," he said.

Benj cleared his throat. He had been expecting this toast for a long time. He had spent years considering what to say at this moment, but now that he was up there, he had forgotten everything he had planned. He began anyway, "To the men who have gone before us, to the women they left behind, to the wild animals who didn't get us, and to the women who will. Cheers!"

The crowd erupted in applause as he drank from the long, smooth ale horn. He was surprised to find that it wasn't ale at all but a light mead. It was easy to drink, at least for the first half. Either his appetite had shrunk in the last few days, or the horn was bigger than he had always thought. People began to cheer his effort, and he pressed on. When he was finished, he slowly turned the horn upside down. The crowd broke out into applause and then laughter as he fell over. Benj stood again, slightly embarrassed, and handed the horn back to the mayor.

"You did well," the mayor said, taking the horn.

"Thanks!" Benj said and then lowered his voice. "I saw your name written-"

"Yes, you did," he cut him off. His smile grew serious, "and don't mention it."

Benj smiled conspiratorially, cheeks flushed from the mead and nodded.

"Benjo!" Sephus called out from the crowd. Let's get you home. I've seen pigs cleaner-looking than you."

"I never thought I would say this, but it's good to see you," Benj said through a sincere smile and spotted Mel. "I'll catch up."

Sephus noticed where Benj was looking, gave a wink, and left.

"Hi Mel," he called after her.

"Welcome back!" She exclaimed, weaving herself through conversations about weather predicaments and farming matters.

"Thanks!" he said, stepping off the circular stone platform that held the town bell. "I'm honestly not going to believe I'm back until I'm physically in my bed and wearing clean clothes."

"Now that you mention it," she said, gesturing up and down, "You look awful."

He gave a hearty chuckle and thanked her.

"No, I'm not just referring to your clothes," she said, concerned, "You look like you got in a fight with a sawmill or something."

"You really know how to compliment a guy." He said ironically.

"I'm sorry, it's just... Your face!" Mel poked his scratched cheek where blood had dried and crusted. "You should take better care of yourself."

"Ow! What was that for?" Benj said, holding his face.

"For not taking care of yourself." Mel said, somehow managing a frown and a smirk simultaneously, "And I've missed you."

Benj felt his cheeks get hot. *Don't blush, don't blush, don't blush,* he thought, and said, "I've thought about you once or twice, maybe."

"Oh, stop," she said, slapping him on a bruised portion of his arm, "As soon as you are done recovering and bathed, let's catch up... There's something I want to tell you."

He asked what it was, but she refused and promised

85

to tell him the next time they were together.

"That sounds good," he said and stepped back before she had the opportunity to attack any more of his bruises, "I would hug you, but I'm sure I smell worse than a street urchin sock."

"Then you owe me one," Mel said, turning to leave.

Benj felt his heart burning in his chest after her. He wanted nothing else than to recover fast so he could spend time with her. Though something in the back of his head told him, he wasn't as charming as he could have been.

"Benj," Mayor nudged him and lowered his voice. "I don't think you realize this, but you're staring."

"What? Oh," he said, pulling his attention away from Mel.

"This is a small town," the mayor said through the corner of his lips. "If you don't want to give them something to talk about, I recommend you try looking in a different direction."

Benj beamed an embarrassed smile towards the man. "Thank you, I had no idea."

"It's ok," the mayor smiled. "I can keep a secret. If you want to have that conversation, come to my estate at any time."

"Thanks! I will!" Benj said and made his way home.

When he opened the door to the bakery, he found a young kid putting a pot of water over the fire. The kid stood up straight and said, "Master Benj, my name is Taft, and I'm your new apprentice!"

Ideally, apprentices were never picked for you; you were supposed to interview interested people, spend some time with them, and decide which candidate to select, if any. Unfortunately, Benj wasn't afforded the opportunity to pick an apprentice because apprentice day was the first of the year, which was when he left on his journey. Instead of waiting a whole other year, Sephus chose the only person interested in being a baker. By the look of his waistline, there wasn't any mistaking the reason why.

"Taft, what's your last name?" Benj asked, looking him over.

"That is my last name, Master Benj," he said, still standing straight, wringing his hands. Nervous.

"Just call me Benj; none of this 'master' business as long as you follow orders and learn fast. Are you a fast learner, Taft?"

"Yes, Mast- uh, sir."

Benj sighed, "What's your first name?"

"Teft"

"Your name is Teft Taft?"

"Technically, it's Teft T. Taft."

"What's the 'T' stand for?" Benj asked, already regretting doing so.

"It's, uh, Taffetas," he said. "The third"

"Taft it is then," Benj said abruptly. "What do you enjoy doing in your free time?"

"Eating and probably burning things."

"Any good with an ax?"

"I'm better at burning things."

"Then I would say you are in the right place," Benj said.

"Lord Sephus said I was born to be a baker."

"Lord Sephus said that did he?" Benj couldn't help but smile. The only title Sephus had was 'Baker.' He had given himself the title 'Master Baker' in the past, but the only thing he was truly masterful at was the ability to do absolutely nothing. Not many people shared his rare gift of laziness. It was harder than it looked; Benj had tried it once. He pondered this when, as if on cue, Sephus popped his head around the corner.

"Benjo, I drew you a bath. It should be hot by now. I left you the good soap, so those wounds don't fester." He said and then made a sniffing sound, "You're going to need a lot of it."

"Thank you, lord Sephus," Benj said.

"No problem," he said with a guilty smile. "Are you hungry?"

"Yes, very," Benj said.

"Taft, go make him something to eat."

"Ok!" Taft said, "What do you want?"

"Something to soak up the alcohol," Sephus replied.

"I'm quite enjoying the alcohol thanks."

"I was talking about me," Sephus said with a concerned look. "I got an early start this morning. You're going to want it too when all that sweetness kicks in, and your head is pounding before sunset."

"Sausages and hot cakes then," Benj said and left to bathe.

He peeled off his clothes, uncovering a filthy and battered body, then closed his eyes as he slipped into the scalding hot water. He hadn't had the luxury of a hot bath for what seemed an eternity. He scrubbed the dirt free of his wounds first, being gentle not to reopen the scabs. He removed the earth from his hair and the rest of his body and then fell asleep.

"Ahem."

Benj awoke with Taft hovering over his bath, holding a tray of food.

"Oh, thanks, just set it over there, I'm about to get out

anyway." Benj stood up, grabbed his towel, and wrapped it around himself.

"Does that have a meaning?" Taft asked.

"What are you talking about?" Benj asked in return.

"A good friend of mine said that every tattoo he got has some kind of meaning." Taft said thoughtfully, "like when he got a spider for his wife, something about either "venomous lies" or "web of deceit.""

"Oh, I've never gotten a tattoo," Benj said, "I don't think I ever will."

"What about the one on your back?" Taft asked patiently.

"I don't have a tattoo on my back," Benj said.

"Then, that is the weirdest, coolest birthmark I've ever seen."

"What birthmark?"

"Hang on," Taft ran out and came back with a polished silver plate and held it up.

Benj looked at his back through the reflection. In the center of his back, below his shoulder blades, there it was. It was a light blue circle as if painted in a single stroke with very little paint.

"Oh, that!" He said, playing it off like he had forgotten, "I got that for a girl. She was... Well rounded." That was the best he had. At least until he found the real meaning of it or managed to scrub it off.

Benj sat in front of the sausages and hot cakes. "You really are good at burning things." He remarked, "Tomorrow, we have a lot to go over." With that, he ate and slept in his own bed for the rest of the day and night.

When morning came, Benj got up to find Taft sleeping in a cot a few feet away from him.

"Taft," Benj said.

"Yeah?"

"It's time to rise and shine." He said, sitting up.

"I'm up."

"Up is what I'm doing; what you're doing is what most cultures would consider down."

Taft yawned and groaned at the same time and then rolled out of bed.

"Can you put a kettle on and meet me outside?" Benj asked, putting clothes on.

Taft did what he was told and then met Benj outside next to the wood pile.

"Every morning when I get up, I chop wood," Benj said, holding his axe. His body was too injured to give him an example. "Have you ever chopped wood before?"

"Sephus had me chop it while you were gone," Taft explained. "He didn't let me do much else. I mean, I did everything else, but I could chop wood unsupervised. For the most part. How much do you need?"

"Maybe a couple of logs worth, to start," Benj said, handing Taft the axe.

"There should be enough over there," Taft pointed towards the other side of the house where chopped wood lay in a neat and massive pile to the roof.

Benj whistled, took the ax, and hung it back up.

Inside, the kitchen was the cleanest it had ever been. Benj kept it clean, but this was nearly perfect. Everything was exactly where it belonged. All containers were perfectly aligned with each other, and there was no hint of flour or sugar anywhere. "Sephus didn't do this," Benj said.

"He supervised," Taft recounted.

"That makes sense," Benj said, remembering Sephus drinking ale and barking orders when he had first started baking. "Will you bring an arm full of wood inside? It's time to start a fire."

Taft brought an enthusiastic armload of wood.

Benj started a fire in the furnace while Taft watched. "Getting a good fire going and controlling it in such a small area will take practice. You have to move the coals to the outside to maintain even heat. The flames move up and heat the oven in a separate compartment above." He opened the oven door above the furnace and gazed at it. It was also spotless.

"Not too hot, or you'll have burnt dough. If it's not hot enough, then you'll have dry bread." Benj took out two buns, hollowed out a small space in the top of each, cracked an egg into the hollowed-out area, and tossed them in the oven.

"There's a difference between cooking and baking," he continued, "I'm going to need you to know how to do both, so I'm not stuck making us breakfast every morning."

Taft was absorbing everything he said, or at least he looked like he was.

"How many recipes do you think you can memorize in a month?" Benj asked.

"I don't know," Taft said, "How many should I?"

"Zero."

Taft, surprised, just looked at Benj questioningly.

"I am not going to make you memorize a single recipe," he said, "because it's better to have the recipe in front of you for the fiftieth time than to make one mistake the forty-ninth time. You might want to memorize where the recipes are. Baking takes time; finding where everything is should not, at least not eventually."

"Also," Benj took one of the well-worn recipe books

off the shelf, "this belongs to Sephus. Do you think you can find his favorite recipe?"

"How?" Taft asked.

"You'll see," Benj said and left the room.

Moments later, Taft called out, "I found it!"

"Oh, did you?" Benj came in, holding two tankards of char leaf tea, and placed one in front of Taft.

"Venison pie." He said.

"That's right," Benj said, "how did you find it?"

"These dark smudges here on the top of the paper," Taft said, beaming. "There's a lot more of them on this page than the others."

"Do you want that nasty grime inside your mouth?" Benj asked.

"I'm inclined to say no."

"That is why I expect you to wash your hands before touching any food, and try to do a good job," after a few moments he added, "or touching recipes." He opened the oven, took out an egg bun he had made, and tossed it to Taft.

"Ouch, ouch, ouch." Taft tossed it up and down before setting it on the counter. "Why did you do that?" He asked.

"It's... Tradition."

# Chapter 8

## Ceremony

K ey woke while it was still dark. Four of the five men who shared his barracks room let out soft snores and whispered breathing. One of the cots lay empty; Alrick was probably on watch. He put on his bathrobe and walked out into the common room.

Each room in the barracks slept anywhere from four to nine people, depending on the size of the room or the rank of the individual. The only exception was Trudie - the only female guard. She slept by herself in the smallest room. Women were encouraged to join the Royal Guard, but not many answered the call. Key thought it was a shame; it was hardly fair that Trudie got a whole room to herself.

The common room had two hearths that burned day and night in the winter. Food was usually available, though the selection was poor. Key poured himself some tea and took a small loaf of bread and ham before walking to the bathhouse.

Contrasting to the giant barracks built with warm-smelling timber, the bathhouse was a smaller structure made from old stone. Figures chiseled from columns lining the walls offered sculpted towels, oils, and other stone-shaped amenities. Earlier in his career, Key marveled at the bathhouse. He considered how nice the king's bath must be if simple guards were privileged enough for this one.

He entered and disrobed, laying his garb on a bench before rounding the corner. Steam billowed out from the bath; Alrick sat in the water across from a newer guard he recognized as Borjani.

"Alrick!" Key said, stepping into the warm water and holding his meal high enough to avoid the splashes. "I thought you would be on watch."

"Just got off," Alrick said. "Played some cards, broke even. It was a good night. Borjani here cleaned everyone else out."

"You guys were at the armory tonight?" Key asked.

"Where else?"

"Isn't Borjani a little new to be playing with the big boys?" Key said before facing the younger man. "No offense."

"None taken," Borjani admitted, hiding any potential hurt feelings.

"He's alright," Alrick said. "I vouch for him."

"Thank you," Borjani beamed.

Alrick ignored him and looked at Key with concern. "I heard your name spoken a few times from the higher-ups. I couldn't tell if it was good or bad. Is everything alright?"

"Normally, I would assume the worst, but this time, as crazy as it sounds, I think it might be a good thing." Key took a sip from his mug and then recounted his last two days. He started with the discovery that his armor had been shined and talked about double duty, finding a dead body in the street, and what happened to the man's house. He ended the story by explaining how he walked into the bathhouse only to find the two ugliest tossers he had ever seen.

"Hey," Borjani said. "Your mother thinks I'm handsome."

"You discovered a murder, saved two beautiful women, and got sent home early? All without taking a nap?" Alrick said, eyebrows reaching upward. "They'll probably make you an officer after that."

"I doubt it," Key admitted. "They wouldn't waste the money on my commission. And even if I did, who would want to be a stupid officer?"

"Good point," Alrick said, playing with the water. "Not me."

"What I want to know is, how did it feel blowing the whistle?" Borjani asked. The question caught Alrick's attention, who had stopped splashing around.

"You know when you're doing something you're not supposed to, and it feels good?" Key asked.

The two nodded in unison.

"It felt like that," Key proclaimed. "This whole time, we've carried these things around, but nothing ever goes wrong, so we can't use them."

"And we just carry them around like the forbidden fruit with fear and reverence," Borjani interjected.

"Uh, sure," Key turned his whole body towards Alrick. "I think your guy here is a poet."

"He gets excited sometimes," Alrick waved him off. "You should have seen him bluff with some of the ugliest cards I've ever seen. Went on about how he gave a dying monk his last coin, and now the spirit of the monk gives him good cards or some such."

"It worked, didn't it?" Borjani asked.

"We'll see if it works next time," Alrick said doubtfully. "If you're ever in a card game with him, just know that the more confident he acts, the more he's bluffing."

"Or so I want you to think," Borjani said with an attempt at malicious laughter.

"We'll see if I ever stand watch in the Armory again," Key admitted uncertainly. "I think Dilly has it out for me. He didn't seem to like that Castor took me off the watch bill. Not to mention, he needs me again tomorrow. So that's another day I won't be supporting his 'watch bill flexibility.' On top of that, I haven't even told him yet that I won't be at muster tomorrow."

"You're just going to no-show and hope your good behavior covers for it?" Alrick's tone was clearly sarcastic.

"Good behavior or not, Dilly is going to beat you silly," Borjani predicted.

"Here's the thing," Key made an arbitrary circle with his fingers. "Captain Castor told me not to check in. He told me to skip muster and show up at his office and not to tell anyone."

"That's funny because he's not in your direct chain of command," Alrick pointed out. "Captain or not, he can't really do that. Or at least I don't think he can. What does he do anyway?"

"He is in charge of investigations, but I don't really know what he does," Key admitted. "Even then, I would be hard-pressed not to obey the direct order of a captain. Especially when it suits my interests."

"Even if the captain does fight your case for not

showing up in the morning, he'll get you eventually, one way or the other," Borjani shrugged. "Dilly always remembers."

"See?" Alrick pointed both hands towards Borjani. "Hardly a new guy anymore. Already knows Dilly up and down."

"I'm learning," Borjani tapped the side of his head. "Alrick explained the great Key and Jory feud today. I honestly believed he was buying perfume for a girl when it spilled all over himself."

"I would have believed it if he was buying it for himself," Alrick said. "I know Key's touch when I see it. That trick reeked of your doing. Know what you're going to do next?"

"I am ashamed to admit that I don't," Key said. "Usually, I have a couple of good ideas brewing before he makes his move, but I've been kind of busy."

"Tie his pant legs together and fill them with sawdust," Borjani blurted out.

"That's not a bad idea," Alrick said approvingly.

"If there were any doubts about Yorbani before, you've squelched them," Key slapped the kid on the shoulder. "Welcome to the big boy's club."

"You're not half bad yourself," Borjani said thoughtfully before teaching him the correct pronunciation of his name. The three finished bathing and made their way back to the barracks. Key explained why they shouldn't repeat anything they had talked about. Oaths were sworn, and the three of them split off to go to their respective beds.

"Key, you slog, this is your sixth-bell wake-up." A voice came from a shadowy figure hovering over him. "I'm not coming back."

"I'm up," Key said, rising to see the barracks watch and leaving his room.

He slipped on his clothes and rubbed a cloth over a few areas to maintain the polished look. *It looks like I have to try to look good for one more day,* he thought, slipping the armor on and clasping the last few pieces in place. He stepped out into the common room, climbed down some stairs, passed a few tired-eyed acquaintances, and headed outside. The air was colder than it had been all winter. Key's breath made rapidly decaying plumes of mist in the air. The rocks he stepped on seemed to hold their ground instead of sinking into the earth as he moved toward his destination.

Arriving, he knocked three times on the door, lighter than usual to preserve his frozen fingers.

"Enter," came Castor's voice from inside. He opened the door to a warm fire and candles; the room was otherwise dark.

"Come in at ease," the captain said, pouring a measure of red wax onto an envelope. "I'm almost done."

He pulled out a spoon, small enough for a pebble, and scooped a silvery white powder from a copper vessel. He sprinkled it over the wax and pressed a round metallic stamp into it. The symbol was generic to his station, three diamonds inside three circles in a delta configuration. He briefly pressed a ring from his right hand in the middle of the impression and blew on it.

Key wandered over to inspect a hand-drawn map of Royal City on the wall. The image showed the castle, roads, alleys, temples, and businesses. He couldn't read the road names in the dimly lit room, but traded the blurry words for the names he knew by heart in his head.

"We have a big day ahead of us," the captain said.

"Well, you do anyway. Care to know what the plan is?"

"Yes, sir," Key answered.

"I'll have none of that when we are working together, save for when there are people around," the captain said. "If you are capable of maintaining airs of courtesy when required, a simple yes or no will do."

"I can, sir," Key said and then corrected himself. "I can, and if I understand you correctly, I believe I am capable of discerning a situation."

"Excellent, then you may talk to me like a regular human being," he said and paused a brief moment to steeple his fingers in front of him. "For the two days I have had you on loan, you've shown me nothing but a high aptitude for leadership, investigatory insight, and humility. Don't misunderstand me; you are not yet in a position to coast on your achievements, but I think that your talents, in all sense of the meaning, might be better spent here than playing cards in the armory."

Hearing the guard's best-kept secret from an officer shocked Key.

"Don't worry, I'm not shutting down the card games," Castor said. "It's my job to know things." He held up the sealed letter in his hands. "It's your choice. Do you want to work for me, or do you want to go back to the caprice of Sergeant Dilly?"

"What is the job, exactly?" Key asked.

Castor eyed him momentarily. "I'm the head of investigations, which would make you an assistant to the royal investigator."

"I'm in," Key committed to the job before it went away.

Castor smiled. "I'm glad to hear it. There's only one prerequisite."

"What's that?" Key asked.

"When you speak of me to anyone, and I mean anyone, you have to make me out to be a heartless slave driver that never gives you a moment's rest," Castor grinned. "If you need to list the things that make you sound overworked when your peers ask, by all means, write it down. As far as you will let on, I only care about the king and getting things done at your expense. If you've ever wondered why there are so many churlish officers in the king's guard, it's because only savages get promoted. A reputation I aspire to cultivate."

When Key agreed, Caster held up a letter.

"Take this to Major Kane and stand by for his instructions. I have plans in motion, but you have to work fast," Castor handed it to him.

Key took the letter and walked out onto a stone walkway. He found the Major's office several moments later and knocked on the door.

"Enter!" the voice spoke from behind the door. When Key was inside, he found an older man sitting behind a desk in an office similar to Castor's. He had a large mustache curled up with wax behind a steaming cup of tea. After seeing Key, he held out his hand for the letter. After taking it, he lifted the seal, unfolded the parchment, and spent some time reading over its contents.

Key stood at attention.

The man let out a few grunts of understanding as his eyes touched every letter of every word. When he was done, he leaned back in his chair and raised his eyes to the ceiling, blinking several times. He then found his quill, and with a few swooshes of penmanship, the letter was signed. Moments later, the wax on the letter was pressed with a new seal and then held out for Key to take.

"This goes to Colonel Chapman." He said as Key took the letter.

"Yes, sir," he said and then left back into the chilled weather. The colonel's office was a little bit more of a walk. He passed a statue of a marble woman standing on top of a dry fountain, hands cupped and held out in front of her, offering no water.

He came to a dark wood door with a plaque stating, 'Colonel C. F. Chapman' and knocked.

"Come in," a voice said.

Key found himself in a room big enough to fit a hundred people at least. An elegant but sturdy table decorated a portion of the room with over twenty chairs surrounding it. The chair at the head of the table looked nice enough to be the king's throne. He felt that maybe the chair was for the king. Swords, axes, and shields, mixed with other battle armaments, hung on walls between the mounted heads of hunted beasts.

The colonel stood with two officers Key did not know. They made small talk near a blazing hearth. The colonel was taller than the two, grey hair climbing up his temples. His voice was soft like melted iron and carried farther than the other two voices. When the other two officers were finished, Key saluted them as they walked out of the office. They didn't appear to see him. When he approached the colonel, he saluted again and made his report. "Good morning, I have correspondence, sir."

The colonel returned the salute and held out his hand. "Good morning, how's the weather out there?" he asked, taking a miniature sword from his desk and slipping the blade through the wax seal.

"It's cold, sir," Key replied. "It might be the coldest morning we've had this year."

The colonel looked at Key as if he were truly listening to him as if his weather report was the most important piece of information he could have received. "I see," he said, giving a further moment of reflection. His eyes went from Key to the parchment he was holding. He took a large feather quill from his desk and signed it at the bottom. Perhaps he was a fast reader, or the other signatures on the paper were good enough to elicit his own. His eyes quickly glanced over the document he had just signed before he was satisfied and handed the paper back to Key, unsealed.

"Carry on," he said and then returned to the fire.

"Yes, sir," Key said, saluting the colonel's back. He made his way outside, open letter in hand.

Without further instructions, Key brought the letter directly back to Captain Castor, who was filling his office with pipe smoke.

"The major and colonel both signed this. I'm guessing it goes back to you?" Key asked, getting used to the feeling of talking to a high-ranking officer so casually. He placed the open letter on the captain's desk.

"Did you read it?" Castor asked.

"No," Key answered honestly.

"Oh, good," Castor said, picking up the letter and holding it in his open palm, "Then this is a good place to start. Lesson one, unsealed letters. In an office that greatly benefits from knowing things, unsealed letters are a wealth of information. How can people like you or I know things if we don't take the time to learn them? I recommend looking at every unsealed one of these tomes of knowledge. You would be surprised at the information you can glean from them. Keep in mind that it looks poor for a messenger to be seen snooping around. Barring that, there are plenty of places one could go to investigate the contents of any piece of correspondence.

"This one, for instance, can tell you a lot. Here, at the top, I have added an introduction so mundane that anyone reading it would likely skip it altogether. It also explains what gives me the authority that I have. Under that, I put in some literary cheek-kissing. Let me ask you this, what is better, physically kissing someone's cheeks or convincing them that you've already kissed them?"

"Probably the option where I don't have to physically kiss anyone's rear end, or are we talking about their face?" Key asked, worried he had already left a bad impression by assuming which cheeks he referred to.

"Precisely, and here," Castor pointed to the part of the letter, presumably with the literary cheek kissing, face or otherwise, "I have made it sound as if in all my years, I have been nothing but a humble servant. In person, I wouldn't deign to kiss any part of them, face or otherwise. Remember this, never overtly curry favor with a ranking officer in person. It makes you look weak, and it's bad form. Letters are different; they must embellish your respect, but that is a lesson for another time, I'm sure.

"Under that I made a request. I packaged it in such a way that the colonel would have come to the same conclusion if I didn't mention it at the end. Always form a request in terms of the other person's interests." The captain continued, pointing to the signatures at the bottom of the page.

"Here at the bottom, a keen eye would recognize that I skipped certain people in the chain of command involved. I don't recommend doing that unless you know things. I know things, so I can do them. Care to read?"

After listening to the captain's monologue, Key did

in fact want to read the letter. He took it from the captain's hand and turned his back so the light beginning to creep in from the windows revealing the words. They were written in a swooping script that seemed regal.

Captain Charles Castor, Chief Investigator for the King, protector of the realm of Royal City, son of the late Baron Nathan Castor who was beloved by both King and Creator, and brother to Baron Nathan Caster the second of Brunshold Keep:

To my most esteemed mentors and superior leaders, Major Elton Kane and Colonel C. F. Chapman, a request for your prudence on a matter I believe holds the interest of his Royal Highness the King and you, his mighty constituents.

Under my tutelage, I have worked with one Corporal Eulerous Key who has shown a high aptitude for receiving instruction and performing shrewdly under my edict. He aided me in discovering the Late Mister Templeton after he was murdered in cold blood, and he was the one who charged in for the heroic rescue of Templeton's household servants. I believe it is within the King's best interest and, therefore, our best interest as servants of the King's peace to place him in a more impactful position.

For your judicious decision to allow a lateral transfer of Corporal Eulerous Key from the Office of the Guard to the Office of the Royal Investigator, please sign.

Submitted: Captain Charles Castor
Approved: Major Elton Kane
Certified: Colonel C. F. Chapman

Key lowered the letter, emotions between excitement

and uncertainty. "So, I work for you now?"

"Yes," Castor said.

"Where it says," Key held up the letter and read, "Under your tutelage... I've shown a high aptitude for receiving your instruction and performing shrewdly under your edict," he lowered the letter. "That doesn't seem entirely accurate."

"This conversation we are having right here is why I prefer to do away with propriety when I'm having a discussion one-on-one," Castor said. "If I held you to the strict standard of not speaking until spoken to, standing at attention, keeping my cards hidden from you like so many other people of position do, and all of that "yes, sir," "no, sir" nonsense then I would miss out on some of the most important pieces of information the other person can offer. And I do love information. You spoke to me honestly, but anyone else would only hear petulance.

"When a king conquers a territory, do they say, "It was the army that won the war," or do they say that the king won?" Caster asked.

"They say the king wins," Key replied.

"That's right. Even though the king rarely sees a single battlefield, he is still claimed as the winner. In the same regard, everything you do from here on out will be reflected on me. Had you not rescued anyone but decided to get drunk and walk around the city naked, they would blame me for it," the captain said. "They would say, "Captain, why was your man walking around with his balls out?" I am ambitious, but I am also fair. When I am promoted, it will be because the men under me got me promoted. Right now, the men under me is you. Do you understand?"

"Yes, and I am grateful," Key said. "Does this mean I

don't have to go to the morning assembly anymore or stand watch?"

Castor smiled. He reached for his pipe with one hand and a leather pouch with the other. The pouch was empty. He frowned. "That is correct, but as often as I don't need you, I expect you to continue improving. There's still a lot more we need to go over before you are half the man my last assistant was. Speaking of the morning assembly, guess who wasn't there this morning?"

Key looked at him, puzzled, "me?"

"Correct," Castor said. "If Frederick, erm, I mean if Captain Watford pursues the right channels, he will have Dilly check your barracks before bringing the matter to the office of investigations. Oh, wait, that's me."

"But you told me not to tell anyone or report it," Key formed the statement like a question.

"I haven't told them yet," Castor said. "I will let them know soon enough." He rummaged through his drawers and cabinets before finding another leather pouch. He pulled the contents out and meticulously loaded his pipe, making sure no flakes were left on his desk.

Key sat and watched him light his pipe with a candle on his desk. Wax dripping on a silver plate.

There was a knock on the door. The captain glanced at Key, who was already moving to stand in his position next to the desk, eyes forward.

"Enter," the captain said.

Sergeant Dilly walked into his office and saluted. "Good morning, sir,"

"State your business, sergeant," the captain said, setting down his smoking pipe.

The sergeant eyed Key, standing at attention and looking forward. "I was going to report a certain individual who missed muster, but I see you have already detained him."

"The corporal isn't detained as much as he is working on pressing matters in the service of the King. Furthermore, he will be in my service until I am done with him." The captain said, proffering the letter signed by the colonel. "It says here," he cleared his throat. "For the lateral transfer of Corporal Eulerous Key from Office of the Guard to the Office of the Royal Investigator, signed Major Elton Kane and certified by Colonel C. F. Chapman."

The sergeant held out his hand.

The captain turned the letter around and pointed at the bottom line and signatures.

The sergeant leaned forward to read. A half moment later, the captain retracted the letter, placed it on his desk, and took his pipe. "Is there anything else?"

"I have him standing a double today," the sergeant said. "You can't possibly expect me to make last-minute changes when lateral transfers require two weeks' notice."

Captain Castor rose from his chair, face filling with anger. "Do you forget yourself, sergeant, or has your time in the company of Captain Watford made you as soft-headed as he is?" Before the sergeant had a chance to respond, the captain held up his hand. "Corporal, wait outside."

Key saluted and silently left the office. From outside the door, he could hear the captain yelling at Sergeant Dilly. The attacks were a constant berate of accusations and insults. He could hear things like, "No respect for your superiors," "Your mother must be ashamed," and "When was the last time you even bathed?" The one-sided conversation seemed eternal. When it was over, a red-faced Sergeant Dilly rushed out of the office. His face was a depiction of pure torment. He did not spare a glance at Key as he walked quickly back to where he came from.

After a cautious moment, Key knocked on the door.

"Come in," the captain said.

Key gingerly opened the door and made his way to his chair, careful not to get swept into the same current Sergeant Dilly had.

The captain composed himself, "Normally, I would say something like, "I'm sorry you had to see that," but in this circumstance, I'm glad you were there. I've been working on that speech for the last two days."

"You knew the sergeant was going to come looking for me and that he would be an 'unbathed, slovenly disgrace to the uniform' before I even started working for you?" Key asked, quoting the captain.

"I knew that I would need a new assistant, and that the sergeant would make it difficult for me when I tried to get one. I was correct. I also made you absent from your duties and responsibilities this morning, intentionally, might I add, so that this very conversation would take place," Castor said matter-of-factly. "I accomplished four things by humiliating that sorry excuse for a sergeant. I should say that I truly enjoy efficiency.

"First, I reminded him that I am not one to be trifled with and that it is not in his best interest to work against me. Second, I broke a rule to prove that I could get away with it. The sergeant was right about the two-week lateral transfer notice. Your heroics the other day made it easier for me, but I would have gotten around it either way. When he saw that I had the power to ignore that rule, he assumed that I was close-knit with the powers that be. There are a lot of rules I am going to break in the future, and I don't want anyone to think they can stop me. Third, someone who is flustered is, mark my word, incapable of holding a logical conversation. By setting him off, so to speak, I was able to show him the letter without showing him my cards. My cards being a very disgraceful display of ass kissing that was above the part that I showed him."

Key waited a moment before speaking. "You said there were four reasons."

"Ah yes," Castor said as if acting like he forgot. "The fourth reason, and probably the most important, is a selfish one. I further developed my reputation for being a conspicuous blighter."

"Is that a good thing?" Key asked. "Just wondering."

Castor relit his pipe. "Have you ever heard anything about the quality of friends you keep reflecting who you are as a person?"

Key shrugged.

"It's not only true, but it is my personal philosophy that I would rather fall off a bridge than get roped into the same category as most people in this city." He said before taking three more quick draws from his pipe. "A reputation is a tool. Like a lever, it does all the hard work with minimal effort. If you have a reputation for the sword, no one will challenge you. If you have a reputation for honesty, a simple point of your finger will damn a man to death. The trick is to stand on the long side of that lever. If you have a reputation for cheating, even if you win honestly, no one will believe you. You might even find yourself confronted by someone with a reputation for punching cheaters in the face."

"So, you want people to think you're a..." Key circled his hands for a word.

"A giant lobcock, yes."

"Can I be one too?" Key asked.

"I'm afraid not," Castor said. "You have to be seen as polite, competent, and restlessly hardworking. That is, until you're a captain, then you can do whatever you want."

"The sky will rain baby dragons before that ever happens," Key said. "I couldn't afford a commission in a hundred years based on my salary. How about a sergeant?"

"Now that's a tricky question," Castor said. "Remember those rules I talked about breaking earlier?"

Key nodded his head.

"As a captain, I'm supposed to have, at a minimum, a company of twelve or so people with a residing sergeant under me, at a minimum. When I took over this office as a lieutenant, I rewrote my job description so I wouldn't be bogged down with so many people also attempting to act busy."

There was a knock at the door. Key leaped up and stood at attention in his spot.

"Enter," the captain said.

A tall, dark-haired youth walked in wearing a blue coat over a pale blue sash and matching vest. "Good morning. I have correspondence from Major Kane."

The captain took the envelope and cracked the seal with his thumbs. After he finished reading, he put the letter in his drawer.

"By your leave, sir," the messenger said, requesting to go.

"One moment, Corporal Singer," he said.

"Yes, sir?" Singer replied.

"Where did you get the idea to wear the formal dress uniform?" He asked.

"Major Kane, sir," Singer replied. "He requires all his runners to wear this while in a messenger status. It's for the case that we have orders to the castle during formal events."

"Where did you get it made?" the captain asked.

"Gretta's Sewing Shop on Alpenrose, sir." He responded.

"Then, you are dismissed," the captain said.

Corporal Singer saluted and left the office.

"Do try to not jostle around so much next time someone pays a visit. It sounds suspicious," Castor said. "Where were we?"

"I believe you were explaining the woes of having a company," Key replied.

"I don't want one, and if I had a sergeant working under me, that would make two people negligent of a division," Castor admitted. "If you keep trying to get promoted, I'll have to figure out some kind of workaround."

"So, I just work here? Like, I'm in the family now?" Key asked.

"Did you want a ceremony?" Castor asked.

"I don't know," Key said. "I'm just trying to wrap my head around all of it."

"Ceremony it is," Castor said, reaching into his drawer. He pulled out a white candle and held it across his desk. He moved it back and forth until Key took it. He then held up his lit candle and walked around his desk.

' "This flame represents the light that shines forth revealing murderous crimes, embezzlement, and other evil deeds. To you, I pass the light."

With that, he lit Key's candle, made his way back to his desk, and sat down. "Does that quench your ceremonial thirst?"

"I don't remember asking for a ceremony, but yes. That was actually quite nice." Key said.

"Good," Castor said. "Now blow out that candle and go get measured for four formal uniforms at Gretta's. Charge it to my office. If Major Kane's doing it, I want to do it too.

"Oh, and get a red sash. The royal investigators only wear red sashes from here on out."

# Chapter 9

## The Crucible

K ey left the office and made his way down to Alpenrose Street. He walked past stone structures with tents pitched in front selling trinkets and baked goods. A cool breeze blew past him, cleansing his smoke-sodden clothes. Tomorrow was supposed to be his day off. Instead, he had had something better than a day off. He wasn't sure how his new role as the assistant to the royal investigator would look. Still, he was certain it would be better than his monotonous life patrolling the city, the city walls, or playing cards in the armory. He would no longer have to stand at attention at the palace doors, bending his knees so he wouldn't pass out. He wished his mother was still alive to tell the story to. She would have been proud.

His mother, Maddie Key, was the reason he joined the Royal Guard in the first place. She explained how his father had been a gallant knight who died at sea, returning home from one exotic place or another. She explained that service to the king was in his blood. Stories of battle, honor, and glory made him hungry to experience it for himself, and a week after his eighteenth birthday, he enlisted.

The dullness that ensued was unexpected, but he returned home as often as he could to tell his mother of all the high points. He tried the best he could to leave out the boring parts. His mother would laugh at his stories and would slap his arm whenever he let slip a vulgar word picked up from his peers. Then, just one year after he had enlisted, she died from a cough. Her sudden departure cut him deeply, but at the time, he had seen enough death to understand the inevitability of it. Eventually, he recovered from his dejection but would never fully heal.

Jostling a bell overhead, Key pushed open the door, revealing baskets of cloth and half-finished garments. Spools of colorful fabrics lined the wall, the floor, and everywhere else, border-lining chaos. A middle-aged woman peered at him from the back.

"Hello," she chirped. "Here for the Major Kane uniform?"

"Uh, I believe yes," Key said, slightly off guard. "The formal uniform with the sash."

"Oh, good. I was beginning to think preparing extras was a bad idea," she said, closing the distance between them. She moved almost cat-like, effortlessly avoiding the obstacles that lay haphazardly in her way. She wore simple, black-on-black attire that was loose in some areas and tight in others.

"Armor off," she commanded.

Key began unclasping his gauntlets, and she moved around him, helping him unbidden with his armor. In an instant, his armor was lifted over his head and set gently on a pile of discarded fabric. He felt a sense of awe at her keen familiarity with it.

"Arms up."

He lifted his arms to the side, and she began taking measurements with a knotted string. He smelled rosemary on her breath as she wrapped her arms around his mid-section in three places. She placed a knee on the ground and unapologetically measured his more personal areas. He took a deep breath, silently exhaling as her hands lightly peppered his inner and outer thighs.

"This is a new experience," he admitted, feeling vulnerable.

"Lighten up," she said, swatting his behind. "It's not like I'm measuring you for a codpiece."

"Measure?" Key laughed nervously, "I thought those only came in one size, as big as possible."

Gretta smiled at the comment, which caused the crow's feet lines to appear around her eyes. They were not unattractive. She turned and made some entries on a piece of paper. "How many would you like?"

"Four, please," he requested. "Red sashes. Oh, and bill them to the office of investigations."

"You work for Captain Castor then?" she asked.

"That's right," he looked at her curiously. "You really know your way around."

"What's that supposed to mean?" she crossed her arms.

"I was just saying that-" he tried recanting his compliment.

"I'm kidding," she smiled. "I've been dressing the royal guard longer than you've been alive."

"I'm twenty-two," he said, lifting the plate over his head and lowering it across his shoulders.

"I'm sure you are. I'll have your uniforms ready in a

week. Don't gain any weight, or I'll have to measure you all over again," she winked.

He left in high spirits and returned to the office.

"What do we do now?" he asked.

The captain was reading a dusty old book. "We look busy until something interesting happens," he replied without lifting his eyes. "For you, that means sword training."

"And then?" Key asked.

"More sword training," Castor replied.

"Suppose I sword train until I can't lift my arms, then what?" Key asked, used to a life where every action he took was delegated to him by his commanding officers.

"Do you see why I don't want a whole company of people asking annoying little questions all day?" Castor asked, setting down his book. "Let me set some goals for you because you are clearly incapable of setting them for yourself. First, I want you to develop a reputation for swordplay. I want you to best everyone in the training field, especially the person with the reputation for being the current best. You'll need a lot of training to reach that goal, so make it a habit to go at the same time every day. Pick any one-hour block that suits your fancy and stick to it. Eventually, I want you to work up the stamina for a two-hour block.

"Second, it would be good for you to work on your calligraphy. There is power in professional handwriting. You should develop your alphabet letter by letter until every word looks like it came from the King's personal scribe himself. I have endless correspondence saved up and categorized for reference. I should also say now that when writing a letter, refrain from reinventing the wheel. Anything that you want to say, request, announce, or any time you want to attempt to change a person's mind, or anything you can think of, has already been signed, sealed, and saved neatly in a box for your viewing pleasure. Find a letter that says the thing you want to say, and then copy it, word for tried-and-true word.

"Lastly, I want you to focus on developing your new reputation. Continue going to great lengths to look presentable. Get a shave at least three times a week and a haircut about once a week. Put it on my account. Ensure your boots and everything else are shined. When the new uniform comes in, I want it to always be crisp and clean. If you must walk around aimlessly, carry something in your hand so it looks like you are completely indisposed. In fact," he considered thoughtfully. "Once a day, I want you to carry a different package through the city, take a different route each time. Thus, inspiring an element of mystery and workmanship."

"Swords, writing, and walking around randomly with a box, got it," Key reiterated. "Since we are investigators, shouldn't we investigate something?"

"Go investigate sword training. I'll let you know if I need you for anything. Don't forget to check in before and after your important tasks. If I'm not here at the end of the day, neither should you be." Castor shooed him out of the door with his fingers.

Key was tempted to ask about when his day off would be but then thought better of it. It appeared there wasn't much to take a day off from. He left the office and headed toward the training grounds.

"Eulerous Key," a giant man greeted him from across racks of wooden swords, shields, and spears. His name was Sefulu Fa, or Sef, and he stood taller and broader than any man in the king's retinue. Despite the chill, he was dressed for warmer weather, and his obsidian skin glistened under a sleeveless doublet.

"Good to see you, Sef," Key greeted his training coach. "It's just Key, though."

"Care to duel for the honor of choosing what I call you?" Sef asked.

"Actually, yes," Key said. "What would I have to do to beat you in a duel?"

"You could stab me in my sleep," Sef offered. "Or you could… no. Just stab me in my sleep. I'm a pretty heavy sleeper, but you should still make sure you're not too loud."

"I'm going to be training much more than usual," Key explained. "Have any ideas for me?"

"Have you practiced the siva?" Sef asked.

"You mean the thing where we slowly dance in a circle and wave our swords around?" Key asked wryly. "I don't think that's going to help me challenge the strongest person here. Plus, if he also knows how to dance around and wave a sword, how does that help me?"

"You're really getting serious about fighting, huh?" Sef asked.

"I guess so," Key said, looking around, finding it strange to be there without the rest of his battalion. The place felt empty.

"When you can do a full crucible in an hourglass, I will show you the black dance," Sef said. "It can be done."

"What's the black dance?" Key asked.

"It's pretty much the same as siva but has a few extra moves," Sef said in an under dramatic voice. "Maybe it will give you an edge over Trudie?"

"Wait, you're telling me that Trudie is the best fighter out of everyone?" Key asked, astonished.

"Why not? She trains more than anyone else," Sef said. "In my country, a lot of women are stronger than men. Keeps us on our toes."

"Did you teach her the black dance?" Key asked.

"Not yet," Sef said. "She never asks for help. But, if she did, I would show her."

"You could beat Trudie, right?" Key asked.

"In a fair match, yes. In a battle situation, I would throw a rock at her." Sef admitted.

"That means a lot coming from you," Key said in disbelief.

"My people know that it's best to fight unfairly if you have to fight a woman," Sef stated.

"Fair enough," Key started unfastening his armor. "I'm off for some exercise then. Don't tell her about the black dance."

"I'm going to tell her, so you better hurry," Sef said. "Oh, and it will help to practice the siva. Like I said, it has a lot of the same moves."

Key dressed down to his doublet and went through his memorized routine of stretching. Normally, the sixty or so in his old battalion would stand around the sergeant who would lead them through the stretches. He then walked to the wooden crucible and mentally created a course of action. The wooden crucible was a large structure made with crude logs, ropes, nets, and iron stretching upward to a staggering height. It was designed to strengthen a different muscle depending on how you climbed up or down. It had multiple knotted and unknotted ropes that reached horizontal beams at the top of the structure netted ladders with wooden bars, a steep slope with sets of stares for shouldering sandbags, and parallel walls with hand and foot holds. Thirty-two people could climb the crucible at the same time without two people bumping into each other. A full crucible was when one person climbed all thirty-two ways up and down again in a single hour. It wasn't impossible, but it wasn't easy by any stretch.

Key carried four sandbags to the base of the staired slope and set them down in a neat row. Sef approached carrying a wood-framed hourglass.

"I'm going to leave this for you here so you can check your time." He set it down on a bench. Key thanked him and asked him not to watch. He turned the hourglass, allowing the sand to start pouring precious seconds into the lower bowl.

"You're up." He said and walked away.

Key threw his first sandbag over his right shoulder, allowing his left hand free to climb the first incline. With each foothold he gained, he splashed water and mud off the steps. He made it to the top, chucked the sandbag over the ledge in front of him, and started over. He alternated shoulders and climbed the second slope. His legs burned as he dropped the second bag down near the first one. When he had reached the last bag, his heart was hammering in his chest. He threw it over his shoulder and made his way up. When he reached the bottom, he collapsed to the ground. There he lay on his back, gasping for air. He looked at the hourglass; it was still mostly full.

Deciding the knotted rope looked less intimidating than the rest, he picked himself off the ground and moved toward it. He grabbed a knot and pulled himself up, allowing his feet to stand on the lower knot. Grabbing the knot above him, pulling himself up, and clasping the next knot up with his feet, he climbed four of the eight ropes.

The other four ropes were not knotted. The hourglass was about a quarter of the way, and he quit.

"Come on then," Sef yelled from across a rack of wooden swords. "You're almost halfway there!" Key did not have breath in his lungs to yell back. Instead, he waved his hand for him to keep it down. Then, he picked up the hourglass, allowing the time to continue running, and walked over to him. "I'll try again tomorrow; I just need to get back into fighting shape, is all."

"It's because they only train you guys once a week," Sef asserted disappointedly. "And even then, they don't really push you. Sometimes, only half of you show up. It's a pity."

Key shrugged. "You're probably right."

Sef offered to spar, but Key declined. Instead, he decided to practice the siva while he got his heart rate under control.

Sef moved out of the fighting circle. "I'll be over here, silently judging."

"As long as you're not showing Trudie the black dance, you can judge me all day for all I care," Key windmilled his arms. He picked up a two-handed wooden sword and positioned himself in the middle of the ring. Opening his legs shoulder-width apart, he held the sword in front of him and began the siva.

He began moving the sword in a series of slow attacking motions. He stepped forward, attacked and then backward blocking with the tip of the sword pointing down. He shifted all of his weight to one foot. His left shoulder spun deliberately backward allowing him to strike behind him. His blade moved to a blocking position once more before slowly stabbing the air in front of him.

Key had completed the twenty or so movements with ease. It had been years since someone corrected him on his posture, blade angle, or footing. He began the movements again, this time nearly doubling his speed. When he finished, he started again, moving faster. The blade nearly sang in the air as he swung out several arcs through                    the                    air. When he finished, he looked at the hourglass and found it empty. It seemed like a good start. He picked it up before walking over to replace the sword on the rack.

"Your form is good," Sef praised.

"Thanks, I figured perfecting my form was the best way to get them to stop yelling at me," Key wiped the sweat out of his eyes.

"Your breathing needs work," Sef said.

"How could you tell?"

"By the way, you didn't breathe," Sef continued, "If you exhaled on outward motions and practiced breathing in on inward motions, you would have better power and more stamina."

"What If I do five outward motions in a row?" Key asked.

"Try this," Sef said and assumed a hand-to-hand combat position. He punched out with a "Hah!" and breathed in. He then did a series of punches with both hands, producing a rapid projection of the same grunts. He breathed in and punched with a final "Hah!" He held the position, fist asserted in front of him.

"Doesn't that make you lightheaded?" Key asked.

"With practice, you will find yourself in an optimal condition," Sef said. "It also gives you power."

"Alright, I'll give it a go tomorrow," Key tried to

return the hourglass.

"I'll keep it safe for you," Sef took it and turned it over in his hands. "You'll need for the crucible."

Key left the training grounds and headed to the barracks. After bathing and redressing, he returned to the office but found it locked up with no sign of the captain. He took that as a sign that he was done for the day, so he went home, ate bread and cheese, and slept. It was a restful sleep that wouldn't be disturbed to pick up a shift in the middle of the night, or ever again.

Evan Kvalvik

# Chapter 10

## A Wedding Cake

I n the weeks that followed, Benj immersed his apprentice, Taft, in the intricacies of baking. He guided Taft through the nuances of following recipes, adjusting quantities for larger batches, mastering unfamiliar tools and techniques, and managing the oven's heat. As Benj was in the midst of explaining the corrections needed for a particularly tricky recipe, the bell at the front of the bakery rang, signaling a customer. He was surprised to walk through the kitchen door and find Brahm standing there looking impatient.

"Good morning, Brahm," he greeted cordially, "What brings you in?"

"Morning, Benj," Brahm fidgeted with his hat, "Is Sephus around? I need a quote for a cake."

"Sephus isn't in, but he rarely knows anything when he is," Benj used his favorite cliche for moving things along. "What kind of cake are you looking for?"

"A wedding cake." Brahm said awkwardly, "I suppose white. Enough for maybe fifty people or so."

"Well, congratulations!" Benj said with a smile,

"Who's the lucky goat?"

"Ha, very funny," Brahm replied unenthusiastically, "Her name is Mel, and she's a girl."

Benj's heart sank, but he masked his disappointment with a forced smile. "A cake for fifty will range between five and fifteen silver talents."

Brahm whistled. "That's pretty steep."

"I know," Benj said, struggling to stay calm. "They take a lot of time to make. I could ask Sephus about a discount, but I already know his answer. When do you need it?"

"Two weeks," said Brahm, "but I need to know the exact price."

"How do you want it decorated?" Benj asked and then explained the various options.

"I'll have to check, but at the very least, it will be five marks per person," Benj calculated silently. "For fifty people, that's... five talents."

Brahm agreed to the price and left.

Benj returned to the kitchen, where Taft was engrossed in a recipe book.

"You're in charge today." Benj hung up his apron. "I have some errands to run." It was a trick Sephus would always use whenever he wanted a day off. Hand over some unearned responsibilities and leave. It didn't matter how well Taft managed the kitchen; he had some feelings to sort out, so he made his way to the Golden Stag.

Pushing through the double doors, Benj took a seat at the bar.

"Benj," the bartender, Tegan, greeted.

"Tegan," Benj replied.

"What'll it be?" Tegan asked, pulling out a glass mug and inspecting it with exaggerated care.

"Dark ale," Benj ordered.

"How dark?"

"The darkest," Benj replied, "And spirited."

Tegan poured a measure of clear liquid into the mug, then topped it off with thick, dark ale from an old barrel. Benj downed it in one go, setting it back on the bar.

"Another?" Tegan asked.

"Actually, I'm pretty sure that was a mistake," Benj slid the empty mug away, "I'll take a regular ale."

Tegan filled a fresh cup with cool amber ale from his largest barrel. "You're in here early," he remarked.

"I've got a lot on my mind," Benj admitted, taking a long sip of the ale.

"Anything I can help with?"

"You already have." Benj raised his glass in a toast to Tegan before taking another sip.

"I've got something that might cheer you up," Tegan said. "Come with me." Benj, feeling the effects of the ale, followed Tegan to the back of the tavern.

They passed shelves of preserves and sacks of potatoes until they reached a large, hissing contraption.

"What's this?" Benj asked, awed by the gleaming metal beast.

"This," Tegan said proudly, "makes the spirit."

"How does it work?" Benj asked.

"You put your mash in there," Tegan gestured to a round covered vat. "Heat it up from underneath," he traced the path of some winding tubes, "and it goes up, around, and down through here. Cold water cools the steam, turning it into spirit that comes out there."

"When did you get this?" Benj marveled at the bronze monster.

"A few seasons ago," Tegan said. "A master distiller

needed money more than he needed the spirits. He taught me how to use it. I'm getting better at it. Do you want to try my latest batch?"

Back in the tavern, Tegan set three small glasses before Benj, each filled with uneven shades of silver spirits.

"I made one of these," Tegan said, "The others from the Parquist Distillery in Royal City, and the third is a surprise. Two are free, but you owe me six marks for the secret one."

Benj agreed and sampled the spirits, giving each a thoughtful evaluation. "This one," he said, pointing to the left, "tastes common. Compared to the others, it's not that impressive."

"And the others?" Tegan implored.

"This one," Benj said, indicating the right, "is smooth, complex, and excellent. The one in the middle," he sipped, "is interesting. It has more flavor than the others and tastes kind of like distilled ale. Is this distilled ale?"

"You got me!" Tegan threw his hands in the air. "I've been trying different things, and you know what I thought? I thought, why hasn't anyone tried distilling ale? So, I tried it, and it foamed so much I had to stop, clean everything off, and wait until it went flat to try again. What you are drinking now is the first success out of three attempts."

"It's good!" Benj took another sip. "What are the other ones?"

"The common-tasting one on your left is from Royal City," Tegan revealed. "And the one you owe me six marks for is Sorte Diamante. Very expensive and very good."

As Benj tried capturing the flavor of the expensive

spirit, Tegan explained the intricacies of distilling. "The trick is, treat every spirit like a woman, and she'll be good every time. You get the temper first, vile and poisonous. That's the first to get distilled. You'll want to dump that out. If you drink it, your teeth will fall out. After the temper is burned off, her heart comes next; that's the good stuff. After the heart, it'll distill, but it turns into the arse-end. That's what you want to avoid."

"How do you know when it's the arse-end?" Benj asked.

"Because it tastes like arse!" Tegan roared with laughter. The two friends enjoyed the joke, their laughter echoing through the empty tavern. They continued talking until patrons began filtering in, marking the time for Benj to go.

"I have something important to say," Benj declared.

"What's that?" Tegan asked.

"I know what I have to do," he said firmly. "And I'm going to do it. How much do I owe you?"

"Eleven marks," Tegan said. Benj dropped a handful of coins on the counter. Tegan took eleven marks and slid the rest back. "Keep it," Benj said, struggling slightly as he left the tavern.

Instead of heading home, Benj walked towards the flower shop where Mel worked. Despite the wisdom of avoiding conversations with love interests while intoxicated, he was too inebriated to care.

"Mel!" Benj called out as he stumbled into the shop.

"Benj! What brings you here?" Her face brightened.

"I think I'm drunk," Benj admitted. "I came to buy you a flower, but since you'd be the one selling it, I think I'll take my business elsewhere." He turned to leave.

"You don't have to go," Mel said, "What better place

to buy me a flower than where I work?"

"Do you often help people buy flowers for you?" Benj asked.

"More than I'd like to admit," Mel said with a smile. She was so easy to talk to, even now, that it gave Benj a bitter feeling in his stomach.

"Like Brahm?" he swayed slightly.

"How did you—" Mel began.

"Are you going to marry him?" Benj cut her off.

She looked at him, unable to respond.

"Well, congratulations," Benj said. "I just wish you would have given me a chance. Maybe you would have found that we could have liked each other."

"I do like you," she said, meaning like a friend. "It's just complicated."

"Not as complicated as—Never mind. It doesn't matter," Benj said, his voice tinged with defeat.

"Not as complicated as what?" she asked.

"Listen," Benj said, his heart pounding in his chest, sobering him. "It might not make a difference, but I like you a lot. I don't want to marry you right now, but I don't want you to marry Brahm in case we decide to later on in life."

Mel looked stunned. "That's very sweet of you. Let's promise to always be friends."

"I don't know," Benj said. "On the one hand, I would love to be your friend. On the other hand, friends wouldn't let friends marry Brahm. He isn't a good person."

"I think it's already too late for that," Mel said despondently. "I was going to tell you about it, but I never got the chance."

"It's never too late," Benj said, allowing hope to rise

and die in one brief crescendo. "But I wish you the best. Let's forget this conversation, okay?"

"Sure," Mel said. "I don't even know why I'm standing here talking to you."

"Perfect," Benj gave a perfectly real-looking smile. "I'll see you around."

"Ahem," Mel cleared her throat. "You still owe me a hug."

"There are people who'd pay good money for that hug. Maybe I'll sell it and buy a bakery," he continued walking.

"You wouldn't," she said, crossing her arms.

"Maybe I will, and maybe I won't. I'll see you around." He continued walking until he left the village, his mind a swirl of thoughts. He found a rock ledge, climbed up, and jumped off, repeating the process over and over.

"Always remember," Tegan had said with a serious expression on his face. "You have to cut it off while it's still good. If you get any of that arse-end into your batch, it'll spoil everything."

He thought about Mel, and he thought about leaving. Why should he stay here? What was there worth staying for? He backflipped off the ledge and angled backward towards the ground. Again, he climbed up, jumped, and skidded to a stop until his already tattered shoes fell completely apart. He made a decision, "I'm getting new shoes, and then I'm leaving." So, he picked up his shoes and walked home.

Evan Kvalvik

# Chapter 11

## A Fish with a Scarf

The following morning, Key got out of bed and rubbed his legs. With the bit of exertion, he did the day before, he was paying for it. After a slower-than-usual morning routine, he managed to hobble to the office. The captain was sitting in his chair, sipping a mug of something hot.

The office had changed. In the far-left corner sat a desk and chair. The desk had a neat stack of paper and writing tools. Key tried to walk normally to the desk, but his slight limp did not escape the observation of the chief investigator.

"You're walking funny," Castor pointed out.

"I went a little overboard at the training field yesterday," Key admitted, trying to keep any pained expressions off his face.

"It's a good thing we don't have errands in town today. Anyway, I got you a desk to start working on your handwriting." Castor nodded towards it. "Go on, try it out."

With effort, Key walked over to the desk and lowered himself into the chair. "I like it. Anything you want me to start with?"

"How about the letter A?" Castor suggested before reaching into one of his drawers, taking out a stack of papers, and holding them up. "You can use these as a reference."

Key put a hand on the back of the chair and the desk and began to push himself up.

"Please," The captain motioned for him to stay in his chair, "Allow me." He stood up, walked over, and plopped the papers on the desk.

"Thank you."

"Don't mention it." Castor added, "Or I'll call you a liar and challenge you to a dual."

Key found an 'a' he liked and began the painstaking process of teaching his hand to recreate it. He started as slow as possible, capturing the muscle memory in his hand the best he could. He started with a loop that formed a small hole, followed by a loop that ran to the bottom of the letter and then a sharp, up and down that pointed to the top. He then made one more loop that went up to the left, down, and up to the right. He compared the original to his counterfeit. It looked like a child wrote it. He tried again.

By the time he had finished the alphabet, his hand and wrist were as sore as his legs. "I think I'm going to go down to the training grounds before my hand is permanently stuck like this," he said, holding it up, making his fingers look as disfigured as possible.

"Very well," Castor dipped his quill in ink. "See you tomorrow."

The very phrase, "See you tomorrow," put a jolt of

excitement through Key's whole body. "See you tomorrow" meant that Castor didn't expect to see him again today. It was an official release from work, and the sun was still in the sky.

Key decided that to keep his position working for this captain, he would be the best assistant to the investigator he could possibly be. If that meant becoming the best sword fighter, having the best handwriting, and looking busy, he was going to make sure he was the busiest-looking person ever to walk the streets of Royal City.

For the next two weeks, Key got settled in. He practiced calligraphy and swordplay and delivered letters. When he wasn't doing either of those things, he spent his time looking for new ways to look busy. He worked hard to complete a full crucible within the span of an hourglass, however slow his progress was. Whenever the sand ran out, he pressed forward until all thirty-two obstacles were complete; then, he would go home, bathe, and bask in the wonder of free time. He also found himself enjoying the mythical and coveted midday nap.

After a particularly strenuous day, he climbed the stairs and pushed into his shared barracks room. Not bothering to put in a wake-up, he got undressed for bed and collapsed on top of it. The room was starting to smell like old socks. He would have to address the situation with the rest of his flat mates if it continued. He let his mind wander as he slowly drifted off to sleep. The smell brought him back around; it was as if it was getting worse. It was as if…

Key stood up and crouched to look underneath the bed; he suspected foul play. He began searching the room, picking up clothes, coats, and bags. He felt and looked under all the beds to no avail. He was rummaging through Naldo's foot chest when Alrick walked in.

"How's it going?" Alrick asked, and then, after a moment, added, "What are you doing?"

"Do you smell that? I think Jory planted a fish in here." Key said, holding an armload of Naldo's clothes. "I'm looking for it."

"It does smell kind of fishy," Alrick said before walking around the room smelling. "I thought someone started developing the foot rot."

"It's Jory," Key stated. "I know it is. Plus, I was going to plant a fish in his room, so it only makes sense that he would have the same thought. It's also his turn."

"Let's think about this logically," Alrick considered. "If this is an attack on you, then it would be placed where it would affect you the most. The rest of us would just be casualties of war. Did you look under your pillow?"

"Yeah, but I didn't look under the floorboard," Key said, walking around his bed and investigating the hardwood floor. "Alrick, give me your sword." Alrick drew his sword and presented it.

Taking the sword, Key jammed the tip between the floorboards and lifted. The wood creaked as it pulled up enough to look under. Not finding anything suspicious he moved and tried the next one. He found a spot that looked like it had been pulled up before. "I think this is the one," he said, jamming the sword in. He lifted the board, and the smell of rotten fish wafted into the room.

"That's awful!" Alrick put his tunic over his nose.

"I need something to grab this with," Key said. "Give me your shirt."

"You are not using my shirt to pick that thing up!"

Alrick exclaimed. "Hang on, I'm going to go grab something." He left the room and came back with a plate and two forks.

Key pried the wood up further while Alrick set the plate near the opening and tried to remove it with the forks. After a few failed attempts, he finally pulled the fish out and set it on the plate.

"Is that a scarf?" Alrick asked, pointing at a yellow cloth wrapped around the fish's gills.

"Rusted relics, man, it is!" Key swore, full of awe. "I hate to say it, but that's a really nice touch. To think I was going to merely put my fish under his bed and not his floorboards, and unscarfed. It's times like this that really make you look inward, you know?"

"The only thing I'm looking for is getting rid of this thing," Alrick said, handing the plate to Key. "Make sure it gets a proper burial."

"Do you want to say a few things first?" Key said, holding the fish plate.

"He had the nicest scarf I've ever seen on a fish," Alrick feigned a tear. "Now, can you please get rid of it?

The next day, Key sat at his desk, recreating various letters. His handwriting had come a long way in the last couple weeks.

There was a knock at the door. Key set down his quill and began to stand. Castor waved him to stay seated. "Enter!"

A winded sergeant poured into the room. "Snatch and grab, sir. Down at the market. It sounds like the purse taken was substantial enough to warrant a hanging."

"The offender apprehended?" the captain asked.

"Yes, but he doesn't have it," the sergeant replied. "We searched him. He must have handed it off. He's not talking."

"What does he look like?"

"He looks about twelve, dirty red shirt and brown trousers," the sergeant recounted. "He's also got big ears."

"Imprison him," the captain ordered. "I will question him after he's had some time to sweat it out.

"Yes, sir," he said and waited for a dismissal.

"As you were, sergeant."

He saluted and left.

"Go fetch me a piece of pie," Castor ordered.

"Pie?" Key asked. "Any specific flavor?"

"No," Castor said plainly.

Key rose from his chair and walked towards the door.

"Never mind," Castor said. "Just get it tomorrow before you come in. If there's pie in here, I'm probably just going to eat it."

Key sat back down in his chair. "What's the pie for?"

"It's a rather inexpensive and, in my opinion, fun interrogation                                          technique," Castor said but would say no more.

The following morning, Key's legs still felt sore, but the more he walked, the better his legs felt. By the time he had purchased the pie, he was walking nearly as typically as anyone else. He brought the pie to the captain.

"Mincemeat?!" Castor asked incredulously. "You had the choice of an entire bakery's worth of pies; you brought the one that belongs at the very bottom of the trash can?"

"I've never had it before," Key said. "The lady said it was her favorite."

"The lady was trying to push her otherwise unsellable product on you," Castor sneered. "Like a

138

chump, you fell for it. Mincemeat pie."

"How was I supposed to know?" Key asked.

"You aren't supposed to know; you listen to the words "mincemeat" and "pie", and you put one and one together." Castor held up two fingers. "I guess we're just going to try to work it. How are your legs this morning?"

"Usable," Key answered.

"Let's go then," Castor said turning to leave. He paused, patting his upper left pocket before moving towards the door. "Out of all the pies in the world. Unbelievable."

By the time the captain finished listing all the pies he could think of, the two arrived at the prison. Keebler was standing guard outside.

"Keebler," Key said. "You're off bridge duty!"

Keebler saluted the captain, who didn't deign to lift a hand in return.

"Someone else got in trouble finally," he said. "I heard you got transferred. How's the new station?"

"Corporal Key," the captain said over his shoulder. "Remind me to submit a letter pertaining to a certain individual talking on watch today."

"Yes, sir," Key replied with a twinge of remorse. He had to remind himself that Keebler broke the brotherhood of the guard and ratted on a number of his colleagues. Also, Castor probably had no intention of following through; he was building appearances.

Keebler's face showed a darker shade of depression than usual.

"Go on then," the captain flicked a hand. "Open up."

Keebler opened the thick metal door as quickly as he could and stood silently at attention as the two walked in. The prison was a series of long passageways in the shape of a four-pronged fork. Normally, only one of those hallways was used at a given time. If the king needed somewhere to hold hundreds of wartime enemy hostages, he would still have room for the constant inflow and outflow of common criminals. To further ensure full capacity was never achieved at the prison, weekly hangings helped thin the herd.

Key had spent countless hours patrolling these halls or napping in one of the unused cells. The sound carried so well that the locks, creaks, or shutting of the doors were loud enough to arouse anyone from their slumber. Just in case, Key closed the door louder than necessary to signal all the guards to be alert. The prison wasn't inspected often, which made it one of the better places to stand watch.

The two walked towards the occupied portion of the prison. The echo of conversational voices mingled with the twin footsteps. One cell had the chalk words 'to be hung' with an arrow on the wall pointing at three sleeping men. The next four cells held a single person each. The guard on patrol strolled up, saluting the captain. "Can I help you find someone, sir?"

"We're looking for a boy that was brought in yesterday," the captain explained. "He should have red pants and big ears."

"If he got here yesterday sir, he'll be in the cell this way," the guard said and brought them deeper down the corridor. "Everyone from yesterday is in this cell."

They stopped next to a cell holding six people, including a drunk, three thuggish-looking men, and two young boys. One of the boys had a red shirt and large enough-looking ears.

"Watch and learn," the captain said to Key, who was

140

standing with a paper-wrapped pie piece in his hand.

"You there," the captain said to the angriest looking man out of the bunch. "I have a few questions to ask you."

"Ask away, mate. I'm not telling you more than "piss" and "off," he said with a missing tooth grin.

"Take him to the interrogation room."

The interrogation room was at the end of the passageway, past several more full cells, one of which included a bunch of whistling women who demanded they turn over the key. Castor raised an eyebrow and pointed to Key questioningly.

"What can I say?" Key shrugged. "I'm popular with the ladies."

The interrogation room had a table with a pad-eye for looping chains through and a single chair. Grated sunlight poured in through an opening in the ceiling crossed with iron bars.

"I have a story you might be interested in hearing," the captain said in a conversational voice.

"If it's about your mum, I can tell you from first-hand experience that it's true," the man laughed, testing the strength of the chains.

"Some time ago, a man matching your description was seen with a boy who also has distinct qualities," Captain Castor began. "The two were witnessed at a temple vandalizing and committing crimes against the church, too egregious to mention. If you name your counterpart, I will do my best to have those crimes acquitted. At the very least, the court looks favorably on those who help the cause of justice."

"Never been to a temple a day in my life," the man said. "So, you can take your egregious crimes and put 'em in your prison purse."

"I know that the food here can be bland at times," the captain said. "So, I took it upon myself to bring you a piece of pie for your cooperation. First, tell me a name of your little accomplice." he nodded at Key.

Key unwrapped the pie and held it aloft.

"Is that mincemeat?" the man said. "It would have worked better if you offered me my own foot!"

"I've heard enough from him. Return him to his cell," the captain said. "Oh, and bring the boy with the red shirt."

A while later, the guard hauled the boy in. His face and hands were caked in dirt. He sat in the chair as the guard connected his chains to the table.

"Let's cut to the chase," the captain said. "I'm about to ask you where the items are that you stole yesterday. Unfortunately, you're not going to tell me and probably say something insulting. Anyhow, I doubt it will be anything clever. I will then explain how It would behoove you to tell me everything I want to know. You won't believe me yet, and that's okay; I am prepared to show why you want to work with me rather than against me. Are you following?"

"I don't know where they are; they just disappeared!" the boy said. The captain rubbed his eyes. "Let's start with your name."

"I go by Crumb," he said.

"Crumb, huh?" the captain asked. "Is that the name your parents gave you?"

"I don't have parents. It's just me and m..." the boy cut off. "it's just me."

"Oh, so it's just you and someone else, huh? I know you kids usually work in pairs. You stole the purse and handed it off. I don't care about your partner; I just want

142

the purse."

The boy was silent.

"This is the part where I tell you why it's in your best interest to work with me," the captain said patiently. "In a moment, I'm going to move you to a cell directly across from your mortal enemy. Then, I'm going to leave. When I come back, if you don't tell me what I want to know, I'm going to put you in his cell."

"I don't have any mortal enemies," the boy explained. "People like me."

"Not this person," the captain said gravely. "But by all means, let's wait until I return."

The captain had the boy put in a cell directly across from the one he was previously in. In chalk, he wrote, "to be set free" on the wall next to the bars.

"Thank you for your help," the captain said patting the boy's head. "Corporal Key, give him the pie."

Key handed the confused boy a piece of pie through the bars.

Castor turned to the man they had previously questioned. "We caught you, Gerard, you temple mutilator!" the captain growled, pointing at the man.

"I told you; I've never been to a temple, I swear by all the… Erm, nobody. I don't even know what to even swear by." he said. "Besides, my name is Donohue, not Gerard."

"Tell it to the ropes, Gerard, you vile scum. Your little accomplice told us everything." the captain said, reaching into the boy's cell and patting him on the head once again.

"Why, you little prick!" Donohue shouted at the boy across from his cell.

"If I ever get out of here, I'm going to beat you into a bloody pulp; you mark my word!"

As they walk towards the exit, murderous shouts

and accusations rose above a small voice of defense.

"When we come back, Crumb will be ready to tell us everything." Castor said, stepping out into the fresh air. "Or he might not be alive enough for his hanging."

"Isn't that a little cruel for a kid?" Key asked. "I mean, if he does give back the purse, those guys are going to kill him if they see him in the city."

"Precisely why we are going to arrange him a trip out of the city," Castor began counting on his fingers. "He has no parents, no gang, and there's nothing for him here. Even if he's released, he'll be back in a cell before not too long. That's why I lit the proverbial fire under his feet. The creator didn't invent pain to make us suffer, he made it to drive us into action. You'll see."

"Where are we off to then?" Key asked, following the captain through the city's winding streets.

"I have a friend that lives north of here," Castor said. "He runs a small shipyard, an Inn, and a farm. It seems impossible for one man to do all that, but he has a gift. It's this gift that helps a lot of the street urchins around these parts restart their lives. Every so often, I send a failed pickpocket to him, and he puts them to work and pays them honestly. Not all of them make it, but a lot do. Most of his businesses are run by reformed street thieves."

"Oh, I see," Key looked thoughtful. "You're planning on sending Crumb down there?"

"Correct," Castor lifted a finger. "Well, technically, it's up there, but yes. If he returns the money. Otherwise, I won't have the power to get him out of his sentence in the first place. Ah, here we are."

The pair arrived at a building called "Skipper's Transport" with a wooden cart in front with arches covered with a patchwork of sheets. Castor knocked on the side.

"A moment," a heavily accented voice announced from inside.

"Take your time," Castor said. "We'll just stand here in the street until you're done powdering your nose."

"Who is that?" The man asked, popping his head through the curtains. His face was round and framed by thick mutton chops down either side of his face. "Charles, is that you? How in the blazes are you?"

"Oh, just fine," he said. "I have some business to discuss."

"Is it business we have time to smoke about?" the man asked, climbing out with a box in his hands.

"We really shouldn't stay too long," Castor said. "We are on the king's time, so to speak."

"That's a shame because I am holding in my hands a box of a very rare, imported flake I just got from the islands of Fanara a week ago. It was so good I had to get a new pipe."

"If you put it that way," Castor said, producing a pipe seemingly out of thin air. "I would hate for you to have to smoke it all by yourself."

"That's the captain that I know!" the man said, opening the box. "I've already let some of it dry a bit, so it's ready to go."

"I believe some introductions are in order," Castor held a hand towards Key. "This is my new corporal, Key. Key, this is Grant Barlow. He's a former skipper of a small trading vessel."

"Call me Grant," the man said, filling Castor's pipe with tobacco. "Where's your pipe? You'll want to try this too."

"I don't believe I've ever seen him smoke," Castor

mentioned solemnly before Key had the opportunity to decline.

"Doesn't smoke?" Grant asked in bewilderment. "Don't you know the health benefits of smoking? Saved my life on more than enough occasions.

"My mother always said the opposite," Key recounted. "She said it makes you hard of breath and that it makes it hard to taste good food."

"If you had ever tried my third wife's cooking, you wouldn't think that was such a bad thing," Grant guffawed. "If you ever change your mind, you can come over, and I'll teach you how to smoke a proper pipe. I'll even give you one."

"That's very generous of you, thanks," Key said allowing the matter to drop.

After the pipes were lit, Castor explained the situation with the young thief and how he would need to leave town.

"So, you saved another one?" Grant's words were wisps of smoke. "This makes three in one year."

"It might be four," Castor corrected. "I got the feeling like he has a sibling or something like it. They might be a package deal. That is if he accepts my offer."

"I suppose I'm due for another trip up North," Grant thought out loud. "When do we need to leave?"

"That all depends," Castor blew a failed smoke ring. "How soon can you leave?"

"I have some deliveries to make in the morning," Grant said. "I would need to pick up some supplies, but I suppose I could be out of here before noon. Is this kid going to try to stab me in my sleep like the last one?"

"I don't think so; he says he's likable," Castor shrugged. "Just don't leave your knife lying around this time."

"It was in my belt!" Grant exclaimed. "Well, lessons learned. I've sailed with enough riff-raff to know better anyway."

"Take this," Castor said, handing over two silver coins. "If, for whatever reason, the boy doesn't want a better life, just count it towards the next one we try to save."

"Alright, just do what you can," Grant pressed.

"Oh, and one more thing," Castor said, drawing from his pipe. "How much for the tobacco? This is incredible."

"It's not for sale," Grant said. "But you can come over whenever you want, and I'll smoke it with you. Maybe you'll come shoot the bull when you're not on the king's time, huh?"

"I'll visit when you get back," Castor regarded the man. "Besides, I'll want to know how the rest of my street urchins are doing."

The three clasped hands in turn and separated ways.

"To the prison then?" Key asked.

"To prison," Castor replied.

When they arrived, Keebler saluted and opened up the door without a word. The two walked down the dim corridor until they reached the cell holding the teary-eyed Crumb.

"Guard, I will need to interrogate this boy one more time," Castor said, stealing a glance toward Donohue, or rather, the temple desecrating Gerard. "His story checks out. We just have one more question about Gerard."

"Can't you see he's lying," Donohue said from behind his bars. "You can ask anyone what my name is. I didn't desecrate any temples."

"Tell it to the hangman," Castor spat.

The guard unlocked Crumb's cell and ushered him to the interrogation room.

"Leave us," Castor said to the guard. "We'll take it from here."

The guard left and closed the door behind him.

"Why did you tell that man I turned him in?" Crumb asked. "I didn't say anything. You lied to him, and now he's going to kill me!"

"I don't think you get it," Castor crouched down so he was eye level with the boy. "You are dead anyway. The purse you snatched apparently had enough money in it to afford you a swift hanging. The only reason why you're not swinging on a rope right now is because someone out there believes that they can get it back.

"Now, I'm in a position to make you a pretty substantial offer. If you get the purse back, I will arrange your freedom. I will also arrange for you to leave the city and see that you are given honest work. I have a friend who helps people like you resurface from the streets and become valuable members of society. But I need something from you."

"What?" the boy asked, nearly in tears.

"I need honesty," Castor demanded. "Not just about the purse, because there's no chance of you living without it, but I want you to answer some other questions. Help me understand that I'm not wasting my time trying to help you."

The three sat in silence for a brief moment before Castor continued. He asked the boy how he felt about honest work and if he would ever be able to put thievery behind him. Crumb didn't seem to know. He explained that he had never had honest work before, but he would be willing to try.

"That's what I was hoping you would say," Castor smiled. "I've arranged you a ride. Tell me where the purse is, and you and your friend will leave tomorrow to start your new life. It's going to be hard work, but you will be in good hands. You'll be working for a close friend of mine. He has a kind heart and treats people with respect."

"How do I know I can trust you?" the boy asked. "And how do I know you're not just going to arrest my sister too?"

"Let's weigh your options," Castor said. "Either you help me so I can help you, or you can keep silent, and I put you in the same cell as your mortal enemy out there. With one option, you have a chance of living, and you and your sister can make something of yourselves. With the other option, you have no chance of either. When your sister runs out of money, and you're not around to help her, what happens to her then? She'll have no more family, no more friends, and no more options. Do you know what happens to girls out there who don't have the means to support themselves?"

Castor could see by the look in the boy's eye that he did know. "I'm asking you again, where is the purse?"

The boy didn't move.

"May I?" Key asked.

Castor gestured towards the boy in a way that said, "Go ahead."

"In the king's guard, we have this rule called, "the brotherhood of the guard." It means that we are not allowed to snitch on anyone. It also means we keep our word even in peril of death. I can see that same strength in you. You don't want to turn in your sister even though it could cost you your life. I respect that more than you could ever know.

"So, I will give you my word under the oath of the brotherhood of the guard that we will not arrest your sister and that my captain is being honest when he says he wants to help you. Give me your arm."

The boy lifted his shackled wrists and held them out.

He took the boy's forearm. "I swear by the brotherhood of the guard that your sister will not be arrested, and you will be set free if you help us."

A tear started welling in the boy's eyes as his resolution had unexpectedly upturned. "Okay, I'll tell you, but please don't frighten her."

Castor lifted two approving eyebrows towards Key, who promised, "I will do the best I can not to frighten her."

"My sister's name is Marie. She's nine. You can find her on the poor side behind Blanton's bakery. If you tell her, "Your brother said you can trust us or he'll eat twenty dirty rat tails," she will give you both purses."

"There's two?" Key asked.

"Yeah."

"Okay, we'll be back."

"Hey," the boy said. "The brotherhood of the guard is a real promise, right?"

"More than you'll ever know," Key replied.

# Chapter 12

## Trading Bread for Gold

C astor and Key made their way to the poor side. Houses were built close together and on top of each other, with tents and shacks connecting them together. The street was thick with putrid-smelling mud in an uneven pattern. A carriage would get stuck if it tried to go down this street, so none did.

"Do you know where this bakery is?" Key asked.

"It's just around the corner," Castor motioned right. "Another reason why you should explore the city more with your fake deliveries."

"I thought you were just kidding about that," Key said, lifting his boot out of the mud. "You really want me to walk around the city on fake official runs?"

"Yes," Castor said. "And I don't play around with official orders. It will be good for you anyway. Explore the city, learn new shortcuts, look busy, and so forth. The more I think about it, the more I'm tempted to pat myself on the back for being so brilliant. Speaking of which, that was quick thinking about the brotherhood of the guard promise. Good work back there."

"Thanks," Key beamed. "I just understood what it felt like to think you were possibly turning someone in. He just needed reassurance, I think."

"Okay, no one likes it when you toot your own flute," Castor admonished. "Ah, here we are."

They stopped outside a small brick house with smoke coming out of the chimney. A wooden sign out front read, "Blanton's baked goods," in red letters. There didn't appear to be any way of going around to the back. Temporary structures were built on either side of the bakery, hanging with tarps and sheets for walls.

"I guess we go through Blanton's," Castor looked at the bakery dubiously. He walked up the stairs and knocked on the door.

"How can I help you?" a voice said, opening the door to reveal a rather plump man wearing a dirty white apron. His chubby face showed visible signs of discomfort when he saw the two sentinels at his front door.

"Good afternoon," Castor greeted. "We are interested in speaking to one of your neighbors out back. Do you mind if we pass through?"

"I would be hard-pressed to turn the king's guard away," Blanton admitted, turning to his side. "Come in, come in."

"Our thanks," Castor said as he attempted to slide past the man's protruding belly. Seeing that entry would be unsuccessful without becoming uncomfortably acquainted with the baker, he stopped and made a shooing motion with his hands.

"Beg your pardon, sir," Blanton said, turning and leading the way through the house. "It's this way."

As they passed through the house, Key noticed that it was more kitchen than home. A small table, cot, and chair leaned against the wall to make room for flour bags and firewood piles. Shelves holding small loaves of bread and even smaller cakes lined the walls near the oven.

"Here you are," Blanton said, opening the back door with a creak. "Just let yourself back in when you're finished.

"Thank you," Castor said as he exited the tiny bakery.

The two entered the back quadrangle. Tents and shanties spread out in every direction in disarray. Castor started looking near the smallest tent to the left and lifted a linen tent flap. He immediately dropped the flap and straightened his back. A look of alarm spread across his face.

Key lifted his hands and silently mouthed the word, "What?"

Castor motioned with his hands to say, "For the love of anything good in this world, never mind."

The two broke out, searching in either direction. Key noticed little trails in the dirt leading out into all directions to the right of the bakery. He followed them until he noticed a tent flap hanging from two knee-high rafters connected to the bakery and another shanty. He lifted the flap and found her. A little girl, wrapped in a brown blanket, was curled up into a ball with her back against the bakery.

"Marie?" Key asked. The blanket moved. Key called out her name again.

The blanket unfolded, and Key could see two bloodshot eyes peeping up at him.

"Hi, Marie, I spoke to your brother," Key said, trying to use his most disarming voice. "He's safe, but he needs

153

your help."

In recognizing Key's uniform, Marie's eyes turned wild, and she tried looking for a way out. Noticing she was trapped, she moved away from the entrance as far as she could go.

"Look, I'm trying to help you," Key tried keeping the exasperation out of his voice. "Your brother told me not to scare you, so if you could please not be scared, we can have a conversation."

"What's my brother's name?" She asked.

"Crumb," Key replied.

"Okay, what's his real name?" She pressed.

"I, uh," Key stammered. "Look, I'm not here to arrest you. I made your brother a promise. It was a sacred promise. We are going to get him out of prison, but you have to help."

Marie's eyes brightened after hearing her brother was going to be released. "What do I have to do?"

Key could hear Castor's footsteps from behind him. He quickly put out a finger, gesturing him to approach slowly. "In order for us to release him from prison, you have to give us the money back."

"You can't take the money; it's all we have. Besides, there is no money."

Castor leaned down behind Key, "You found her!" he said in a voice that wasn't quiet or disarming.

The girl looked like she was going to panic.

"Your brother said if you can't trust us, he would eat a bunch of rat tails," Key interjected.

"How many?" the girl asked.

Key turned to Castor with a silent plea for help. Castor shrugged.

"Was it fifty?" Key asked.

"No," the girl replied.

"Now that I think about it, twenty," Key said triumphantly. "He said that he would eat twenty dirty rat tails."

"That was just a lucky guess," The girl said. "Besides, you already got it wrong the first time."

"You can't blame me for having a bad memory," he reasoned. "Do you remember what you had for breakfast two weeks ago?"

"I don't usually eat breakfast," She replied.

"Do you remember what you ate two weeks ago?" Key asked, frustrated.

"Probably bread and an egg," She replied.

"But do you actually remember?" Key replied.

"No," she said forlornly.

"Okay, so I forgot it was twenty, but now I remember," Key proclaimed, vindicated. "Besides, we have to get your brother out before it's too late. Do you know what they are going to do to him if you don't help us?"

"What?" The girl asked.

"They are going to hang him," Castor said from over Key's shoulder.

Key continued, "I don't want your brother to die, and you don't want your brother to die. So, can you give us the money, and we can help him escape?"

"Can I give you half?" She asked.

Castor started tapping his foot.

"You'll have to give us all of it," Key said.

"But I'll starve!" the girl said.

"How about we get you some bread from Blanton's?" Castor suggested.

"I hate his bread," the girl said. "It's too hard, and it

tastes like grease."

"I'll make sure he makes you good bread," Castor promised. "Besides, you only have to eat it for one day; I'm going to get you and your brother out of town tomorrow, so you'll never have to eat Blanton's bread again."

Castor explained his plan to the young girl. After some creative descriptions of where he was sending them, she finally relented and handed Key the two money purses her brother stole.

"Okay, but I don't want stale bread," she said. "I want it freshly made and without grease."

Castor tapped Key on the shoulder and motioned him to go talk to the baker. "Do you know about a place called, "Skippers Transport" on Alpenrose..." Castor explained to the girl as Key made his way to the door. He went inside and found the baker building up his fire.

"Blanton, I need you to do me a favor," he said. "I need some bread for the little girl out back."

"Are you kidding me?" the baker asked. "The last time I gave that little urchin some bread, she gave it back to me with two fingers holding her nose! I'm not giving that ungrateful rat anything else for as long as I live!"

Key held up his hands. "Look, if you make her the best bread you've ever made, you'll never see her or brother again. They are leaving tomorrow, but only if you do this one thing."

The baker thought for a moment. "Okay, but it'll cost you                              four                              coppers."
Key reached into one of the money pouches he was holding and pulled out a gold royal. His eyes bulged as he looked at the coin. He pulled open the drawstring and noticed they were all gold royals.

"Where did you get money like that?" the baker asked, shocked.

"Uh, taxes," Key lied, not wanting to explain the story. He reached into his own coin purse and produced five copper coins. Here are five. Keep all of this to yourself." After a moment, he added, "And don't use grease."

The baker accepted the money with a huff and tucked it away. "Anything else?"

"Can you deliver it to her once you're done?" Key asked. "And be nice to her. She has no parents."

"Fine, fine," the baker said. "If you'll excuse me, I have to make a special bread for a special little princess."

"That's the spirit!" Key cheered as he made his way to the back door. At the same moment, Castor stepped inside. "Let's go. We need to catalog this money and get it to the treasury."

Evan Kvalvik

# Chapter 13

## The Soul of a Shoe

B enj woke up, walked outside to chop wood, observed the mountain of wood he had forgotten about, and then went back inside. Some habits would always stay intact.

"Good morning," Taft greeted. "I've made you breakfast." He held out a plate of warm fresh bread with two golden eggs on top, and a golden-brown sausage.

"Morning, and thanks," Benj replied, not wanting to mention how surprised he was to find nothing was burnt. "Wow, you didn't burn it this time," he said anyway.

"I watched it the whole time," Taft gleamed with satisfaction. "Some could say I made it with love."

"It definitely tastes like you made it with love," Benj said between bites. "I have to get shoes today and need you to take care of everything while I'm gone again."

Taft agreed, and after he finished breakfast, he left the bakery with his shoes in hand. He walked through town, feet pattering on dirt and cobblestones until he reached William's Shoe and Leather Repair.

He saw William in the window drinking something hot from a wooden Tankard. The shop's front door still had a sign that said closed, but Benj did not have time to mull around all day. He made three hard knocks on the thick oaken door, which made three soft sounds, betraying his efforts. The door made an unlatching sound and opened slowly.

William had straight grey hair down to his shoulders. He had leathery features around a square nose and a strong jaw. He was old but not old-looking.

Before William could say anything, Benj started, "Good morning, Master William, I'm sorry for coming over so early, but I'm in a little bit of a bind." He held up his broken shoes. They were tragic to look at, even for William, who had seen every broken shoe in town for the last thirty years. "Do you think you can help?"

"Come in, let's take a look," William spoke, trying desperately not to portray the tone of being inconvenienced.

Benj walked through the door and into a small, well-lit room with two chairs, a table, and a shoulder-high shelf with three rows of shoes.

"Please, have a seat," he gestured to a chair before leaving the room and returning with a warm drink. "Let's take a look," he said as he removed the shoes from his hands. "I can fix these up quickly," he continued, holding up a shoe to show the separated sole, fraying threads, and worn leather. "They should hold up until I can make you a new pair, but not much longer."

"That sounds good," Benj said.

"These look like they've lasted a long time." He said, pulling out a curved blade, cutting the remaining threads, and holding the soles to the shoes. From there, he inspected the black foot imprint on the frayed leather soles. "I see you had to grow into these a bit. And you tend to put more pressure on the outside of your foot and your toes."

"I didn't know that," Benj said.

"You can tell a lot about a person by looking at their sole." He said with a smile. It was probably a shoemaker's joke.

Benj smiled at him, "What do you get for me?"

"That depends on if you're planning to do much dancing?" William raised an eyebrow.

"No," Benj answered.

"Then, I have nothing on hand, and I will have to make the shoes from scratch." William said and asked, "When do you need them? "

"Less than two weeks," Benj said, knowing the wedding was in two weeks.

"Do you want soft, silent shoes for feeling the earth beneath your toes or strong, sturdy shoes for walking over rocks and rough terrain?" William asked.

"If it's possible," Benj began, "I would like them strong enough to endure a carriage travel from here to King's Gate, dragging me behind on my feet. I need something strong. Really strong."

"That is an odd request," he said before finishing his drink. "Do you drag behind carriages often?"

"Not yet," Benj replied. "I haven't had the right shoes for it."

William laughed and retreated to the back, "I think I have just the thing." He came back a moment later with a large wooden box.

"I believe this is the leather you're looking for," he said as he lifted the lid. "Hide of the snow bison. Hard as a dragon's flank." He pulled a white leather sheet from the box and hit it against the table to prove his point.

"It's pricey but durable. After cutting out enough to size your feet, there would be some extra left over. I could fashion you some boots. I would say that I could make them as fine as any boots you've ever seen. I'll put softer leather in layers for comfort. I could do it in two weeks for eight and a half talents."

Benj considered his finances and renegotiated, "Four talents, a pie, and a sausage bread."

"Six talents, two pies, and I'll finish your boots in less than a fortnight. I'll fix your shoes, too, but you have to bring me the sausage bread today." William countered.

"Name your pies," Benj demanded.

"Apple and elderberry."

They both agreed, and William held out his hand to shake. Benj reached in and noticed a light orange circular tattoo on his forearm.

"I have that same mark!" Benj said, clasping his hand, "But a different color."

"Any man worth his own grit has that mark," William said. "I'm assuming you went all the way up?"

"I thought it wasn't polite to talk about it?" Benj said questioningly.

"Oh, that's only for the people who don't go all the way up, or worse, the people who camp out of the bottom for a few days and then turn around," William's voice seemed to hold no mercy for such people. "Can I offer you something to drink?"

"I appreciate it," Benj said. "But no, thank you."

"The real tradition is to keep the conversation we are having right now to ourselves," William explained. "This is just between you and me. This journey, or "trek" as it's called, is not what makes you a man. If you're not a man when you start, then you won't be when you get back. This trek isn't about becoming a man; it's about reaping the rewards of being a person who goes that extra mile and reaches the highest peak when they don't have to. It's about being an outlier."

"So why aren't women allowed to go?" Benj asked. "I'm sure they can be outliers too."

"Who said they weren't allowed to go?" William asked.

Benj shrugged. "They aren't a part of the tradition."

"And yet, how many women's names did you see on the mountaintop?" William asked.

"I don't remember most of the names," Benj admitted.

"There are some women's names," William assured him. "But you are right to consider rethinking our little tradition. I've argued this point with the mayor. It keeps coming down to forcing someone to do something that they don't want to, even though it might make them a better person. Men have died from the tradition, and women haven't.

"It's a complicated subject, but ultimately, we decided to encourage all women to go on the trek regardless of whether they are required to or not. You should do the same. Make sure not to be too pushy or give any hints. This journey is about finding yourself with as little information as possible."

"So, did you make the mistake of jumping off the mountain, too, or did you play it safe and climb down?" Benj asked.

"I'm sorry, what?" William asked.

"Did you jump off the mountain?" Benj asked. "With your powers?"

"Ooooh," William exclaimed. He slapped his knee and laughed. "From what I understand, all the abilities are different. For me, I got really strong. I can crumple a copper mark with my fingers. That's why I'm so good at making shoes. The mayor can feel what the weather is going to do. I think he could sense a whole season in advance if he wanted to. That's why he's head of the farming committee. You said you could jump off the mountain?"

"Yeah, it's more like gliding off a mountain. Pretty much any time I jump in the air, I don't fall straight down anymore," Benj said, standing on a chair and jumping down the hall. He glided downward until his feet touched the ground and caught himself on the far wall. "I'm still learning how it works."

"Wow! I'll admit, one part of me is jealous because that sounds like a lot of fun," William affirmed. "The other part of me wonders how that will help with you and baking. That snow bison leather would be too hard for most cobblers to work with. For me, though, I won't even need special tools to bend it into shape. All I have to do is work it with my hands."

"I could always climb back up again and rewrite my name," Benj plotted. "Maybe my next power would be to magically clean the kitchen."

"That's a good one," William seemed to agree. "Unfortunately, you can't write your name twice. I've tried... What? Don't look at me like that; I have an inquisitive mind. It's like after we write our name once, we can't bring another knife to the surface or anything to the surface again."

"Like there's some kind of invisible wall?" Benj asked.

"Kind of; it's like the closer you get, the more it

164

pushes back," William tried explaining. "Try it for yourself one day; it's pretty interesting."

"I don't know if I'll ever go back up there," Benj confessed. "At least not any time soon," he said, and then he told him about his run-in with the mountain wolf and how he almost died.

"That's quite a tale," William declared, shaking his head. "I'm glad you made it home. Ah, speaking of making it home, I should give your shoes a quick fix so you can bring me sausage bread." He took a needle that was threaded with a leather cord and sewed his shoes together. He made fast work and then handed them to Benj after they were finished. "Try that out."

Benj took the shoes and slid them on his feet. "It works, thank you!" When he returned home, he made the sausage bread and had his new apprentice deliver it.

Over the next week and a half, Benj hadn't figured out how to tell anyone he was leaving. Instead, he trained Taft hard every day. He made lists and schedules and had sales on items he wanted his apprentice to make over and over. Taft was keeping up but was not happy about the intensive workload.

"Taft," Benj said, "I have something to tell you."

"Out with it then." He said, scrubbing a pot.

Benj sighed. *I really should have hazed him more*, He thought. "I'm leaving soon."

"How soon?"

"Right after the wedding cake," he specified.

Taft asked when they were planning on making the wedding cake, and Benj told him it would be tomorrow. There were only two days left before the wedding. The closing deadline felt more like a dull sore than the gut punch it used to feel like now that he had time to process everything.

"Ok then," Taft accepted it and continued on working.

"Taft, I have something else important to tell you," Benj said again.

Taft tossed the sponge into the pot he was washing and gave Benj his full, undivided, and slightly irritated attention.

"What?"

"If I'm not back before your ceremony... I just want to tell you that in all things, especially baking, always put in your best work." Benj advised, "Go all the way to the top. You got that?"

"Yeah."

"And don't worry about how long it takes you to make the dough." he continued, "You aren't going to beat anyone's record. There is no record. There is sloppy dough and perfect dough, and I'm not training a sloppy dough bread baker."

"I got it, I got it," Taft said.

Benj took a handful of flour and dropped it on the counter. "Hey, Taft, if this is the mountain of success and I was climbing up and I made it here," he pointed in the middle of the pile. "Did I put in enough effort?"

"No," Taft said.

"If I went here," He pointed close to the top, "Did I do a great job?"

"Yes," Taft said until he saw the look on Benj's face. "No," he changed his answer.

"How about here?" Benj pointed to the top of the flour mound.

"Yes!"

"If Mabry comes in for a pie and she doesn't feel like

kissing you after she tastes it, did you put in enough effort?" Benj asked.

"NO!" Taft yelled.

"When you bake that pie," Benj said, "don't just kind of bake it; bake it all the way to the top. But don't burn it. I'm looking for a flaky, golden-brown crust. Oh, and bring a bow and arrow to keep the wolves from eating you."

"Wait, what?" Asked Taft, but the magic was gone, and the bell rang.

"This is your show now, champion," Benj waved him forward. "Go see to your customers."

Taft went through the door to the front and came back a moment later.

"Mabry isn't having it?" Benj asked with a smile.

"This one's for you. It's Melisandra."

If strings were holding up Benj's smile, they were both clipped at once.

"Tell her I'm not here," he said.

"I can hear you," Mel said from the other room.

"Tell her I'm busy and to come back in a week," Benj said quieter.

Taft went through the door and said, "He said he's busy and-"

"I know; I heard him the first time," she cut him off. "Benj, let me come in and say something really fast. Then, if you really want me to go, I'll go."

Before Benj could respond, Mel pushed her way past Taft, and by the look on Taft's face, it was a tight squeeze.

She wore a traditional green and silver dress that looked like it would be ugly had anyone else been wearing it. She wore a white ribbon in her hair and had thick masculine boots on her feet. She was living proof that it was possible to look rugged and beautiful at the same time.

"Sorry to interrupt your... pile of flour," she said playfully. "I really am."

"Alright, Mel. What can I do for you?" Benj asked, cleaning up his mountain of success that was secretly Mt. Asven.

"I was wondering if you wanted to take a walk with me?" Mel asked sweetly.

Benj wanted nothing else but to spend time with her, but he realized it was just going to make it harder. Whatever she had to say, it would have to wait until after he had left town.

"Sure," said Benj, contrary to his own resolve, "I'll grab my jacket."

The two followed the river that led out of town, walking, and talking about everything, but nothing significant.

"Did you know one of the stipulations to this marriage is I can only take half my clothes with me?" She asked.

"No," Benj answered, curious of the strange requirement. "How many clothes do you have?"

"How should I know?" She asked, "Do you count how many shirts you have?"

"Five," Benj admitted. "Well, four now, I caught my sleeve on fire a week ago, showing Taft what not to do."

"You caught on fire?!" She exclaimed, "Are you alright?"

"Yeah, but you didn't answer my question," he smiled. "How many?"

She started saying that she really didn't know, but Benj glared at her until she crumbled like a dry scone. "I don't know exactly; I just know there isn't room in the new house for all of it, including a living area."

Benj cursed. "You have enough dresses to take up an entire living area? What are you going to do with all of them?"

"Keep them at my parent's house until we decide what to do, I suppose," she said, casually.

"You know what I would do," Benj started, "I would learn how to sew so I could alter them, and then I would sell them."

"I know how to sew, but I'm not selling them!" She said indignantly.

"It's not like you're going to wear them, you can't even take them with you." He tried convincing her.

"I might need them later." She supposed.

"For what?"

"I don't know, maybe you're right."

"You're only telling me I'm right because you want me to drop it."

"Yep, so drop it."

"You really are the worst."

"It's part of my charm." She said, smiling and batting her eyelashes.

"Maybe a small part of your charm; the rest should be around here somewhere." He said, kneeling next to the snaking river they were walking along. "Ah, here it is."

"What?" She asked and moved closer to him curiously.

Benj cupped his hand and scooped water into it. "It's in the river!" he said, splashing her in the face.

"You beast!" She yelled, half angry.

"Good thing you have so many extra dresses; I'm pretty sure that one is ruined," Benj said, feeling satisfied with himself.

"I think it is ruined. Help me get it off," Mel said, unclasping a strap going over her shoulder. She smiled wickedly, "Made you blush!"

Benj hadn't realized he had blushed, but he was certain he was blushing more just thinking about it. She put the clasp back on.

"I wasn't blushing. I had to sneeze!" he defended himself, but Mel laughed at him more.

"Made you blush, made you blush!" she said and then splashed him with water.

Benj felt even more in love with Mel than he had the day before. She was easy to talk to, she was fun, and he couldn't leave without trying to stop her from marrying Brahm.

"Mel, do you love him?" He asked. It was his last chance to find out before she went off and made an unfixable mistake.

"Like, love or," She lowered her voice, "love?" She asked with the face of an angelic devil.

"Just yes or no," he said.

"I'll tell you, but it has to be a secret." She spoke.

"Ok," he said and looked around. There was nobody, "what is it?"

"Closer." She said, and he stood close enough to kiss. She cupped her hands over his ear and whispered, "You're awfully curious for a fish," and pushed him towards the river.

Benj let out a yelp and grabbed onto her for balance. The two fell into the ice-cold river. After the initial shock of what had happened passed, they looked at each other and laughed.

# Chapter 14

## Sandstorm

T he bell on the front door rang, and Taft went to check on the potential customer. Benj was standing just inside the door, soaking wet from head to toe. "Can you get me a towel, please?" Benj asked, "I don't want to get water over everything."

Taft brought him a towel that he wrapped around himself. After drying off and eating some food, he realized he still had to tell Sephus he was leaving.

The old wooden stairs creaked with memories of a past life. A life Benj had put behind him piece by piece as each day aged him further into the person he was becoming. He stood in front of the door to the room he had stood in front of so many times before. This time was possibly the last. He was there not as the street urchin taken in out of charity but as someone strong from a good upbringing, strong from failures as much as successes. He loved Sephus as a father and knew he was about to tell him that his son was about to leave.

He knocked. "It's open," Sephus said. Benj cracked

the door open wider and wider, peeking through with only one eye open. Better to see something you can't unsee with just one eye. Sephus was dressed. Benj relaxed.

"What is it, boy?" He asked, lounging in his chair, turning a ring over in his hand. Benj took a breath to say something, but Sephus said something first.

"I was about your age when I met my first wife," he said, "She was a beautiful redhead, and you know what they say about redheads?"

"I think so," Benj walked in further and shut the door behind him.

"Well, that wasn't true for her," Sephus said. "The fifteen years we had together before she died, I had seen her lose her temper only once. It was when she was pregnant with our son. I had taken the leg off of her chair to sand it down. The chair was a little lopsided, so I had the leg in my hand, fixing it when she sat. I didn't have time to say anything. All I could do was watch her as she sat and fell backward." He started laughing. "She chased me around the house with a knife, yelling at me until she was out of breath."

"I can't imagine that was the only time you pissed her off," Benj supposed out loud.

"What do you want, boy?" Sephus asked.

"I'm leaving," Benj admitted at last.

"Perfect, bring me back some onions and mushrooms," Sephus reached into his coin bag.

"I'm leaving town," he corrected.

"Then bring me back some out-of-town onions and mushrooms."

"I'm not sure when or if I'll be back."

"You taking the other one?"

"No."

"Good, but he is your apprentice."

"He's making a wedding cake tomorrow under my supervision. If it's good, I'll graduate him or certify him or whatever it's called." Benj said with a wave of his hand. "If it's not good, we'll be up all night until it is."

"You can't graduate him until he's of age," Sephus contradicted him.

"It's not hard to follow a recipe," Benj stated.

"I'll give you that, but it's still not lawful to beat someone else's apprentice," Sephus declared.

"Then, don't beat him!"

"What if he's out of line?"

"You've never beat anyone in your entire life."

"I suppose not," Sephus said thoughtfully. "When do you leave?"

"Tomorrow," Benj answered, "I'll pack up my things as soon as the cake is finished."

"Aren't you invited to the wedding where they're serving the cake? It's in two days, right?" After seeing the look on Benj's face, he understood. "Oh, leaving before the wedding and not after."

"Yes."

"Where will you go?"

"Probably the city."

"Which one?"

"Which one do you recommend? I was just going to walk until I found a good place to settle down."

"I'll see about getting you a horse so you're not walking," he stated. "Do you want a big city or something small like here?"

Benj explained that he had no idea what he wanted because the village life was all he knew. He tried articulating his preference for a new home, but "good food" and "a good place to swim" were hardly distinguishable qualifiers.

"The way I see it, you have three options," Sephus offered. "Thannon, Faerwin, or Royal City."

"So, which one is better?" Benj asked, ready to make a quick selection.

"Depends on how you want to die, in my opinion," Sephus said and, after a moment, continued. "In Faerwin, you're likely to be killed by pirates or accidentally insulting a fisherman who always feels like he's not respected enough for all of his hard work. Honestly, how hard is lounging around in your boat all day with a line in the water? Anyway, there's a good chance you'll also be stabbed by a drunk or a prostitute. Thannon is pretty much the same. In Royal City, you are more likely to be killed by a thief. They have a lot of them there. A noble will kill you if they feel like your eyes lingered on their wife for too long. They can get away with it by simply flourishing a fake little story. There are assassins. They don't like working for free, so don't piss anyone off that can afford it... You can also get stabbed by a drunk or a prostitute. Mostly, just don't mess with drunks or prostitutes. Be careful of the guard. They'll kill you and call it the king's work.

"They're each about a seven-day ride from here, but they're close to each other. So, if you don't like one place, it's about a several-day ride to the other... Do you like fish?"

"What?" Benj asked.

"Do you like eating fish? Sephus asked clearly.

"Not particularly," Benj admitted.

"Then I would choose Royal City," Sephus

announced his recommendation. "It's a little cleaner and smells better. Don't get me wrong, it still stinks, but there aren't as many decaying fish lying in random places."

"Okay, Royal City, then," Benj said, wishing he wasn't leaving or that staying didn't hurt so much.

"Just follow the sunset. You're going to need money," Sephus reached into his top drawer and pulled out a handful of half talents. "I've been saving these for such an occasion."

"Thanks, I have money, though," Benj said, "I'll have about three talents after I buy my shoes."

"You're going to need it for taxes, tolls, room, supplies...," Sephus started ticking off fingers.

"Supplies for what?" Benj interjected.

"For when you start your own bakery. So, don't spend it all on hooch and loose women." Sephus said, probably from experience.

"This means a lot," Benj took the coins. "Thank you,"

"Why are you wet?" Sephus asked.

"I had the most amazing time with the woman of my dreams two days before her wedding," Benj said wistfully.

"Well, it's a good thing you're leaving then. Situations like that only lead to trouble and running home in your undershorts."

"Thanks again, Sephus."

"Don't mention it, boy. Now get into some dry clothes and get dinner going."

"Taft is on it already."

"What's he making?"

"I don't know, but something tells me you're going to complain about it." Benj said with a smirk, "Or die trying."

The following day, Benj woke up early, went to the

kitchen, and laid out three large mixing bowls on the counter. He then made breakfast, sat, and ate while Taft walked in to find the kettle was already hot.

"Taft!" He announced abruptly, startling Taft, "Today is your final test before I graduate you as my apprentice."

"Don't I have to be of age first before you can do that?"

"No, all you need to do is make this cake." Benj pointed at an empty cake pan. "We'll cross the other bridges when we come to them. Does that sound easy enough?"

"Sure."

"Well, it won't be," Benj paused, waiting a few heartbeats before continuing. "Okay, let's get started. We have to make a cake for fifty people. The cake in question is going to be our least expensive option. What recipe are you going to use?"

Taft slowly reached for a recipe book while looking at Benj for approval of his selection. He found stone features. Benj wasn't going to share anything or help in the slightest. Taft took a book out and flipped through the pages until he found the one he wanted and pointed.

"Okay," Benj said, "Not my first choice, but a few nuts in a wedding cake isn't unheard of. However, we are making the most inexpensive cake possible. So, are you going to use this recipe and leave out the nuts, or are you going to find a different recipe?

Taft scanned the recipe, flipped forward a few pages, and then returned to the nut cake. "I'll do this one."

How many layers will you use?"

"If I make two layers and use the large pan, it'll be perfect," Taft said with a smile.

Benj stared blankly.

Taft's smile faded. So, I'll make it three layers."

"Good," Benj approved. "Nuts can sometimes add their own oil to the texture, so just be cognizant of that. You may or may not need to add extra oil. This cake is in your hands. I'll be back." He left before he headed to the shoemaker's house.

William sat outside smoking a pipe, staring blankly at the wooden goblin holding a sign that read, "Leather, Shoes, and Repairs," when Benj walked up.

"Good morning!" Benj greeted.

William held up a finger and went into the house. A moment later, he came out holding a knife and said, "Give me your shoes."

"These?" Benj said, pointing towards his feet.

"Yes, your boots are ready, and you're going to throw those away anyway, right?"

"I suppose," Benj said and took off his shoes.

William took them and put them on the wooden goblin, making cuts in the back of the shoes to slide them on. After making a few adjustments, he walked around it and was satisfied. "Let's go inside. Come on in."

William walked to the back with the boots in his hands. "I almost forgot how hard it is to work with this leather," he said, clapping the boots together. They were white and thick, with a single metal clasp on each side over the ankle.

"They're amazing!"

"My thanks; you'll have to clean them every once in a while, to keep them sharp," William added, "But at some point, you might get them dyed."

"If it lasts that long," Benj countered, feeling the sturdiness of the boots.

"Those will last," William said easily. "I almost forgot!

177

You said you were going on a trip of some sort, so I took it upon myself to make a very special addition to these. Right here," he pointed to a row of slots on the inside of the boot. "Fits five coins per boot. Give me a couple, and I'll show you."

Benj gave him two silver talents. William took them and placed each one snugly in two of the slots inside, where a layer of leather overlapped. "Just slide them in here," William said, pointing to where he placed the coins, "and they won't fall out. They'll stay perfectly hidden. Just don't get your boots stolen."

"These look fantastic," Benj said, handing him the other four talents. Thank you."

"No problem, Benj, but where's the rest?" William said, holding the coins in his hand.

"It's in the boot."

"I'm not talking about the two in the boot; I'm talking about my two pies."

"The two pies are ready to be picked up. All you have to do is take the two out of the boot, let me put the boots on, and then you can go pick up your pies. I'm not stupid, William. You would have me deliver the pies, but we both know that pie delivery wasn't part of the deal."

"How about I keep your two boots until you deliver the pies?"

"You wouldn't do that."

"Why not?"

"Because the second you make me walk home without shoes, I'm going to take the two pies that I made for you and eat them while I watch my apprentice make two more pies for you." Benj threatened, "The only problem is, you don't want two of my apprentices' pies; you want last year's Winter Festival pie-baking champion to make your pies. So, I suggest you take the two in the boot, give me my boots, and walk back to the bakery with me so you can pick up your pies."

"Fine," William admitted defeat, "Just try them on and see if I need to make any adjustments."

Benj tried the boots on and walked around. They were sturdy and fit perfectly. "Nice work!"

"Let me know how they are when you get back."

"I'm probably not coming back for a while," Benj confessed. "But if I do, I will stop in and say hi."

"If that's the case, here." William twisted a copper Mark into a spiral with his fingers. The amount of strength it must have taken to do that sent Benj reeling.

"For good luck."

After William left with his pies, Benj went back into the kitchen to see how his apprentice was doing. At that point, everything had been going smoothly. The batter was made, and Taft was pouring it into a large cake pan.

Benj poked a finger in to taste it. "Not bad."

Taft smiled, and the bell attached to the front door rang. Sephus called from out front, "Benjo, you had better come out here and check this out."

Sephus lead him outside where there was a man was standing next to a horse. Benj recognized the man as Curtis, but he had never seen the horse. It was a rich brown with white spots and a white main.

"He found you!" Curtis waved. "And you got some new boots, I see."

"Yes, sir," Benj replied. "Picked them up this morning."

"We got you a little going away present," Sephus gestured towards the horse. "This is Sandstorm."

"Old Sep here drives a hard bargain," Curtis said,

slapping Sephus on the back. "He says you're heading to Royal City?"

"That's right," Benj replied.

"Well, she's an older girl, but she's faster than my midrange horses," he said, patting her cheek. "She did her fair share of racing back in her prime. She could probably get third place if she wanted to, but I don't like pushing her too hard anymore."

"She's a racehorse?" Benj asked, "I can barely ride a slow horse. I can't ride a racing horse."

"Sure, you can!" He said, "Just talk with her and build her trust up. She'll only go as fast as you want to. The only difference between her and any other horse is she has more feelings. I offended her once, and she ignored me for a week."

"Thank you very much," Sephus said, shaking his hand.

"It's my pleasure," Curtis said genuinely. "Oh, and one more thing. She knows a trick from her previous owner. I don't know what their relationship was, but I don't think she likes doing it." He handed Benj a folded piece of paper with the word 'Halu' written on it.

"Ha-" Benj started before his mouth was cupped with a big beefy hand.

"Hi, how are you? I'm fine!" Curtis cut him off loudly. "Don't, boy," he warned in a low voice. "She'll start bucking around, and, in my opinion, it puts her in a bad mood. Besides, it wouldn't make a very good first impression now, would it?"

There was a tense moment of silence before Benj spoke, "I guess I should thank you."

"Thank me for taking good care of her. She's one of my favorites." With that Curtis waved and headed back home.

Sephus handed Benj a quartered apple. "Feed her these, one by one. You have a lot of trust to develop with her and little time to do it."

Benj took the pieces and placed them one by one on his open palm as Sandstorm ate them. "She's beautiful," he said, "How much did you pay for her?"

"Never ask how much a horse costs," Sephus scolded.

"What if I'm buying a horse?"

"You're about to be if you keep it up." Sephus tossed him another apple. "But I'll tell you I paid significantly less than I should have. I called in a favor."

"Sephus, I can't tell you how thankful I am," Benj said, overwhelmed with emotion.

"Come inside, there's more."

On the front counter sat two saddlebags filled with supplies.

"I took the liberty of getting your supplies ready." Sephus opened the saddle bag flaps. There's no way you were going to be ready in time, seeing how this wedding is tomorrow."

"Sephus, this is-" Benj cut off.

"I know," he said, taking Benj into his embrace. "You're going off to do big things, and I'm proud of you."

Smoke rose from the top of the door into the kitchen. Benj started to go through the door when Sephus held up a hand to stop him.

"I got it from here," he said stoically. "You go and pack up." He then walked into the kitchen and took charge.

Benj could hear him shout from inside, "What's going on in here? Are you Daft Taft? Take that thing outside before you smoke us out and burn everything down. Are you trying to make a wedding cake or a funeral cake? Don't smart-mouth me, boy; get that pan cleaned up and start over!"

Benj listened for a moment longer and then made his way upstairs to his room. He set his pack on his cot and began filling it. First, he packed a small wooden box with two compartments, each with a stone inside. Then he packed all three of his remaining spare shirts and two extra pairs of pants. He wrapped a bar of soap with a beeswax cloth and gently added it. Finally, he packed his recipes. He had two folded pages of parchment with small writing on the front and back. Then he put his extra money in the secret slots in his boots. Realizing he had nothing left to pack, he went down to help in the kitchen.

On the morning of the wedding, Benj woke up to Taft nudging him.

"Yeah?" Benj croaked.

"Breakfast," Taft replied.

Benj got up, put his blanket and pillow in his bag, and climbed down the stairs. On the kitchen counter was a plate with eggs, sausage, and bread with melted cheese. He dug in.

"I made that bread last night after you went to bed," Taft bragged, eating his own piece.

"Mh, Mhm!" Benj murmured his content.

"Thanks," Taft said with a smile.

"I have a feeling you'll do just fine without me," Benj said finally. "Is there any cake left?"

Taft brought out the remainder of the sample cake. It was baked in a pie pan. Benj stuck his fork and took a bite. The white glaze gave way as he pulled up a yellow sponge with nuts.

"I only put nuts in the smaller one," Taft explained.

"Sephus," Benj called, "Get in here and try this cake before I eat it all."

Sephus walked into the kitchen, fork in hand, scooped up a piece of cake, and ate it.

"Do you think we should get smaller cake pans?" Sephus asked. "I just don't know how I feel about using pie pans for our sample cakes."

"I don't care anymore," Benj admitted, "Taft, you are no longer my apprentice; I acknowledge you, this day, as an equal."

"What would have happened if we never finished the cake?" Taft asked.

"I would still be leaving," Benj said, "but I would have slapped you first."

"I thought I had to be an apprentice until I come of age and all that," Taft trailed off.

"Traditionally, yes, but I have to go," Benj proclaimed. "Don't burn the place down. Sephus, thank you for everything."

Sephus gave him a hug. "I'm going to miss you, son."

"I'll come back and visit."

"Come on," Sephus said, "I'll help you saddle your horse."

After the horse was saddled and packed up, Benj, Sephus, and Taft said their goodbyes. Benj had ridden horses before, but getting up on Sandstorm proved challenging.

"What do I tell the girl when she inevitably asks about you?" Sephus asked, referring to Mel.

"Tell her the truth," Benj said considering what the truth really was. "Tell her it was time to move on. Just don't tell her the whole thing about me being jealous and angry that she was marrying a prick and not me."

Sephus smiled, Taft waved, and Benj rode West. The sun rose behind him, over the town where he grew up, and over the only family he'd ever had. He left everything behind in clouds of dust as he started his long journey west.

# Chapter 15

## Gallows Reese

During the day, Benj would ride and stop to set up camp when the sun set into his eyes. There, he would gather dead leaves, fallen wood, and logs for a fire. He would fall asleep next to the fire and dream of baking bread and flying through clouds of flour.

He woke up more saddle sore than he had ever been. He was also sore from where he slept on tree roots. Not in any particular hurry, he built a fire back up from the coals and moved his joints around.

He took a roll from the travel pack and placed it near the fire for warmth. He then cooked two eggs in his skillet, which was smaller than the one he had tossed off the mountain all that time ago. He had learned his lesson traveling with a heavy pack.

On the seventh day, before he had the opportunity to pack up camp, he heard whistling coming from down the road. He looked past some trees to find a man walking quite cheerfully, heading in the same direction Benj was. The man was about as tall as Benj but perhaps ten years his senior. The way the man dressed made him look wealthy, or at least not impoverished. He wore a white shirt with buttons under a light brown jacket that went down his waistline. His pants had regal embroidery stitched over the front and a sword waving to the rhythm of his gait.

"Ho, there, friend!" The man called towards Benj as he walked close enough to see the fire and campsite.

"Ho," Benj replied.

"May I beseech upon your goodwill and ask to share that charming-looking fire of yours?" the man asked through a red beard contrasting with his short blonde hair.

"Sure, come warm yourself," Benj replied, thinking how it was a weird way to ask.

The stranger drew near and held out his hand. "The name Gallows Reese."

"Benj," he said, shaking the man's hand. "Interesting name. Were you born with it?"

"Terrible, isn't it? Hah!" Gallows laughed. "Haha! I wasn't born with it as much as I nearly died with it. You see, if a man had theoretically escaped the Gallows as many times as I have. Eventually, they would call him Gallows, too. For me, it's a constant reminder of how incredibly lucky I've been."

*Black ashes,* Benj thought, this guy is a criminal.

"So, what brings you east of Royal City?" Gallows asked, sizing Benj up.

"I'm Looking for work. You?" Benj asked and began packing his bags. He tried not to look like he was hurrying to leave the conversation; however, the participants were questionable.

"I was heading to my Grandmum's when I got

robbed on the road two days back towards Thannon."
Gallows Reese warned, "You better travel safe, or the
same thieves will get you too."

"Thanks," Benj said, taking note of the man's sword.

"You're not traveling alone now, are you?" Gallows
asked, looking around the campsite.

"Yes, but I can handle my own." Benj said, then
considered him, "If you got robbed, how do you still have
a sword?"

"Everyone has a sword," Gallows said, putting his
hand on the black jeweled hilt. "They didn't have room
for this old rusty blade."

Something was off about this stranger, and the story
wasn't adding up. That sword was probably worth more
than Sandstorm. Benj slowly picked up his skillet as if to
pack it and held it idly in his hand. He heard metal on
metal as a sword was slid from the sheath.

"T'was nice of you to pack your bags for me." Gallows
Reese said, holding the point of the sword to Benj's throat.
"Now put that pan into the bag nice and easy."

His mind raced. The stranger only wanted to know if
he was alone to rob him. He flipped open his pack, slowly
putting the skillet inside when his hand brushed against
a small wooden box. An idea struck him. He unlatched
the box with the tip of his finger, opened it, and dumped
two palm-sized stones into the bottom before removing
his hand. "Here." He said, closing the flap and handing
the bag carefully to the thief.

"Ah, I see you have saddled your horse for me too!"
the man said, taking the bag and pulling the strap over
his sword hand and head. He said, "Nice and easy," or
"Easy now," arbitrarily, the same way someone might say,
"There you go," or "I dare say."

Benj stood defeated.

"Don't worry, I'll give him a good home."

"Her," Benj corrected. "It's a her."

"Easy now," he said while he untied the horse and jumped on. "I suppose I'll give her a good home."

"Oh, one more thing," Benj said, watching the touchstones work their magic as smoke began billowing out between the seams of the bag. "Do you smell that?"

"Smell whaaaaaaaah!" Gallows Reese screamed.

The distraction bought Benj time to pull a piece of paper from his pocket and read the single word that might help.

Gallows Reese reached for the smoking bag strapped diagonally across his shoulders. He held his sword, pointing it in Benj's direction.

It was time.

Benj ran towards the thief and yelled, "Halu!"

The horse reared up, kicking Gallows Reese into the air, sword clamoring to the ground. Benj grabbed the sword and began to yell for him to stop.

The thief, getting to his knees, tossed the bag off his shoulders and charged.

"Wait, stop!" Benj yelled, holding the sword. He didn't want to use the blade; he had never used one. He just wanted to agree, disagree, and have them go their separate ways. The sword in his hand felt foreign and heavy; its cold steel was a stark reminder of the seriousness of the situation. His fingers trembled around the hilt, and he swallowed hard, trying to find his voice amidst the chaos. "Let's talk this through," he pleaded, hoping to defuse the tension before it escalated further.

Gallows Reese lunged toward Benj, face contorted, making a low growl.

Benj swung downward like he had done every morning since he became a baker. "Depends on how you want to die," he remembered Sephus saying. The sword buried its steel into the man's forehead. Gallows Reese's body went limp while blood poured from his head a deep burgundy. Arms and legs twitched uselessly on the ground.

Benj threw up.

He went to his pack to put the fire out and empty the contents. After some effort and a few singed hairs, he got one of the touchstones to roll free. Hot embers glowed red on all his earthly possessions. All his clothes, recipes, and gold mixing spoon were in a smoldering heap.

After an hour, he had salvaged his coins, a half-melted bar of soap, a skillet, and both touchstones. The stones had saved his life. He made room in the saddle bags and packed them away. Next, he went to the dead body and checked his pockets.

He found a money pouch with three half talents and tucked it away. He took the belt and scabbard from around the dead man's waist and put it on. It had two dragons on the belt facing in opposite directions. He picked up the sword and went to wipe the blood off on the man's jacket but paused. It was a nice jacket. All his clothes had burned up, and he could use the clothes. He wiped the sword on one of his half-burned shirts and sheathed it.

The blade was double-edged with textured steel where it had been folded. The handguard was a slightly curved symmetric cross beam jutting out from a braided leather hilt. Five spikes curled around a massive black jet in the middle of the hilt. It was both beautiful and sinister. Whoever this man was, he didn't spare expenses, or at least whoever he stole it from didn't.

He bent to remove the jacket. Fortunately, the body had fallen, and blood gushing from the head wound flowed downhill and not on his clothes. Once removed, he paused, looked at the shirt, and debated taking that too.

Thirty minutes later, Gallows Reese was lying face down in nothing but his undershorts. A tattoo of a snake and a three-point crown over two stars was all that took the attention from the corpse's shame.

He packed the reallocated clothes into the saddlebag with the oats. The clothes didn't smell dirty, and he hoped they wouldn't ruin the oats' flavor for the horse. It was time to move on, but there was something he needed to do first. He pulled out an apple, took a bite, and gave the rest to Sandstorm. He looked around the campsite and the dead body one last time and shuddered. It was time to leave.

The longer the day went on, the more people he saw walking on the road, and Benj ignored every one of them. When Royal City finally came into view, the sight was magnificent. The city was in the middle of a giant river that forked around walls, acting as fortifications from the North, East, and South. In the West stood an arched stone wall curving outward, protecting the city between the two river bends. Two bridges stood - one to the northeast and one to the southeast - wide enough to fit a merchants' convoy and made the only two entry points into the city. Although large and regal, the palace was overshadowed by several large cathedrals and a domed building to each side that stepped down into shorter and shorter rooftops. The city's canopy sloped up to other massive structures and landmarks. Steeples, spikes, golden-winged statues, and bulbous roofs rose to a point. Each rooftop bore a unique identity with grey stone, black marble, or gold-plated granite.

Benj stared at the distant city in awe. He felt overwhelmed and realized he wasn't as ready to live there as he thought earlier. He swallowed the lump in his throat.

"You ready, girl?" He asked Sandstorm.

She glared forward. She seemed like she was still upset about the commotion earlier.

"I know," he told her, slapping the reins and pressing forward. "Me too."

The closer he got to Royal City, the larger it got. When he got to the bridge, people queued in front, and he took a place in the back of the line. As the line progressed, each person stopped in front of a stout, red-faced guard.

"Afternoon, ma'am," a red-haired guard greeted an elderly woman in front of him. "State your business in Royal City."

The woman wore a scarf over her head and carried a basket with the contents covered.

"I'm here to visit my son. He just g-"

"Two Marks," The guard cut her off.

She handed him the two copper pieces, and he waved her through.

"State your business." The guard said to Benj.

"I'm here to find work. I'm a"

"Four Marks." The guard cut him off.

"But you only charged the lady in front of my two," Benj said indignantly.

The guard gave an exasperated look. "She didn't have

a horse, so she only had to pay two." The guard paused to let it sink in. "You have a horse, so you pay four; I'm being generous because technically, it's a copper mark for each functional leg stepped on my bridge, and I see six."

Benj tossed the guard a half-talent coin. The half talent was a smaller silver coin with a hole in the center. "Can you make change?"

"As sure as I can spit," the guard assured him, then spat to remove any doubt. The guard flipped the coin in the air to listen to the sound it made. Benj had no idea whether it was possible to tell if a coin was real by the sound it made, but it was impressive, nonetheless.

"'Here you are." The guard handed him eighteen marks. "Now, move along."

"You owe me three more," he said. "You only gave me eighteen."

The guard let out a sigh. "That's two for you, two for the horse, and three for the money-changing fee." He said, putting his hand on the hilt of his sword. "Now, move along."

Benj paused as if he would say something further but thought better of it and moved forward.

The city grew before him as he drew closer and made his way through the musky streets. People clambered in all different directions, around, behind, and past him. It was odd to be in the midst of such activity, but he didn't let it distract him from his goal. He needed to find a bakery to see if he could get some work.

He arrived at a crossroads where a signpost indicated four directions. To the back was the East Gate, to the left was Castle Road, straight ahead was Brighton Road, and to the right were the Slums. He chose the left path, immersing himself in the city's vibrant sights and sounds.

"Sir, sir, sir."

Benj looked down to see a dirty-looking street urchin.

"Excuse my presumptions, sir, but you look lost."

Benj felt embarrassed to have been called out so blatantly for the newcomer he was while the boy continued.

"This is no problem, sir," the boy assured him, seeing the look on his face. I am a man of many qualities; one of those is helping foreigners navigate our most complicated city."

The boy looked twelve years old and wore a large white smile in contrast to the light brown face darkened with streaks of dirt.

"No, thank you, ah-" Benj started.

"Samir, at your service, but my friends call me Sam. You, my friend, can call me Sam." He said without taking a breath.

"The last time a stranger called me friend, I got robbed. So, thank you, Samir, but no, thank you. If I ever need your services, I'm sure I will call on you." He said, gently nudging Sandstorm forward. "Good day."

"Good day, sir," Samir said. "However, are you sure you want to go that way?"

"Yes, I'm sure," he said and then stopped the horse. "Why?"

"That road leads to a very dangerous place. You're either very brave, or you are in need of my services more than I thought."

"It's Castle Road; it leads to the castle," Benj stated.

"Oh, haha!" Samir faked a laugh. "Very funny, sir. You had me going for a moment."

"If Castle Road doesn't lead to the castle, where does it lead?" he asked, confused.

"This leads to thieves and murders," Samir said seriously. "Half of the people are Crownsmith; the other half are dead."

"What's a Crownsmith?" Benj asked, irritated.

"Pardon my unwarranted advice, sir, but please, for the sake of our lives and your mother's prayers, do not say that so loudly next time. I am pleased to show you the castle, sir. It is right this way." Samir walked in front of Benj and gestured with his hand and that overly happy smile again.

At that moment, unbidden memories surfaced in Benj's mind. He remembered living in the streets as a young orphan and relying on strangers for food. He remembered the loneliness, the insects, and the cold nights. If Sephus had never saved him, he would have been in Samir's position. He saw himself in Samir's dirt-streaked face and decided to help.

"Samir, instead of the castle, do you know of any bakeries?" Benj asked.

Samir smiled. He was knowledgeable in many things, but his knowledge of bakeries was about to pay off. He led the way, talking about which bakery made the best cakes, which one was closest, and which owners were nice or not nice.

Benj's thoughts drowned him out as he was led through road after road, each offering a strange new sight, smell, or piece of culture. Street merchants sold colorful rugs with intricate designs under sheets roped up between buildings. A small troupe of entertainers juggled bottles of spirits. At the same time, one acted drunk, casually snatching them out of the air for a sip and then placing them back into the juggled loop without dropping one. A woman sat behind a table made of wooden boxes, offering to tell Benj his future, "I see you have a gift hidden away," she promised. "I will tell you how to find it for a price."

"No thanks," he smiled and moved forward.

Samir took him to a street baker who was pulling large wheels of flatbread out of a movable oven with a long, thin paddle.

"Get your weevils! Hot toasty weevils!" The man shouted.

Samir smiled and gestured towards the man. It wasn't quite what Benj had in mind; in fact, it wasn't anything like what he had in mind. He hopped down from his horse anyway and approached the street merchant.

"Ah, there's a man who enjoys the finer things in life; how many weevils can I get for you?" The man asked, setting his sizeable wooden paddle aside.

"I am actually here to see about the possibility of employment," Benj said, wishing it didn't feel so awkward to say it.

The merchant looked at Benj and then Samir.

"No, but thank you. This is pretty much a one-man operation."

"How much for one?"

"Five Marks for one weevil, seven Marks for two."

"I'll take two," Benj ordered, giving the man seven copper Marks.

He had wished he only bought one weevil as he followed Samir and pulled Sandstorm behind him. He was full after eating half. He gave his other half to Samir, who smiled and accepted it graciously before tucking it into his pocket. They began approaching another street baker, and Benj came to a halt.

"I'm more looking for a bigger establishment." He told the boy.

"Yes, sir!" He said enthusiastically. "But if I may speak freely, sir, they won't hire you."

"What?" He asked, shocked at the statement. "Why wouldn't they hire me?"

"There are very nice places on the other side of town," He said carefully, "and well... Begging your pardon, sir, but we don't look like we belong on that side of town." He lowered his head and shrugged.

Benj was confused. Of course, he belonged in the better parts of town; it's not like he was dressed like... He looked at what he was wearing. He was tattered, dirty, and travel worn. He looked like he could have been a street urchin himself if he didn't have a sword and a horse — the look of confusion left his eyes.

"You're right, Samir; we need to get cleaned up."

"You're right," he said, hesitating, "and you will definitely need to clean up."

Benj pulled out a single mark from his bag and held it up. "If you're going to be my guide," he breathed on the coin and polished it on his sleeve, "you're going to need to get cleaned up for tomorrow too."

Samir's eyes got big. "Oh, I see! I will be as clean as the king's stable boy, and for four Marks, I'll smell just as good."

Benj lifted an eyebrow.

"I met him once," Samir said, "He smelled very nice."

"That's kind of strange, but I believe you. Do you have any nice clothes?" Benj gestured up and down.

"Yes, sir!" He beamed. "I only wear this shirt because it matches my pants; these are my best pants."

His pants were raggedy and held up with a rope.

Benj groaned inwardly.

"Alright," He said, "Do you have any plans tomorrow?"

"No sir," Samir said with a big smile. "My services are yours for as long as you need."

"Alright," Benj said, digging out coins from his pocket. He leaned down and handed four Marks to Samir. "If you take me to a nice inn, come back, and we can get started first thing in the morning. Do you know of anywhere quiet?"

"I know of this place; it is very close," the boy said. The owner is very nice."

Samir took Benj through the poor area of town and then finally reached The Stonegarden Tavern and Inn.

"Sure, this looks quiet," Benj said, trying to stay optimistic about the run-down place. Can I trust you to watch my horse until I come back out?"

"Yes, sir!" Samir said, excited, either to be useful or to rob him.

Benj would have to leave Sandstorm outside anyway, so there was nothing he could do. He walked through the front door just in time to see the barmaid pick up a half-drunken ale off the bar and pour it into the barrel through a latch on the top.

"How can I help you?" She said as she wiped her hands on a dirty towel hanging from her apron.

"Hello," he said obligatorily. "I would like to see about a room, please."

"Will you be…" She pointedly looked at his sword, "causing any problems tonight?"

"No, ma'am," he said, patting his sword. "Just got here, and I'm not into any…" He trailed off. "No, ma'am."

"Four Marks a night," She said.

"That sounds fine," Benj agreed to the price and set the coins on the bar. "I also have a horse that needs stabling."

The lady slid the coins on the bar toward her, "That's an extra mark. Bring the horse around back and stable it yourself. Your room will be upstairs, and the second room will be to the left. There are no locks, so don't leave anything in there you don't want stolen. The bog is out back. If you use the chamber pot, dump it out yourself. If you want a bath-"

"What is a bog?" he asked, cutting her off and placing the mark on the counter. "Yes, I will need a bath."

"It's where you piss. Are you new?" She asked and continued, "If you want a bath, it'll be first thing in the morning. If you want a hot bath, get there early. If you want the first bath, get there first. Breakfast is whenever I make it, so don't run down here barking orders before I've had my morning tea. Got it?"

"Got it." Benj said, "I have clothing I would like washed."

"It'll be ready first thing in the morning," she said, holding out her hand. "One mark per article of clothing, I don't care how small. Too small, and it's two marks if you get my meaning?"

He was down to his last two marks, but he had three articles of clothing that needed to be washed. "Is there a money-changing fee?"

"What?" she said, making it more of a statement. "Good money is good money; I should be paying you to pay me, not the other way around, I say."

Benj almost sighed in relief as he slid a half talent towards her and got the appropriate change back. He picked up his money before she could take any more of it.

"I'll take the horse around back now."

He walked outside to find Samir talking to Sandstorm. "It's not so bad out here, I think you'll like it."

Benj took the reins. "Samir, thanks for the help today. See you in the morning?"

"Yes, sir, I will be here bright and early."

When he finally collapsed onto his bed, he intended to nap briefly before exploring more of the city. Instead, he ended up sleeping through the rest of the day. When he awoke that evening, he meant to think and plan, but he drifted back to sleep once again.

Evan Kvalvik

# Chapter 16

## Conflict of Interest

A t the office of investigations, Castor sat, writing a letter next to neatly stacked piles of gold coins. After signing the bottom of the page and sealing the folded letter with red wax, he gave it to Key.

"This goes to Major Kane; make sure the money goes directly into the Major's hands," he said, sliding the fortune-worth of gold coins retrieved from the thief back into the two purses. I would take the satchel... Just a recommendation."

Key took the satchel and dropped the two coin purses inside. He then took the sealed letter from Castor. "What does it say?"

"Oh, the usual," Castor began, reciting the letter from memory. "Here's the money and how much money it is; make sure whoever's money this is gets taxed for our efforts of retrieving it. I also requested that he release the prisoner in question into my immediate custody for further investigations. I didn't offer any other information on the matter, so I don't want you to either. Also, you don't have to wait around for correspondence back; he'll send Singer after he's drafted the prisoner release form."

"Alright, I'll be back in no time," Key said, putting the letter in with the gold and leaving.

Key felt uncomfortable carrying so much money around. When he arrived at the Major's office, he felt a sense of relief as he knocked on the door.

"Enter!" a voice sounded from behind the door.

Key opened the door to the office and found it empty except for who he remembered as Corporal Singer. He was a head taller than Key and wore the dress uniform with a blue sash. The uniform looked crisp, and it gave him an air of superiority, even though they were the same rank.

"I have correspondence and a delivery for Major Kane," Key announced formally.

"He's out of the office, but I can take it," Singer said, holding out his hand.

"I've been instructed to put it directly into his hands," Key remembered what happened the last time he said that phrase and hoped it wasn't some ill omen for the Major.

Singer looked annoyed. "He should be here soon if you want to wait."

"Thanks," Key said, adjusting the shoulder strap. "But don't look so upset. You don't want this package any more than I do."

"What is it?" He asked.

Key reached into his satchel and pulled out one of the coin purses. It was heavy in his hands. He opened it and showed Singer. "This is fourteen gold royals. I have another one with fourteen more."

Singers' eyes got wide. "Can I hold it? I've never held

so much money in my life."

Key hesitated and then handed over the coin purse.

"It's so heavy!" Singer said, hefting the purse. "What would you do if you had this much money?"

"I don't know," Key thought about it. "Probably buy a commission."

"You could do more than that," Singer said, tossing the bag up and down in his hand. "You could probably buy a whole Dutchy. That's what I would do. I would be a Duke." He plucked a coin out of the bag and flipped it in the air. "Duke Alexander Singer," he said.

Nervous about him dumping the coins everywhere, Key held out his hand. Singer returned the coin to the bag and handed it back. "I can see why you looked so nervous. If any of these went missing, you would probably hang."

"There is no doubt about that," Key agreed. "This money almost got someone hung already."

There was a quizzical look on Singer's face. Key relayed the story of retrieving the money, skipping over the parts Captain Castor would prefer to keep secret.

"So, it was technically you who found the money?" Singer asked, surprised.

"It was a team effort. Besides, if I wasn't there, Cas-" Key almost slipped. "Captain Castor would have found the money by himself. Don't tell anyone I told you this, but he's kind of a genius."

"Nobody's here," Singer waved a hand through empty air. "You don't have to pretend to brown-nose your superiors around me."

"I'm not," Key said, remembering to say something negative about the captain. "He might be smart, but he's a giant lobcock," he borrowed Castor's word. "Always, corporal do this, corporal do that, and if there's nothing to do, I have to stand at attention for the rest of the day and stare at the wall. If you ask me, the guy needs a piece of his own pie. How's it working for the Major?"

"He's a slave driver, never a moment of rest. Sometimes, I wish I was back on guard duty."

Key wondered if all of the officers wanted their corporals to refer to them as "slave drivers" and openly talk about how much they hated working for them.

"Oh yeah, same here," Key responded, gaining inspiration for the game they were playing. "It's like I have an everlasting mound of chores to do. I would jump in an instant to trade places with Keebler for a day."

At this, the two laughed when they heard footsteps. Their laughter was cut short when the door opened.

"Attention in the room!" Singer called out, and both of them stood, feet together, as rigid as a board.

"At ease, men." Major Kane said, then directed his attention toward Key. "What do you have for me today, Corporal?"

"Correspondence from Captain Castor and two bags of gold, sir," he said as he dug into his satchel and handed the Major the sealed letter. He then pulled out the two bags of coins and set them on the desk with a clink.

The Major cracked the seal on the letter and briefly scanned it with his eyes. "Alright, let's count it up." He then motioned towards Key to count the coins.

Key upturned the bags and dumped them on the table. He then began stacking the coins in piles of five and began counting: "Five, ten, fifteen, twenty, twenty-five, twenty-six, twenty-seven...." He stopped. A coin was missing. He checked inside his satchel; there was nothing in there.

The Major calmly rescanned the letter in his hand,

looking for the appropriate amount.

A bead of sweat formed on Key's forehead as he searched the bags and then the ground around the desk. There was nothing. He glanced at Singer, who stood stiffly off to the side.

"It says there's twenty-eight," the Major said. "It looks like you only have twenty-seven. Maybe there was a mistake?"

"I know it has to be here somewhere," Key said, nearly frantic with worry.

"I'm sure it is," the Major replied. "Corporal Singer, why aren't you helping look?"

Singer walked over to the desk, bent behind it, and pulled a gold royal up in his hand. "He must have dropped it when he was dumping out the bags," he stated matter-of-factly.

Key knew he didn't drop any coins. Furthermore, he had already checked the ground around the desk twice.

"Keen eye, Corporal," the Major praised. "You just saved your fellow corporal a lot of heartache."

"Thank you, sir," Singer replied.

Key stared daggers at Singer, who did not return the eye contact. Had he pilfered the coin when he was holding the coin purse?

"It looks like this is settled then," Key observed. "By your leave, sir?"

"Cary on smartly. Tell your captain that I'll be sending correspondence shortly."

"Yes, sir," Key said and then left.

The air cooled Key's face as he stepped outside. He had been sweating and for a good reason. Being in charge of so much money and then coming up short would mean terrible things for him. He tried remembering what

Singer's hands were doing when he reached inside the purse to inspect one of the coins. He shouldn't have given it to him. He would have to be more careful next time.

He began taking the satchel off as he entered the office. He heard voices inside. He slung the satchel back on, pushed the door open, and saluted with a fist to his chest.

"Corporal Key, reporting back from orders, sir," he said formally.

"Ah, Corporal Key, come in." Captain Castor beckoned. "This is Major Thomas. He oversees public relations. I was just talking about how you were quintessential to ascertaining our rather large quantity of gold earlier."

Key dropped his salute and saluted the Major.

"At ease, Corporal," the Major said. "It sounds like you have a gift for investigations. I told the captain that I would have delivered the gold myself, being such an important package, but he assured me that you were the right man for the job. It turns out he was right."

"Thank you, sir," Key responded.

"It ought to be me who is thanking you. You made the Royal Guard look good out there," The Major said. "I'm keeping my eye on you. I expect great things."

"Yes, sir," Key replied gratefully.

"Charles, I'll see you around," the Major said as he stood to leave. "I almost forgot: Here's the two talents I owe you."

"Always a pleasure, Major," Castor said, standing in tandem and taking the money.

After the Major left, Castor collapsed in his chair.

"What was the money for?" Key asked.

"Oh, nothing," Castor said. "Sometimes we make

friendly wagers over this or that. How did it go?"

"It turned out fine, but there was an issue. I might have dropped one of the coins on the ground," Key said, apprehensive to say what he actually thought happened.

"I think it's only natural delivering that much gold to have a shaky hand," Castor said. "I'm just glad you didn't decide to run off with it."

"The thought struck me once or twice," Key joked. "How far do you think I would have got?"

"I have no doubt you could have gone all the way and settled down somewhere in the country with plenty of acreage and lots of cows," Castor said. "Now, when are you planning on going to the training field? Or would you like to practice your letters first?"

"Actually, I wanted to discuss the five copper Marks I spent for the girl's bread today," Key admitted.

Castor's face lit up. "I am so happy you brought that up. Let me explain how that works," he tapped joyously on his desk with all his fingers.

"Frequently, we have to spend money in the name of service to the king. The king understands, the treasury understands, everyone understands. So, after spending money, just like you did today, you have to draft a monetary requisition letter."

"A what?" Key asked.

"It's a request letter for money. You just put the date, how much money you're asking for, why you're asking for the money, and any further information that could help the office of investigations - my office - investigate the validity of these requests. For instance, remember the uniforms you ordered and had the expenses billed to my office?"

Key nodded his head.

"As soon as that bill arrives, I will write a monetary requisition letter, take that letter to the treasury, and they will pay it. Now that I think about it, you'll be proficient enough to write one for the uniforms after you ask the bank for your five Marks back. You'll also have to deliver the letter, and probably deliver the money. Anyway, once every so often, we audit the requests and see what everyone's been up to. There have been times when I had to approach some of the other officers to tell them that "stocking your office with expensive wine every week is not an official expense and to stop trying to ruin it for everybody."

Key motioned for Castor to slow down. "Are you telling me that you can make requests for money based on facts that you, yourself, investigate the validity of?"

"That's right," Castor said, happy to have gotten through.

"Doesn't that create a, you know?" Key asked, trying to describe the word with his hands, but the best he could do was depict a pulsing ball.

"A conflict of interest?" Castor replied, guessing what the hand motion meant. "Absolutely."

"Does anybody know about it?" Key asked, feeling scandalized.

"We all know about it," Castor explained. "Royal City, in a way, operates on the honor system. I haven't done anything to warrant extra security measures, and I don't plan to. No one else wants it to be more strict either."

"Okay, where do I start?" Key asked.

"Remember when I told you every letter that you want to write has already been written?" Castor asked, not waiting for an answer. "It just so happens that I have a request for money over something very similar." He dug in a drawer, pulled out a creased letter with a broken seal attached, and handed it to Key. "There are some minor details you need to change. For instance, the date and the approximate time, and instead of "to purchase lunch while interviewing a suspect," put "to purchase bread for a thief to lure her into returning the thirty-some pieces of gold she stole. Make sure to give the Baker's address. The resolution should be, "She returned the gold." You got it?"

"I think so," Key said, dipping his quill to begin copying the letter. Shortly after, there was a knock on the door. Key began standing up.

"Oh, sit down," Castor said. "As long as you appear gainfully employed, you don't need to bother pretending to be alert. Enter!"

Key settled back into his seat as Corporal Singer entered.

"I have correspondence from Major Kane, sir," Singer announced handing Castor a letter. He remained at attention as Castor broke the blue seal with a snap and started reading.

"Excellent," Castor said. "You are dismissed."

"Yes, sir," Singer said and turned to leave. He turned his head to address Key, "Close call with that gold you nearly lost today. You're lucky I was there to find it," and then he left.

After a moment of silence, Castor spoke up. "I do believe that was a direct attack on you just now."

"You caught that too?" Key asked, setting his quill down.

"Yes," Castor said. "Not too much escapes me. I suspect he was hoping that was the first time I heard about the incident, and he just nonchalantly told on you."

"What a prick," Key said.

"What a prick, indeed," Castor repeated. "If you want, as soon as you can swing a sword well, I can arrange a duel between you two. It could be a fun way to win some bets. He's taller than you, but I happen to know for a fact that he hasn't visited the training field a single day since he started working for the Major."

"That's not a bad idea," Key said, picking up his quill. "We'll see how my training goes. I'll try to get some extra sparring in."

An hour later, Key handed Castor the monetary acquisition letter he had written for his five Marks.

After scanning the letter, Castor let out a deep sigh. "I can look past the fact that it looks like it was written by a nine-year-old girl, no offense to young Marie, but there can be no mistakes. Do you remember the axiom that appearances create credibility? That applies to every aspect of this office, especially its correspondence. You crossed out three words and misspelled "Acquisition." It's the second word the treasury will read! You'll have to redo this; try to go slower next time."

There was a knock at the door, and Castor gave the command to enter.

A small boy with a dirty face walked in with a piece of paper. "A letter from Gretta's, sir."

"It seems your uniforms are done," Castor said, reading over the paper.

"She did say she had extras on hand," Key remembered.

The boy cleared his throat.

Castor reached into his drawer, pulled out two copper Marks, and handed them to the boy.

"Pleasure as always, sir!" the boy said, and left.

"I'll also need Acquisitions for the two Marks for the

delivery boy and the uniforms, of course," Castor said. "Practice makes perfect."

Key made a list of the letters he would need to write and then stood up. "I'm going hit the training ground."

"Very well," Castor said. "Swing by and pick up those uniforms first, Gretta will let you have them. I'm sick of hearing you clink around in that armor anyway. When you're finished, take the rest of the day off; we have a big day tomorrow. Care to make any bets on whether our pickpocket takes my offer for a better life or makes a run for it?"

"I think he'll go for the better life," Key said. "He has his sister to think about."

"I would gladly lose a silver piece to see those two make a better life for themselves," Castor said.

"I'm not betting a full talent," Key nearly yelled. "I'll bet the five Marks I'm writing an acquisition for and not an empty hole more. That means I can't pay you until I get it from the treasury if Crumb walks, deal?"

"That's a wager," Castor said, leaning back in his chair. "One I hope to lose."

Evan Kvalvik

# Chapter 17

## Street Thieves

B enj woke from his room in the Stonegarden Inn and recollected the events from the previous day. It all felt like a dream or like he had imagined it somehow. He knew he had a lot of work to do, so he climbed out of bed and went downstairs. The sun was peeking through the windows at a man sleeping behind the bar on a cot. Benj walked past him without waking him up and snuck out through the front door.

The air was thick and humid. People were sluggishly walking towards their respective places of employment or already setting up their shops. He walked around the back to check on Sandstorm. The horse stood in a stall of four poles driven through the ground connected with crooked wood planks. Despite her drab surroundings, the horse seemed content.

The innkeeper was lighting a fire under a metallic tub in a similar stall, except it had a four-foot wooden wall for privacy. The wall was only on one side, threatening to leave him vulnerable on the other three.

"The Bath'll be ready in an hour or so unless you want

it cold," the old woman informed him, striking her tinderbox. "Don't suppose you'll need soap or a towel?"

He had soap and wasn't a stranger to cold water, but he might enjoy something to dry off with. "A towel would be nice. I'll be out in a few moments." He told her, "I think I'll take it cold. Do you have my clothes ready?"

"I'll bring them out." She slipped the tinderbox back into her pocket and stalked off.

He left and came back with his half-melted bar of soap from the incident with Gallows Reese and two touchstones. He removed them from the charred blue fabric they were wrapped in and placed them together at the bottom of the tub. When he felt the stones start to heat up, he carefully lifted his hands out of the water.

The single wall protecting him from possible side glancers in the 'bathing room' made him feel only a quarter of the way comfortable. He was three-quarters uncomfortably exposed as he peeled off his travel-worn clothes.

He splashed himself with the frigid water and began lathering himself with the bar of soap while he waited for the water to heat up. The blue suds turned black as dirt pulled free from his face and hair. When he was finished, he decided not to wait for the water to finish heating before getting in. It felt warm enough as he reached to separate the stones before sliding in himself. He took a deep breath and pulled his head under the water. When he surfaced for air, he was met with two big eyes and an even bigger smile.

"Morning greetings, sir!" Samir greeted from over the single privacy board. He was surprisingly clean and would be considered semi-well-dressed if the colors and patterns he was wearing were not at war with each other.

Benj, not entirely unaccustomed to being reported to while he was in the bath, leaned back and donned a comfortable smile.

"Samir," he acknowledged the boy. "You found me."

"Oh yes, I first went to check to see if your horse was properly taken care of, and to my wonderful pleasure, I found you!" He beamed a look of self-satisfaction, "I will look after your horse while you finish."

The innkeeper draped his laundered clothes over the privacy wall with a muted thump.

"Your clothes are ready," She said and directed her attention to the boy poking around the stables. "Hey!"

"It's okay, he's with me." Benj lifted a hand out of the water to calm her. He knew who she was yelling at.

The innkeeper gave a cautious look and relented. "If you say so, then fine."

"Ma'am," Benj noticed the towel she was holding. "Is that for me?"

"It can be for a Mark." she said, holding the towel in one hand and her other flat palm facing out, "Pay now."

Benj looked at his pants where his money bag was and then looked at the innkeeper's line of vision over the privacy wall. He groaned inwardly and then climbed out of the bath, dripping water into pools where he stepped on uneven clay bricks, covering himself to the best of his ability. He pulled his dirty pants up in front of himself and rummaged around until he found the copper coin he was looking for.

Glancing over, he found her next to the wall, staring directly at him. He continued holding his pants in one hand and offered her the coin with his other. She slowly held up an old, wrinkly hand and accepted it. After the transaction, she scanned his wet body with wizened eyes and smiled.

As soon as she left, Benj jumped in the bath, causing water to splash out on all sides. He didn't care about the mess as long as he was out of eyeshot of the curious city and all of its nosey old women. When he was all dried off and, most importantly, the old innkeeper was done watching him dry off, Benj put on the freshly cleaned clothes that he had gotten from the dead thief. They fit him impeccably.

"You look fantastic, sir!" Samir said excitedly. "A significant change from how you looked yesterday if I am not so bold to say, sir."

Benj thanked him but told him not to be so formal as he packed his meager belongings into the saddlebag. Before long, he was walking down the road with Samir, leading Sandstorm on foot.

Samir was explicitly instructed to go to the nicest bakeries first. The buildings along the road looked as if they had been constructed hundreds of years ago, with intricate swoops, patterns, and spiritual figures carved into and out of the stonework. Newer buildings alongside the ancient ones were made in a similar style of architecture, with bronze and iron inlays into the masonry.

The beauty of the city came with a price. There was a constant clicking and hammering from stone and chisel that resonated through the air from a hundred directions. Samir ran ahead and stopped under a low-hanging sign that said, "The Flaming Loaf," in brown letters on a whitewashed background. It was clearly a bakery, though the building from which the sign hung was more beautiful than the town hall back home. The surrounding businesses were also operating out of historic architectural masterpieces they had no right to be in.

"Samir," Benj said, preparing to go inside. "Will you wait out here with Sandstorm?"

"Sir, if it's no trouble to you, the streets are very safe, and it would be my greatest pleasure to assist you inside."

"Fine," Benj said and tied the horse to a pad eye jutting from a lamp post just outside the bakery. At this point, he was too excited to argue or even care.

The two walked into the bakery, and a warm, familiar smell filled Benj with a sense of home. Other foreign smells filled him with awe and wonder.

A middle-aged lady stood behind a marble countertop covered with glazed and sprinkled delights. His stomach reminded him that he had not stayed around to eat breakfast at the inn, intentionally or not. Samir looked spellbound. He ignored the world around him and walked slowly, transfixed on each delicate bread and pastry.

"Hello and welcome," the lady greeted. She was wearing all black with hints of powders and spices on a small apron around her waist. "How can I assist you?" she asked.

Benj took a deep breath and spoke. "I am a master baker and wanted to inquire about the possibility of working here."

"You?" The lady scoffed. "A master baker? I don't know anything about that, but my husband is out for the day and won't be back until this evening. He would be the one to talk to, but we don't need help."

"Oh, well, thank you for your time," Benj said, trying not to sound crestfallen after the rejection.

Samir stood before the baked goods, oblivious to the conversation, and didn't move.

"Samir," Benj called. There was no reply, so he called louder. Samir jerked his attention away from the pastries with practical indifference.

Benj saw the look on Samir's face and crumbled. "How much for an apple tart?"

It was ten marks, which was expensive. He would have sold twice as many pastries back home for half as much. He agreed to the price and asked her to cut it in half.

"It would be my pleasure," the woman said, taking the pastry and dividing it. She handed Benj the two pieces, who gave one to Samir. The delighted look in his eyes almost made the over-priced pastries worth it.

"I know of a place much better," Samir said when they were finally outside. "We just came here first because it was on the way."

Benj untied Sandstorm and ignored shouting coming from down the road. He started to say something but stopped when the shouting grew closer. Both he and Samir turned to see what the commotion was all about.

Everyone along the street turned to watch as two guards chasing a girl ran past them. The guards seemed in better shape than the girl but wore heavy armor that slowed them down. The girl had dark, unkempt hair and a leather vest showing more of her feminine features than Benj usually saw from girls back home, except for one. She ran past him, and he instantly recognized her. The two guards followed close behind.

*Smoking Shields!* Benj thought, "It's Lucia!" He would be hard-pressed to forget the spice merchant's daughter who had tried to rob him. He handed the reins and his half of the apple pastry to Samir. "Take this, I'll be back," he said and ran after them.

"Can I have it?" Samir asked before Benj was out of earshot.

"Yes but watch the horse!"

Benj was as far away from the guards as they were from Lucia. He had no idea why he was pursuing her. Mainly because if the guards couldn't catch her, he wouldn't be able to either. And, if they did catch her, what would he say to her before they took her to prison for whatever she did this time. All he knew was he was curious. Maybe he wanted to know why she was in trouble, or perhaps he wanted someone to talk about home with, or maybe that kiss left a strong impression. He chased those thoughts away as he ran after the guards through alleys, jumping and gliding over trash piles and sleeping transients.

The guards chased her upstairs, leading to the top of a building. Benj followed the guards up and down a stairwell on the other side. He gained on them by jumping off and twisting down a light pole.

One of the guards slid on horse dung and almost lost his footing. The man cursed loudly. Lucia ran into the middle of the street and slid under a carriage. The guards pushed people away as they followed her, causing one pedestrian to topple over. Benj tripped over the man who had just been pushed over but recovered, leaning as he drifted in the air and touched down with running feet. The man shouted after him, but there was too much distance between them to do anything else. He saw the guards turn a corner and then another one. He began to wish he had finished the pastry as his energy started to dwindle.

Lucia climbed up another ladder.

"Another one?!" The guard with horse turd on his

shoe protested before reluctantly following the first guard up.

Benj climbed up after they cleared the ladder. He peeked over the roof of the building and saw all three of them standing there, catching their breath; she was cornered.

"Looks like you ran out of luck, missy," The first guard gasped. "Don't try anything you'll regret."

"Ain't nowhere to go, love." Horse Turd said, hunched over with his hands on his knees.

"Listen," He heard Lucia say, sounding more composed than the others, "I wasn't taking her purse, I just noticed the clasp was broken, and I was trying to help her fix it so she didn't lose any of her belongings!"

"Then why did you still have it?" The first guard asked. "And if you're such a saint, why did you run from us?"

Lucia was desperately trying to explain herself, but even Benj could tell that she was floundering.

"I think we should teach her a lesson." Horse Turd said, straitening up. "Hold her arms, Burns; we have to make sure she's not hiding any contraband anywhere else."

"I think I'll double-check her when you're done," Burns replied. "Just in case you miss something. We have to make sure we're real thorough."

There was a high-pitched scream, and Benj came up with a plan to try to prevent whatever he thought was about to happen. Lucia might be guilty, but she didn't deserve this.

"Hey!" Benj shouted, climbing up the ladder. "What are you doing on my roof?"

The two guards stopped. One was holding Lucia,

and the other was reaching towards her.

"This is a matter of official business mandated by his majesty the King," The guard holding Lucia said, "This is none of your concern."

"If it's a matter of the king's majesty, then I will be on my way," Benj said, feigning to turn away. "Wait a moment. That's the thief that stole my horse!"

Both guards looked at her as if looking for guilt written across her face. She gave him an odd look and stared at him in bewilderment. Benj winked and gave the slightest hint of a smile. He dropped the smile as soon as the guards looked back at him.

"Again, pardon my intrusion," Benj held up his hands innocently. "Before I go, let me just take one good swing at her. It will be quick, and after, you can use my roof for as long as you like."

"That sounds like a reasonable idea to me." Roger said, looking at Horse Turd, "What do you say, Givens?"

"Come on and take your shot then," Givens said, taking Lucia's other arm.

Benj felt his heart pounding in his chest as he slowly walked towards them.

"I can handle myself against a girl. You don't need to hold her," Benj said, lifting his hands into a fighting position. "Just cover the exit so she doesn't make a run for it."

The guards laughed and released her.

"Likes a little bit of a fight, does he?" Roger said, releasing her and joining the other to block the exit.

After the guards stepped away, Lucia searched again with little hope for an exit down the side of the building. Benj approached her calmly and looked down the side with her.

"I'm here to help." He said in a hushed voice.

"Great help you are, there's no way down." She said, not indicating whether or not she recognized him.

"There is a way down over here," Benj pointed down the side next to him.

"Are you going to take a swing or have a tea party?" The guard asked, getting impatient.

Lucia walked on the ledge to where Benj stood and looked where he was pointing. She was thin, and Benj had jumped off smaller ledges holding heavier things. He hadn't hit the ground hard enough for injury before, but this would be different. This was going to be a lot higher of a jump. He hoped it would work.

"I hope you're ready for this." He wrapped his arms around her waist and jumped off the building. She screamed and squirmed the whole way down but didn't break loose. The extra weight of the girl sharpened the angle of descent. With effort, Benj leaned back as much as he could to slow their fall. The building was tall enough that he had to kick off the opposite alley wall before touching the ground. Holding on to each other, they slid to a stop, resulting in both of them falling over with Lucia on top.

She cried and hit him frantically. "Why would you do that? You almost got me killed; you're awful! You're the worst person ever!"

"Lucia!" He yelled her name, hoping he remembered it right. "We need to run!"

The guards were still atop the building, raging and yelling down, "Catch them!"

Lucia snapped out of her terror, put her hands to her body, and gave a surprised look. The shock wore off at once, and she scrambled into action.

"Come on," she said, helping Benj up. "I know a place where they won't follow us."

The two of them ran through alleyway after alleyway, turning this way and that. The guards were surely lost for good, but they kept running. There was less and less pavement underfoot when they finally settled into a quick-paced walk.

"We made it," she said, gasping for breath. "We're safe now."

Benj was relieved. He had a thousand questions and worked desperately to formulate his thoughts into coherent words. He was about to open his mouth to speak when he saw something that made him lose all concentration.

It wasn't that anything was threatening about a place that sold meat from a potentially questionable source, and it wasn't that there was blood splattered on the front porch of the establishment. It was the name. On the front hung a yellow and red painted sign aged through the years that read "Castle Road Goat Pies."

"Lucia, someone told me this road is dangerous and that I should never go down it," he said, still looking at the trail of blood that ended at the door.

"Of course, it's dangerous." She said, shaking her head, "That's why the guards won't follow us here. Besides, this is where I live. Don't worry, you are safe with me."

"We lost the guards a long time ago; maybe we should turn back now," he recommended, looking behind him for rogue stalkers.

"Don't be silly; we're safer here than literally anywhere else in the whole city," she smirked and became serious. "What kind of relic did you use back there?"

Benj fell silent. At first, he was confused by her question. He hadn't used a relic. When he realized she was asking about how they survived jumping off the roof, his silence continued; he was now trying to consider the best way to lie to her. He had gotten his ability on Mt. Asven on a journey he could not talk about.

A short, rotund thug came around the corner and eyeballed Lucia menacingly. "Oi, Jafa!" He said, "It's Bash and someone else."

"Looks like Bash brought a newcomer," a voice came from behind Benj, startling him. He turned to see a tall man who had probably cut his own hair with a pocketknife and was covered in gaudy tattoos.

"Guys, he's a friend," Lucia said nonchalantly. "He's with me. Leave him alone."

"A friend?" Asked the tall thug. "Well, any friend of Bash is a friend of mine. What's your name, then, friend?"

"Benj," he responded stoically. "I assume you're Jafa?"

"You assumed right," the tall thug said, hooking his thumbs under suspender straps. "Come on, any friend of Bash is a friend of mine. Welcome to the family."

The man held up his arms to give Benj an awkward and, quite frankly, unwarranted hug. Benj didn't move.

"Don't," Lucia warned.

The man didn't listen. Instead, he wrapped his arms around Benj, and a moment later, his money bag flew into the air for the heavier thug to catch.

"You look like you've had a tussle," Jafa said, brushing Benj off and deftly drawing away his attention while going through his pockets with nimble fingers. "What's this now?" he asked, producing a ring out of one of Benj's inner pockets and inspecting it.

Benj had no idea he was being searched until he saw

the ring come out. It was black and had a gold three-pronged crown etched with a dot above the outer spikes.

"Pots!" He said, flipping the ring to his companion. "Take a look at what Bash brought home."

Pots snatched the ring out of the air with the same coordination that he caught the money bag with.

"It's our symbol," He commented, looking closely at the ring. "But how does he have it? I've never seen him before."

"Where did you get the ring?" Jafa asked seriously. He looked as if he was on the verge of deciding whether to be happy or very angry.

"A friend gave it to me," Benj replied, unaware of the ring's significance.

"What friend?" He pressed.

"A friend, what difference does it make?" Benj regained some confidence in his composure.

"The difference is, you give me a name, or I cut off your thumbs."

Having no other option, Benj recalled the name of the man that he killed on the road. "Gallows Reese." He hoped for the best.

"You're telling me," Pots said, holding up the ring, "You married Gallows Reese?"

"No, no, no," Benj said, embarrassed at the implication. "We're not like that. If anything, it's a friendship ring. No reason to make things weird."

"Why didn't you just say so in the first place?" Jafa asked before snapping his fingers and pointing from Pots to Benj.

Pots tossed the money bag into the air, and Benj caught it. He didn't know why they were giving him money until he realized it was his. He hadn't noticed it missing it in the first place.

"I've got someone who would really like to meet you," Jafa said, putting his arm around Benj and leading him forward. "Let's go."

Benj shot Lucia a sharp look that seemed to say, "This is all your fault," but she shrugged it off as if to respond, "How should I know this would happen?" They both followed the street thieves.

# Chapter 18

## The Crownsmith Cathedral

T he four walked down the street, turned left into a thin alley, and right into a courtyard surrounded by buildings. The road finally ended in front of two huge double doors guarded by a large man with half his face tattooed like a skull. The man had his hand on the hilt of his knife and looked ready to draw it at a moment's notice.

"Stand down, Bones, he's with us," Jafa said with several indistinct hand gestures and continued forward. Bones nodded and pushed on a massive door that swung open inward. The four walked in.

The inside opened into a vast domed chamber adorned with stained glass windows and sculptures of saints from some long-forgotten religion. In the center stood a table featuring an upside-down crown, echoing the black ring, with the letters' E,' 'P,' and 'T' etched at the tips of its spikes. A golden skull was resting atop the intricately painted crown, its hollow eye sockets fixed intently on the room's entrance. Surrounding the table were chairs that seemed insignificant compared to the grand throne that dominated the head of the table. Colorful light poured through the stained glass, casting vibrant patterns across the otherwise empty space.

The four made their way past the table and through a long corridor on the right. Benj noticed paintings of burning corpses and bloody weapons pulled free from destitute warriors. Jafa came to a stop in front of a door and waited. Once everyone caught up to him, he threw open the door and gestured for the others to go in.

Benj felt his pulse quicken as he took in the scene. The room was filled with a motley crew, the air thick with smoke and the scent of stale beer. They were gathered around low tables, engrossed in games of chance and spirited conversations. The walls, draped in animal skins, seemed to close in, but the atmosphere buzzed with an undercurrent of camaraderie.

"Reese!" Jafa's voice boomed, causing Benj's stomach to drop. *Not Gallows Reese,* he thought, anxiety knotting in his chest.

"Not now, I'm winning!" a man replied from the back table with voice too familiar for comfort.

"This bloke says he knows Gallows. Even got his signet ring!" Jafa announced, throwing a casual glance over his shoulder at Benj.

The room froze. Eyes turned, assessing the newcomers with a mix of curiosity and skepticism.

"If you peek at my cards, I'll tie your legs apart and hand you over to Bash," the man called Reese retorted, rising from his seat. He moved with a fluid grace that suggested a sense of authority.

Benj exchanged a glance with Lucia and mouthed, *You're Bash?* She dismissed the question with a wave.

"So, my brother gave you his ring, did he?" Reese stepped forward, taking the ring from Jafa. He was dressed in light linen pants and an open vest that revealed an array of tattoos. The crown insignia over his heart mirrored the ring he held in his hand. His long blonde hair was tied back, framing features that bore a striking resemblance to Gallows, albeit more adorned.

"He doesn't usually work well with others," Reese remarked, inspecting the ring with a mixture of intrigue and wariness. "People can find him… difficult."

"You're telling me," Benj replied, gesturing at the ring. "You can't crack a joke without him pulling a sword on you."

Laughter erupted from the group, and the tension began to ease. Benj felt a flicker of relief. Maybe he wasn't in as much trouble as he'd thought.

"Sit, sit!" Reese beckoned, motioning to an empty space at the table. "Let's hear your story, then."

Benj hesitated but felt a pull of curiosity mixed with apprehension. He took a seat, and Lucia joined him, the two of them flanked by the others. The atmosphere shifted; it was no longer a hostile interrogation but rather an invitation to share tales.

"Gallows and I had… an understanding," Benj guessed at his make-believe story. "We met under unusual circumstances. I had something he needed, and he had something to trade for it."

The group leaned in; their interest piqued.

"Something like a barter?" Pots asked; his gullible expression made him appear the simple sort. Maybe he was?

"More like a life debt," Benj blurted out, recalling the tense moment when Gallows had drawn his sword on

229

him.

"Life debts don't come cheap," Reese cut in, his tone shifting to one of respect. "So, what was it?"

"A wedding cake," Benj said after an unsure pause. "I'm a baker."

Everyone in the room laughed. Benj rapidly devised a story about Gallows and a wedding cake, but the subject changed when Reese asked what he was good at. Benj began explaining how he makes good cinnamon rolls when Reese cut him off.

"We're all outlaws here. You don't have to pretend to be something you're not around us," Reese stopped himself. "Wait, are you taking a piss at my expense?"

Before Benj could think of anything to say, Reese continued, "No wonder he likes you; you're just as big of a rotter as he is! You two even dress the same!"

Benj looked down at his clothes; they were Gallows' clothes. He had almost forgotten.

"Where is that little weasel anyway?" Reese asked, letting down his guard.

"I thought he would be here by now," Benj improved as if his life depended on it. "He said he was going to meet up with me yesterday. When he didn't show up, I assumed he came here instead."

"That's odd, he never came here." Reese considered, allowing silence to fall on their conversation. "Let me make the introductions for him. I'm the Front Lieutenant Larkin Reese of the thief's guild. You might have heard of me, but if you haven't, If I ever catch you calling me Larkin, I'll hand you over to Bash. Which I see you've already met.

"Some of these people don't matter," he pointed at two women and a darkly dressed man. "They're from different guilds, assassins mostly. This is Priest, Draiden, Pots, and Jafa."

Benj greeted everyone at once. "I'm Benjos B-" he realized he did not want to say anything about baking ever again. "Bird, but I go by Benj," he continued, "And if I ever catch you calling me Larkin, you'll be spending time with Bash first."

"You have yourself a deal, Bird," Reese laughed and slapped him on the shoulder. "Since my brother runs point, I assume he's taught you everything he knows?"

"I know some stuff," Benj said, thinking better than to extend his index finger.

"A man with humility is a rare thing. You certainly didn't learn that from my brother."

"There were some things I taught him," Benj said, making a mental note not to be humble.

"It's settled then!" Reese flipped the ring towards Benj, "If my brother doesn't return before tomorrow night, you'll get a trial by fire. I assume that's why you have his ring, is it not?"

"You are absolutely correct," Benj said, trying to sound confident. "I already have a job lined up," like getting *the blackened ashes out of town.*

"With Gallows?" Reese asked, "This is that job."

"Alright, I'll go get my belongings and come right back then," Benj tried extricating himself again.

Reese asked where his belongings were. After Benj told him about his horse near the bakery, he snapped his fingers and pointed to Jafa and Pots. "Did you hear that? His horse is at The Flaming Loaf. Retrieve his things and pay the boy. I'll reimburse you later."

They reluctantly agreed and left.

"Bash," Reese said, watching Pots and Jafa leave. "Put

231

him in the guest room for now. Are you hungry?"

"I am," Benj said honestly.

"Lunch is in an hour," Reese announced, "Bash, make sure you show him around."

Lucia nodded her head and beckoned for Benj to follow.

She took him to a room, calmly shut the door, and quietly yelled at him, "You never told me you worked with that scum! You said you owned a bakery! Who are you anyway?"

"You mean Gallows Reese?" Benj asked quietly with a quivering voice, "I've never met the guy. Somehow, I have his jacket. It's a long story. But all I was trying to do was to keep you from getting felt up by those guards when you brought me into a den of dangerous-looking people. Then I went into survival mode. I don't know; I just freaked out and started agreeing with them. I need to leave now. How do I get out of here?"

"Look," she said, placing a calming hand on his arm, "They are bringing your horse here. Now is not a good time to leave. Trust me, I've tried... It's also a long story. Just keep up the act, and when you have a horse, I'll tell you when it's a good time to leave. In the meantime, I'll teach you what you need to know, but don't go all rogue and leave. It will not go well for anyone."

"Cursed pikestaff," Benj swore. "Smoking ashen shields," he swore again, stretching the creases out of his forehead with the palms of his hands.

"It'll be okay," she said, calmly now in a low voice. "You saved my life back there. I'll make sure you survive here."

Benj had no other option except to trust her. He followed her around as she gave him a tour of the

Crownsmith Cathedral. An hour later, he found himself sitting around a large table surrounded by pickpockets and petty thieves. Lucia sat to his left, and the man whose brother he killed sat across the table.

Reese took his knife and tapped on the side of his wooden cup.

"Attention, everyone," he said, but a low murmur continued from around the room. "Shut your ever-loving mutton holes before I shut them for you!"

The room got silent and stayed that way before Reese started speaking again.

"Now, as some of you know, we have a new prospect for our team. This is Benjos Bird. He comes to us from Thannon where he spent time with my brother. Some of you know Gallows Reese-"

"I bet most of us wish we didn't know him!" One of the men said, cutting Reese off.

There was a laugh from around the table. Reese picked up his knife and threw it with precision at the man's face. The man dodged in time to allow it to pass at the last moment. It was almost as if he expected it. The knife hit the wall behind him and clattered to the ground.

"Someone get that for me," Reese demanded while he scratched the knife tattoo under his eye. "As I was saying, Bird here is a point, so if my brother doesn't show up tomorrow, we're going to have a good old-fashioned trial by fire."

The table cheered and made a whooping noise.

"Benj here has told me that running Point isn't his only quality," Reese continued, looking at everyone at the table in turn. "He also enjoys long romantic walks in the sand and kissing under the stars."

Some whistled at this, others made kissing sounds.

Reese pointed with a fork around the table. "I believe I introduced you all earlier, so without further delay, I present the newcomer's first toast. Bird, will you do the honors?"

Reese lifted his cup. The rest of the table followed suit. Benj stood and tried to remember the speech he gave at his coming home ceremony after the long trip to Mt. Asven. He started speaking before remembering all of it, "To the men who have gone before us and to the women they left behind..." He froze and couldn't remember the second half. Two heartbeats passed, and he said finally, "More women for us!"

Most of the table gave a loud "Here, here!" and drank; Lucia gave a deadpanned expression. Benj sat down, relieved it was finished.

A man sitting to his left with premature gray hair complimented him on his speech. He was the same man that dodged the knife earlier. He was older than the rest of them or appeared so with his short, cropped beard and long mustache that hung lightly combed to either side. His thick grey hair was neatly combed in some areas and braided in others. He got halfway through a story about Jafa's first speech when he had to dodge another knife. Benj was starting to understand why he was good at dodging knives in the first place.

"Stuff it, Priest!" Jafa said, cutting the meat on his plate with a spoon. "Your first toast was so bad that everyone who heard it is dead."

Priest winced, held up his hand, and rocked it back and forth to critique the insult and everyone continued their meal. They ate, drank, and talked excitedly about everything from almost getting caught in their dangerous endeavors to actually getting caught and running from the Royal Guard. Even Lucia told her how Benj had come to her rescue. Benj was relieved when she changed the story so as not to reveal his hidden talents. This got a good reaction from the table.

"He's ugly, but he's got some balls!" Draiden announced on Benjo's behalf.

Draiden's dark skin was made darker by his many years sailing various pirating vessels. He had colorful beads twisted and braided into his hair, which he kept tied together in the back.

"We'll see how he does tomorrow," Priest said, swirling a glass of dark red wine with his fingertips.

"I'm also excited to see what kind of point my brother brought me," Reese said, pulling a piece of bone out of his mouth.

Benj wrung his hands anxiously under the table and forced a neutral expression. He thought about how he was going to escape. If he ran "point," whatever that meant, he would be found as a fraud and probably killed. If he was found as a fraud and then charged with the murder of this man's brother, he would probably be tortured before he was killed. He was going to need to have a long conversation with Lucia to figure everything out. He was glad he had someone he could trust. The way she kept his secret was a relief because he had few other options except to rely on her.

"Bird, what relics are you good with?" Reese asked, breaking him out of deep thought.

He had heard countless stories about relics, but he had only ever seen three in his whole life, technically two of which were his touchstones. The other was the one Lucia wore when he met her. "There's so many."

"Can you use a sound sight? Windpunch? Or a

torch?" Reese asked.

"Yes, but I am perhaps rusty," Benj replied with a lie.

"Right now, we only have the Soundsight," Reese said, tossing Lucia a small wooden box. "After dinner, take your boyfriend to the training hall for some practice tonight."

"Sure, but he's not my boyfriend, " she said, smiling. "Yet."

"I'm sitting right here!" Benj said, holding up his hands.

"Real cute," Draiden said flatly. "What time are we meeting tomorrow?"

"I would want to change the subject too if Bash had turned me down," Priest said, folding his hands in front of him.

"Twice," Lucia held up two fingers.

Draiden gave an embarrassed smile, "It was cold; I only asked if she needed help keeping warm."

"Grabbing me around the waist and asking me if I was into bad boys isn't keeping anyone warm," she said frankly.

"It could have," Draiden retorted.

She turned toward Benj, put her hand across his shoulder, and spoke loud enough for the whole table to hear. "I would love to help you train, even if it takes all night."

# Chapter 19

## Soundsight

After eating, Lucia took Benj by the hand and led him down a passageway toward the middle of the building to a red door. She opened the door to a round room with a domed ceiling made of Iron and wood. In the center, a tall, angry-looking man leaped over a wooden barricade, rolled under a log suspended by two ropes, and stabbed a dummy with a long, sharp dagger. He pulled the thin blade from the dummy's straw heart and slowly turned his head toward them.

"Sorry," Lucia apologized, backing out of the room and pulling Benj after her. "Thought no one was in here."

"What was that all about?" Benj asked as she shut the door after him.

"Come on, I'll tell you when we're in private." She whispered, ushering him away.

They walked through several passages. Benj tried to remember every twist and turn to escape later, and he took mental notes as one turn led to another. Lucia took a lantern off a desk and led him up a spiral staircase that seemed to take forever. He felt they should be nearing the top as the stairs got more and more narrow. Lucia stopped on a small platform leading farther up and rested, waiting for Benj to catch up.

"Tired?" Benj asked when he had caught up to her.

"Dizzy," she replied and added, "Don't worry about the boyfriend comment from earlier. It's hard to explain, but I thought that if everyone knew I had chosen you, then maybe the idea of me being taken would solidify in their minds."

"It's no problem," Benj said, leaning back to make more space between them. He was conscientious about how close they were standing to each other and nervously tried to put distance between them. The platform they both stood on was a slightly bigger step in the tight circular staircase. She stood close, and her breath cooled the skin around his face and neck. He felt his body wanting to draw closer to her despite also wanting nothing to do with her or her gang of thieves.

"Come on. It's not that much further," she tugged on his shirt and continued upward, causing the steep staircase to twist around the lantern light. At the top, she unlatched the door and swung it outward, spilling soft sunlight on their faces. Through the door, Benj could see the rooftops and spires of the entire city. The sun was setting behind the mountains in the West, leaving behind a vibrant orange and violet hew.

"Welcome to the roof," she said, walking out to showcase the view. The wind blew gentle gusts of cold air that seemed to change directions at random intervals.

"It's nice up here," Benj said, awestruck by the city's canopy.

"And it's secluded enough to talk." She added,

waving him forward. "There doesn't seem to be any unwelcome assassins lurking about."

They sat on the ledge of the building, feet hanging over a massive drop to a busy street below. A moment of silence passed as they both collected their thoughts and soaked in the view.

"You told me you were John's daughter," Benj said in a slightly accusing voice.

"I am John's daughter," Lucia crossed her arms. "I didn't lie to you about that. I thought you said you owned a bakery. Why are you here?"

"I am a baker," Benj replied carefully. "But I was only an apprentice when we met. I'm a full baker now, if that makes a difference, but I did lie to you about owning the place. I might have been trying to impress you. I don't know what I was thinking when I did that, but I'm sorry."

"I hope you're sorry," she huffed. "I was going to run away to that little village and marry you. The only thing that kept me from leaving was caring for my dad. He's in some trouble."

"John's in trouble? What kind of trouble?" Benj wondered before registering the rest of what she had said. "And who said I would marry you in the first place? Two people have to agree to be married."

"I guess I was looking for a way out," she muttered, half to herself. "And then I met you. I thought, "I could enjoy the simple life as a plump, old baker's wife," so I planned to come back as a last resort.

It got quiet between the two.

"What happened to your father?" Benj asked, but then remembered the question that was really burning in his chest, "Was that man back there an assassin? Is that why you were so afraid of him?"

"Now isn't the time to talk about my father's problems. Maybe we will soon," Lucia positioned her body on the ledge so she could face him. "And first of all, I wasn't afraid. Secondly, if anything, I want to know about how you saved my life back there."

"Now isn't a good time to talk about how I saved your life," Benj retorted with the same tactic she had just used. "Why do they call you Bash?"

Lucia shot him a look of irritation. "I'll tell you about Bash if you tell me how you got Gallows' ring. You're not even from Thannon; I know where you're from."

Benj let the offer hang in the air.

"Don't worry, you can trust me." She added, putting a hand on his shoulder. "And you need me if you're ever going to learn what a 'point' actually does."

"You make a good point," Benj said accidentally, resisting another urge to extend his index finger.

"And you will, too, when I'm done with you," she laughed once. "Just so we're clear, you're an imposter who has saved my life, and I'm a woman of great mystery, but if we don't get you up to date on how everything works around here, nothing will matter. Until then, you and I will just have to trust each other with our lives."

Benj agreed, and they shook hands.

"Where do I start?" She asked herself out loud, "The Crownsmiths are an organization started a couple hundred or so years ago to rid the city of some horrible tyrant. The goal was to remove a bad king from the throne and replace him with a good one. The organization has evolved but has fancied itself a political equalizer ever since.

"There are three factions within the Crownsmiths, the Overseers, Executioners, and Levelers: basically, planners, assassins, and thieves. Reese is the head of the thieves, which is consequently the guild you just got involved in."

Benj shot her a doubtful glance. "I can't help but feel like you're not giving yourself enough credit for that."

"Now, now," She objected and continued, "The executioners are the assassins. That man you saw earlier who was stabbing the ever-living straw out of the training dummy was one of them. Don't worry; they won't bother you if you don't bother them."

Benj seemed to recall someone saying that once about mountain wolves.

She raised a finger and corrected herself, "But stay away from them as much as possible."

"Got it." He said, gently pushing her finger out of his face.

"The Overseers, or planners," she continued, "Are made up mostly of the upper class and gentry, but we don't really know who they are, so they could be anyone. When crooked people enter court politics, the planners put that person up for a private vote. If the vote is unanimous, they make a plan to get rid of them. They also oversee other aspects of the community; I'm not sure what they do; the thieves' guild never meets them."

"So, they're kind of the good guys?" He asked.

"Oh no." She laughed cynically. "Some are, maybe, but there will always be someone who takes advantage of their position. I've heard some overseers write up jobs for relatively good people just because the target is wealthy or won't sell their property to them. I've heard there have been jobs for people over simple offenses. Sometimes, I wonder if the planners even exist and if we just do these jobs to keep the organization alive.

"Tomorrow, the job is for a noble who bought the assassinations of several Crownsmith members. We only found out because, apparently, their assassin knew ours. Somehow, word got out, and now it's back to the Creator for him and another day of work for us. You have to take the good with the bad sometimes.

"As the Crownsmith has evolved, they added another faction into the mix. They refer to it as an investment branch. They do stuff like lending money to people like my father for wild interest rates, building brothels, and selling protection. Gallows is in charge of most of that branch. He also works some jobs with us."

"How did you become a part of all of this?" He asked,

"I can't very well be a woman of mystery if I told you that on our first date." She teased.

"I wouldn't call this a date, but if anyone asks," he continued, "how should we tell them we met?"

"We met while I was traveling through Thannon," She said, adding, "You were quite smitten with me, as I recall."

"Now, now," Benj had been waiting to say that back to her. "You came through with your wagon, and we talked. That's all there is to it."

"I can agree, but we will have to work out the rest later," she said before continuing her lecture. "Before I forget, a basic team consists of three parts, locks, baggers, and a point. The person in charge of locks is responsible for getting in. That's usually me. If I have time to pick a locked door, I will try my best, but most of the time, I'll sneak in through an open window or smash through it. Baggers are just people with bags. It's their job to grab everything that will fit in it and stuff it in. The point has maybe three jobs. First, you are responsible for going in and looking for people. If you are spotted or chased, simply leave through of the door you came in from, stay in sight, and someone will hit them over the head. After the place is clear, your job is to find all the very expensive and hidden treasures while leaving the easy-to-find items alone. Check behind paintings and bookshelves and look for secret compartments."

"If a housekeeper is in the house, what do I do?" Benj asked for clarification.

"By the time we show up to sack the house, anyone who is supposed to be dead will be dead already. Anyone else just needs to be tied up for the evening."

"Oh," Benj said. "That-" he cleared his throat, "makes sense."

"If the house is confirmed empty by the point, we all go in as baggers. There's a little bit more to it, but I want to show you this first," Lucia said, pulling out a small box and offering it to Benj. "Here, take it."

Benj took the box and opened it to find a bracelet of thin twisted rope with a grey metallic orb in the middle. The orb had a foreign script engraved in small letters wrapping around from one string point to the other. He picked it up and inspected it, holding it by the string.

"You have to blow on it for it to work," Lucia instructed.

He blew on it. "Like this?"

"Harder." She corrected.

Benj blew in loud huffs. He blew until he was lightheaded. Lucia's smile grew bigger until she couldn't contain her laughing.

"Okay," She said, wiping a tear from her eye. "I think it's good now."

Benj looked at her with a cautious eye and then realized he had been tricked. "You don't need to blow on it, do you?"

"No, silly," she said, still recovering. "Just put it on."

He coiled the bracelet around his wrist, and the world exploded with movement. The air around him mixed in chaotic and rhythmic patterns like the flames and heat of a fire. There wasn't a color, but somehow, he could see waves as if seeing the wind for the first time.

"Weird, right?" She said with an assault of words that bounced harmlessly off him in close circles, rippling around and off him. He took the bracelet off.

"What is this thing?" He asked, holding it pinched between his fingers like a dead rat.

"It's a Soundsight," she said. "It mixes what you hear with what you see. I personally hate using it. It makes me sick to my stomach. Now, turn around, plug your ears, and count to ten. Then, put it on and see if you can find me."

Benj turned around and complied. As soon as he was finished counting, he put on the bracelet and looked around. The roof had many places to hide; there were old clay pots, pieces of bricks, and debris in piles scattered everywhere. Various waves of sound bounced up and around the walls of the building. Every footstep and conversation from the street twisted up and around the roof's edge and blended.

He looked carefully around until he saw what he was looking for - small, almost imperceptible lines came from behind a wall holding a small brass bell.

"Found you," he said, walking toward the wall.

"That was fast," Lucia said from behind him.

Benj froze and slowly turned to see her standing

behind a large clay pot. It wasn't where he expected she was.

They met eyes. Lucia saw the look of concern on his face.

"What is it?" she asked, with waves of sound protruding through her mouth.

He pointed toward where the sound had come from, where it was still coming from. She stepped back and waved to him to follow, but Benj pressed forward. Lucia made frantic gestures to stop him, but all her efforts fell on deaf eyes.

Benj moved soundlessly towards the wall. Thick boots stepped between rocks and chipped mortar, creating waves of distractions. He moved his head slowly, glancing around the corner to see what or who was back there. He saw movement, and then two eyes shot right at him. He jumped, and Lucia dove back between the clay pots where she had first hidden.

The eyes belonged to a grey cat that scurried away after being surprised.

"You can come out now," he said, watching the cat scamper off.

"What was that?" She asked, standing up with relief.

"A cat," he replied. "What did you think it was?"

"I don't know," she said, carefully navigating the obstacles around her. "There are plenty of dangerous people here. I don't like taking any chances. Don't scare me like that."

"I've never seen anybody move so fast to hide from a cat," Benj jabbed at her pride.

"You're the one who turned white," she accused. "It's getting dark anyway; we should start moving down."

Benj followed Lucia down the stone stairs and

through the Crownsmith Cathedral until she reached an intersection and stopped.

"You're that way," She gestured. "They have you in the first door to the left. That's where they put all the guests. I'm this way." She leaned in conspiratorially, "I'm in the second door to the right if you need somewhere to hide from another cat."

Instead of pointing out that she would more likely need to hide from a cat, he wished her good night. She wished him likewise and went to bed.

Benj found his room. It was small but cleaner than the inn he slept in the previous night. He found his saddlebags on the floor beside his bed with the sword on top. He wondered if the sword would be recognizable. He could always say that he borrowed it if anyone asked. As he sank into bed, he couldn't help but feel his future loom ahead like the gallows loomed before a damned man.

# Chapter 20

## A Formal Disguise

K ey woke up excited to try on one of his new uniforms. He had never worn the dress uniform before but liked how they looked. He had to remember to keep them somewhere Jory couldn't mess with them, but where could they go?

He got out of bed and promptly opened his footlocker. Inside, his new uniforms lay neatly folded, stacked in a pile, and ready for him. He pulled his tunic on over his head, pulled his trousers up, and began pairing his many buttons to their rightful slots. The jacket proved harder to button, as there were more of them and a more complex system of flaps and folds to navigate. The knee-high boots were simple enough to tie, if not tedious.

He couldn't remember if the sash went over the left shoulder or right, so he picked one at random. He completed the uniform by placing his two-cornered hat on his head and looked in the mirror. The sight of himself all decked made his pride tingle with excitement. He practiced some crisp salutes and a few debonair poses before pulling himself away from the mirror.

Everyone in the barracks had turned their heads and watched him as he made his way downstairs. He endured the attention as he ate a plate of eggs and bread and walked to the office. He had received eight compliments, not counting a whistle and a wink, before leaving the building. Granted, they were all compliments from his friends, but it felt good, nonetheless.

As soon as he got to the office, he opened the door, and Castor frowned.

"The sash goes over your other shoulder. Like this," he said, gesturing towards his own sash. "It's left to right, so we can-" he drew his sword and made some stabbing motions followed by slashing ones, each accompanied by various sound effects and voices with his mouth. It sounded like, "Ching, ching, no, please don't hurt me, oh yeah? Shing shing, ohh, my eyes! Ha-ha! Swish, thunk plop plop, dead..."

Key removed his hat but paused mid-motion at Castor's theatrical performance. He made a mental note to check the captain's tea whenever feasible.

"Anyway, if your sash is over your left shoulder, you have more freedom with your sword hand," Castor said, sheathing his sword.

"I don't think I'll ever forget," he said, removing his sash and switching sides. "Thanks."

Castor inspected him. "You look perfect. Are you ready to make a small difference in the world?"

They walked in silence until they arrived at the prison. Alrick was standing out front, guarding the entrance. Key realized that he didn't recognize him in his new uniform.

Alrick saluted and opened the door, "Good afternoon, gentlemen."

Key stopped in front of Alrick, who still hadn't made eye contact with him. "Captain, did you hear that? He called us both gentlemen."

"Well, I suppose you look gentle enough," Castor replied. "Probably couldn't hurt an old woman with her own cane."

A look of confusion overcame Alrick's face before he noticed who he had addressed. "Key, is that you? You look like a flaming peacock in all that."

"Thanks, how's the watch?" Key asked.

"A lot better not that I've seen you all cleaned up," Alrick said. "Begging the Captain's pardon, sir."

Castor raised an eyebrow at Key.

"He's good, sir," Key said, vouching for Alrick.

Castor nodded towards Alrick and walked past him, stepping inside.

"Talk later," Key said, following the captain's lead.

As Key stepped inside the prison, he made his footsteps louder than necessary to wake up anyone who might be sleeping in one of the spare cells. He had been woken similarly too many times not to pay the courtesy forward. However, after getting close to Crumb's cell, they still hadn't seen the guard on watch.

Key stomped his foot, claiming that he still needed to break his boots in. Oblivious, Castor agreed that the knee-high boots take some time to get used to. They continued forward until they finally stopped in front of Crumbs' cell. The boy was lying on the ground, staring at the ceiling with his hands behind his head.

"Good morning, Crumb," Castor greeted with gentle authority. "Are you ready to go?"

"That depends," Crumb said, standing up. "Are you going to release me, or are you going to chop my head off?"

"You made good on your promise, so we are going to make good on ours," Castor informed him. "Today, you go free. Also, we talked to your sister; she's going to meet us at the wagon."

"If you were going to kill me, you would tell me, right?" Crumb asked, nervously fidgeting.

"No," Castor said, cocking his head as if listening for a word from the almighty. "I don't think I would," he said before looking around and asking, "Where is the guard?"

"I'll find him," Key said and ran towards the sleeping area.

He rounded a corner to find his archenemy in a cell, snoring on a cot. He shook him awake. "What are you doing?"

"Huh? Oh, I'm just," Jory said, stalling for time while trying to remember where he even was. "Oh, I'm just cleaning out this cell."

"Hurry. I have a captain over there who needs to get a prisoner out," Key urged him quietly. "Slap your face a few times so it doesn't look like you were sleeping. You're lucky you were on your back."

It was common knowledge that if you were going to take the risk of sleeping on watch, you should never sleep with your face, cheek, or forehead touching anything that would leave a sleep print. Even while standing, if you were to lean your head against anything, it could leave an incriminating mark called 'cot burn.' It was evidence that you were resting your face against something for longer than necessary and enough evidence for several lashings.

"Thanks," Jory said, standing up, slapping his face, and opening his eyes. He started walking out of the cell.

"Jory, where's your helmet?" Key asked urgently.

250

Jory turned around, walked back into the cell, and reached under the cot. He quickly pulled out the helmet, put it on, and joined Key, walking back toward the captain.

It would be bad news for Jory if he was caught by a captain sleeping on watch. Key would not wish that kind of punishment on his worst enemy, which, it turned out, was Jory.

As the two walked back, key coached him, "Remember to salute, and make sure you ask for the letter before releasing the kid. Just because he's a captain doesn't mean he can set people free whenever he wants."

"Ah, captain," Key said as they approached the cell, "I found him cleaning out the unused cells."

"Good man," the captain applauded. "I am here to take this prisoner into custody."

"May I see the letter of release, sir?" Jory asked, sounding as if he had been alert all day.

"Very well, corporal," the captain said, handing the letter to Jory, who, in turn, pretended to read it before handing it back.

"Everything checks out," Jory said, and then, searching his key loop, he found the right key to unlock the cell. After it was unlocked, he opened it and ushered the street urchin out.

Crumb cautiously walked out, looking untrustful towards the three other men.

"Let's go," the captain ordered and led the way outside. The others followed.

Key winked at Jory, who still hadn't conveyed recognition for the man he had played countless tricks on for the last two years.

"Thank you, sir," Jory said graciously and saluted.

Key lagged behind and waited for Castor and Crumb to walk ahead. As soon as they were out of earshot, he quickly told Alrick how he found Jory.

"I just didn't know it was him," he concluded. "He was sawing lumber back there like I've never seen my whole life. You guys keep him up late?"

"I'm not sure what he was doing last night," Alrick admitted. "Did you turn him in?"

"A full captain finding a lowling sleeping on watch? Come on, I wouldn't put that on anyone," Key confessed distastefully. "I helped him get on his feet, made him slap his face a few times, and then told the captain that he was back there cleaning."

"You are truly worthy of that uniform," Alrick praised. "But I'm not sure he would have done the same for you."

"You know what the best part is?" Key asked with a cunning smile. "Because of this uniform, I don't think he even recognized me. He even called me 'sir' on my way out. I didn't tell him I wasn't a sir; I just walked away."

"That's brilliant!" Alrick shouted. "When we get relieved tonight, I'll make him tell the story in front of everyone. As soon as he's done singing your praises, I'll tell everyone who really saved his life."

"I like that idea," Key said, turning to leave. "Let me know how it goes."

When Key caught up to the other two, he found Castor telling the boy what to expect. "The most important thing is always to be honest. Don't take anything that isn't yours, or he'll find out. And work hard. As soon as he sees you are hardworking and reliable, he'll give you bigger and better responsibilities. If it gets difficult, just remember that nothing is as bad as starving on the street."

"So, what if I don't want to go yet?" The boy asked.

"The choice is yours," Castor shrugged. "You're free to leave whenever you want. Even when you get there."

"So, I can just run off right now, and you won't chase me?" Crumb asked.

"Yeah, try it out. Stretch your legs and go for a run," Castor said, gesturing forward with his hands. "We won't chase you."

The boy sprinted forward, disappearing down the street.

"He didn't just run away for good, did he?" Key asked.

"It's important for these kids to know that they are making the decision for themselves," Castor said, not breaking his pace. "I'm not going to force him to do what I know will make him happier. He has to want it for himself."

The two walked in silence until they reached Skipper's transport. Crumb still hadn't come back, but his sister, Marie, was already sitting inside of the carriage.

"Hi, Marie," Castor waved. "Did Grant tell you to wait in the carriage?"

"No, but Mr. Barlow said I could," She said. "Where's my brother?"

"I'm sure he's just packing up," Castor guessed. "As soon he realizes you're here, he'll probably come as soon as possible."

"Is everyone ready to go?" Grant asked, carrying a small crate around a corner.

"The boy ran off. He probably went home, I can't imagine why he hasn't shown up yet," Castor said, looking around for him.

"It probably wouldn't be good separating them," Grant figured. "What do you want to do?"

"We could always send Marie back home to see if her brother even wants to go," Castor offered. "In the meantime, we can have a smoke."

Before the pipes were lit, Marie yelped, "Corbin, you're back!"

The three men turned their heads to see the young boy walking towards them carrying a small pack.

"Your name is Corbin?" Key asked the boy.

"I guess," Corbin said and lowered his head.

"That's a good name," Key said. "I think you should introduce yourself with it from now on."

"Especially so the temple mutilating Gerard doesn't recognize the name 'Crumb' if he ever comes looking for you," Castor added helpfully.

The boy's face turned red, and he balled his fists.

Key turned to the captain, "It might be better if you go now."

Key was right but before leaving Castor reached into a leather pouch and took out five Marks. He placed them in Key's hand. "Here's a lesson for you. Always pay your debts as soon as possible; It sharpens your reputation." When he was finished saying his goodbyes and walked off cheerfully.

"It's been a pleasure meeting you, Master Corbin," Key said sincerely. "Keep your sister safe and do the right thing out there. Here," he said, offering the boy a small carver's knife. "Take this just in case."

Grant made a loud, frustrated noise. He walked over and plucked the knife from the boy's hands, "I'll make sure to give you this when we arrive. We should go now."

Key said goodbye and watched the cart lurch

forward until it was moving North at a steady speed.

Evan Kvalvik

# Chapter 21

## The Robbery

A shadow passed over his eyes, and Benj snapped them open. Priest was standing over him with an infuriatingly cheerful smile.

"Good morning, sugarplum," Priest cooed patronizingly. "Slept well last night?"

"Yeah," Benj croaked. "I think so. What time is it?"

"Mid-day, you lethargic lout," Priest ridiculed. "Do you want the good news or the bad?"

"Bad news, I guess," Benj said, sitting up in bed.

"The bad news is you missed breakfast and will have to…" Priest waved a hand in circles, "fast until lunch."

"And the good news?"

"Why, it's lunchtime time now," Priest said with a flourish. "You should hurry before you miss that too."

The two walked into the common room and sat at the table. In front of them lay bowls of steaming sausages, potatoes, fruit, and hot bread. Benj picked up a berry, and Priest slapped it from his hands.

"All here?" Priest asked as Reese walked into the room.

"You're worse than your brother's boyfriend over here," Priest directed the insult at Reese. "Where were you at breakfast this morning?"

"Don't act like you've never missed the prayer before," Reese replied, sitting and folding his hands. "The creator forgives when the heart is humble. Isn't that what they taught you in monk school?"

"I just don't know you have a humble bone in your whole body."

Jafa slapped the table, "Well, let's get on with it then!"

"Bow your heads," Priest said and then continued. "Great Creator, we know that you don't answer the prayers of the criminals, but if you did, we would ask for a successful robbery and offer to give the church six percent of our takings. Well, we would give you six percent, but five percent will be easier to calculate, so we'll do that and throw in an extra half of the talent for your supreme favor. All who agree say aye."

The table sounded with a unanimous "Aye," and Benj followed suit.

"What's the whole prayer thing all about?" Benj asked, leaning over towards Priest.

"It's like this; we commit crimes of a very specific nature. It's not as bad as other things, like killing your grandmum's dog..." He said, casting an accusing look at Jafa.

"It peed in my boot!" Jafa explained. "Not on; in. The thing had it coming."

"Well, anyway," Priest said, giving a disgusted look. "Like I was saying, our crimes aren't as bad as other crimes because we usually have a semi-good cause. Because of that, the Creator might be more inclined to bestow his blessings on us in contrast to, let's say, the common thug. But he might be less inclined than your common do-gooder, so we try to sweeten the deal a little bit."

"That sounds a little bit like bribery," Benj blurted, causing the table to look at him. He tried correcting himself by adding, "But alas, we're all thieves anyway, right?"

"In this business, you are faced with your own mortality enough that you either get religious or superstitious," Priest explained. "For us, it has become a combination of both. It helps to stick to the same ritual even if it is religious in nature."

"We haven't had a single death since Priest showed up," Reese said from across the table. "It was working for us, so we made it a part of the routine."

"Now he appropriates our hard-earned money to a bunch of bald-headed monks after every job," Draiden complained, stabbing a sausage and putting it on his plate.

"I would rather be a bald-headed monk than have your ratty, unwashed hair," Priest retorted.

"You're not supposed to wash it," Draiden said, holding one of his matted locks. "It would lose its form."

"So, why do you call Lucia 'Bash'?" Benj asked, changing the subject.

Lucia shot a furious look around the table, daring the first person to speak.

The table broke into an uproar of nervous laughter.

"Keep that up, and you'll find out sooner than you'd like," Reese warned, stabbing a sausage on his plate.

"Now that everyone is in a good mood," Priest said, "Let us conduct business."

"Right," Reese agreed, "We have a big job tonight,

and as you know, my brother hasn't shown up yet. This means Bird here gets a trial by fire."

The table murmured comments and jokes.

"I'm sure he'll be fine," Reese continued. "My brother has trained him well enough, I'm sure."

"Or Priest should have offered ninety percent," Draiden mused.

"We would offer you if we knew you would have any value," Priest said offhandedly. "That's not a bad idea. Do you have any gold teeth, or are they just yellow?"

Draiden threw a spoon at Priest's head, but he dodged it without looking up from his plate. *He must get that a lot,* Benj thought.

"Calm down, Draiden," Priest said. "We're running low on cutlery as it is without you tossing them around all the time."

"Anyway," Reese said, "Bash, I have you on locks, as always."

"Got it," Lucia responded neutrally.

"Pots and Jafa," Reese got the pair's attention. "The goal is to hit them over the head. Let's leave the killing to the assassins, hmm?"

"Guy pulls a knife on me, he's going to get it in 'is heart," Jafa made a stabbing motion with his fork, "As always."

"Priest, Draiden, I don't care if you cheat, but if you're going to make a wager," Reese said. "For the love of dumplings, don't cry about losing; just pay up."

"Wager?" Draiden asked.

"Two silver talents, colored ropes, and if you get caught cheating, it's four," Priest wagered. "Cheating includes anything like what you pulled last time. We'll put it up for a vote if you think of something new."

"It's a deal."

"Good luck."

"Last and most interesting," Reese said. "Benj, you run point. Focus on people first. Only move to the hidden stashes after the all-clear. None of this run in all crazy before you checked the place out. That's how people die."

"Got it," said Benj.

"Are we bringing a loader?" Draiden asked.

"Not this time," Reese said, shaking his head.

"New guy then," Draiden pointed at Benj. "Bird, you're loading the cart."

"We're all loading the cart tonight," Reese overruled. "That reminds me, the house has two floors. It's big, and it has a stone wall around the perimeter. Don't take anything you can't lift over the wall. Bird, if you find anything that you need help collecting, get a bagger and move on."

"Blue rope it?" Draiden asked.

"Yes," said Priest. "If I catch you pulling ropes, Draiden, you're going to need a bigger spoon to defend yourself with."

"Meet out front at sundown," Reese said with finality. "Oh, and dress for the occasion this time. I don't want any style points tonight."

When they were finished eating, Lucia stood up, "Benj, walk me to my room?" she asked.

Draiden cocked an eyebrow at them.

"Calm down, Draiden," Lucia scolded and left with Benj close behind.

She opened the door to her room. Blue and gold tapestries hung from the walls, and a simple dresser and bed sat to each side of an otherwise small and empty room. She quickly picked up several delicate pieces of clothing off her floor and put them in her bottom drawer.

"So, are you really good at picking locks?" Benj asked, nervous about being in a girl's room.

"Not as good as I can smash windows," she said bluntly. "Are you ready?"

"No," Benj said, "I didn't understand half the things they said in there. What are blue ropes?"

"Priest and Draiden are competing over who gets the most valuable items. After they fill a sack, they tie them off with their own personal ropes. The blue rope means that you - the point - found them, so they can't take credit for it when we count everything up. At the end, they will see how much each has bagged, using their own-colored ropes, and name a winner. You only have one bag usually, but you're expected to beat both of them."

"Yeah, I'm not so sure I'll be able to do that," he admitted.

Lucia explained what to expect, and she told him that his biggest problem was making sure no one was in the house. It seemed that the more she tried to help, the more concerned he became.

"How do I spot them before they spot me?" He asked, feeling his time rapidly approaching.

"Don't worry," Lucia tried to calm his nerves, "The Soundsight will help you find people. It will also help with false walls, just knock on things and watch for changing sound patterns. Breaking things usually helps. Oh! And always check the bookcases. Behind books, inside of books, on the top or around. You get the point. You'll do fine.

"One more thing, use signals. Point with one finger for one person, two for two people, and so on. Rock your hand back and forth for sound coming from wherever you point. Make sure you don't miss anyone before waving anyone in. A thumbs up means it is free and clear, and punch your hand to bring in Pots and Jafa."

"Got it," he said.

"You'll do fine," she said again. "Just be confident and appear to know what you're doing."

"How am I doing so far?" He asked.

"Awful," she said, sitting on her bed patting the spot next to her.

Benj walked over and sat on the furthest part of her bed, away from her.

"I don't like talking about this, but if I don't tell you, someone else will…" she said slowly. "Two years ago, my father borrowed money from Darius."

"Who?"

She looked at him incredulously, "The Grand Marshal of the Crownsmith organization. He's the one in charge of everyone."

"Oh, good to know."

"So, my father borrowed money from him and used it to build a spice cart so he could take his business on the road. You know the one. Everything was just fine until he missed some of the payments. Business was slow for a while. Anyway, they took me to pay off the debt."

Benj was silent.

"They gave me to Gallows Reese, who put me in a house to work off the debt. I couldn't, uh, you know. I was scared, and there was this man looming over me, so I-" she paused, "I kicked him in the balls… Twice."

Benj smiled. "That's why they call you Bash."

"Yeah, but then," she continued, "after that, I ran out; this man tried to stop me, so I kicked him in the balls, too. They found me trying to leave the city. They were going to kill me when Reese, this Reese, suggested that I could be useful to his crew. While I was learning the ropes, my dad got sick and couldn't run the spice route, so they had me take his place. They said if I tried anything, they were going to kill him. He's all I have left. That's how I met you."

"They needed you to take over selling spices so you could pay them back for the money they loaned your dad?" Benj surmised, "That's why were you cheating people?"

"All the money I brought back they would keep," she said, "They would even check the ledgers to make sure I wasn't keeping any money from them. I also needed the money to take care of my dad. When he was sick, they beat him for not working. They were going to just let him die. If he did, I would run away tonight. I've been planning an escape. Then I found you. So, if something ever happened to my dad, I was planning on running away to your bakery. It sounded romantic, a baker and a spice merchant. It gave me hope. Even if it didn't work out in the end, it was nice knowing that I had a backup plan."

"How do you work for people that did this to you?" Benj asked, incredulously.

"Reese is a good man. He's not supposed to let me keep my share of the loot from jobs because it's supposed to go towards the debt," she explained. "He's been paying me out of pocket, so I have enough money to take care of myself."

"But you're technically a slave?" he asked.

"It's not so bad," she explained. "But, if I ever get the chance, I've come up with a hundred ways to get back at Gallows Reese...." Tears welled up in her eyes.

Benj moved next to her on the bed but thought better of touching her, "You don't have to worry about him."

She put her head on his shoulder and cried softly, "Do you see why I don't like to talk about it?"

"Lucia, listen to me," Benj said, heartbeat warning him to tell her. "Gallows Reese isn't coming back."

Lucia snapped her head up, eyes slightly swollen, "What do you mean?"

"He's dead," he whispered.

"Dead?!" Lucia yelped.

"Shh!" Benj silenced her and dropped his voice to a low whisper, "I killed him."

"You killed him?" she repeated with a surprised whisper.

"Yes," Benj said. "With his own sword."

Her eyes got wide and serious.

"Benj, if you lie to me about this, I swear," Lucia said.

He assured her that it wasn't a lie. He explained to her that was one of the reasons why he wanted to leave.

"You're my hero." she said simply. "But you can't tell anyone, ever."

The two spent time talking until sleep unexpectedly took them both.


A loud knock came to the door in rapid succession. *Knock, knock, knock!* The door opened. Benj lifted his head surprised to still be lying next to Lucia, and even more surprised she was holding his hand.

"You two, quickly now!" Priest bellowed in, "It's almost time, and neither of you are ready!"

Lucia jumped off her bed, rushed to her drawers, and pulled out a set of neatly folded black clothes."

"Come on, come on, come on," Priest said, snapping

his fingers. "Get your stuff together. We're meeting outside now."

Lucia looked at Benj standing next to the bed like he wasn't sure what 'get ready' meant. She pulled out another set of neatly folded black attire and tossed them to him.

"They're men's clothes technically, put them on," and with the same breath, looking at Priest, she said, "The door?!"

Priest shut the door.

"Turn around," Lucia ordered and turned herself to change her shirt.

Benj was slow to react. By the time her words registered she had already begun to disrobe. He turned away, face flushed red. He quickly began putting his own set of clothes on. They were tighter than he normally would wear, or ever wear for that matter. He would have to work that out later.

When he was dressed, he turned to see Lucia standing facing him with a devious smile.

"Tight clothes really bring out your," she coughed, "Eyes."

"You think so?" Benj asked, widening his eyes, oblivious.

"Never mind," she said, opening her door. "We have to go."

The two of them ran into the main hall; it was empty. They made their way outside.

The sun was setting over the City's rooftops. Everyone was standing next to a horse and a rather large black carriage.

"Glad you two decided to make it," Reese said with a grim expression.

Everyone was wearing black and had serious faces.

"Found these two in the kitchen trying to get a pre-operation snack," Priest said nonchalantly. "A couple of stress eaters if you ask me."

"Next time," Reese held up a finger. "Pack a meal."

The two gave mismatched acknowledgments, and Reese opened the carriage door.

"Everybody in."

The trip was slow and bumpy inside the surprisingly spacious carriage, even though it was packed to capacity. A single lantern hung from the overhead, casting faces into shadow in a circular succession. Benj wouldn't have hated sitting next to Lucia, but he was next to Draiden and beginning wondering why Priest had chided him about not bathing. The man smelled like a field of flowers growing in the middle of a cedar forest. With what little fresh air spilled through the cracks, Benj was tempted to lean closer to the man to purify the air. After a long while in silence, the cart stopped.

Jafa passed out sacks and different colored ropes to Priest and Draiden. Benj was given a single sack with strands of blue rope. Pots held similar items. Benj noticed some of them using a single strand to tie the rest to their waistline. He copied them.

The carriage became dead silent. No one moved. The anticipation hung heavy in the air like pipe smoke in a tavern. Three taps on the outside of the carriage signaled Pots to dim the lantern. The darkness swallowed everything but the sound of steady breaths and the smell of Draiden's hair.

Two taps. Everyone stopped breathing.

A single tap. Draiden's leg tensed.

The carriage door swung open, flooding the inside

with fresh air that bit at the sweat beads on Benj's face. Everyone spewed out in one fluid motion. They were parked in front of a stone wall, twelve feet high with a rope draped over the side lazily swaying in the breeze.

"Point first," Lucia whispered to him. "Wave us in when the front is clear. Wait for me to open the door before you start clearing the house."

Benj walked past the crew, who were diligently adjusting their gear, and put a hand on the rope to climb over.

"Don't forget this," Reese handed him the Soundsight.

"Not on my life," He took the bracelet, put it on his wrist, and climbed the rope with the sound of his hands and feet moving with every motion.

At the top, Benj saw the house. It was large and surrounded by a rich green garden with trees blocking any outside view that had been unimpeded by the surrounding wall.

All lights were off.

Benj waved the 'Clear' Signal and jumped, gliding across the yard. He waited on the back porch while Lucia made her way across the lawn towards him.

"Did you try the door?" she asked.

"No, I thought you were on locks?" he asked.

"It's a common courtesy," she said, pointing at the door. "Not all doors are locked."

"Fine," he said and put his hand on the latch. He was fully prepared to ask if she was satisfied if the handle was locked, but it gave way, and the latch clicked open.

"You were going to say something rude if it was locked, weren't you?"

"No!" he whispered loudly.

"I don't care, either way," she said quietly, "You should probably get going before everyone gets here."

Benj touched the bracelet unconsciously and made his way into the house. The sound patterns bounced off the latch where the door came shut. He stepped through sound patterns as they bounced off chairs and walls. Having the Soundsight made it easier to see where the moonlight didn't shine through the windows.

At the end of a large seating area, two flights of stairs jutted up to a tall balcony overlooking the long open area towards the back door. Sound patterns tumbled in from the top of the stairs and gently bounced around. He investigated the sounds, moving up the stairs and down a hallway.

"-It had his address on it. So, I took it and tossed him into the river." A man's voice from another room. "Lucky find I think."

Benj peaked around the door from where the voices came from.

"Why 'ello mate," A man's voice came from behind him.

Benj spun around just as a man grabbed him. Two others came out from behind the door.

"What's this?" One of them asked.

"Caught this one lurking around. Looks like he had the same idea," The first man said. "What do you think you're doing? We got dibs."

"I uh…" Benj stammered, "…Saw this place. It looked like a good place to lay down for a nap."

"What should we do with him?" One man asked.

"Kill him," the first man said.

"Wait!" Benj said, "I'll make you a deal."

"I'm listening."

"How far down do you think the drop from the balcony is?" Benj asked, nodding towards the railing. "Long enough to break someone's legs?"

"Yeah, so what?"

"Toss me off, and if I survive, let me go," Benj said.

"What a creative little idea," one of the men said. "I haven't heard a more reasonable offer in all my life. Toss him!"

The two men picked Benj off the floor, hoisted him over the guard rail, and released him on the third swoop. Benj turned around and coasted down and forward towards the back door.

*I just need to get to the others, he* thought as he hit the ground, slid, and ran.

"That little twat just tricked us!" Benj heard from behind him. "Get that floaty little pinprick and find his relic!"

Footsteps stomping downstairs enveloped Benj in a cascade of waves as he fled toward the entryway. When the door was within reach, he swung it open and launched outside. The cool night air rushed away the stale smell of the house.

"We have company," Benj said and stood in front of the door, far enough back that the chasers couldn't knife him before they were taken out.

"Three of them."

The door swung open, "You little ba-" The first man started saying before collapsing limply on the ground. The other two followed suit, landing on top of each other as Jafa and Pots clubbed them each of them over the head.

"How did you dig these guys up?" Jafa asked, pointing at the mound of men with his club.

"They were robbing the place," Benj said,

overwhelmed with excitement. "I think they found the guy dead and had the same idea we did."

"Good work, Bird," Reese slapped him on the back. "Finish clearing the house. Jafa, Pots, search these three. Anything they have gets a blue rope."

When Benj found the rest of the house empty, he gave the 'clear' signal. He immediately went into the room where the three thugs were searching and picked up where they had left off.

He searched the bookshelf. It was four tiers high and lined the entire wall of the space. He began pulling out stacks of books and placing them neatly on the floor. There was a thin book hidden behind some others. It was labeled, 'The Dark Magicks." He put it into his bag and kept searching.

He needed to move faster. Books fell on the floor as he slid his hand, shoveling the books off the shelves. Three books stuck together fell on the floor in unison. They were lighter than any single book and hollowed out in the middle and made an airy thump. Inside was a gold ring with some kind of curly-horned animal, a smaller light-colored metal ring, and nine gold royals.

*Found it,* he thought as he picked each off the ground.

He put the gold and the small fortune into his bag. As soon as he picked up the smaller ring, the sound waves vanished. The Soundsight stopped working. He tossed the ring into the bag and the waves appeared again, from all directions.

Benj curiously picked up the ring again, and the waves stopped. Already feeling queasy from the sound sight, he put the ring on his middle finger and continued searching the other books. He found nothing and started searching the desk.

He pulled out drawers and dumped the contents out on the floor. Papers of no importance poured out and settled effortlessly around him.

Draiden walked in and asked, "Find anything?" His question failed to form waves in the air.

"Yes, but I don't think there's anything else in here," Benj said looking around, "Unless you want to double check the pile of books on the floor."

Draiden nodded, turned to leave, and then paused. "Well, well, well," he bent down and picked up a black coin purse off the floor, presumably from one of the robbers. "Nothing else in here, huh?"

Benj swore to himself. How could he have missed something so obvious?

"Looks like I found this fair and square," Draiden said and opened it, "Not bad, looks like I owe you one for helping me out here." He took a rope off from around his waist, tied it around the sack and walked out of the room.

Benj began searching other places. There were spare bedrooms, sitting rooms, drawing rooms, offices, and dining rooms. He found a drawer with four ornate knives and a small sack of coins when a single whistle sounded. It was the sign that it was time to go.

Benj made his way down the stairs. After looking around to see if anyone was looking, he jumped down the last flight of stairs. Instead of gliding down them, he landed halfway down the stairs, tripped, and rolled onto the floor.

Priest came around the corner carrying three large sacks, "What happened?" He asked.

"I, uh, tripped," Benj said, confused as to why he had fallen.

"Are you okay?" Priest asked.

Benj searched himself for injuries. He was fine.

"Just my pride," he replied.

"Well, stop lying around and help me carry these bags."

"Sure," Benj said and held out his hands. He was still shocked that he didn't glide down the stairs as expected. He figured that it must be the ring. He made a mental note to play around with it later and tried helping Priest with his bags. *Not only did I only fill half of a sack, but Priest had three,* he thought to himself.

"Not these," Priest said, "those." He pointed behind him.

Benj looked behind Priest and was shocked to find two large sacks filled with items and wrapped with Priest's black ropes. He took them and walked out of the house.

The whole crew was passing out sacks, hand over hand, over the wall. Benj handed off Priest's bags and finally his own, tied with a single blue rope, and passed it over with the rest.

Benj was the last person to climb over the wall. Again, he didn't glide but landed straight down when he jumped. *This ring must be some kind of anti-magic relic,* he thought.

The doors closed on the carriage with all the bags inside. Reese took the reins and moved forward without them. Another carriage moved up to take its place. Everyone got in.

"Eleven and a half bags," Pots declared.

"Get anything good?" Jafa asked Priest.

"Maybe," he said vaguely. "I guess we'll just have to find out. Bird?"

"Same," Benj said, still upset about not noticing the

robber's coin purse on the floor. "Whatever happened to those three in the house?"

"Let's just say they're going to wake up with one dastardly headache," Jafa said, rubbing his head. "It would be a shame if they didn't wake up and leave before anyone goes into the house. Otherwise, they'll get landed for our robbery."

The ride home seemed shorter than the one there. Everyone was more relaxed. Benj sat next to Draiden again. This time, he wasn't upset about it.

# Chapter 22

## Counting the Spoils

T he thieves all sat around the dinner table with anticipation. Twelve sacks tied off with various colored ropes sat at the focal point. The anticipation of opening the bags and counting the loot inside made everyone giddy with excitement.

"Okay, before we start, I need a volunteer for the ledger," Reese announced. "Put your hand down, Bird. I don't know how you did things in Thannon, but we don't have points or baggers take ledgers on their own bags."

Benj lowered his hand.

Lucia raised her hand.

"Bash, go ahead and take station." Reese pointed her toward a writing desk.

"Who wants to go first?" Reese asked the table. "Bird, if you raise your hand one more time, I'm going to use it to wash Draiden's chest hair."

"No need for that, I'll go," Draiden volunteered. He stood up, picked up a bag, placed it in front of Reese, and sliced the brown rope off with his knife. The bag contained four bronze candle holders and a box full of silver cutlery.

"Mark him down for…" Reese inspected a silver cheese knife, "Five and a half talents."

Lucia dipped a quill into ink and made an entry.

"You can melt those down and get at least Seven," Draiden argued.

"It'll cost one to melt them down, and it will barter down at least one more," Reese explained. "The candle holders are worth half a talent at best, and that's me being generous. Next."

Draiden tossed another bag on the table and cut the rope. Inside were four rolls of silk and the coin purse from one of the robbers.

"Nice," Reese said, after counting the coins and feeling the fabric, "A royal and eight talents. Next!"

Lucia continued to scribble entries into the ledger as Draiden opened his sacks.

Priest went next and sliced his black ropes. Opening his bags, he revealed Swords, boxes with pipe leaves, wines, and spirits.

"What's the tally?" Reese asked, "Fourteen royals and about two talents for Draiden, and Thirteen and Three for Priest."

Reese began to announce the winner as Draiden when Priest interrupted him.

"Oh, silly me," he said, reaching into his jacket pocket and pulling out a crystal bottle with gold inlays. He set it gently on the table. "I almost forgot this."

"What is it?" Reese asked, reaching for the bottle.

"It's a bottle of Elden Spirits, and if I'm not mistaken by the markings here, this bottle is remarkably old."

"That's not fair," Draiden grumped. "It has to go in a sack!"

"Oh, sure, let's put this priceless and fragile artifact in a burlap sack and see how long it takes for you to break it. Especially with you tossing these things around like you do. I'm surprised any of my other bottles made it at all."

"I'll accept it," Reese declared, picking up the bottle and scrutinizing it.

"I call a vote," Draiden demanded. "It's not in a bag, so it's cheating. If you agree that Priest is cheating, raise a hand."

Draiden sat there with his arm in the air, looking around the room awkwardly before Priest chimed in.

"All opposed?" he said, and the hands went lazily into the air around him. Draiden sat frowning with crossed arms.

"It's settled then," Reese said, "how much can you sell it for?"

"I'll have to ask the consultant, but I would venture to guess at least four gold royals," Priest guessed.

"We'll still need a buyer. Mark him down for two royals. And it looks like we have a winner."

"This is bollocks!" Draiden exclaimed, "That cheating son of a fairy was going to keep it if he beat me."

"You realize if I was going to keep it, I could have easily lost our bet, paid you two talents, and still made out ahead," Priest asserted.

"But you would have to avoid running into Darius for the rest of your life," Reese said, placing the bottle with the rest of the loot. "No one seems to be able to manage that."

Draiden threw two silver talents at Priest.

"Why would he have to avoid running into Darius?" Benj asked.

"He has three relics that come with the position," Priest said, picking up his coins, "One of them makes it so you can tell if someone's hiding something from you. It's a way to ensure we are honest criminals. Basically, whatever you do, don't lie to him."

Benj tucked that last piece of information away. He had a lot of lying to do, so it was probably better to avoid Darius altogether.

"Bird, you're up," Reese said, pushing a blue roped bag towards him.

"Uh, can I borrow a knife?" Benj asked.

"By the looks of it, I think you'll need to borrow one of Priest's bags as well," Jafa scoffed at him.

Reese pulled out a knife and cut the blue rope. Benj reached in his bag and pulled out the book called, 'The Dark Magicks' and set it down.

"This is fantastic!" Reese affirmed, picking up the book.

"Really?" Benj asked.

"Yeah, for a wizard," he said and threw the book at Priest's head. "For us, it's completely worthless."

Priest ducked out of the way, "What was that for?"

"Just practicing. One of these days, I'm going to hit you."

"Fair," Priest shrugged.

"Uh, next, I have some of these." Benj pulled out four daggers.

Reese looked over them and handed the plainest looking one back to him. However, it was anything but plain. The dagger was as long as his forearm, point to hilt of folded metal with silver decorations. The sheath itself could have been completely silver with a woven pattern and a single green gem at the point.

"Now you can cut your own ropes," Reese explained, "Put him down for five royals."

"Here's this," Benj said, dumping out a coin purse on the table. Nine Marks rolled out of the bag.

"Nine Marks," Reese said unenthusiastically.

"And nine more royals," Benj said, reaching into his bag and slapping the heavy gold coins on the table. Benj reached inside the bag to see if there was anything left and pulled out the heavy gold ring.

"Very nice!" Reese said, approvingly, "Looks like my brother wasn't wasting his time after all. Anything else?"

"I almost forgot. I also found this," Benj said, holding up the ring on his middle finger and moving it towards Reese.

The table burst out in laughter.

Benj took it off his finger and set it on the table. Patterns of waves splashed around him. He looked to where the Soundsight was still on his wrist and then took it off.

"Have you been wearing that this whole time?"

"I guess so," Benj admitted. "I hardly noticed."

"Hardly noticed?!" Reese exclaimed, "Any normal person would have tossed up last week's dinner if they wore it half as long as you!"

"I get sick just looking at it," Lucia interjected.

"I kind of like it," Benj lied and tossed it across the table to Reese.

"You are a crazy person," Reese said, placing the relic into a pouch. "Let me see the rings."

Benj slid each ring across the table toward Reese.

"Put him down for another royal for the sheep ring. This other one isn't silver," Reese said, looking at it distastefully. "Put him down for two Marks."

"I'll buy it for two marks," Benj offered, interested in experimenting with it more and certain it was priceless.

Reese tossed the smaller ring back to him and said, "Sure. Minus two marks."

Lucia made the entry.

"You did good," Reese said, looking over everything on the table. "Priest, take him to get some ink. Make sure he gets the royal treatment."

Before Benj had the opportunity to ask what Reese meant, the room grew uncomfortably quiet. He had noticed the heavy footsteps stop outside the door. It seemed everyone else had noticed it, too by the pensive looks on their faces.

The door swung open, revealing the largest man Benj had ever seen. He had to slightly duck to get through the door. Turning to shut the door, he revealed a single, long dreadlock hanging from the back of his bald head that hung down, alongside a double-sided war axe strapped to his back. Thick eyebrows that curled upward to a point on either side of his brow gave him a Nefarious look. He wasn't thin, but his face seemed to outline skeletal features.

"What do we have here?" he asked, moving toward the group of them.

"Just tallying it all up," Reese reported with an edge of discomfort. "Is there something I can do for you, Darius?"

"Has there been any word from your brother?" He asked, eyes scanning the room and landing on Benj. "His absence is beginning to make me feel uncomfortable."

"I haven't seen him," Reese stated, annoyed. "But we have a new prospect. His name is Bird. He was the last person to see him."

"Then I will ask him," Darius said, motioning to Benj to come closer. "Where is Gallows?"

Benj momentarily froze; Priest had talked about Darius and had said not to lie to him. *How do I not lie to him?* He asked himself. "I'm not exactly sure," Benj said. It was the truth.

"You did not travel with him?" Darius asked. Showing two lower teeth on either side of his jaw that were longer than the rest. It looked like the opposite of fangs, but unlike fangs, these were thick and straight.

"No," Benj answered.

"Do you know where he might be?" Darius asked, looking at Benj with a concentrated stare. It was as if he was looking for something.

"I'm certain he is still east," he answered, relying on the fact that he was certain he was, in fact, in that direction.

"Very well," Darius said and moved his attention back to Reese. "Make sure to address his absence at the council meeting tomorrow. Oh, did you find anything of... interest at the job tonight?"

"Yes, in fact," Reese said, "Benj, show him the ring you showed me."

Benj held out his hand.

"Show him how you showed me," Reese said, smiling.

Benj slowly lowered his other fingers. Darius stood for three heartbeats with grim features. The room fell silent.

Darius reached for this axe and held it up in a jerking motion, causing the whole room to flinch back. Abruptly, Darius let out a large barrel-chested laugh and slapped Benj on the back, nearly knocking him to the ground. The tension in the room shattered as everyone else laughed along.

"I do enjoy our little visits," he said before stepping out of the room.

The room waited until his footsteps diminished down the passageway before anyone spoke.

"As I was saying, take Benj to the Spitting Serpent tomorrow. He drinks on me, so make sure he tries everything." Reese held out his hand and took the ledger from Lucia. "I'll schedule a meeting with Archer and Carmello."

Priest stood up and scanned the room, "Pots and Jafa," he said, "You're coming with."

"What about me?" Draiden asked with mock hurt. "I want to go to the Spitting Serpent."

"Then take a bath. I don't want any of your stench keeping any of the barmaids away. Benj needs a bath, too. Take him with you and give him something nice to wear.

"He really doesn't smell that bad," Benj defended him.

"Thank you, Bird!" Draiden celebrated, ushering Benj out of the room. "Finally, someone who appreciates tree resin-based oils and soaps. Just for that, I have something I would like to give you. Do you know how hard it is to turn pine sap into a usable oil? Let me tell you...."

# Chapter 23

## Grave Details

The sixth bell wake-up came, and Key conducted his morning routine. He was still getting used to wearing the new uniform, but at least he knew how to wear it right. When he was dressed, he took his hat off of his lamp table and found something under it. There was a flask with a note under it that said, "Thank you. -Jory."

He uncorked the top and smelled the contents. It smelled fine, but there was no way he was drinking something that came from Jory, even if it wasn't too early in the day. It didn't matter how appreciative he thought his archenemy was. The flask was nice, though. He tossed it into his footlocker, remembering to empty the contents later and wash it thoroughly.

Downstairs, he found bread, chicken gravy, and watered-down beer. He made himself a plate and sat down at one of the tables. Trudie sat down across from him.

"What's with the uniform?" She asked, eyeing his triangular hat.

"It's a long story," he warned her. "I'm not entirely sure myself. It has to do with castle formalities and how, if I deliver a message there, I won't offend the King."

"It looks good," she said sincerely. "I heard about you saving Jory's tail the other day. We all heard about it. You've become quite a topic of conversation lately."

"What are they saying?" Key asked, eating a bite of dried bread with gravy.

"Besides, the fact that you ended The Great Key and Jory Feud with a single act of kindness?" she asked, trying to remember what all else happened. "They are also saying that you saved two beautiful women who were kept in a secret manor's dungeon. They also said that you discovered who did it and killed him with his own sword."

"I should clear some things up," Key said, steepling his fingers. "I didn't kill anyone, and I didn't save two beautiful women. When I told that story, I might have embellished it a little. Only one of them was worth looking at, but she was old enough to be Dilly's grandmother."

Trudy let out a laugh, "So you're saying it's true?"

"No, I'm saying it's not true," Key corrected her. "And they weren't in a dungeon; they were tied to the bed,"

Trudy blushed slightly, "You didn't just save two damsels in distress; you also saved their honor?"

"It wasn't like that at all," Key explained, feeling that he was making matters worse. "They were bound and gagged, and their eyes were all red and puffy from crying all night. It was terrible and the complete opposite of a romantic rescue."

By the look Trudie gave him, she didn't appear to be listening. He decided to change the subject. "Sefulu says you are the best sword fighter we have."

"He says I'm the best?" She asked, surprised. "He's never told me that."

"Well, don't tell him I told you then," Key said, wiping his hands on a napkin. "But yeah, he says you show up and train with him more than anyone. What makes you train so hard?"

She looked around, noticing everyone else had left, "I should probably go before I'm late for the morning assembly," she said before gulping down the rest of her ale. "Next time I see you, I'll tell you about it."

Key stopped her from clearing her dishes. "I'll take care of these. You don't want to be late."

"And he's a gentleman," she said out loud before standing and leaving.

Key sat for a while longer, enjoying the fact that he didn't have to go to another morning assembly. After a moment, he cleared his and Trudie's dishes off the table and sauntered towards the office of investigations.

He spent the morning writing financial acquisition letters. When he had finished his third one, he handed it to Castor for inspection.

"Not bad," he said after closely scrutinizing every letter of every word. "Your handwriting has certainly improved. I think it's time to give you your own official seal of office."

"So I can write the letters, seal them, and take them to where they need to go?" Key asked, leading to something. "What would you do?"

"It will certainly open up my schedule a little more," Castor admitted. "With all the extra time from not proofreading your work or sealing your letters, I could probably afford to stop and smell the flowers a little more.

Maybe I'll start a family or an underground fighting ring. Anyway," he reached into his drawer and pulled out an older-looking, wooden-handled stamp. "This is for you. Don't worry, we can have a ceremony."

Key held up a hand to stop him. "It's okay, you don't have to...."

"Attention in the room!" The captain called out.

Key's body acted on instinct drilled into him since training camp. He popped to attention, standing ridged with his arms to his side.

"This seal that I bestow into the capable hands of Corporal Eulerous Key is a symbol of the King's security and trust. With it, may he seal acquisitions, correspondences, and other things that require secrecy and a safeguard from prying eyes. May he stamp out unruliness and deliver justice into the hands of the just and righteousness into the hands of the right.

"Now, hold out your hand and repeat after me," Castor continued with his oration. "I receive this-"

There was a knock at the door.

"A moment!" He called before continuing a little faster, "I receive this seal as a servant to the king with great honor, humility, and justice."

"I receive this seal as a servant to the king with honor -"

"With great honor, humility, and justice," Castor corrected him.

Key repeated him word for word. When he finished, Castor handed him the stamp.

"The office of investigations only uses red wax," he added and called for whoever had knocked to enter.

A guard that Key did not recognize entered and removed his helmet. "Sir, we found a body in the Basin

Street River. I was told to inform you."

"Has anyone identified the body?" Castor asked.

"No, sir," the guard said. "All I know is there was a stab wound. It looked like one of those wealthy types."

"Show me," the captain said as he followed the man out. Key placed the seal his desk drawer and tried the lock for the first time. It turned smoothly and clicked in place. He placed the key in his pocket and followed after the two.

"Let's make a quick stop at the stables," the captain said, changing direction. "I don't feel like walking today."

After a brief visit to the stables, the three had arrived on horseback at the scene. There were several other guards either standing around or interviewing the surrounding people. After salutes and introductions, Castor handed his reins to Key, walked over, and looked down at the body. He knew exactly who it was.

"This is Waller Barley," the captain said. "Played cards with him once or twice; bad bluffer."

"Should we check his house?" Key asked, holding the two horses. "See if there's any more people tied to a bedpost?"

The look of stark realization passed over Castor's eyes, "If there are, we have a big problem on our hands."

"Like what?" Key asked.

"Like, a group of rogue thieves and assassins working together to make my job harder than it needs to be," Castor said before barking orders at the surrounding guards and putting them all into action.

The two mounted their horses and made their way down Basin Street. It wasn't even midday and there were drunk people shouting, women standing half clothed outside of shanty looking shops, and bodies passed out on the road. The captain had shouted at disorderly people more than once to remind them to keep the peace.

"Reprehensible," Castor sneered," I would recommend stationing more guards here if I wasn't worried they would all get stabbed."

Key rested his hand on the hilt of his sword. "I just try to avoid Basin Street."

"I suspect that everyone avoiding this place is why it has gotten so out of hand," Castor considered. He finally turned down a side street and continued forward. After they arrived at the house, they tied off their horses and made for the front door.

After several knocks with no response, Castor directed Key to check the back. The back door was unlocked, so he drew his sword and entered. He noticed the house had clearly been ransacked. He walked quietly to the front door, unlocked a latch, and opened it."

"The place has been looted," Key said, walking out of the front door. "Are we going in alone or getting back up?"

"In light of past recent events," Castor said, drawing his own sword. "Let's call for backup and then make sure there's no one inside. We have to get to the bottom of this."

An hour later, the house was swarming with guards. There were no clues about who had conducted the theft, but Castor had a plan. As soon as his investigation was complete, he directed a sergeant to ensure that the proper reports were made and to inform Mr. Barley's nearest living relative of his passing.

The two saddled up, and Key followed Castor back to the office.

Inside, Castor drafted a letter, pausing every once in

a while to think out loud. "If we were going to stake out an estate, how many people do you think we would need?" he spoke to the ceiling.

"I don't know, fifteen?" Key replied from behind his desk.

"It would be hard to hide fifteen guards, even if it was dark," Castor said and then put his quill to paper again. "But eight… That will do the trick."

When he finished writing, he gave the letter to Key. Who began reading it.

"Flaming balls, corporal," Castor cursed. I didn't give you the letter to read; I gave it to you to seal it with your new stamp."

"Oh, I wasn't sure," Key said, holding the letter. "Do you have a candle?"

Castor sighed, stood up, and lit the candle on his desk. He placed it carefully on Key's desk and added a small wooden box next to it.

"What's the box for?" Key asked.

"Sprinkles," Castor replied. "It makes the seal look more official."

Key opened the box to find a silver powder and a small silver spoon. He then refolded the letter and dripped wax over the flap in the middle. He sprinkled the powder on top of the wax and pressed it with the seal. After a moment, he lifted the seal and displayed the seal of the office.

"It's crooked," Castor critiqued. "Look, the top of the handle indicates which side is up. Fortunately for us, Sergeant Dilly has no standards."

Key handed the letter to Castor, who lifted his hands. "What am I going to do with that thing? This is your show now. You're the one with the stamp."

"I really don't want to talk to Sergeant Dilly," Key confessed, refraining from sounding desperate.

"And I don't like mincemeat pies," the captain replied. "Now that we're done talking about our dislikes, you have a delivery to make."

Key gripped the letter and walked outside. The horse he borrowed from the stables was still tied to a stand-out front. The sergeants' offices were not too far of a walk, but Key liked riding horses. Now that he knew he could just borrow one from the royal stables any time he wanted, he was going to ride as often as he could.

At the sergeant's offices, he tied up his horse, walked to Sergeant Dilly's front door, and knocked.

"Enter," came a voice from inside.

The sergeant started rising from his chair before he noticed who had just entered. "Corporal Key?" he asked. "What are you doing out of uniform?"

"I was instructed to wear this uniform," Key defended himself. "Anyway, I have correspondence from the captain, sergeant."

Dilly took the letter from Key's hands, cracked the seal, and began reading it. After a long moment, he spoke, "Does he really expect me to keep eight of my best, able-bodied soldiers off duty to stand around, doing nothing until he decides to call on them?"

"I don't know what the letter says, sergeant," Key told him, not offering further information.

"I will look into this; good day."

# Chapter 24

## A Curse and a Cuss

The sun was setting, and Benj, Priest, Pots, and Jafa walked down Castle Road, kicking up dust in a trail behind them. They went through alleys and across a bridge over a dry trench until they reached a shanty-looking building with no sign out front. It had a snake on the door that seemed to be mid-strike.

"This is the Spitting Serpent?" Benj asked.

"There's the serpent, and there..." Draiden spat on the door, "is the spit."

He banged on the door twice and then once more. It opened into the most high-quality tavern Benj had ever seen. Thick candles cased in red glass domes lit rows upon rows of glass bottles filled with spirits, casks, and wine bottles. Similar candle domes lit gambling tables that were surrounded by men and women dressed like nobility, clattering coins and cards on table tops.

Beautiful barmaids dressed in scandalously little walked around with trays holding food and drinks. The barmaids were talking and accepting tips from patrons in places that made Benj blush. Smoke in the air mixed with the scents of perfumes mingled with the sound of stringed instruments, talking, and laughter.

Draiden had given Benj black trousers with a matching black jacket. The jacket came with buttons, but no button holes, and no undershirt. Draiden wore a loose-fitting white silk tunic with a grey diamond pattern untucked from loose light brown pants. The others wore rich but casual garments, making the group look the part of the rogues they were.

They sat at the bar, and a different drink was served to each of them except for Benj. The Barkeep looked at Benj with a slightly raised eyebrow.

"He's drinking on Reese tonight," Priest said, sizing up his violet drink that looked black from a nearby candle.

"Which Reese?" The Barkeep asked.

Priest cautiously looked left and right before leaning in close and whispering, "Larkin."

"Did you say Larkin Reese?" The Barkeep asked in an obnoxiously loud voice, assumedly on purpose.

The other Crownsmiths shared uncomfortable glances.

"Yes, you big oaf," Priest said, mildly irritated. "You're lucky he's not here tonight."

"Alright, alright, don't get your unders in a twist," The Barkeep laughed, "What'll you have?"

"I'll have the house ale, please," Benj requested.

"Get him a Big Bertha," Draiden ordered from across Priest.

Benj looked at Draiden, but he just smiled and sipped his drink.

The Barkeep put a giant glass bowl filled with a red concoction in front of Benj and watched him until he took a sip.

"It's good," Benj said, "Is there alcohol in this?"

The Barkeep smiled, nodded, and moved down the bar to help other patrons.

A man stood up, four chairs down, and yelled, "A curse and a cuss!"

On stage, a bard responded to the outburst with a shake of his head and continued twisting the tuning pegs on his lute. There was a unanimous agreement throughout the tavern, and more people repeated the shout.

"Alright," the bard relented before tuning the rest of his lute strings. "A curse and a cuss." He continued and began plucking the strings for a while before he abruptly started.

A cuss isn't much, but it could always get worse, so beware.
A curse is worse than a cuss. But a curse and a cuss is worse.
A swear or a curse is worse than a cuss, but it could always get worse with the more that you curse and you swear.
A stab is worse than a swear and a frown and a stare.
A stab and a smile beats a stab and a glare.
A stab and a glare is worse than a swear and a curse and a cuss, so take care.
A stab and a curse is worse than a stab and a kiss.
A stab and a kick is worse than a stab and a curse and a cuss and a glare,
but a stab and a punch is as bad as a stab and a kick… But it could always be worse, so beware!

A kick in the crotch is about as bad as it gets.
You'd give a curse and a cuss and wish for a stab
and a kiss.
A kick in the crotch is not worse than a stab, but on
a list of what hurts, a stab is not worse.
Baring a stab, and a kick in the crotch, and a curse
and a cuss and a swear and glare,
It could always get worse, so beware!

The bard strummed his lute one last time, and the room erupted in applause and laughter.

"Get him another!" Draiden yelled at the Barkeep.

A moment later, another large, red drink sloshed in front of Benj.

"So let me get this straight," Benj said, forcing his eyes to focus on the dice before him. "If you roll a five, six, seven, eight, or nine, I take a drink. But if I roll a one, two, three, four-" Benj silently counted the next numbers, "nine, ten, eleven or a twelve, then we all have to take a drink?"

"That's what I'm saying, It's a win, win!" Jafa said rolling the dice on the table, it was an eight and Benj took another long pull from his drink.

"Wait!" Benj said with absolute clarity, "There's two dice so you can't roll a one!"

"But think of all the other numbers!" Draiden said with a big drunk smile.

"Roll again!" Benj said.

It was a seven. Benj drank.

"I think you guys sare cheating," Benj slurred his words together.

"Then you roll the dice," Draiden said slapping the

dice in his hands.

Benj rolled; it was an eight. He drank.


"Finish your drink," Draiden said, "It's time to go."

Benj looked over at his Big Bertha and noticed it was full again. *When did that happen?* He took as many drinks of it as he could and then stood up.

He found himself on the ground, lying on top of a toppled bar stool. Four hands hefted him up and led him out of the door.

"What happened bachthere?" Benj asked sloppily as his vision spun.

"When you got out of your chair, or when you joined the table down there and started telling them about your dog back home?" Priest asked helping him outside.

"Remember when you rolled snake eyes all those times in a row?" Draiden asked, encouraged helping.

"I rolled snake eyes in'th spitting snake three times!" He yelled as they walked across a small bridge. "If'thas not luck, there'snosuch thing."

"You're a pretty lucky guy, mate," Jafa said. "Do you think you can walk without help?"

"I can fly w'thout help!" Benj tossed off their hands and started jumping. The ring prevented him from gliding, but no one looked.

Benj slowly lagged behind as the three men walked in front.

"Wait up y'guys!" He yelled.

"Well, come on then!" One of them shouted behind his shoulder.

They walked around a corner ahead. Benj took the time to relieve himself in a bush. By the time he rounded the corner, they were gone.

He stumbled and walked in the dark, singing what lyrics he remembered from the "a curse and a cuss" to himself, determined to find his way back home when he heard footsteps.

"Isabout time," He said as he walked toward the sound. When he got there he looked up to find three dark figures glaring at him with rope in one hand and a black bag in the other. One man threw the sack over Benj's head, tied him up in spite of his protests, and dragged him away.

Benj found himself shirtless, strapped to a table, and blindfolded. He could hear the sound of indistinct voices, feet shuffling on the floor, and the squeak of a door hinge.

"We know you work for the Crownsmiths. We have some questions for you. If you answer our questions, we'll let you go. If you don't give us the answers we want, we'll start with your toes and work our way up."

"I don't know anything!" Benj pleaded, "I'm a baker! Let me go!"

"Who is Larkin Reese?" The man asked with a calm voice.

"I don't know, but if you call him Larkin, he won't like it."

Benj was slapped in the face. The effects of the alcohol absorbed most of the blow.

"Ow!"

"Let's try this again. What do you do with the Crownsmiths?"

"I don't do anything. I'm a baker. I bake bread. I invented sausage bread. If you tried it, you would be kissing me on the face right now and not slapping me." Benj said, sobering up. "What do you want from me?"

He was slapped again. "Where are they located?"

"If I knew that, I would be in bed right now, not talking to you lardheads."

Before they were able to slap him again, Benj threw up red juice all over the floor.

"I'm not cleaning that up," One of them said. "I've got my own job to do."

The room got quiet.

"All right, put him under. Let's get to work."

"Put me under what?" He asked trying to move his arms. Someone pinched his nose. When he opened his mouth to breathe, they dumped a warm, bitter solution inside. He was forced to swallow it. He heard them talking about birds when his vision blurred. He saw a bird land on his chest. It sang to him as the room darkened and he drifted off to sleep.

Evan Kvalvik

# Chapter 25

## The Worst Guards

T he next morning, Key arrived at the office. The door was unlocked, but the captain was nowhere to be seen. He settled into his chair and began looking through letters.

They contained a treasure trove of information. For a while, he got lost in a sea of correspondences, acquisitions, and requests. He found one that mentioned Corporal Ellsworth. He had heard the name before; he must have been the captain's former assistant. Rumors of his death had spread like wildfire. Each story brought on a different scenario, leaving more questions than answers about his death.

There was a knock at the door.

"Enter," Key said. It almost sounded like a question.

"Corporal Givens, reporting as ordered." The man said, saluting Key.

"At ease, Givens," Key said, uncomfortable at being saluted.

"Key, is that you?" Givens asked, squinting at him. "I thought you was some kind of officer with how you're dressed."

"That's okay," Key said, uncertain what to do. "The captain isn't in right now. What did they tell you to report here for?"

"Dilly said we are being transferred," he smiled. "There's more of us outside."

Key stood up and walked outside and found a group of some of the worst guards in Royal City. The only exception was Trudie, who was standing among them. Some weren't standing at all. Three of them sat on the cobblestones, and the others stood around talking loudly, unsettling the otherwise quiet atmosphere of the officer's district. Two had started wrestling. None of this would bode well for the captain's favorite axiom.

He cleared his throat and greeted them. "Hi everyone, I'm not sure why you are here, but I'm sure the captain has his reasons. He should be here soon if you all want to try pretending to be orderly until he arrives. It will look better if you do. I recommend forming up in loose ranks."

"Hey, Givens," Roger called out, "It looks like Key's new uniform has gone to his head!"

A few of them laughed, one of which was Jory.

"We weren't sent here to report to you," Poulson said, still sitting on the ground.

"You guys are going to piss him off if he shows up and you're sitting on the ground." Key's warning elicited more laughter and a few curse words.

"Trudie," Key said, ignoring the jabs, "Can I have a word with you inside?"

Trudie stepped into the office after Key, followed by whistles and innuendo.

"What is everyone doing here?" Key asked, shutting

the door.

"I'm not sure," Trudie said, looking around the office. "Sergeant just told us to report here after the morning assembly."

"But why are you here?"

"The same reason everyone else is?" Trudie formed her statement as a question.

"I mean, clearly, Dilly sent the worst guards he had," Key said, struggling to finish his thought. "You're not on the list of the worst guards."

"I don't think he likes me," she admitted.

"That makes sense," Key said, understanding how easy it was to get on Dilly's bad side. "The group out there is going to get both of us into trouble if they don't reign it in a little. You might want to wait in here with me. When the captain gets back, you don't want to get roped into whatever's coming their way."

Trudie started to reply when her words were cut off by the sound of yelling.

"What are you doing on the ground? Stand up, fall into formation, all of you!" a voice yelled before the door swung open, and an angry Major Kane walked in. Trudie and Key stood to attention.

"Where's your captain?" the man asked abruptly. "And what is the meaning of this?"

"The captain isn't here, and I'm not sure what they are doing out there," Key said. "I'm working that out now."

"Your men were out there being a disgrace to the uniform," he said. "You need to keep a higher standard."

"He told them to form up, sir, but they wouldn't listen," Trudie said in Keys' defense.

"Is this true, corporal?" the Major asked.

"Yes, sir," Key answered.

"Come with me," the Major said and walked outside to the formation of guards. "This is Corporal Key; he is the assistant to the investigator. That means when the investigator isn't here, Corporal Key is in the office of investigations. Whatever he says will be treated as if the captain spoke it himself. Do I make myself clear?"

"Yes, sir!" The formation said in unison.

The major directed his attention back to Key, "When your captain gets here, tell him to report to my office immediately."

"Yes, sir," Key said as he stormed off.

Key found himself standing in front of a glaring formation before he made his way back inside. He opened the door to find Trudie still standing at attention.

"You can relax now," Key informed her.

"You weren't kidding about getting roped in with the group out there," she said. "You saved me from that one."

"Thanks for speaking up for me."

Before not too long, Key heard a familiar voice say, "Gentlemen." Before the door to the office opened, Captain Castor stepped inside.

"Why is there a whole company of guards standing outside my office?" He asked, noticing Trudie.

"The Sergeant sent us a group of his absolute worst guards," Key said and then added. "Except for Trudie, I mean, Corporal Logan."

"Well, send them back," Castor ordered with a flick of his hand. "I have no need for them at the present."

"I tried. They said that they have direct orders to report to you, sir," Key said, remembering to speak formally. "Speaking of orders, Major Kane wants to see you. He sounded urgent."

"What does he want?" Castor asked.

"Sir, I might be able to explain," Trudie said. "Request to speak freely?"

The captain nodded, and Trudie walked him through the series of events that had happened before he got there. She explained how they were to report to the captain and await further orders from him.

After she was done, the captain took a moment to gather his thoughts. Finally, he said, "Corporal, I'm going to tell everyone to report back to the sergeant then you and I are going to go pay a visit to the Major."

"Yes, sir," Key acknowledged and followed the captain out.

Key and Trudie stood off to the side as the captain addressed the guards standing in formation, "Thank you all for coming, now fall out and report to Sergeant Dilly." With that, he turned on his heel and made his way to the Major's office with Key in tow.

"Come in," the Major said after the captain knocked.

Key and Castor went inside.

"Ah, Captain Castor," the Major said as if he had just been thinking of him. "I take it you've met your new company?"

"I stumbled across some random guards on my way back to my office," Castor said, keeping a neutral face. "I sent them back."

"I see," the Major said producing a letter from on top of his desk. "I have here a request letter from you asking for eight guards to standby for further instructions. There doesn't seem to be a time frame for how long they would stand by for. Captain Watford paid me a visit yesterday and came up with a quite generous offer.

"He offered to transfer eight of his guards into your

service. Seeing that your office has had an increased workload as of late, I believe it prudent to accept the captain's offer. I signed the transfer letter this morning."

"Sir, I assure you, the guards I requested are a solution to a temporary problem," the captain said. "I will have no need for them once I catch a singular group of murderous thieves."

"Be that as it may," the Major started, "you are still negligent of a full company, even with the extra support."

"Corporal Key, will you please explain to the major the first thing you noticed about the extra support we received this morning," the captain said.

"Yes, sir," Key hesitated. "Permission to speak freely, Major?"

"Go on."

"The first thing I noticed was the guards that Sergeant Dilly sent are the worst guardsmen he has," Key stated. "Every single one of them, save Corporal Logan, are all the biggest troublemakers in the force. The only reason Corporal Logan was added to the bunch is because she is a girl. The rest are the lowest form of human ever to don the uniform. I've worked with them. I think Sergeant Dilly is just trying to rid himself of a headache."

"I'll admit, they did seem an unruly bunch from what I noticed," the Major recollected. "But that's only because they lack proper leadership. All guards are equal in the King's eye, and until they are discharged, whether honorably or otherwise, they are considered equally valuable members of the King's service. I will not be withdrawing my authorization for the transfer. Besides, the better team you make them, the better it will look for you come promotion time."

The three stood for a long, silent moment.

"That will be all captain," the Major said. "Go forth and do good things."

Key followed his disgruntled captain out of the office. He knew the captain had been avoiding picking up a company at all costs. He was able to avoid it for years.

"If I can't give them back, I'm going to have to figure out another way to get rid of them," the captain said thinking out loud. "I could always make it so difficult for them that they quit...."

"Remember what you told me about playing people off of their strengths?" Key asked, pausing a moment to work his thoughts out. "You could always play them off their weaknesses. I know that Dilly won't put Foiler on bridge duty because he can't be trusted to handle money. If you have coins lying around and you leave him unattended, you could catch him in the act of taking them. I'm sure we could find similar scenarios for each of them."

"That's not a bad idea," the captain said, arriving at his office door. "Tell me everything you know."

"Keebler broke the brotherhood of the guard once, so everyone tells on him. Poulson lies about everything, Roger and Givens act like they are the law, and Lambro just smells bad."

The two sat at their desks while Key talked nonstop about the other guards past offences. Part of him wondered if he was technically betraying the brotherhood of the guard himself, but with the way they treated him earlier, it seemed only fair. He didn't have much to say about Jory considering his pranks were the cause of him being one of the worst guards.

Castor scribbled down notes as fast as Key spoke. Before they were finished, a knock came at the door.

"Enter!" Castor said.

It was Givens. He explained how they were all sent back.

Castor told Givens to fall in and wait for further orders. After Givens left, he let out a huge sigh. "I better go speak to them." He said and walked outside.

Castor stood in front of the small company and addressed them, "It appears that you all have been transferred to the office of investigations. Welcome to my world. Everything you say and everything you do is a direct reflection on my office and me. When you are in my service, you will act with professionalism and integrity. You have an important job. I am currently working on a course of action. I need you all to stay on your guard and be prepared to move when I say move. As the Major explained earlier, Corporal Key is my voice when I am not present. If he says jump, you jump. If he says fall in, you fall in. If you have a problem with that, you come to talk to me so I can get you some lashings. Do I make myself clear?"

"Yes, sir!" the company said in unison and remained where they were standing.

"Very well," the captain said, looking at each of them in turn. He went back to the office and collapsed in his chair. "What do I do with them?" he asked himself.

"Sword training?" Key suggested. "Trudie trains pretty much every day. She can take them down to the yard."

"That will buy at least a little time," Castor admitted, loading his pipe. "Go out there, put Trudie in charge of taking them down to the training grounds. I'm going to draft a letter of acquisition for all of their past writeups. Maybe we'll find something inspirational."

# Chapter 26

## Bird, Crown, and Star

B enj woke up with a startle. His head pounded from the drinking. He vaguely remembered leaving the bar, and he had a feeling that there was something he had forgotten. He wasn't in his room. He panicked as it all came back to him. His wrists were raw from the ropes, but all his fingers and toes were still there, and he was no longer tied up. He got on his feet, and the room swirled around him. He was still drunk.

The door opened, and Priest came in with bread, dried fruit, and two drinks on a tray.

Benj sat up slowly in bed, confused, "What happened last night?"

"After you eat something and get your head straight, you'll be better for a conversation," Priest said warmly.

"Where are we?" Benj asked.

"The Cellar Inn. It's just down the street from the cathedral. It is a safe place." He set down the tray. "Here, drink this. It'll help with your head."

Priest handed him a large cup of salty, bitter-tasting tea and encouraged him to finish all of it. "Make sure you eat something before you come out. If you have to throw up, do it in here," he said, sliding a pot over with his foot.

"I don't get it,' Benj said, "Why am I here?"

Priest sighed. "It was your initiation. Everyone does it, even me."

He left the room while Benj ate small bites of bread and drank water. The bitter drink had made his head bearable, but he still felt awful. After a while, he opened the door and made his way to a staircase that led down into the common room. There, sitting around tables, eating, and drinking was the entire team. Everyone cheered.

"Let's see it!" Draiden yelled from the crowd.

"See what?"

"Open your shirt!"

Benj lifted up his shirt and found a raw tattoo of a black bird holding a three-prong crown over his heart. There was a star under the left crown spike. He was bewildered.

The crowd cheered for him as he made his way to the tables and sat down.

"Here's the little baby now," Draiden chided, "You should have seen yourself blubber when they said they were going to cut off your precious little toes!"

"As I recall," Priest lifted an eyebrow, "You pissed yourself all over the table and cried for your mother."

"Congratulations, Bird," Reese said with a smile, "You're official now, but you'll probably want to sleep it off for the rest of the day."

Everything was too much for Benj to take in. The sound hurt his ears, the light hurt his eyes, and the drumming in the back of his head kept him from getting upset and throwing chairs." Yeah, I think some sleep would be good."

"I'll walk with you," Lucia offered and escorted him out.

Reese watched Benj and Lucia as they walked out and then spoke, "You mean to tell me he didn't say anything?"

"Not a single word," The tall man said from across the table. His name was Archer, and he was the man who purchased the stolen goods from each job and redistributed them among the city's jewelers, merchants, and weapons dealers. He also had connections with every alchemist in Royal City.

"He seems trustworthy," Archer said, "He defended you when I called you Lar-" He caught himself, "Well, you know. Pretty impressive. Kept to his story, and then he threw up all over the place."

"Thanks, what do I owe you?" Reese asked.

"I owe your brother enough to call this one a favor," Archer said, lifting the lid off a box. "Let me see these wares. Maybe you can cut me a deal."

Reese redirected his attention to Bones. "That was probably one of your best works of art."

Bones nodded gratefully. There was almost a smile, but not quite.

Reese whistled, and everyone began arranging the tables into a semicircle. Items were then taken out of wooden crates and set on the tables. He and Archer walked around, stopping at each table and negotiating a price. After a price was agreed upon, Archer would pay Reese, and the items were placed back into crates and taken away.

By the time Archer left, Reese ended up making slightly less than he tallied the first night. He had a council meeting later, and the anticipation of it distracted him. He still had Priest's bottle of spirits, which gave him hope for a better turn-out.

"Priest, what are you doing about that bottle?" He asked.

He held up empty hands and gestured around the room. "Carmello hasn't shown up yet, and he should have been here an hour ago. So I guess you could say I'm resisting the temptation to open it."

"He's late?"

"Yes, but not unexpectedly. We'll give him another hour before we send someone."

"I'm putting you in charge of that," Reese said and stood. "I have a council meeting to go to."


Lucia had helped Benj to his room and laid him on the bed. He had thrown up everything in his stomach, but she put a pot next to his bed just in case.

"It's part of the initiation. It happens to everyone."

"Even you?"

"Kind of," She hesitated. "Because I'm not really here out of my own free will, Reese told me what was going to happen and assured me the men would respect me when they tied me up."

"He really is a good man, isn't he?" Benj asked.

"I think so," She said noncommittally, "Do you want to see?"

"See what?"

Lucia pulled her shirt down around her left shoulder, revealing the Crownsmith tattoo.

"He asked me where I wanted to put it; I told him here." She pointed at her shoulder.

"It looks good on you," he managed before dry

heaving into the bucket next to the bed.

"You really are a charmer," she said, lying down next to him on the bed.

"This is nothing," He said, eyelids hanging heavy. "You should have seen the mess I made last night."

At the Celler Inn, a man in his thirties entered. He had long brown hair tied meticulously back behind handsome features. He wore a blue jacket with matching blue trousers and spoke with an air of pretension.

"Hello?" He called out. "Did I miss the festivities?"

"Carmello, you pompous old prick, you're as late as a skeleton with an antidote," Priest greeted him.

"I was held up in court or some such thing," he excused himself. "So sue me."

"No need to involve the law. What can you tell me about this?" Priest set down the crystal bottle in front of him.

"Ohhh, what is this indeed?" He squeaked with pleasure as he picked the bottle up to inspect it. "Elden Spirits, if I'm not mistaken, at least fifty years old. This is quite the find."

"It was a gift from an old friend."

"You don't have to lie to me, old chap," Carmello held the bottle protectively. "No one would give the likes of you a bottle of this quality. I would say this bottle is worth at least two royals and fifteen."

"I'll pay that much right now and drink it myself," Priest countered, recognizing the start of the negotiations.

Carmello looked affronted, "Fine. I'll give you three royals of the selling price, but that's because I'm certain I can find a buyer."

Priest held out his hand, "I'll do it."

Reese walked into the Crownsmith Cathedral and approached the large round table in the center. The gold skull sitting in the middle of the table reflected the stained-glass windows and shined radiant colors on Kahl Stau, Tannus Reginald, and Darius Balat. By the time Reese sat down, a single bell rang out in the distance, designating the thirteenth hour.

"Glad you could make it," Darius said, folding his fingers across the table. "Let us begin. The first order of business is from last night's reports. Reese?"

Reese stood up, "We just got a new member; his name is Benjos Bird. He worked with Gallows before coming to us. He led this last operation as a point, and it was a success. We were running a skeleton crew there for a while after the recent deaths of my other members. Bash continues to be valuable to the team. I plan on keeping her. The total estimated earnings from last night come to forty-eight royals and just over five talents. After the sales with Archer, it came out to a little less. There will be one or two royals after Priest sells the last of the wares through Carmello. There were no casualties. There were three robbers in the house when we got there. Odd, but not unheard of. Bird found them and led them to Jafa and Pots, who took care of them."

"The money?" Darius held out his hand.

Reese set the heavy bag of coins on the table and slid it over to Darius, who separated the coins into four piles and slid the smaller stack toward Reese. He then slid two of the larger stacks towards Kahl and Tannus.

"You can keep your last royal pending the sale," Darius said, and then, before Reese could protest, added, "Have you done nothing to find your brother?"

"I am many things," Reese said dispassionately, "My brother's butler is not one of them."

"I see," Darius said solemnly. "Anything else, Reese?"

"No."

"Kahl, do you have anything to report?" Darius asked the leader of the assassins.

Kahl Stau rose from his chair, "I have arranged our next target; our assassins are drawing up the plans as we speak. They should be ready within the next few days. I have nothing further to report."

Tannus slammed his fists on the table and raised his voice angrily. "What do you mean you've arranged our next target? The only thing the assassins should be arranging is their collection of knives while the overseers do the planning. What are you arranging?"

"I am familiar with the rules, Chancellor. We are allowed to conduct inside jobs without the involvement of the overseers in special cases, but I will consider your argument." Darius made brief eye contact with Kahl before continuing. "Is there anything else you would like to report?"

Tannus stood and took a deep breath. "The overseers and I are concerned about the state of the area surrounding Canal Street. The brothels, smoke dens, and money lenders have been turning what used to be a nice area of town into a garbage pit. Homeless gather in the street, and trash and waste have gathered to a ghastly degree. We have decided that hosting such establishments is no longer viable for our community."

"I understand your concern, chancellor," Darius stated grimly. "But those establishments have become our primary source of income. The overseers haven't drawn up any plans as of late, and that is costing us. So, we have

313

been taking contracts."

"We haven't drawn any plans because there are no plans to draw. The king has no open opposition, so the kingdom is now our primary mission. That means Royal City, and that means getting rid of the refuse." Tannus insisted. "Furthermore, I don't appreciate you going off and conducting assassinations without consulting the Overseers. We are here for a reason, and you cannot continue taking contracts out on our citizens for revenue!"

"Do you enjoy your little payments, Tannus?" Darius asked, gesturing towards the stack of coins in front of him. "It appears as if you are unhappy with your cut."

"This isn't about money," Tannus said, pushing the coins away. "You can keep it. This is about preserving our king and preserving our people. If you neglect your responsibilities, you will not enjoy the outcome."

"Then I will look into cleaning up Canal Street," Darius said. "Is that all?"

"Yes." Tannus took his seat.

Darius composed himself in his chair. "It appears we all have some challenges ahead of us. Kahl, I want you to cancel your plans for now; we have to rid ourselves of some refuse first."

"Yes, lord," Kahl acknowledged without a hint of irritation. This brought a satisfied look from Tannus.

"Reese, I want you to go to Thannon tomorrow and find your brother," Darius ordered.

"That will take over two weeks!" Reese exclaimed.

"I believe I was telling you to go to Thannon, not asking how long you felt it would take," Darius said, staring at Reese with a level eye.

Reese bit his tongue. "I will go tomorrow."

"Excellent. I don't care who you put in charge while

you're gone. We will arrange our next meeting upon your return. You are all dismissed."

Evan Kvalvik

# Chapter 27

## The First Stone

K ey entered Sergeant Dilly's office and was welcomed with a smug, self-satisfied smile.

"Ah, Corporal Key," the sergeant greeted. "Are you coming in to argue about the captain's new company?"

"No, sergeant," Key said, handing him a letter. "Just bringing correspondence from the captain."

The sergeant took the letter and waved for Key's dismissal. Key stood his ground.

"You are dismissed," the sergeant finally said.

"Sergeant, with your permission, I believe I will stay until you've read the letter."

Dilly broke the seal on the letter and began reading. After a few moments of silence, he abruptly slammed the letter onto his desk with a violent force. "What does the captain want with his new company's writeups?"

"You would have to take that up with that captain; I'm just following orders," Key replied levelly. "I would assume it has something to do with them being his responsibility now."

Dilly sat thoughtfully until his glare finally softened. "Yes, I suppose they are his responsibility now." He began digging through boxes of documents.

Key's legs were stiff from standing, and he began shifting his weight from one leg to the other before the sergeant placed eight stacks of paper on the desk in front of him. Each stack was tied with brown twine and had a written name on the top of each. The sergeant held up one more that hovered over the pile ominously. It had the name Eulerous Key scrawled across with disappointing penmanship.

"I'll have this last one delivered to the captain myself," Dilly said, holding the exhaustive history of Key's offenses in his hand. "You can take those and leave."

Key gathered up the documents and walked out of the door with a slight feeling of unease. What would the captain think if he read all the documented times he had gotten in trouble? Granted, most of the instances were due to his and Jory's career-long feud. It would probably be safe to say that all of Jory's writeups were because of Key. He contemplated how he was going to explain all of it to the captain when he inevitably asked. Would he tell Castor about all the pranks he and Jory played on each other? If he didn't, the captain might think that he was a troublemaker and send him back to standing watch.

Deep in thought, Key stepped into the office of investigations carrying the packets of paper. Before he had the chance to place them on his desk, he noticed a small black letter on the floor just inside the door. Castor sat staring at a coin purse on his desk as puffs of smoke diligently rose from his pipe.

"Did you know you have a foreboding-looking letter lying here on the floor?" Key asked, bending over to pick it up. He held up the black parchment sealed with red wax with the shape of a crown. "Are you expecting a letter from the king?"

Castor took the letter and turned it around in his hands. "I don't think this is from the king, but it does appear foreboding."

He cracked the seal and unfolded the black parchment. Key walked past, trying to see what kind of ink would show up on black parchment. From what he could tell, it was blank. He continued to his desk and set down the packages. "Who's it from?"

"No one," Castor said, putting the letter in his inner jacket pocket and changing the subject. "Come count these coins with me. I decided to give your plan a try. I took the liberty of borrowing a few coins from the treasury."

Key walked over to the coin purse and opened it, spilling its contents on the table. There were fifteen silver talents and a gold royal. Key counted the coins, and after he said the amount he counted, Castor directed him to place the coins back and tie the bag with a loose knot. He did so.

"Put this in your desk," Castor said, nudging the coin purse with the stem of his pipe. "As soon as our new additions come back, we are going to send Foiler to prison. I mean, on a little errand."

The two signed for the money on a piece of paper, which the captain promptly folded and sealed. They discussed their plan as well as possible before there was a knock at the door.

"Back from training, sir," Givens reported, stepping into the office. He was breathing heavily, and he glistened with sweat.

"Very well. Send in Corporal Foiler." The captain ordered and considered Givens with narrowed eyes. "And inform my men that if they ever report to this office out of uniform or without properly bathing first, it will not go well."

After Givens had left, the captain made his desk look messy, unbuttoned the top few buttons of his uniform, and lifted a leg over the arm of his chair. Key lifted an eyebrow, but before he had a chance to ask what he was doing, a timid knock came to the door.

"Come in, come in," he said jovially.

"Captain, sir, I wasn't sure if you wanted me to bathe first before I came or if I'm supposed to report to you now," Foiler said, apprehensive to fully enter through the door's threshold.

He was a thin man with a hooked nose that gave him a hawkish look. His sandy blonde hair was still damp and messy from his efforts at the training grounds; he had not bathed.

"It's fine; just remember it for next time. I honestly forgot why I called you in," the captain said, lounging sideways in his chair. "How was sword training?"

"Corporal Logan is a taskmaster. No one likes her, sir," Foiler replied, rigid under Castor's scrutiny.

"Is she now?" Castor replied, happy for the news. "Well, that's all I needed to know. You can leave." He waited a half breath before adding, "Ah, I suppose there is something you can do for me. Do you know where the treasury is?"

"Yes, sir," Foiler acknowledged, looking more at ease than he had before.

"Good, we caught a purse-cutting street rat earlier, and I just need someone to take this stolen money to the treasury. I put it somewhere in here," the captain said, looking through his drawers and lifting papers from his disorganized desk. "Corporal, do you have the money purse?"

Key opened his drawer, pulled out the coin purse, and set it on his desk. "It's right here, sir."

"Oh good," the captain said. "Did you count it yet?"

"Not yet, sir," Key replied, trying to hide any hints of playacting from his voice. "I thought the treasury could just count it when we gave it to them."

"So, you're telling me the money in that coin purse is uncounted?" the captain reiterated, solidifying the fact.

"Correct, sir," Key said. "it's probably not that much anyway. I'm sure it will be fine."

"Very well," the captain said, turning his attention toward Foiler. "Can you take this to the Treasury? Oh, and take this," he said, producing a sealed letter, "This letter will explain where the money came from if they ask."

Key handed the coins to Foiler and noticed that he was already considering the weight of the bag. He and Castor didn't move for a long while after Foiler left. Finally, Castor then sat up in his chair, buttoned his uniform, and began organizing his desk.

"Why did you make yourself look messy before Foiler got here?" Key asked.

"Because perceptions, young Eulerous," Castor said, squaring his papers on the edge of the desk. He offered no more on the subject. "I've never been so excited to get robbed in my life. He's probably hiding around a corner looking in the purse now."

Key cleared his throat. "Captain, there's something I need to tell you."

"Captain, is it?" Castor asked, clearing crumbs off his desk. "It must be pretty serious."

"It's going to take some back story. Jory and I joined the guard at about the same time. When we were at camp, Jory planted a flower on my footlocker, and I retaliated. We've pretty much retaliated against each other, back and forth for around two years...." Key continued to explain his and Jory's history with pranking each other. The only details he left out were the part about the old fish he had purchased and his shined armor.

Castor's eyebrows were lifted in shock. "That's-"

There was a knock at the door.

"Enter!"

"Delivery from Sergeant Dilly, sir." The guard said, placing a twine-wrapped stack of papers with Key's name on top into Castor's hands. He saluted. The captain thanked him, and he left.

"I have to say, that is one of the better stories I have heard in my whole career," Castor said, gauging the thickness of Key's stack of papers. He reached under his desk and placed Jory's twine-wrapped papers next to each other.

"About the same size."

"Most of the writeups in mine are his fault, and most of the writeups in his are my fault," Key explained. "I just wanted to explain the story before mine got here."

"That is very wise of you," Castor acclaimed. "Let's return to this later. Who's next on our list?"

"Lambro is known for lying about everything," Key said, referencing a list they had made. "I'm not sure how that will help us, though."

There was a knock at the door. As soon as the captain permitted, a plump sergeant walked in, slightly out of breath. "Captain, a guard was delivering a large sum of money to the treasury, but it was less than the amount you specified."

"Ah, that would be Corporal Foiler," the captain said with mock sorrow. "Detain him, search him, and arrest him for theft."

"Yes, sir," the sergeant turned to leave.

"Sergeant," Castor said, stopping the man before he could leave. "Bring me back the money and keep this quiet for as long as you can. I'm going to see if I can't kill more birds with the same stone."

Evan Kvalvik

# Chapter 28

## Arranging a Marriage

B enj woke up and noticed he was by himself. He gathered his clothes, bathed, and walked down to the dining area. Everyone was at the breakfast table eating and cracking jokes with each other. Upon seeing Benj, the room went quiet. Draiden stood up, raised a glass, and toasted to their newest member. There was a mixture of agreement and cheers around the table as Benj found a seat.

Lucia leaned close and whispered, "I would have woken you earlier, but I wasn't sure if you still needed time to recover."

"Yeah, how are you feeling?" Draiden asked, implying that he had overheard the comment."

"A lot better. What did I miss?" he asked, scooping cold eggs and sausages onto a plate.

Draiden looked pleased. "Reese left this morning, and he put me and Priest in charge while he's gone. I'm not sure why he couldn't just put me in charge."

"Because he doesn't want everything to burn down in his absence," Priest responded, walking into the room.

"It's not like we'll be doing anything, so you're all free to scurry around and do whatever it is that lowlifes do when they aren't robbing houses."

"I'm going to go visit my dad," Lucia announced. "Benj, do you want to come with me?"

"Sure," He smiled. "I keep forgetting that John is your father. That's something I still need to get used to."

"You already know her father?" Jafa asked suspiciously. "How?"

Benj paused. With the story he fabricated, there would be no reason why he should know her father.

"We weren't going to tell you this," Lucia said, cutting in. "But Benj and I have been courting for some time now. He's already met my father."

Benj shot her a surprised look. That wasn't what they agreed their story would be. However, he had made a blunder and her story did make sense.

"Two thieves find more than just loot while plundering their assassinated victims," Priest mused. "Isn't that romantic, Draiden?"

"Sounds eerie, even to me," Draiden admitted.

"You'll want to get some new clothes then. You should find yourself something respectable to wear for the father-in-law." Priest tossed Benj a bag of coins. "This is your cut from the job. I'm sure Lucia knows some good places to go."

"We can go right now if you're ready, sweetie pie," Lucia said, smiling at him.

Benj stifled a laugh at the absurdity of the pet name. There was a part of him that was excited to pretend to court her. He had started liking her even though she was just a friend. She was the only person he was able to trust. Having someone to talk to and share secrets with was a good feeling, but their closeness only complicated his plans for leaving. She wouldn't leave without her father, and he wished he had left days ago.

"I guess I'm ready," Benj said, trying to think of a pet name to use at the last moment. "Uh, sugar balls."

"Hey, Pots," Jafa said with a nefarious grin. "Can you pass a sausage, sugar balls?"

The table laughed.

Jafa took the sausage and held it to Pots' mouth. "Say 'ah,' my little flower peddle."

"You guys keep that weird stuff to yourselves," Draiden said and then smacked the sausage out of Pots' hand. "All of you."

"You're the best, sugar balls," Pots said and then laughed.

Lucia stood and pulled on Benj's arm. "Alright, we're leaving."

The two walked outside and were well down Castle Road before she broke the silence, "Sugar balls? Is that the best you could do? We need to work on that."

Benj looked at her indignantly. "I'm sorry I didn't think of a cool nickname to call you twenty seconds after finding out that we're courting. That was not part of the plan. Besides, sugar balls are a real thing. They're little cakes, and they're delicious."

"Little delicious cake balls, huh?" Lucia asked. "Is that how you feel about me?"

"What? No, I was playing along," Benj said, exasperated. "Anyway, I don't know the first thing about courting. I thought people just decided they're going to get married and then order a cake."

"I'm not sure how it works either," Lucia confessed. "But I think we have to hold hands."

"It's okay, we don't have to hold hands," Benj said, involuntarily blushing.

"No, we have to hold hands," she demanded, taking his hand. "Just until we get out of here. Then you don't have to pretend to like me anymore.

Benj stopped, released her hand, and faced her. "Lucia, I really do like you. I haven't really had a friend like you before. I've always worked too hard at the bakery to go out and do things like have friends. I would really like it if we could stay friends after this is all over."

"If you're trying to get out of holding my hand, it's not going to work," Lucia said, retaking his hand. "Let's get you some new clothes.

Stau knew someone was approaching from behind him, but he didn't need to be a veteran assassin to hear or recognize the heavy footsteps coming his way. He continued watching his younger assassins train as the giant man stopped behind him.

"Did you draw up the plans I requested?" Darius asked, stopping next to him.

"I started putting things in motion as soon as I noticed Tannus was going to be a problem," Stau said. "All you have to do is say the word."

"Tonight, then," Darius told him. "There's no need to delay. When it is done, I will send in the thieves."

"This one is going to be messy," Stau warned. "It's hard to make it look like an accident when you also need to kill a palace worth of guards."

Darius watched as one of the assassins jumped toward a straw dummy, stabbed it through the chest, and landed with a roll. "This isn't the first chancellor we've killed, and it won't be the last," he said with finality.

Stau creased his forehead. "Have you considered what Reese will do? He's not going to agree with you dispatching his dear old friend Tannus."

"That's why I sent him away."

Stau asked, "What happens when he gets back and starts connecting the dots?"

"I'll leave that to you," Darius said, turning to leave. "By the time he gets back, I'm sure you will have planned a perfectly acceptable tragedy."

"I will look into it."

"See that you do."

Benj and Lucia walked inside a store called, "Amelie's Apparel." Clothes laid folded across racks and wooden crossbeams. The smell of cotton and leather filled the room. A small lady with dark skin peered at them from around a wooden crate stacked with folded tunics.

"Welcome to my store!" she chimed happily. "Can I help you find anything today?"

"Yes, please," Benj said, taking in the room. "I'm looking for something for me."

"He's meeting my father today," Lucia added.

Benj shot her a glance. They didn't always need to pretend to be courting.

"Oh, how exciting," the lady said. "What colors do you like wearing?"

"Brown, mostly," Benj shrugged.

"Let's try green," Lucia interjected.

The lady relaxed into a knowing smile and waved for them to follow her to the left of the shop. They followed her as she led them to assorted colors of tunics and vests.

"Most of these should be about your size," she said digging through a crate and pulling out a couple loose fitting shirts. One was tan and the other was off-white. She handed them to Benj and kept moving around looking at various pieces of clothing and holding them up to him for sizing. She gave him two vests, one brown and one green, and then handed him several matching pants. One was cotton; the other one was leather.

Benj took the clothes and looked around for a privacy curtain.

The lady pointed towards the corner of the store. "You can try them on back there. Do you need help?"

"I'm sure he can do it himself," Lucia said on his behalf.

He brought the clothes back and closed the curtain. When he was dressed, he walked out wearing the green vest, green trousers, and white tunic. "How does it look?" "You look like a proper gentleman," Lucia complemented with a smile.

The lady clicked her tongue, walked over, and began fussing with his trousers. "I'll need to take these up. If you give them to me, I can start doing that now."

Benj went back in the room closed the curtain and when his pants were removed, he held them out of the curtain. When the lady took them, he put on the brown leather pants, tan tunic, and brown vest. When he came out Lucia fixed him with an odd look.

"That was fast," she said proudly. "It takes me forever to shop for clothes, and here, in a matter of minutes, you found the exact perfect look with no effort whatsoever. Obviously, you have to get them."

"I don't even know how much they are," Benj admitted, looking around for a price.

"Four Talents and five," the lady informed him from across the room.

Benj opened his new coin purse, anticipating the need to put some of his items back. He was astounded to find two silver Talents, twelve copper Marks, and one very large gold Royal. He had never had this kind of money in his life. He looked at Lucia, who, seeing the look on his face, said, "We'll take them. Oh, and do you have anything black?" ---

Reese slowed his pace to a trot, giving his horse time to rest. He would need to go easier on his horse if he was going to make it all the way to Thannon. He had been upset that Darius sent him to find his brother when his brother could look after himself. If Gallows didn't want to come back to Royal, that was his problem.

It was past midday when he stopped to eat and take a few sparing sips of water. As upset as he was about the unexpected journey, he was happy to be out of the city and on the road again. It had been too long since he had gone anywhere.

Deciding he was content to take his time, he scanned the horizon for any sign of water and green pastures for his horse. He decided that when he got to Thannon, he would stay a while regardless of if he found his brother. He noticed a dark circle of birds in the distance, except they weren't flying like normal birds; they had to be vultures. He decided to take a closer look, just in case.

Reese found he had guessed correctly as he watched vultures soar overhead. He kept a cautious eye on his surroundings. Dead animals meant other, more dangerous animals. He drew his sword and nudged his horse closer.

He moved his horse through a cluster of trees and saw where the large birds were landing; it was the dead body of a man. The corpse's clothes were gone, and the man was lying face down in the dirt. His decomposing body was ripped to pieces from the vultures, but one thing stood out, a tattoo of a snake and a three-point crown over two stars.

"Brother," was all Reese could say. Though he hadn't gotten along with him, he felt the pain of loss as he stared down at his brother's lifeless body.

He began searching the surrounding area for anything that would identify his brother's killer. There had been a fire. Around the charred remains lay a half-burned leather satchel. He opened it and found burned clothes, a broken and burned wooden spoon, and some damp papers. Most of the words were written too small, and the rain made them illegible. He peeled the papers apart to reveal the words "Benj's Recipes."

Benj and Lucia walked down the busy streets carrying folded clothes tied together with string. Benj was grateful that his hands were too preoccupied for Lucia to try walking hand in hand again. They talked and walked together until they approached a cart that he recognized. It was the spice cart he had seen come through his village so many times, except for it looked dingier than he remembered. Their laughs and smiles turned into a solemn silence as they approached.

"Father?" Lucia asked, calling towards the spice cart. There was silence at first, followed by a rustle within. Sound of glass bottles and shuffling noise. The back of the cart opened, and John dragged himself out.

Benj watched as the familiar man slid out, carefully maneuvering a hurt leg with his hands. He was a shadow of the plump and happy spice merchant he had shared breakfast with so many times before. He had become thin, and his beard was longer and unkempt. His dark skin had become paler, and he was covered in fading bruises.

Lucia ran to him and threw her arms around him, causing him to groan in pain. "I came as soon as I could; how are you feeling?"

"The leg still hurts, but the rest of me is doing better," he said before noticing who she had come with. "Is that" he paused for a moment, "Benjos Baker? What are you doing here?"

"I just wanted to see what life was like outside the village," Benj said, clasping hands with the man.

"He saved my life," Lucia blurted out excitedly.

John looked at Benj, surprised, "How?"

"It's okay. You can tell him everything," Lucia said, adding, "I do."

"It's a long story, I hope you don't have anywhere to be," Benj warned.

John laughed, "My schedule just cleared up."

"I was looking for work at a bakery when I recognized Lucia...." Benj continued recounting the story, explaining how the pickpocket found Gallows' ring in his jacket pocket. He also expressed his desire to leave the city as soon as possible.

"I see," John said with a troubled look on his face. "When are you planning on leaving?"

"I'm not sure," Benj said honestly. "I was going to leave as soon as I got the chance, but I'm worried they'll chase me down if I do. To make matters worse, someone decided to tell everyone that we're courting today, and it won't look good for her if I just disappear."

"It's not my fault you constantly need someone to rescue you every time you open your mouth," Lucia argued, crossing her arms.

"At any rate, I'm happy for you two," John said, beaming. "You couldn't have picked a finer or more hard-working man then Benjos. You have my blessing."

Benj opened his mouth, but nothing came out. Lucia looked as if nothing had happened.

"We've mostly just come to a mutual understanding that we need to stick together in order to get out of here safely," Lucia clarified. "We're not actually planning on getting married."

"If we did, it could buy us some time to escape," Benj mused satirically.

Lucia sat up. "That might actually work. If we tell them we're getting married, they won't come looking for us right away. That should buy us enough time to get out of their reach."

"If I got my cart fixed and got a horse, all we would need is about a three-day head start," John said in a quiet voice, leaning forward slightly.

"I have a horse in the stable," Benj offered. "But I'm not sure how pretending to get married will buy us three days."

"We'll just tell everyone that we are staying somewhere in town to celebrate or whatever," Lucia devised out loud.

"There's no way they'll believe it," Benj said uncertainly. "We've only known each other for like…" he started counting the days on his fingers.

"As far as they know, we could have known each other for years. We'll just have to speed things up a bit."

"Speed things up, how? Do we start wearing matching outfits or something? Because you're flirtatious enough without speeding things up." "Just do your part and leave the rest to me," Lucia said with a smile. "In the span of ten days, they'll be begging us to get married."

"Thankfully, we already know a fake priest," Benj added. "That solves at least one problem."

"Are you sure he's fake?" Lucia asked. "It would be safer just to tell people we already got married out in town."

The conversation bounced back and forth between Benj and Lucia as they arranged their fake wedding. John observed quietly, looking like he was enjoying himself.

"Benj, promise me to be good to her," John said when the conversation had lulled. "She's all I have in the world."

"We're not really getting married, John," Benj reminded him.

John leveled his eyes at him.

"I swear to be good to her," Benj promised. "You have my word."

John motioned him closer and then wrapped his arms around Benj in a hug. "Whether your wedding is real or fake, welcome to the family."

Benj gently patted Johns back. "Thanks, John, now let's try to get out of here."

After the two pulled away from each other, Lucia emptied her money pouch and placed the coins in her father's hands.

Benj followed suit, adding the rest of his coins to the pile. "I have some more back at the cathedral."

"You two are incredible," John smiled proudly at the pair. "If you already have a horse, this will be more than enough to fix the wagon and get supplies."

"Just be ready for us," Lucia advised. "I'm not sure how long it will take, but when it's time to go, we'll have to rush."

Evan Kvalvik

# Chapter 29

## The Same Stone

After an expected knock sounded through the room, Key and Castor assumed their positions like actors preparing for a performance. They had rehearsed their lines meticulously, but that preparation quickly fell by the wayside. With each encounter, Castor grew increasingly unpredictable, and by the third round, he was improvising far more than sticking to the script.

"Ah, Corporal Poulson," the captain said, rolling up little balls of paper and tossing them in a cup at the end of his desk. "Come in, make yourself comfortable."

"Yes, sir," Poulson said and apprehensively walked towards the center of the office.

"There was something important I needed you to do," the captain said uncertainly, tearing the corner off a piece of parchment and rolling it into a ball. "Do you remember why I called Poulson in here?"

"The money from the thief, sir," Key offered, pretending to be engrossed in a letter.

"Ah, yes," Castor said, stretching lazily on his chair.

"We caught a thief today, and we need someone to take the stolen items to the treasury. Now, where did I put that bag?" Castor said, shuffling around his already messy desk. "Did I give it to you?"

Key looked up at the captain, thinking about how best to keep up with his unplanned dialogue. He opened some wrong drawers before finally opening the one holding the coin purse with fifteen silver talents and one gold royal.

"It's right here, sir," he said, hefting the bag on top of his desk. "Do you want me to count it first?"

"You haven't counted the money yet?!" the captain nearly yelled, desperately trying to fight back a smile.

"I apologize, sir, I see so many of these that I forgot about it," Key responded. "I haven't even looked inside. Do you want me to count it now?"

"No, no, the treasury can handle it. It's their job to count coins anyway." The captain straightened in his chair. "You haven't taken any of them out, have you?"

"No, sir," Key replied.

"Well, you lost your chance," Castor pointed at the bag. "Poulson, will you take that money to the treasury before Corporal Key gets any wild ideas?"

"Begging your pardon, sir, but I have more honor than to pinch a few Marks from a street rat's coin purse," Key said, improvising as Poulsen took the bag off his desk.

"You should take one of these," Castor said, proffering a wax-sealed letter, "They aren't expecting it, so this letter will explain where we got it from and remind them to pay their taxes and such."

Poulsen took the letter from Castor, saluted the best he could with his hands full, and left the office.

"If I had known having a company of thugs would be this much fun, I would have done it significantly earlier," Castor said, not waiting to hear fading footsteps. "Any bets on whether or not he's our third in a row?"

"I think he's going to take the bait," Key guessed, buttoning his shirt. "Unless he's outside listening to us now. You didn't even wait to see if he left or not."

Castor stood up, moved to the door, and swung it open, revealing an empty doorway. "I would take that bet if he didn't look so eager to take a peek at the coins."

"Too bad, I was about to bet a full talent," Key said carelessly.

"That's a big increase from your last bet," Castor said, noticing the sky through the doorway. "I would be willing to make that bet with you just to see you bet some real coins for once. In fact, you have yourself a deal."

"It's okay," Key said, holding up his hands in defense. "I might have been bluffing when I said that."

"There are no takebacks," Castor informed him, pulling out a silver talent and setting it on his desk. "The rule with betting is if one person makes a wager and the other accepts, the bet stands. Besides, the odds are in your favor, and I fully intend to lose.

"I have to be somewhere at sundown. Stay here, and don't leave until one of us wins the bet." He took out a key from his inner pocket and placed it next to the silver coin. "If you lose, just leave your coin on the desk before you lock up. I will be very disappointed if I find two coins here in the morning, but don't let that deter you from losing nobly."

Evan Kvalvik

# Chapter 30

## Black Cloak Meeting

B enj walked into the thief's dinner hall, hand in hand with Lucia, earning odd looks from Pots and Jafa. The table was set with roasted lamb, potatoes, and two golden brown loaves of bread. Benj went to sit down, but Lucia pulled him back with a slight shake of her head. Looking around, he noticed no one was sitting.

Lucia put her hand to Benj's ear and whispered, "Technically, we have to wait for the head of the table to sit first; right now, that's Draiden and Priest."

"What are you two love birds whispering about?" Jafa asked from across the table.

"I was just telling him how much I love him," Lucia said, pulling Benj's arm closer to her. "I didn't think you guys wanted to hear all that stuff."

"Oh, we love hearing that stuff," Jafa said, elbowing Pots. "In fact, I have a secret too," leaning to pots ear, whispering, "pst pst pst pst" and then giggling. The two shared fake whispers to each other and giggled for what seemed an eternity before Priest and Draiden walked in.

"Please, don't wait for us," Priest said, gesturing for everyone to sit down.

After everyone was seated, Draiden spoke, "We have some news."

"I got some news too, but it's a secret," Jafa said, once again making whisper noises in Pots' ear and then laughing with him.

"We have a job tonight," Priest said, looking troubled.

"A little short notice, huh?" Jafa asked. "I could have been two sheets to the wind already. Luckily, I'm only one sheet in the wind. Pots here is a sheet and a pillowcase."

Pots agreed. He didn't speak often, but whenever he did, it was never remarkable.

"Darius called us in tonight," Priest said solemnly. "He said some noble was caught trying to sneak into the queen's chambers." He paused for the reaction.

Draiden jumped in, "If anyone was wondering, it didn't go well for him, and now his place is up for grabs. Who's in?"

"I'm up for a little fun," Jafa said and asked, "Who is he anyway? That sounds like something Pots would do."

"His name is Thomas Fralvais or something like that," Draiden answered.

Pots whispered noises into Jafa's ear.

"Sugar balls says he's in," Jafa announced, wiping his ear off.

Lucia looked at Benj and said, "I'll go where you go, my love."

"We're in," Benj said, flushing.

The table sat in silence as they watched Benj try to stop Lucia from serving him. Finally, Benj took the serving utensils away from her and began serving her.

"Is that enough for you, my heart?" Benj whispered.

"Yes, dearest," she said and then spoke in a lower voice. "Nice one. Have you been thinking about that all day?"

"You know me too well," he cooed back at her.

Priest cleared his throat, "I uh," he started to say but decided not to bother with it. "Oh, never mind."

The sun was almost behind the mountains as Captain Castor made his way through the city streets carrying a black leather bag. He dodged through an alleyway, scaring off a few ragged-looking youths playing dice. Taking a quick glance to ensure no one was watching, he reached into his bag and pulled out a black hooded robe. Quickly as he could, he donned a robe, fastened it in place, and lifted the hood over his head to conceal his identity.

He picked up the bag and continued walking, making his way through dark alleys and darkening streets until stopping in front of an unlabeled door between a butcher's shop and an apothecary. He opened the door inward to find an empty hallway that reached for a red door beneath shadows of stone walls and a dark blue sky. He passed through the red door to find similar hoods sitting around a long table; only half of the members had arrived. Without a word, he sat down at the table and waited.

Chairs slowly filled up as more silent, hooded people entered, including a man who did not match the others. Instead of dark robes, he wore a dirty apron, and instead of a hood, he wore a brown wash towel over his head. No one spoke. Only eleven people were accounted for, and one chair remained empty.

The people sat patiently for as long as they could

before Wash Towel said, "Shall we just begin then?"

There was a general agreement from around the table.

"Is anyone here for the first time?" The leader asked. When no one responded, he removed his hood. After a moment, the hoods all came off, reveling faces lit by the soft yellow light of candles. "Terrence, where is your robe?"

"Some of us work for a living, your historyship," Terrence said bitterly, taking the cloth off his head. "I nearly had to kick everyone out of my shop to get here on time, and that's without me having to walk all the way back to my house for a robe. We weren't supposed to meet for another three days anyway."

"Very well," the man at the head of the table said. He was the leader of the overseers. He was also the king's cousin, official historian, and fourth in succession for the throne. The fact that he was the leader of a Crownsmith sect remained a conflict of interest that fascinated Castor to no end. If the man truly wanted to be king, he had all the necessary tools at his fingertips to ensure his position. It was a known fact that Marcus Tal'el did not want any part of the physical throne. He believed he could make more of an impact from a more subtle advantage.

After all, the hoods had come off, revealing the faces of the more secretive faction of the Crownsmith. Marcus cleared his throat. "I called everyone together this evening because Tannus has brought to my attention something alarming. It's something that I've feared would happen for a long time. I was going to have him share more details about it tonight, but it appears he could not join us. I wanted to have this meeting several days ago, but the chancellor's schedule wouldn't permit."

"Maybe he didn't get the invitation?" Mika said with a soft feminine voice.

"I put the black letter in his hands personally," a man said from across the table by the name of Ingot Bracerman. "If he had previous engagements, he would have told me."

"What is the news?" Terrence asked, eager to get back to his shop.

"Our request to clean up Canal Street was poorly received," Marcus announced. "Furthermore, it seems that Darius has abandoned all sense of protocol and has taken his own matters into his own hands. Captain Castor has informed me of the deaths and robberies of several of our city's residences and described his suspicion of Darius. The news from Tannus confirms it. I'm afraid this has all gotten out of hand." "What does this mean for us?" Terrence asked.

"Darius will have to stand in front of the council and answer for what he did. This will most likely result in expulsion from the organization," Marcus said gravely. "He knows this. Historically, those with power do not give it back willingly. So, we have all found ourselves at a crossroads where we will have to turn our heads away or fight him, and he knows that we are not going to turn our heads."

"And yet, the one he would attack first failed to show up this evening," Castor said, realizing the immensity of the situation. "What exactly did Reginald say when you spoke to him?"

Marcus recounted the private conversation with Tannus Reginald.

"I'll set a guard," Castor said before stopping to consider something. "That is if they haven't gotten him already. Sergeant, go find Corporal Key and tell him to assemble the company. Grab as many extras as you can and meet me at the office of investigations, swords at the ready."

"Yes, sir," Sergeant Allister said.

"By your leave, Tal'el," Castor said, waiting briefly at the door before receiving the word to go.


"How do you feel about children?" Lucia asked passively, brushing the lint off her black garments.

"How do I feel about children?" Benj asked incredulously. "I feel like I'm a flip of a coin away from getting my throat cut out by someone who thinks it's just another day on the job. I'm scared, Lucia. Somehow, I haven't yet come to terms with my own inevitable death. My fate is sealed in a coin that is already in the air."

Lucia walked over to him and put a hand on his shoulder. "We're all scared, and we all have a decision to make. Are we going to lay there and accept it, or are we going to fight until our very last? When I was scared, I didn't accept anything; I kicked the first man I saw in the balls as hard as I could. Now it's your turn. I hope that helps."

Benj straightened his black tunic and looked in the mirror at himself, "In a strange way, it does kind of help."

"Good," she said. "Now, back to my question."

A knock at the door came, and Lucia jumped into Benj's arms for effect. The door opened, and Draiden addressed them both. "It's time," he said, and without another word, he left.

"I kind of expected some kind of remark from him," Benj said, still in her arms.

"Yeah, I think I prefer serious Draiden," she said,

pulling away slightly.

"We should go before..." Benj trailed off.

"Before you decide you want children?" She asked with a coy smile.

"Lucia, what would you do if I told you I started actually liking you?" Benj asked.

"I would be overjoyed by the idea because it would mean your acting skills would improve. In which case, we might actually pull this thing off," she said. "Wait, why? Did you start liking me?"

He smiled and said, "Of course, I like you," tapping the side of his nose with a wink.

"I'm being serious," Lucia said.

Benj walked to the door and opened it with Lucia in tow, calling after him.


Key had just come up from the bathhouse when a sergeant he had never seen before ran into his room and gave him the message. He was to gather the company and meet at the office as fast as possible he mentioned having to go gather extra support and left.

He quickly dressed in everything but his plate, which he carried down the stairs and set on top of the common room table. He knocked on Trudy's door first, several times in quick succession. The door opened, and a groggy-faced Trudy came to the door.

"Suit up and meet me out here as fast as possible," Key told her. "The captain is mustering us. I think there's some kind of emergency."

Her eyes perked open, and she acknowledged him before slamming the door in his face. He then repeated the process, without knocking, to the other barracks rooms where everyone else slept. He had stood the barracks watch enough times to know where most of them slept.

Some were already awake, others were sleeping. Givens growled at him and then turned over to go back to sleep. Key shook him and then explained the emergency. "There's a good chance you'll get to stab

# Chapter 31

## A Grave Trap

B enj and Lucia were too excited to pretend to be in love; they at least sat together. The pendulous lantern rocked faster than before. It coruscated, lighting and unlighting nervous faces in rapid succession.

Draiden cleared his throat, "we didn't pray."

"What?" Jafa asked, playing with the handle on his wooden club.

"We didn't pray," Draiden shook his head. "Like we normally do. We were too busy watching those two gawk at each other," he threw a frustrated hand in Lucia's direction, "That we didn't even think to pray first."

"You're right," Priest said, "on both accounts. Those two have been gawking."

"His name is Bird, and you're all surprised when he gawks?" Jafa asked jokingly.

"Well," Draiden said expectantly. "What are you waiting for?"

The carriage came to a stop, the doors flew open, and all focus shifted. Everyone began climbing out of the carriage, and slipping into the shadows.

A large stone barrier towered over head. Jafa made a loop with his rope, and after his third try, he got the loop around one of the massive pillars connecting iron bars. He tied a knot around one of the ropes and then pulled it to the top, tightening the loop to the stone.

"Up you go," Jafa motioned towards Benj.

With some effort, he climbed up the wall and sat on the top, looking around. The house was enormous and completely empty. He gave the signal and said, "It's clear." Then, he removed his ring, tucked it into an inner pocket, and jumped.

Red eyes stared at red flames as his campfire illuminated his brother's final resting place. A mound of dirt bordered by rocks marked Gallows' unfinished grave. One day, he would come back when he found a proper grave marker, but first, he had to ask Benj a few questions.

He decided he was going to ask Darius for the Truthseer, a relic that supposedly made it possible to see if someone was lying to you. If Benj had been working with his brother, it's possible that Gallows, or rather, Gimble, had been carrying Bird's things when he was attacked. He had also learned through years of experience that people, especially thieves, were dishonest by nature. He needed to be certain.

He brought dry bread with a basque paste, which was a fermented mixture of herbs and oil, but he had no appetite for it. He had seen a lot of death in his life, but he was ill-prepared to lose someone this close to him. He and his brother had fought before; they had even raised swords at each other. Now, everything that seemed to anger him about his brother transformed into a sorrowful light through a macabre prism.

He laid down on his bedroll. He would set off tomorrow and deliver the news. He closed his eyes to the raspy screams of distant vultures and welcomed the sounds as they lulled him to sleep.


"Gentlemen, I want to thank you for arriving at such short notice at this hour," Captain Castor said, addressing his six men and the seven others in Sergeant Allister's company. "Tonight, there is a chance that you'll have to use your swords. Do not blatantly stab anybody unless they pose a direct threat to you or your fellow man."

Trudy cleared her throat.

"Or woman, thank you, Corporal Logan. In my experience, thieves will give up if and only if they recognize that they have no hope of escaping. The Chancellor's house has one gate and a wall surrounding it. I want to first secure the wall and then, second, secure the doors. There are three. A front door, a back door, and a servant's entrance. Be quiet. The more surprises we have, the better our chances are. Let's move."

The group followed at a fast pace after the captain. Their journey was partially lit by street lanterns. When they walked out of the circular light, it was so dark that the cobblestones could have dropped into an endless void, and they would have walked right into it. Only the feel of their footsteps and the sound of the surrounding footsteps were evidence that the ground was even there.

"What's the story?" Trudy asked, keeping up with Key.

"I'm not sure," Key replied, controlling his breathing at the fast pace they were keeping. "You know as much as

I do. Now that I think about it, it might have something to do with the murders and house robberies that have been happening."

"Like the time when you rescued those two women tied up to the bedpost?" Trudy said with a hint of something he couldn't quite put his finger on.

"I think so."

"You know, when you came to my room tonight, you had a look in your eye," she said. "I've been imagining it was the same look those women saw when you ran into their room with your sword raised."

"Uh, I'm sure the only thing the women saw was me standing there stressed and sweaty. I didn't even know what to do with my sword," Key said. "I doubt it was anything like tonight."

Trudy made an undiscernible sound. "Go on."

"That's pretty much it," Key said, not understanding what she wanted to know. "I'll try to look less aggressive or whatever next time I have to wake you up in the middle of the night."

Trudy squeaked.

"Are you okay?" Key asked. "Did you step on something?"

"I'm okay. Whenever you knock on my door, you can look as aggressive as you want," Trudy told him.

"Hey guys, what's all this about?" came a voice that Key recognized. It was Ansel Jory - an oddly welcome newcomer to his strange conversation with Trudy.

"We're not sure," Trudy said, sounding winded from their quick pace. "I guess we're going to try to catch a thief."

The door was locked, and Benj motioned for Lucia to

open it. After several long minutes, Jafa took her lock picks, nudged her out of the way, and, with two quick motions, opened the door.

Benj entered the large house through the back door. The size of the place swallowed him up in darkness and silence. He regretted not asking about the Soundsight before they left, but it had been such short notice he was doubtful anyone else was more prepared. He would have to rely on his natural senses.

He explored the kitchens and various rooms. There was food still on plates around the table, and the fire in the hearth had died down to simmering coals. He walked upstairs as quietly as he could. As far as he could tell, nobody was home. He ran downstairs and gave the signal.

The five of them entered. Draiden pulled Lucia aside, "We need you to keep watch," he said. Before she had a moment to protest, he said quickly, "Don't worry, I'm sure your boyfriend will find you something nice. We're short one, and usually, Reese watches our asses."

Lucia gave a curt nod and then made her way back up the wall.

Benj found the main office and immediately searched the drawers. There was nothing but books and papers. There were a few nice-looking items, but they weren't the treasure he was looking for. He went to the bookcases and started dumping books on the ground. Not finding much, he ran his hand over the top. There was nothing to find.

He went to a smaller bookcase and searched it. All he found was a few bookends. He tried to reach the top, but it was taller than the other one had been. He had to climb the shelves to look over the top. There was a small, almost imperceptible opening over the bookshelf. It looked like there could be something behind it.

He got down and started pushing in different directions. The bookcase moved. He put his shoulder on the side and began pushing; it didn't budge. He tried the other side. The bookcase slid sideways, opening into a small, hidden closet.

"Found you," he said, looking into the secret room. It was dark. He lit a candle on the desk and brought it into the room. There were swords in sheaths hanging on the walls alongside a black cloak hanging over a green wooden chest. He lifted the cloak to find the chest was locked. He tried lifting the chest, but it was too heavy. It sounded like it could be full of coins. He needed to find the key.

He started searching for something to unlock the chest when Priest came in holding several half-filled bags. Benj told him about the chest and asked him to tell him if he found a key.

"I'll keep my eyes open," Priest said, slipping some of the gold-plated accouterments from the desk and looking for his next target.

Someone whistled in quick succession. "We have company!" Lucia yelled up the stairs. Everyone dropped what they were doing and scrambled to get out of the house.

Benj descended the stairs and met her. The two ran outside towards their section of the wall that had their escape rope. As they approached, they noticed the rope wasn't there anymore. Benj continued anyway, leaned against the wall, and joined his fingers together. He told Lucia to climb up. She stepped on his hands and raised herself up but dropped down again.

"They're waiting for us on the other side," she said

frantically, grasping his shirt and pulling him away. A guard cut them off in each direction they ran.

"This way," Benj said, guiding her back to the house. "You're going to have to trust me."

They went inside the house and up the stairs. He led her left and right into the bookcase room at the top of the stairs. "This is a false wall. We can hide in here."

The two squeezed into the little room, and Benj began trying to slide the bookcase shut. It was not designed to be shut from the inside. You had to put your whole-body weight into moving it at all.

Benj took one of the swords and handed it to Lucia. "If I don't come back for you, use this to pry the bookshelf open. I'm going to close you in."

"No, we'll go together," she protested.

"I think you forget that I can fly," he said, forcing a smile, and began pushing the bookshelf closed.

"Can you open it?" he asked through the books.

It budged a little. "I think so," she said.

"I'll come back for you," he promised and then ran around the corner, looking for a balcony to jump from.

He found a window and opened it. Looking out, he saw the others. They were running towards a closed gate. They had five guards chasing them; he felt like they had a chance; the guards all wore heavy armor. He had to wait for them to run past him. He began climbing up the window sill. He hoped he would be able to clear the wall. At this distance, he was only halfway certain.

The last of the guards crossed his line of sight as he perched on the window ledge. He heard a noise and started to jump when a hand grabbed the back of his tunic, pulling him inside and causing him to land his back.

"Don't move," a woman's voice commanded as cold steal bit his neck. "Were you going to jump out of this window? You're a crazy one, aren't you?"

The four thieves--Priest, Draiden, Jafa, and Pots--sprinted toward the back gate. Arriving first, Draiden tested the latch, and it clicked open. He pulled it open just in time for the others to catch up.

Priest stepped through the gate first and was met by a larger guard with his sword drawn. The man swung his sword in a wide arch that cut through the open air of the escape route. Instinctively, Priest pushed the gate shut on the swinging sword, jarring the guard's handle on it. The guard's nose flared with anger, and he thrust forward. Priest dodged but was too late to thwart his attack. He looked down and saw dark red blooming from his chest.

Draiden, enraged by the blow, slid his dagger from its sheath and kicked the gate as hard as he could. The gate smashed into the man, causing him to stumble backward and cover his face. Draiden jumped on the stunned guard, flying through the portal and stabbing the man through his left armpit. He pulled the blade free and looked at his friend.

Two lanterns dimly illuminated a glossy stain forming on Priest's chest.

"Come on," Draiden encouraged, hearing the guards catch up from behind, but Priest didn't move.

"You were right," he said, spitting blood on the ground. "We should have prayed." He started falling, and Draiden caught him.

"You'll make it," Draiden said, tears forming in his eyes. "Just stay with me a little longer."

"Offer him six percent for me," Priest choked out with

equal parts blood and breath. He convulsed in Draiden's arms and then slipped out of his grasp, crumpling into a pile on the ground. Swords pointed at them from all around.

"You killed Givens!" One guard shouted and swung his sword at Draiden.

Another guard caught the man's sword arm mid-swing, "It's over! Stand down."

Jafa saw his opening and made to run through the gate but was stopped short as three more swords were leveled at him. They were hopelessly surrounded.

"Take them in," a man said, stepping out from the shadows. "I'll want to have a little chat with them tomorrow. Maybe we'll all share a piece of pie together."

Evan Kvalvik

# Chapter 32

## Runic Poem

L ucia woke with a terrible pain in her neck. She had fallen asleep sitting up, and despite her best efforts, she hadn't found a comfortable position. Light beamed in from the top of the secret room's entrance, reminding her where she was. She heard voices. They were muffled, but she could make out the words as they came closer.

"I believe they were searching for something in this room," a man said. "This is how it looked when we found it."

"Chancellor Reginald would have been furious with people throwing his books around like this," another said, sounding appalled.

*Chancellor Reginald,* Lucia thought she recognized the name, although she wasn't sure how. Another thought came to her. *They said the house owner was Thomas Frival-something.* She had a weird feeling like she was directly in the middle of a set-up.

"Poor Tannus," the first man said. "They found the bodies this morning and said it was too ugly to talk about."

"I think they killed him to rob the place, but they also killed everyone else." The other man said.

"I would spit, but I wouldn't want to further soil the chancellors…" the voices wandered off.

*Did they get caught?* She thought dismally to herself. She decided she would find out soon enough, but she couldn't rush. She was going to wait for as long as she needed to before escaping. Her stomach grumbled, but she had been through worse hunger.

She took in her surroundings, eager to find something that would occupy her thoughts while she waited for the place to clear out. Her hand fell to the lock on the chest. Excited for something to keep her busy, she slipped a small lock kit from her boot and got to work as quietly as she could. She had gotten some training with the kit, but most of what she learned was for locked doors. Fortunately for her, she had nothing but time to learn something new.

Benj sat in the cell and listened to the other prisoners complain about the same story over and over again. The complaints came from three men in the cell directly adjacent to his. At first, the conversation was interesting to listen to, but after a while, it began to wear on his nerves. It also seemed to be bothering the rest of his crew.

"I'm telling you, he didn't even know where the money was, let alone how much was inside," a man with a hawkish nose said from the next cell over.

"When they detained me, I thought I had gone crazy because he clearly said, "This money is uncounted." I just wanted to see if they would notice that anything went missing."

"Give it a rest," Jafa engaged them through the bars. "Someone obviously knows that all three of you are as crooked as a cork hole, and you fell right into their trap. It hurts my heart to hear your story; it really does. So, I'm going to give my sensitive little heart a break while you all shut up about it for a while, eh?"

The three men glared at Jafa, and one of them said, "What are you going to do about it? Bend the bars with your sensitive little hands and come over here?"

"Yeah, you can't just tell your superiors to shut up," another one chimed in. "That's a good way to get your words smacked out of your mouth."

"If I ever see you on the outside, we'll see who is smacking whom," Jafa threatened.

"It'll be us smacking you, is what it's going to be," the man with a bent nose clarified. "What, you get in a few schoolyard scuffles? Is that where you learned how to fight?"

"Draiden, are you going to get in on this?" Jafa asked with the first smile he'd had since they arrived. "I don't want you to miss out on this."

Draiden wiped his puffy eyes, turned towards their newfound foes, and offered, "He learned it from your mother."

The verbal fight that ensued seemed to improve their moods. Draiden's disposition improved as the joys of throwing insults lightened his heart. Even Pots offered a few.

Benj sat horrified at the thought that he would see these three outside of their respective cells.

"Bird, do you have anything to offer?" Jafa prodded.

"Not really," he said and then, throwing all caution to the wind, added. "I don't want spend the next hour trying to explain my insult to them."

Draiden and Jafa hesitated as the meaning set in and then let out a roaring laugh and patted him on the back.

"Yeah, because they're dumb," Pots said, eliciting more laughs.

"Their dumb, meh, meh, meh," Hawk Nose mocked Pots in a petulant voice. "Nice one."

"Did you hear that, Pots?" Benj said with a listening hand to his ear. "He said nice one."

"When I get out of here," the other man said. "I'm going to gut every single one of you like a pig!"

"That's probably not the only thing you'll do with a pig when you get out," Draiden said, smiling.

"Nice one!" Pots complimented.

Their laughter was cut off by the clicking sound of footsteps. The seven of them went quiet.

A uniformed man walked into view and appraised the newest prisoners. "Ah, if it isn't my little thieves," he said. Benj noted that he wasn't looking at the four of them, but at the three they were just exchanging insults with. "And my other thieves," he said, finally looking at the four of them.

"You tricked us," Hawk Nose yelled and then followed it with, "sir."

"I simply gave you three an opportunity to prove you were trustworthy," the man said calmly. "You proved me otherwise."

"You lied!" another man yelled. "You said the money was uncounted. Who's untrustworthy now?"

"Did I?" the uniformed man asked. "I must have made a mistake, kind of like you three."

Another uniformed man approached with the same woman who had captured Benj. She was holding a piece of pie.

"I think I'm going to change this up a bit," the uniformed man said. "I'll take…" He pointed around the cells until his finger landed on Benj. "You."

One of the guards pulled out a key and opened the cell door. "Come with me, and don't try anything."

"Don't tell him nothing," Pots encouraged him as he was led away.

Benj allowed the armed men to click manacles around his wrists and lead him to a back room. The group moved through a heavy door, and one of them motioned for Benj to sit down in a chair across the table.

"My name is Captain Castor," the man said. "Can I interest you in some apple pie?"

The woman who had captured him held out a cloth-wrapped pie for Benj to inspect.

"You know, I'm sure there is a decent baker in Royal City," Benj said, dissatisfied with the baked good. "No offense, but it looks like whoever made this pie handled the crust too much. The trick is to use cold water and just barely mix the dough long enough for it to come together, but not too long that your body heat will melt the fats. That way, when you bake it, you get a crispy crust that flakes off, not crumbles."

"Enough," Captain Castor said, cutting him off. He gestured for the other three guards to leave. "I want to talk to this one alone for a moment."

After a moment of silent protests, the other guards left the room.

"What do you know about pies?" Castor asked, showing a slight irritation.

"I'm a baker," Benj said solemnly, "Or I was one before I got roped into this mess."

"You mean before you joined the Crownsmith?" He asked carefully.

"No, I mean, yes," Benj finally answered. "I kind of joined by mistake."

Castor considered a moment. "Very well then, tell me about your mistake."

"I'm a baker. I was coming to Royal City to start a new life when I was robbed by a man named Gallows Reese," Benj said, recounting his story as concisely as possible. "All my clothes were ruined, so I took his jacket. I didn't know that he had a pocket with a ring inside that was somehow a symbol of the Crownsmith. I was pickpocketed, and when they found it, they brought me in, and I had to pretend that I somehow knew Gallows. I'm kind of stuck here until I can find a way to escape. If they found out that I killed him, I'm as good as dead."

"You killed Gallows Reese?" Castor asked with a skeptical tone.

"Yes, that's where I got the ring," Benj said. "It had a crown on it."

"Did the crown look anything like this," Castor said, pulling up his coat sleeve and showing a Crownsmith tattoo on his forearm.

Benj paled. "I... Oh, pits of ash, I'm as good as dead, aren't I?"

"Don't worry, your secret is safe with me. Gallows was the lowest sort of trash. I just need you to answer some questions," he said, putting his sleeve back down. "Why is Darius targeting Crownsmith members, and why did he put a job on Tannus Reginold?"

"Who?" Benj asked. "I was told we were after some guy who broke into the queen's room and tried to... Well, you know what he did."

"No, I don't," Castor said frankly. "Tannus was a Crownsmith and the representative for the Overseers. Furthermore, he is not the type who would break into anyone's room. Who was leading your operation?"

"Priest was, but your guy killed him last night," Benj said solemnly. "Reese is usually in charge, but Darius sent him to Thannon to look for... Gallows."

"Of course, he did," Castor said, putting the pieces together. "Larkin would never allow Darius to target his friend. It makes so much sense. If what you're telling me is true, I'm going to need your help. I can get you out of town, but I need some time to prepare. If I get you out of here, will you warn me before Darius targets anyone else?"

"Yeah, but if he lied about who we were supposed to rob, then how much help would it be if I gave you a false name?"

"All I need is his timing; I can handle the rest," Castor said. "Whenever you get a job, put whatever information on a letter and seal it with wax if you can. Take the letter to Gretta's on Alpenrose and tell her to take me the letter immediately. I'll pay any associated fees."

"Gretta's on Alpenrose got it. So, you're going to let me go?"

"Oh, no," Castor nearly scoffed. "If I just let you walk free, your life would be forfeit as much as anyone would trust you. You're going to have to break out on your own."

"I'm going to what?" Benj asked incredulously.

Castor leaned back in his chair and pondered his conundrum. "Who's the best pickpocket you have out there?"

"Jafa, by far," Benj said, not wanting to discuss how he had robbed him blindly in broad daylight. "He's the skinny one."

"When you go," Castor held stern eye contact. "Just make sure you get out of here quick."

The lock opened with a click and Lucia could barely believe it. Her hands were sore and smelled like metal from holding the picks. She rolled them back up and tucked them away in her boot. She stood in front of the chest, back against the entrance to the secret room, and lifted the heavy lid open. It squeaked and groaned causing her to stop and listen before lifting it all the way up.

The light coming in from the top of the bookcase had dimmed, but it was still bright enough to see by. Her eyes drank in the chest's contents as she crouched to move things around. She found a silver goblet with jewel inlays. She moved it aside and ran her hand over some books. She held one to the sliver of light; it read, "Complete Runic Sentences." She held the other one up, "Poetry of the Trembling Heart." She could just see the looks on everybody's faces as she and Benj recited poetry to each other. She made a mental note to take that one with her.

She set the books aside uncovering a large, velvet bag. She hefted it up and opened it revealing a gold covered skull. It looked like the one at the cathedral. She put it back in the bag and shivered.

Pushing everything back to the other side, she pulled out a half-empty bottle of spirits. Next to the bottle were three heavy coin purses. She picked them up and tucked them away under her shirt. One of them left a noticeable bulge, so she opened it to distribute the coins better. Her eyes bulged when she noticed it was mostly gold and silver. She tucked the coins in as many places as she could without being too noticeable. She stood up to move around. Nothing jingled if she didn't jerk around too much. Kneeling, she inspected the bottle further. It was a similar bottle that Priest had found and sold for so much. She wanted to taste it, if for nothing else than to see why someone would keep it locked away in a hidden room.

She lifted the elegant-looking bottle and twisted off the cork. It dislodged with a pop. She almost lifted the bottle to her lips when she remembered she had a cup. Placing her hand back in the chest and pushing a book out of the way, her hand found the silver goblet. She poured the amber liquid into the cup and smelled the contents. It smelled of wood and flowers. She took a sip; it cooled as much as it burned. The flavor was hard to describe; it was almost like tasting the colors green and gold. It tasted like late spring or early summer. It teased at her hunger. Before she knew it, she had drunk the entire cup.

"I see why that's so expensive now," she said out loud and then clapped a hand over her mouth. Why did she talk out loud? It dawned on her; she just drank a full goblet of spirits on an empty stomach. That might have been a bad idea, but maybe it was completely worth it.

She stood up, but it felt like she pushed the world down. "Oh no, I'm drunk," she said and then clapped her hand over her mouth again. She stood there listening and breathing. It was dead silent.

She had waited long enough. If someone had been in the house, she would have heard something by now, or they would have heard her. If someone caught her leaving, she would just tell them she was a maid. It was a solid story. Unfortunately, it meant she would have to leave the silver goblet behind for now. A maid can't be seen trying to smuggle silver cups out of the house.

Feeling resigned, she took the sword Benj had left for her and began to pry the bookcase open. She had to alternate prying it from the top and the bottom but eventually opened it enough to put her hands through. She peaked out at the empty room and then pulled the bookcase out of the way. When the crack was big enough for her to squeeze through without dislodging any coins, she grabbed her book of poetry and exited.

The room was cool and refreshing. She quickly put her shoulder to the bookcase and moved it back into position. She would have to come back for the rest one day. Maybe she wouldn't come back at all.

She made her way through the house like a specter, peeking through each doorway before slowly moving through it. She still felt light-headed and had to use the handrails to walk downstairs.

The dimming light over the front door suggested the sun was setting. She opened the door and walked out.

"Halt where you are," a man said to her. She turned to see a guard standing watch just outside the door. "Who are you?"

"I'm a maid," she said, holding up her hands, heart racing in her chest.

"How did you get in here?" the man asked.

"The servant's entrance," she said as calmly as she could, slowly turning to face the voice. She saw a young and handsome man standing with his hand on the hilt of his sword.

"I guess I mean, how did you get in here without anyone seeing you?" the man asked softer after seeing her.

"I was running late," she said, making up a plausible-sounding tale. "I didn't want to get in trouble again, so I snuck in like I usually do when I'm late. Please don't tell Master Reginold. I'll lose my job."

The man relaxed. "Reginold... I mean, the chancellor is uh, well you're not supposed to be here." He spoke. "What is that in your hand?"

"Oh, this?" she said, looking at the book she was holding. "The reason why I'm late. Sometimes, I get so enraptured in these poems that I lose track of time."

"Love poems?" the guard asked, hiding a grin.

"Yeah, they are my favorite, do you want me to read you one?" she asked fearlessly. What was she doing? She should excuse herself, not talk to the lion in his own den.

"I would love that," he said, smiling. "What's your name?"

"Lucia," she said, surprised that she had just given her real name. "And yours?

"Alrick," he said with a half bow. "That's a very pretty name."

"Thank you, the pleasure is mine," she said.

"What are you going to read?" he asked, still smiling.

"Let's see..." she said, opening the book. It was filled with complex paragraphs and runes. She quickly flipped to the first page, it read, "Complete Runic Sentences by Zilez Kalizar." The covers had been switched on the two books she had found. She immediately turned so the guard could not see what she was reading, went to a middle page, and cleared her throat.

"This one is called true love: True love is like spices that you can season things with," she pretended to recite, looking at undecipherable runes. "What would life be like without nutmeg and cinnamon? Mint leaves are herbs, but they can be dried and sprinkled around if you want.

However, a heart can't be dried, crumbled, or sprinkled. If your heart dries out, you'll find yourself alone and then die.

"Anyway, that's one of my favorites."

"I, uh," Alrick reached for something positive to say. "I'm afraid I might never understand poetry. Thank you, though; that was lovely."

"Thanks," she said, tucking the book away. "I should probably go."

Alrick took her arm and stopped her from leaving. "Can I see you again?"

"I'm afraid I am already courting someone," she said. It wasn't a complete lie. At least she was becoming more comfortable with the idea.

"Lucky guy," Alrick said wistfully. "It was a pleasure meeting you, Lucia. I will consider your poetry for as long my mint leaves are fresh."

"That's very sweet of you," she said and then left. She decided to pay a visit to her father and drop off the money before heading back to the cathedral.


"Who killed Tannus Reginold?" Castor yelled at a stony-faced Jafa.

"I've never even heard of him," Jafa replied honestly.

"You're testing my patience," Castor warned, walking around the table and grabbing the man by his collar. "I'll ask you one more time, who killed him?"

Castor had put the spare key to the prison in a place that would be easily seen and hopefully easily stolen. It was attached to a string that dangled irresistibly from his pocket. He held fast to Jafa's clothes, putting the string close to his hands. He looked away a few times to give the thief ample time to take the key. He pushed back and walked towards the door.

While facing away from the prisoner, Castor checked to see if the key was still there. He turned around with a hint of a smile, "I'm done talking to this trash. Put him back with the others."

As soon as the guard removed Jafa, Castor addressed Key and Trudy. "This is going to sound strange to you, but nevertheless, I need one of you to relieve whoever is standing at the prison entrance. When you hear footsteps coming towards the door, I also need to abandon your post. Stretch your legs, relieve yourself around the corner, whatever it is that you need to do to not get clubbed in the head."

"Key, this sounds like something you would be better at," Trudy said.

"I'm on it," Key volunteered. "What do you want me to tell the guy outside?"

"Tell him that I need his help inside."


"They really want to find out who killed this Reginold," Jafa said, standing in the middle of the cell.

"I have the feeling that whoever's house we hit last night was not Thompson Frivolton," Benj said.

"Thomas Frivalvais," Draiden corrected. "But you're on to something. Last night, I saw some things with the name Reginald on them. The name looked familiar, but I couldn't place it. I think someone lied to us, and I think that's why Priest died."

"I just have some questions for you in the back," the captain was saying, leading three guards past their cell. The captain pointed at their three enemy neighbors. "Questions about these three, this could take a while, maybe a whole hour."

After the sound of a shutting door echoed through the prison halls, Jafa let out a satisfied smile and held up a key. "We'll have our whole lives to mourn Priest's death; let's not waste time in here."

Everyone stood up as Jafa stuck his hand out of the bars and put the key in the lock. The lock slid open and the four of them creeped into the passageway.

"Hey!" Crooked Nose got their attention. "No hard feelings about earlier, eh?"

"No hard feelings at all," Jafa holding the key by the rope just out of their reach. "I suppose you want me to stick this in your little keyhole and let you three out, huh?"

"Yeah, yeah, yeah," one of them whispered. "That would be really big of you."

"Come on," Benj rushed. "We have to go."

"First, I want to hear them say sorry for all the hurtful things they said," Jafa smiled, swinging the key back and forth.

"I'm sorry for all the hurtful things I said," another one of them said.

"I want all three of you to say it at the same time," Jafa said, smiling at them.

"We are sorry for all the hurtful things we said," the three of them said in unison.

"Now, say something nice."

"You're a handsome man," one of them offered.

"And you tell really great jokes," another one said.

"Come on," Draiden tugged on Jafa's tunic. "Quit playing with them; we have to get out of here."

"Those were beautiful sentiments from all three of you, and I mean that from the bottom of my heart," Jafa said, laying the key in the center of their empty cell.

"Unfortunately, there isn't enough time to unlock your door."

"Just give us the key," Nose said. "You wouldn't leave us in here like this, would you?"

The four thieves ran towards the entrance and away from the shouts of the three prisoners. At the door, Jafa started formulating a plan to attack the guard just outside. Benj unlocked the door and went outside. No one was there. He waved the others out.

Once everyone was outside, Benj began to run, but Draiden grabbed his arm stopping him. "Now we walk as calmly as if we were browsing the flower market," he lectured, beginning to relax his pace. "No need to run if nobody's chasing us."

They made their way down the street at an infuriatingly slow pace. After rounding a few corners, they all started sprinting home.

Evan Kvalvik

# Chapter 33

## The Grand Council

B enj found Lucia standing in the dining hall eating bread and cold meat. As soon as she saw him, she ran forward and gave him a hug.

"I thought you guys got caught," she said, holding Benj and taking in the others.

"We were caught," Draiden said, holding out his arms too. He lowered them when he realized Lucia wasn't going to hug him also. "Jafa got us out."

"Reese is back," she said, giving him a severe look. "He found his brother dead. He's not happy. I also told him something that made him even more upset. Did you know that the job last night was against an Overseer? And a chancellor. Apparently, it was one of Reese's friends."

Having just been told this by the captain, Benj already knew but acted surprised. "Really?"

"Yeah, that's why Darius sent him away," she explained. "Otherwise, Reese would have tried to stop him."

"That's how I know that name." Draiden snapped his fingers. "They're always having meetings together!

Where is Reese?"

"He went to go talk to Darius," she informed everyone. "I just got back. I had to eat some food before I passed out."

"We have to go find him. We have news of our own that he's also not going to like," Jafa said miserably.

Lucia stuffed more meat and bread into her mouth and followed the party, looking for Reese. They found him standing at the table in the main hall. On the other side of the table stood Darius, Kahl Stau, and the other dark-eyed assassins.

"I did what I had to do for the good of the Crownsmith," Darius said before Kahl Stau leaned over and whispered something in his ear.

"Ah, I see the rest of us have arrived," Darius said, completely at ease. "Come in and join us. I believe we have all the requisite elements for a Grand Council that I myself will answer for some flagrant accusations by our own beloved Reese."

"A Grand Council, from what I know, is usually only for big policy changes or... something bad." Lucia whispered after seeing Benj's blank expression, "We don't have many of these."

"Bad?" He asked. "Like what?"

"Bad, like, I wasn't at the last one, but he was." She said, pointing at the golden skull in the center of the round table they were approaching.

Reese's face was a mask of exhausted determination.

"If there aren't spare seats, just make yourselves as comfortable as you can," Darius said benevolently. "If circumstances were different, I might have delayed the meeting on account of dead relatives, but I see that Reese wants to address this situation right here and now."

With Reese as a focal point, the small crowd parted for him as he sat at the opposite end of the table.

"Is everyone present?" Darius asked, folding his hands pleasantly in his lap.

Reese looked around and asked, "Where is Priest?"

"Priest was stabbed last night," Draiden said uneasily. "He didn't make it."

Draiden snapped his battle axe on the table and said, "Grand council is in session. Reese, make your case."

Reese sat in silence for a long time, shocked, knowing one of his favorite men had died. "You killed one of our own," he said quietly at first, slowly raising his voice as sorrow turned to anger. "Tannus was one of us, and you killed him. You sent me away so I wouldn't try to stop you, and then you murdered him. For what? Because he told you Canal Street is turning into a cesspool of human waste that you know you created? Or was it because he told you to start living up to the code of honor from which your position was established? You killed him because he spoke the truth, and you robbed him of everything. Now you put my whole team in jeopardy and killed another one of my friends. I just found out my brother died. How do I know that you didn't kill him, too? Now that you've refused to give me your little lie-detecting relic, I can only assume it's because I would uncover the web of deceit you've been spinning. How many of my friends and family are you going to kill to sate your blood lust?" Reese stared at Darius defiantly.

"I'll take that as the end of your speech," Darius said as if nothing was wrong. "Kahl, do you wish to add to any of these remarks?"

Kahl stood up, adjusted his sleeves, and cleared his

throat before speaking. "I do have something to add. If Reese was being completely honest with everyone here, I would say he had a pretty strong case to attempt to overthrow Darius and put the proverbial crown on his own head. Except he isn't being completely honest. We've intercepted letters between him and Tannus describing to do exactly that."

Doubts and murmurs came from several people standing around the table.

"You're lying," Reese accused, looking around mockingly. "Where are these letters? I've never written a single word remotely close to what you're describing."

"Silence," Darius ordered. "You've already said your piece."

"It grieves me to tell you that is not the worst part." Kahl stood and met each person's eyes sitting around the table. He pulled out a black book from his pocket. "It's true, I don't have the letters with me, but I have this. I found this in Larkins' possession. It outlines every one of your names and crosses out the names of those who are no longer with us, including his own brother. Do you refute the evidence in this book?" Kahl asked.

"That is not my book," Reese said calmly. His eyes were fierce and bloodshot. "If that book says anything, it doesn't say it in my handwriting. And so, it puts you and Darius at the center of those accusations."

"You must think everybody is as dumb as your dead brother if you think anybody will-"

Reese cut off Kahl as he lunged at him with his knife.

Darius reached out and blocked the blow with his bare arm. It felt like stabbing a marble block, and his attack was easily deflected. He realized it was the relics.

Darius gave a long, bellowing laugh and stood up. "If

378

you want to fight me for your trial, so be it. I would give you an hour to say goodbye to your dead brother, but you'll be saying hello to him so soon enough. I don't want to come between your reunion."

"You'll bleed for this," Reese spat.

"I would like to see you make me," Darius said, almost nonchalantly, as he stood up, taking his axe off the table. The room opened up into a circle surrounding the two.

In the middle of the crowd, Darius hefted his massive axe on his shoulders and began stretching. "You'll need something bigger than that carving knife if you expect to stand even half a chance."

Pots and Jafa ran out of the room and came back with a long halberd and a sheaved scimitar.

Reese held out his hand to Jafa, who answered the unspoken selection for the blade. He tucked his knife back in its holster and drew the scimitar, tossing the sheath to the ground in one fluid motion. The dark leather hit the ground, clattering until it disappeared into the mob of onlookers surrounding the duel.

Reese considered the runes around Darius' neck. *There's only three of them,* he thought. All he had to do was slice the ropes off the one that made him impervious.

Darius held his wicked battle axe at the ready and twisted his neck, producing a series of satisfying cracks. Reese made the first move and lunged in, aiming for the ropes and chains around his neck. The relics clanged together as Darius twisted in a quick motion, catching the blow, half on his axe handle and the other half on the arm. The sword hit the hard surfaces and jogged Reese's grip. He held fast.

Darius continued twisting and building momentum

to swing the axe toward Reese's chest. Reese parried the blow and ducked away. The axe missed Reese, but it knocked his sword out of his hand. Half a heartbeat later, Darius' heavy fist caught on Reese on the chin. The blow knocked him to the ground next to his sword. He lay where he landed, blood pooling under his face.

"On the ground rodent!" Darius yelled out as his boot made contact with Reese's stomach. The kicks left Reese writhing in a daze. Darius lifted his axe into the air and bellowed out a shout, eliciting cheers from the surrounding group; some stood in shocked silence.

"I gave him everything!" Darius circled Reese's unmoving body. "I fed and clothed him, employed him, gave him a position of honor, but that wasn't enough, was it?"

Reese groaned on the floor.

"Are you trying to apologize? Because I didn't hear you," Darius mocked as he loomed over him.

"I said," Reese spat blood on Darius' boot, "You're a lying coward." The words came out slow and arduous.

Darius looked down in mock pity. "So be it," he said, adjusting his grip on the axe handle. He raised the axe slowly above his head. "I sentence you to death."

"No!" Lucia shouted, ran, and jumped, trying to deflect the blow. Darius bent his elbow, landing a blow directly on her head. Her body went limp, and he stepped over to kick her like he had kicked Reese.

Benj did not hesitate. Darius was everything in the world that he hated, and he was about to destroy everything in the world he loved. He charged. Breaking through the crowd with his silver dagger, feeling for the only thing he knew would stop Darius. He put his hand - ring on finger- directly on Darius' bare shoulder and stabbed upwards through his ribs.

It worked. The ring had canceled out the power of the Relics. There was a sense of confusion as Benj pulled the dagger free and stood in the middle of a silent crowd. Blood poured down Darius' side and ran down his leg.

"What did you do? What did you do?!" Darius yelled, furious. "Get him!"

Benj pushed past a single stunned thug standing in front of the table and jumped on top of it. The assassins were already surrounding him and drawing their weapons of precision.

Benj pocketed the ring and picked up the golden skull. It's h*eavier than it looks*, he thought and ran towards the edge of the table, throwing the skull at the assassin in front of him. Benj took advantage of his window of opportunity, jumped over the assassin's head, and glided through the cathedral.

The front entryway door was shut. There wouldn't be enough time to open it, even if it wasn't locked by chance. Skidding to a stop on the ground, Benj ran from the battle cries of his assailants. *The stairs,* he thought as he rounded the corner of the circular stairwell and began climbing. He took two stairs at a time but felt it wasn't enough. Angry voices stomped and climbed after him, getting closer and closer. He wasn't fast enough, and the tip of a sword peeked into sight just behind him.

Heavy breathing like an angry animal followed him closer, sounding louder than his heartbeats. He wasn't going to make it to the top. Benj made a split decision that, given more time to think about, he might not have tried - not in a million years. He turned around and jumped back down the spiral staircase, over the heads of the assailants and over the tips of their swords.

The stair tunnel was dark enough to cause confusion as he slid around the outer wall, hitting a dual knife-wielding assassin on his way down. He gained a footing on the downward-sloped wall and ran sideways over even more heads and swords as he descended.

Shouts came from behind him as two of the men fought over who knocked into whom. Benj slid along and around the corkscrew wall past an assassin who looked at him dumfounded, dagger in hand forgotten.

He flew out of the stairwell sideways, landing on the ground off balance, twisting, and rolling onto his back. He stood up, dizzy from the circling, and began to run. Someone punched him in the stomach. A red flash of pain crossed his eyes. Benj choked out a breath, the world still spinning around him. He heard a deep, sinister laugh and looked up to find Darius standing over him, blood running into a puddle at his feet.

The other assassins spewed out from the stairwell. Draiden rammed his shoulder into one of them, then picked up a cudgel, raising it into the air.

The room came to a guarded halt.

Darius picked up Benj by the neck and held him up. Black spots formed at the corners of his vision, and panic rose in his chest as he fought for air. Looking over Darius' shoulder, he noticed someone coming up from behind. It was a bloodied and tattooed-faced Reese, leveling a sword with both hands.

Benj let go of Darius' wrist with one hand, cutting the support from his neck and reached into his vest pocket, where he kept the ring. A vibration rippled through Darius' arm to Benj. Reese had struck Darius in the neck unsuccessfully.

Benj found the ring in his pocket and managed to put

it on while his vision darkened. Darius gave no sign of discomfort at the jarring blow and attempted to throw Benj by the neck at Reese. As soon as Benj's ringed hand contacted Darius' wrist, his feet began lowering to the ground.

Without the added strength from the runes, Darius strained against Benj's weight. His grip loosened, and Benj touched the ground and took a deep breath. "Now!" He attempted to yell, but his throat wouldn't allow it.

Reese saw the strength leave Darius and, with the added look of confusion, struck at the necklaces again. Darius raised an arm to block the attack and was dumbfounded when it landed. After the blow landed, he swung again, putting everything he had into a reckless attack. The sword cut through his arm and dug into his shoulder. The dismembered hand and wrist hit the ground as he swung again, lodging the sword deep into his side.

Darius fell out of Benj's feeble grip and fell onto his knees. Reese swung again at his face, but the runes protected him once more. The force of the swing knocked the sword out of Reese's hands for a second time. Darius held up the stump of an arm to protect himself from further blows while the sword clattered on the ground.

Reese reached down, took the runes off Darius, and put them around his neck. Power flooded through Reese's veins as he felt the strength of one relic. His skin became solid from another, but the third gave him something different. He could feel the essence of a person. He felt Darius' fear, shame, and bloodlust. "You know, that wasn't my book."

"I know," Darius said, spitting spit blood. "The same way I knew you had to die."

Reese looked down at the bleeding Darius. He felt pity for the man if he even was one.

"Knife," Reese said, holding his hand out towards Benj.

Benj handed Reese the silver knife. Reese took it, cut off Darius's head, and threw it on the table where the golden skull once sat. Kahl slowly made his way towards the door.

"Grab him," Reese said, pointing in Kahl's direction.

"You must know that Darius put me up to this," Kahl explained, holding up his hands innocently as Pots and Jafa approached him.

"Do you admit to giving false claims and accusations in front of the grand council?" Reese asked.

"Of course, you were never guilty. He put me up to it and threatened to kill me." Kahl said.

"Then my innocence is proved, as well as your guilt." Reese said, "Kill him."

Kahl opened his mouth to protest, but instead of sound, only blood came out as a knife was pulled out of the back of his skull. The assassin, Ren, cleaned his knife on Kahl's shirt before he collapsed.

"I am now the Crownsmith Lord Marshal. Does anyone dispute my claim?"

The crowd gathered closer to Reese, but no one spoke.

"For the next order of business, Ren, I promote you to Lieutenant of the assassins."

Ren bowed his head in thanks.

"Draiden, I promote you to Lieutenant," Reese said and then pointed to the ground around him. "I need someone to clean up my brother's mess."

"Very well," Draiden accepted the position.

"Benj, what do you know about my brother's death?"

Before Benj could speak, Reese lifted his hand. "You just saved my life, so I'm going to do you a favor before you make the mistake of lying to me."

Reese looked at his three relics, and after a moment of studying them, he lifted the older of the three and handed it to Benj. "Put it on," he ordered.

Benj removed his ring and put it in his vest pocket before receiving and lifting the relic around his neck. Immediately, he could feel Reese's grief for his brother and friends, his feelings of betrayal from Darius and Kahl, and finally, a deep and astonishing mistrust towards himself.

"First, a lie." Reese proceeded to demonstrate. "I did not enjoy killing Darius,"

Benj could see, like boiling water, the dishonesty of the statement.

Reese spoke again. "If you flourish one detail of the truth, I will kill you."

Benj knew that when he told his story, he would have to be dead honest. He removed the necklace and gave it back. He then told the whole story about Gallows Reese, who tried to rob him, and how he defended himself against a growling attacker. Benj added how he wished things were different. He wished he could have got to know him, not blindly swing a sword to try to keep him away.

Reese stood listening to the story, standing over Darius's dead and broken corpse. After Benj had finished talking, there was a long moment of silence.

"We'll put it to a vote, majority wins. Lieutenants, by raise of hand, who says he's guilty?" Reese asked, lifting a hand. After a moment, the newly appointed assassin leader raised his hand.

"All opposed?"

Draiden raised his hand and said, "Gallows, rest his spirit, had it coming. Creator knows I loved him too, but you can't execute Bird for defending himself."

"I can do as I please!" Reese shouted, "Bird, do you have no interest in voting in your own favor?"

"My what?" Benj stood contemplating, trying to escape through the staircase again.

"You charged Darius when it wasn't even your battle," Reese explained. "Faced with uncertainty, you came to my aid and saved my life. You saved the Crownsmith against the greatest foe any of us have ever taken on. I promote you to the rank of Lieutenant. Now, if you don't raise your hand, I'll have to find someone else with your idiot courage to fill the position... after executing you."

Benj raised his hand.

"It looks like we have an impasse, and Lieutenant Bird's life is saved," Reese announced. "Bash," Reese said parting the crowd around Lucia, "You were the first to run in. Whatever you want you can have it."

"I want my father's debts forgiven," she said without pause.

"Done."

"I would also like to go with him to find a place to settle down," she looked at Benj. "I know of just the place. I would like Benj to come, too."

Reese regarded the two, "You are by all means free to go, but I hope I can entice you to stay a little longer? I'm going to need help getting everything situated, and we lost a lot of key members."

Lucia paused for a moment and then looked at Benj.

"We can wait a little longer, right? We'll have to put our marriage plans on hold if that's okay with you?"

"Yeah, that's fine," Benj said, mostly for putting the marriage plans on hold. Did he really plan on coming back? He did come here to start a new life. It was possible Reese would help him get a bakery started and he could be an Overseer of some sort. "We can hold off on our plans for now."

"Anything else?" Reese asked before removing the relic from his neck again.

"It's Baker," Benj said, not fully committing to the statement.

"What?" Reese asked.

"I didn't have a surname but grew up as a baker."

"Shut up, Bird," Reese laughed, "We have tattoos to get. Ren, Draiden, Bird - come with me. Bash, you too. The rest of you clean up this mess. Keep Darius' head where it is. Grand Council is Adjourned."

Benj followed Reese into the kitchen with Draiden, Lucia, and Ren. Bones was stirring a large pot of stew, presumably for dinner.

"Whatever you're doing, set it aside, Bones," Reese ordered, clearing a spot on the counter to lay down. "I need a third star, and these they need second stars."

Bones stopped stirring the pot and looked at Reese with astonishment. He had been in the kitchen the whole time and missed the Grand Council and everything else. His eyes stopped on the relics around Reese's neck and focused for the span of a few uncertain heartbeats. Finally, he took the large wooden spoon out of the pot, set it down, and wiped his hands on a towel that hung from his belt.

Reese lay down on the counter and opened up his

shirt, revealing an upside-down crown in the center of his chest with two four-pointed stars under the outer points. Other tattoos riddled his body, covered in blood and bruises.

Bones opened a drawer and pulled out a small sack containing an ink bottle, several chisel-like needles and a wooden mallet. He dropped the needles into a bowl and poured a kettle of scolding hot over the needles. He then opened a cabinet and pulled out a bottle of clear colored spirits, and poured a measure on Reese's chest, wiping the area with a rag. He gave the bottle to Reese who took a thirsty pull.

Bones scooped out the needles from the bowl and set them out neatly on a plank of wood. Waiting for an unspoken acknowledgment, he dipped a needle into the ink and held it just over the middle spike of the three-pronged crown on Reese's chest.

Reese nodded, and Bones tapped the needle with the mallet. After a moment, Bones wiped away the ink to reveal the first line but found it clean.

"Almost forgot," Reese said, wrapping off his relics with his shirt. "Try again."

Bones started again. The ink took, and before he knew, Benj was laying on the table wincing as the painful needle repetitiously bore into his skin. He kept thinking, "It's better than dying," and wondering how Reese made it look so easy.

Bones wiped a thin layer of ink off Benj's chest, revealing a finished star below the third crown spike over his heart. The skin around it was red and raw. At that point, he wished he was back home in the bakery. He was homesick and missed his conversations with Sephus. This tattoo would have been one of the things he would have told him about.

Benj got up from the table, and Draiden lifted a pantleg, revealing the tattoo on his shin. Bones went to work. He then put a second star on Ren's throat.

When Bones was working on Lucia's shoulder, Benj looked around the kitchen, smelling the familiar scent of baking bread. He looked in the oven to find four golden brown loaves, side by side. They were finished.

He took a thick towel from the top of the oven and pulled out the loaves, setting them on an empty surface. A bowl of batter sat nearby. Benj stuck a finger in to taste it and habitually added some salt. He then put a thin layer of fat into four more bread pans, poured in the batter, and placed them in the oven. The room seemed quiet. He turned around to see everyone staring at him.

"You really are a bloody baker," Reese said, standing shirtless near Draiden.

"All I did was take bread out of the oven," Benj said in his defense.

"All you did was be the first person to meddle with Bone's kitchen without him breaking one of your fingers off," Ren said in a raspy and quiet voice.

Bones shrugged and then nodded.

"He was watching you intently," Draiden said in a low voice. "It is a good thing you know what you're doing."

"Bird," Reese said, slapping the raw spot on his chest, "I can see many good things for you in the future, or at least in the kitchen."

Evan Kvalvik

# Chapter 34

## After

Hooded shadows sat around a table.

"Two meetings in two days," Terrence said, taking the apron off his head. ."You all can take your secrecy and toss it down a well for all I care. What do you want, and why does our own Marquis always feel like he's exempt from these meetings?"

Castor cleared his throat, but Marcus lifted his hood and spoke first. "Tannus Reginold is dead, and he was killed by Darius."

Terrence's features fought for common ground between anger, sorrow, and pensive. "That's not good."

The rest of the hoods came down revealing concerned and angry faces.

"I'm the one that called this meeting," Castor said, reaching into his jacket pocket. "I have a letter I would like to read to you, but first, I want to give you all some backstory."

Castor told the story about the night following their last meeting. He explained how one of his men had died. He didn't mention his plans to remove the guard from his service just hours before. He also kept Benj's name a secret as he explained the prison interviews.

"I told him to contact me with any updates before one of them stole the key off one of the guards and miraculously escaped," he said with a straight face. "This morning, I got this letter from him through the private channel I had explained earlier.

"It reads: Darius was killed, Stow was killed- I believed he is refereeing to Kahl Stau. He says, Reese is in charge, don't lie to him. Draiden, Ren, Lucia, and I have been promoted to Lieutenant. He has told us we can leave, but not yet."

"Do you think he's telling the truth?" Delina asked nervously, rubbing her knuckles.

"I have reason to believe he is," Castor said. "Nevertheless, we should still be cautious going forward."

"That still poses the question, what are we going to do about replacing Tannus?" Mika offered, pointing at the empty chair. "One of us needs to fill the position."

"I can't," Allister said holding up his hands. "I'm too busy with my company to represent anyone."

"I have my shop to look after," Terrence said and then stalled. "The captain is already in communication with them. Sorry, Charles, but I nominate you."

"I am quite indisposed in my current situation," Castor stated, rejecting the nomination. "So thanks, but no thanks."

"I don't know if that's such a bad idea." Marcus steepling his fingers. "You were the one who caught onto Reginald's assassination. Terrence is right; you've already contacted our other spokes. You pretty much make your own schedule in the office of investigations."

Castor's face paled at the unanimity of the other voices. "I'm trying to take things off my plate, not add more things on. We should consider Mika for the position."

"I'm too quiet," Mika said quietly.

"I'm not interested," Delina said.

"I'm not interested either!" Castor raised his voice, incredulous at the nominations. "I feel like Marcus on this one, I can do more from behind the throne than on it."

"All in favor of making the captain the Marquis and representative of the Overseers?" Marcus said, raising his hand.

Castor sat with his hands in his lap as every other hand in the room raised.

"There you have it," Marcus gestured next to him. "Come, take your chair."

Castor begrudgingly stood up, walked around the table, and sat beside Marcus.

"Now we have another chair to fill," Marcus said with finality. "Marquis, it's your responsibility to find your own replacement,"

"I will keep my eye out for someone," Castor stated blandly. "Now, back to business. If I confirm that Larkin Reese has been elevated to the position of Grand Marshal, what do you want me to do about it?"

"If you can convince him to clean up Canal Streat, that would be a good starting point," Ingot offered. "Only, try not to get yourself killed."

"Find out what he wants to do," Marcus advised. "See if you can't convince him to swear fealty to the king. It's been long since the Crownsmith was loyal to the king."

"I'll try to arrange a meeting," Castor said, inwardly cursing his misfortune. "Now, if that's everything, I have two funerals to prepare for."

When the meeting was over, Captain Castor - Marquis and representative of the Overseers - made his way to the office of investigations. With a heavy heart, he lifted his quill and wrote to his brother, the baron of Brunshold Keep. He wrote of the events that had taken place the last several weeks, his new retinue, and his new position in an organization he had joined so long ago. He finished the letter, "I wish I had father's wisdom on these matters. If he were here today, he could tell me exactly what I would need to do. I look forward to receiving your future correspondence. Whatever wisdom I haven't inherited from father, I often find in your sloppy and, frankly, uncouth handwriting. Until next time...."

THE END OF BOOK 1

# Acknowledgments

Thanks for reading, and a special thanks to everyone who made this book possible. Alexander Brown helped me conceptualize the story after I first had the idea in the missile compartment. Kainoa Stau encouraged me to continue writing the story, even though I intended to kill off his character. I've bounced ideas off my brothers Jens and Micah continually since I started. Charles McAllister helped me with all things esoteric. Ask him to teach you the secret handshake; he won't. You can thank my mom and my sister Eva for going through and taking out all the swearwords. Maudib and Destiny helped edit the rest. Big thanks to Daniele Turturici and D.M. Maloney for the cover art and the graphic design respectively. I also couldn't have done this without Autumn Joy Rumsey. Her infinite artistic talents came at a cost; she doesn't know how to enjoy Blue Grass music. Finally, I want to acknowledge Michael J. Sullivan for inspiring one of the characters. Can you guess which one?

# About the Author

Evan Kvalvik was born in Washington. Skipping the boring parts, he joined the Navy, drove a submarine, became an ordained internet minister, and officiated over twelve marriage ceremonies. Now he is a Notary Public which means he can also officiate weddings in the state of Tennessee. It's a hobby....

He and his wife live in Tennessee where they raise two hairless cats on something that resembles a farm. It's not a farm, not really. Though one day they hope to put up a fence and, I don't know, raise alpacas or something.

Milton Keynes UK
Ingram Content Group UK Ltd.
UKHW020906061224
452240UK00014B/905

9 798991 397629